The Sea People

By Theo Lemos

Text copyright © 2013 Theo Lemos

Cover design by Dino Cozadinos

All rights reserved

This is a work of fiction.
All characters and events portrayed in this novel are used fictitiously and any resemblance to actual persons is coincidental.

ISBN-13: 978-1503083547
ISBN-10: 1503083543

This novel is dedicated to my wife and children for their love, support and encouragement

Contents

Chapter 1: Halia	1
Chapter 2: George Philo	8
Chapter 3: Chris Zacharias	16
Chapter 4: Jake	20
Chapter 5: Alexander Kephalas	42
Chapter 6: The Mystery Lady	46
Chapter 7: Athens	49
Chapter 8: Piraeus	68
Chapter 9: Teresa	83
Chapter 10: Lichas	102
Chapter 11: Diana	119
Chapter 12: The Tour	136
Chapter 13: The Crossing	148
Chapter 14: The Yacht Club	158
Chapter 15: The Cemetery	172
Chapter 16: Paleo Limani	186
Chapter 17: The Sea	210
Chapter 18: Yacht Bay	221

Chapter 19: The Beach Bar	**237**
Chapter 20: The Fisherman's Wife	**260**
Chapter 21: The *Bacchus*	**280**
Chapter 22: Panagia Island	**299**
Chapter 23: The Green Isles	**322**
Chapter 24: Joanna	**337**
Chapter 25: The Old Town	**351**
Chapter 26: The Memorial Service	**361**
Chapter 27: The Sea People	**366**
Chapter 28: The Betrayal	**377**
Chapter 29: The Map	**399**
Chapter 30: Basil	**408**
Chapter 31: The *Trident*	**415**
Chapter 32: Virginia	**437**
Chapter 33: The Wait: Monday	**449**
Chapter 34: The Wait: Tuesday	**455**
Chapter 35: The Wait: Wednesday	**466**
Chapter 36: The Wait: Thursday	**469**
Chapter 37: The Wait: Friday	**478**

Chapter 38: The Street Party	**482**
Chapter 39: The Yacht	**498**
Chapter 40: The House	**514**
Chapter 41: The Tomb	**522**
Chapter 42: Confrontation	**536**
Chapter 43: Natalya	**551**

Acknowledgements

This book would not have been published without the huge contribution from my wife, Jan, who not only encouraged me but was also my proof-reader, editor, and publisher. I am also extremely grateful to our dear friend Jenny Kaluzny for her invaluable input and also to my stepson, Dino Cozadinos, for the cover design.

Chapter 1: Halia

Dawn breaks over the Aegean.

At the north eastern corner of this historic sea, the island of many names prepares to receive the morning sun. This land of peaks and vales, headlands and bays is, more accurately, a group of seven islands forming an archipelago running from the northwest to the southeast. Its arrangement is straightforward. The main island is almost circular in shape, the eroded remains of a group of extinct volcanic vents. To the northwest, two small rocks scarcely thrust their heads above the water, and to the southeast are four rather more substantial neighbours.

There is no wind this spring morning. The surrounding seas are glassy and so accurately reflective of the sky that the separation of one from the other is indistinguishable at the horizon. To the south, beneath the water's surface, large sandy areas are visible, interspersed with dark banks of seaweed and varying tans of rocky reefs. These crystal clear waters are cold though, having been borne by currents from the nearby Black Sea.

The wild and undulating landscape is blanketed with thick vegetation, which at this time of year produces a rich display of wild flowers. By summer these would die down to leave a mundane and uniform brown with infrequent patches of evergreen. The still, morning air is thick with the scent of lentisks and osiers.

Both the southern and western coasts, shielded from the chill north-easterly winds, slope gently from the central peaks to the sea. Here there are occasional fields of grass, clumps of pines and groves of fig trees. On bare rocky hillsides there are shrubs of oregano, thyme and sage. There are also low headlands separating shallow sandy bays and pebbly coves.

The other side, the north and eastern coasts are sheer and cut through by valleys that meet the sea at rocky inlets etched into the cliffs. Here the vegetation is more profuse and the moist ravines are cloaked with stumpy evergreen trees. In contrast to the southern shore, the waters plunge abruptly to inky depths.

The main island is blest with two natural harbours. One is in the southeast and consists of a semi-circular bay protected from the wind and currents by the four other islands of the group. Within the surrounding shores are the remains of an ancient fortified harbour. Its purpose remains unknown.

Further west, halfway along the southern coast and at its most southerly point, a spur of land, curving southeast, forms the other protected inlet. Here is the main town and most recent habitation. The grand villas of the leading families ring the waterside, while the more modest houses and cottages cling to the steep slopes. All but a few of these dwellings are deserted for most of the year. As with most islands of the Aegean, the population swells into the thousands during the summer when families from the mainland and other parts of the world come to stay in their ancestral homes. Now the inhabitants barely number three hundred. Most are retired couples or black-clad widows living off their deceased husbands' pensions. The balance consists of those who run the local services, builders who look after and maintain the wealthier households and an assortment of eccentrics and recluses.

Panagos Magos is one of the dozen men on the island who earns a living from care-taking and renovating properties. He lives on his own, high up in the village and close to the church, in a terraced two-storey white-washed cottage with a red terracotta-tiled roof, which he rebuilt from a ruin. He's in bed, huddled under a blanket. The early mornings are still chilly at this time of year.

Being Easter Sunday, he will not work. He has laboured all week on his main spring project, redecorating one of the mansions in his care, and is ahead of schedule. The owner will not be coming until the end of July. This major job, together with his routine maintenance responsibilities, will see him through another winter, with money to spare. Perhaps next spring he will buy a small boat to run his clients around in.

Originally born and raised on the island, this will be the fifth year of his return. He used to work as a mechanic in a Mercedes dealership in Piraeus until one of the customers, a compatriot, tempted him back to look after his summer house and yacht. The fact that he was a jack-of-all-trades and could repair anything brought him to the attention of others and, within a couple of years, he had as much work as he could comfortably handle.

In his heart he had known that he wanted to come back. He preferred the pace of life here. Events moved too fast in the towns and cities. You couldn't think things through and it was easy to make mistakes. Mistakes that, more often than not, ended in heartache. He preferred being an outsider, a loner; he had to accept that. He was too impulsive, jumping into friendships and relationships, and ending up being betrayed and rejected.

This was paradise in comparison. Here he was focused and everything somehow worked out for the best. For nine months of the year the weather was sunny, pleasantly warm and dry. The local inhabitants were tolerant most of the time, leaving you to do your work at your own pace, and there was no one with authority to piss you off.

July and August were the closest you came to the frantic pace of the outside world. This was when the owners came to their summer homes and each believed that you worked only for them. He was endlessly ferrying suitcases, changing light bulbs, collecting shopping from the ferry, repairing washing machines and air conditioners and driving families to and from the beaches.

Even this hectic time of year had its compensations. There were free meals and drinks, trips on yachts and visits to nightclubs on the nearby island. Had any of them heard about the world recession? In the end, when his customers left, they gave him the contents of their fridges and freezers. It was amazing what he sometimes ended up with: smoked salmon, fillet steak and, occasionally, caviar.

The last week of August was 'list week', as he liked to call it. This was the time his clients gave him an inventory of the repairs and improvements they wanted done over the winter. This could include anything from renovating an entire house to installing a TV aerial. From then until Christmas the weather remained good, and this was the time to get on top of the work he had accumulated.

January to mid-March was the dead time. It was damp and cold. The winds howled continuously, either from the humid south or the freezing north, and the stormy weather often isolated the island for days. It was so far removed from anywhere else that it had its own power supply, having a couple of generators located in a building beside the football stadium. There were frequent power cuts, shortages of fuel, food and cigarettes, and the islanders became depressed and hostile. It was impossible to do any work at this time so Panagos would visit his family and friends, generally travelling around the mainland until the beginning of March.

Panagos stirs and looks at the mobile he keeps handy on the bedside table in case he receives an emergency call-out; not that he gets many at this time of year. It is eight o'clock. In thirty minutes the church bells would call the congregation to worship. For the few like him who didn't attend, the service was broadcast over loudspeakers. It was loud enough to penetrate the thickest walls and shutters. He decides to get up and turn on the hot water thermostat for his shower while he continues to snooze for the last half hour of peace. During the low season nights the local power supply was cut at midnight, so he made a habit of switching his electrical appliances off before going to bed.

He is just about to make his move when he is conscious of something rushing up at him from below. He has a fraction of a second to brace himself.

The earthquake lasts fifteen seconds. During this time, he observes with interest as the furniture in his room wobbles and creaks and one of the doors of his wardrobe falls open. He is surprised to find his bed inching towards the bedroom door. He's never realised there is a slant in the floor until now. Downstairs he can hear cutlery falling and china breaking in his kitchen.

When it is over, he lies still for a few minutes. Living in Greece you get used to tremors and quakes. This was a significant shake, the worst since his return to the island but still not serious. He only becomes anxious when his attention turns to the villa he is renovating. The houses on the island are built to resist such events, yet he imagines cracks in newly plastered walls, or maybe a can of paint falling off a ladder and bursting open on the parquet floor.

These thoughts motivate him to spring out of bed and get dressed. He tries his light switch but, predictably, there is no power. It turned off automatically during an earthquake and probably wouldn't be back for hours. He remembers a joke the locals have about the island; it is surrounded by so many fault lines that they had nicknamed it Atlantis as they expected it to disappear under the waves one day. At least the loss of power would silence the fake church bells and loudspeakers.

Running down the stairs, he doesn't stop to check the kitchen and instead pulls on his shoes and steps outside. The narrow lane of terraced cottages is deserted. His scooter has fallen over but does not appear to be damaged. It starts first time and soon he is gliding down the winding, uneven streets towards the harbour.

The earthquake was a minor event. The epicentre was twelve nautical miles to the north and several miles beneath the seabed, along a well-known fault line. There was little structural damage to the buildings of the island. Panagos would only have one day of extra work to do, replastering a few new cracks. The paved road that ran from the town to the north western end would have gained some more potholes. Several rockslides would have occurred in places that only goats visited.

On a small, rocky isthmus, between two of the smaller islands at the south eastern end of the archipelago, hard by the ancient harbour and below sea level, lies a structure built over three and a half thousand years ago. It was never meant to be found. Today's earthquake, although not very powerful in itself but coming at the end of a long history of seismic events, has caused a major underwater displacement.

Chapter 2: George Philo

Sunday, 24th June 2012

1:00 AM: It is the early hours of a late June morning. The night is moonless, but there is a breathtaking display of planets and stars in a sky that is cloudless save for a thin inky black line above the northern horizon. The brisk southerly breeze originating from North Africa, which has brought hot and sultry weather to the islands of the Aegean for the last three days, has ceased. The wind has been still for several hours, and the dropping temperature has caused a layer of condensation to form on every surface.

On a crescent-shaped beach facing west, the fine sand is pearly white in the starlight. Behind a low dune, a dark area of thick undergrowth and trees is heavy with the chorus of cicadas. The sea is smooth to the horizon, with a thin mist carpeting its surface.

At the southern end of this bay, a low headland separates this sandy paradise from a more modest, pebbly cove. Here there is an ageing concrete jetty with a modern fibreglass motorboat tied stern first to two rusty bollards. Stone steps then lead diagonally up a slope to the top of the cliff and a white-washed, two-storey villa. A castellated parapet surrounds its red-tiled, pitched roof.

The house is a simple rectangular design with a first floor balcony running the length of the front elevation, below which is a raised and railinged porch. The bright blue doors and shutters of the ground floor are closed but those of one of the bedrooms on the first storey are open onto the continuous balcony, which is sheltered beneath an extended yellow and blue striped awning and overlooks the cove.

2:00 AM: The weather has changed and now the wind is picking up from the north, blowing away the wispy mist, throwing ripples across the once calm sea and causing wavelets to caress the sandy beach. The menacing dark line of cloud above the northern horizon has thickened somewhat with invading black fingers spilling across the sky and reaching for the Milky Way. Within the approaching thunderhead, frequent flashes of lightning can be seen.

On the top floor of the villa the breeze has been captured by the open French doors of the main bedroom. Inside, a naked couple lie on the double bed, covered by a single sheet. Both are in a deep sleep brought on by the fatigue of a relationship still in its first passionate throes. Outside, in the cove below, the yacht rocks gently.

3:00 AM: The wind speed has increased to force five. On the sea, white horses are parading down from the north. Ribbons of surf are unrolling on the beach and the sound of the cicadas has been overwhelmed by the turbulent air's rustling of the undergrowth and trees. In the cove the powerboat is seesawing alarmingly and, although not in imminent danger, is pistoning water onto the jetty every time the stern drops. The advancing clouds now cover half the sky, with lightning flashes striking the turbulent waters close to shore. The resulting thunder is loud enough to vibrate the panes of glass of the villa's windows. In the bedroom the man is stirring.

George Philo wakes. His first thought is his need to go to the bathroom. He moves slowly and stiffly after so many motionless hours. In the dark and airless en suite his body smells of the aftermath of intimate lovemaking and his urine reeks of ouzo, wine and spicy food.

When he has finished, he thinks of brushing his teeth, but a rumble of thunder diverts his attention. He goes back through to the bedroom and onto the balcony. He is naked, but there would be no one to see him. He glimpses the approaching thunderstorm. This is not an uncommon event for the North Aegean and the forecasters had warned of it. Within half an hour there would be a deluge. He worries whether the anchors of the boat will hold, but there is nothing he can do about it now. He decides to make a quick check to ensure the shutters and windows of the house are securely closed. He pulls on his trousers, slips on a pair of slippers and picks up the torch from the bedside table. There was never any mains power at this time of the night so he knew to be prepared.

Satisfied with his inspection, he returns a few minutes later to find it darker outside than when he had left, the clouds having obscured most of the sky. He is astonished that Denise is still asleep, probably having drunk more than she should have. He, on the other hand, is wide awake and too restless to go back to bed until after the storm has passed, so he sits on a cushioned wicker chair to observe the spectacle. This panorama of the sea is one of his most treasured pleasures.

Not for the first time he speculates on what his life would have been like if his mother had not made her epic journey across the Atlantic or, moreover, was allowed to return home alive. He would now be an Irish Catholic living somewhere in the north eastern United States. Would they have been discriminated against because he was illegitimate? Most certainly. Would he have had the same opportunities for education and business? Probably not. Would his industriousness have overcome these obstacles? Debateable.

But then the turn of events that had led to his present heartache would not have occurred either. If he had had the choice, which path would he have selected? This pointless and repetitive train of thought, as always, left him depressed. It suggested fate had dealt him an impossible hand, something he was not willing to accept even after all these years. He preferred to believe that his relentless energy and determination could overcome any problem.

He looks back at Denise and smiles. Not bad for a man in his mid-sixties. This was his best conquest in recent years, although he had to admit that if he had been penniless he could not have pulled it off. He was realistic about that. The days of being able to turn a woman's head through his looks and personality alone had long gone.

They had met last Easter at the same Athenian nightspot that over the years had provided him with dozens of casual girlfriends. The procedure was simple. The nightclub in question was renowned for the quality of its live music, especially the singers and the passion with which the regular customers performed the Greek dances. George, despite his age, was one of the best. He was part of the hard core of about a dozen men who turned up regularly and provided the atmosphere for the place. The management needed them as much as the performers. Their unspoken arrangement was that George and the other men would turn up and warm the clientele to the singers with their dancing and partying. The clientele, which consisted of wealthy foreign tourists sent by hotels or brought by taxi drivers, would be inclined to spend more money. In return, the doormen would allow a number of attractive single women in for free. Some nights, if there weren't enough turning up at the door, they would go to the nearby taverns and recruit from there. The women would be placed near the dance floor amongst George and his pals. The music, singing, drinking and tragic-heroic dancing would intoxicate them. The rest was easy.

Denise turned up one Thursday night with three other women. They were part of a larger group, from England, who were on a cultural tour of Attica and the Peloponnese. The four who came to the club were divorcees wanting to experience Greek nightlife and have a good time. The Greek men were only too pleased to oblige and, when you add the money they were throwing around, the girls were easily impressed, especially in these austere times.

George had the appearance of someone in his early fifties. Although tall and well-proportioned, his youthful and athletic figure came at a price: five days a week at the gym for one and a half hours and regular swimming in the sea. He was realistic about his prospects and normally set his sights on women over forty-five. Denise was forty-two. He was surprised how quickly he'd seduced her and, by the following Saturday, she had abandoned her party and their tour to go off with him on his boat to explore some of the nearby islands.

Naturally, he'd assumed it was just another holiday fling but, after she had returned home, she wrote him romantic letters and either called or sent him text messages every day. As soon as she had saved enough money, she returned for a long weekend. This now was her third visit and, with the summer weather, he had taken her for another cruise. His only regret, as he glanced at the approaching storm, was leaving Photis, his handyman, behind. He usually slept on the yacht and made a far better job of securing it than he did. But it was Denise who wanted them to have privacy for once, and it was not long before he discovered why.

Now here they were. He had often spoken to her about this place. How beautiful it was, the view, the isolation, all the time knowing that he should not bring her. Then, on Friday night, after a romantic meal ashore, they were on the yacht at anchor and in bed. After they had made love, she lay on top of him, her rich chestnut locks caressing his face as she showered him with kisses, and asked him to bring her, her large brown eyes pleading. How could he say no? Especially after the news she had just given him.

Yesterday they had eaten a sumptuous fish lunch on Thassos to the northeast, rode at anchor for siesta time, and then motored in before darkness fell. The glassy sea made it seem like a fairy tale. With the food they had brought with them, they had feasted on the yacht while watching the Euro 2012 Football Championships on the television on board before going up to the house, where they had made love in the bedroom overlooking the sea. They would stay just the one night and then in the morning sail back to Piraeus. He would take her to the airport and still be in his office first thing Monday morning. He would then have time to get his head round the news she had given.

He enjoys the euphoria of the moment and almost manages to keep the memories away, but, as always, they come back. 'Ah Anna, my wonderful Anna, my beautiful Anna.' How could there be a greater love than hers? He recalls his last annual pilgrimage to her grave in Cyprus, within the precinct of her family enclosure at the cemetery on the barren, treeless hill. How he'd fallen to his knees and cried. What bitter tears of regret he'd shed. Regret of being deprived of her loving embrace for all the years she was alive. Regret at not being able to give her his love and passion in return. No prison sentence could offer a greater hardship. And then there was Jacob, the only product of their love. 'My son, her son, our son.'

As hard as he tried, he could not forget. All the wine, women and pretend romance in the world were no consolation for what he had lost, for what he had sacrificed. It always came back to this; the total futility of it all.

But now the storm is getting closer and it is beginning to worry him. Not the storm itself, but that there is something else going on. Something does not feel right. He should not have come here with Denise, not under the circumstances. He had fooled himself into thinking that they would not find out. He had sneaked in after dark, but, of course, they would not have to see him to know, and if they knew, so would the other. Why is the storm not waking Denise? His thinking is becoming confused.

Suddenly, with a gust of wind, the rain comes lashing straight into the bedroom. George gets up with the intention of closing the shutters but, as he looks down into the cove, he freezes. The rain is sheeting so hard that he can only see as far as his boat and the surrounding cove. Then, from the turbulent water, a fog begins to rise. As it increases in substance, it begins to glow from within.

He realises he should flee, but his earlier feelings of despair leave him inert, he no longer sees the point. Instead, he watches as the mist continues to thicken and grow, filling the cove beneath and lapping against the house. He hears the front door burst open and shortly afterwards the sounds of movement behind him, but his attention is riveted by the glowing cloud and he cannot move his body. His will has slipped away and he barely has time to acknowledge that this is the end. Involuntarily, he turns round and starts to walk towards the bedroom door, passing the now empty bed.

Chapter 3: Chris Zacharias

Sunday, 24th June

The marble city was coming to the end of a summer's day. As the air cooled, the inhabitants shook off their heat-induced lethargy, abandoned their airless apartments and took to the troubled streets, some to protest, some in search of consolation and companionship and some to look for entertainment. The arteries of the metropolis, radiating from its well-lit and densely populated heart, were humming with traffic.

Away from the shops, supermarkets and boutiques, the clubs, cafés, bars and restaurants, in a green and leafy suburb of detached houses surrounded by manicured lawns and flowerbeds, the peace of a Sunday evening was maintained.

In one of these symbols of status and success, Chris Zacharias had put the phone down for the last time that evening. He was sitting out on his raised porch overlooking the garden. It was well after dark and beginning to get chilly so he would soon need to go inside. This was one of the advantages of living in the northern suburbs of Athens: the escape from the oppressive heat, especially at night. He imagined his wife and elderly mother-in-law sitting in the lounge, watching television, and his two children tucked up in their beds upstairs.

The increasing humidity was intensifying the scents of the many blooms laid out in the beds that surrounded the house; but this was not giving him any pleasure.

Under normal circumstances he would be following the football on the television in his study, but he had little appetite for that tonight. It was only now, with all the arrangements completed, that the sadness of the day caught up with him. George was not only his business mentor but also his best friend. Without his help at the beginning of his career, would he have all this: a two-storey detached house, surrounded by fragrant gardens, in one of the best areas of the city? As a recently qualified solicitor when they first met, his future success was far from guaranteed.

The fateful call had come after he had returned from church and had finished having lunch with his family. It was Photis. He had told him how his boss George had taken his latest girlfriend away for the week, for a tour of the islands, except this time without him. He was completely distraught as he explained that just an hour earlier he had received a call from the policeman of Halia. A local fisherman and his daughter had been cruising along the coast with their boat, inspecting the rocky shallows for octopuses, when they spotted the yacht in the cove. As it appeared to have sustained damage to its stern, they went in for a closer look and to check that it was securely moored. That was when they saw George's body lying on the pebbly beach at the foot of the cliff below his house. The local doctor had been called out and seemed to think that George had suffered a heart attack. He estimated that he had been dead for about six to eight hours.

The local policeman's theory, supported by the doctor, was that, because there was a storm that night, George was worried about the lashings of the boat and went out to have a look at them. At the top of the cliff he had either suffered a heart attack or lost his footing on the slippery path and fallen to the beach below. Despite having several abrasions on his body, it was not the fall that had killed him outright. It was probably the shock of his injuries which caused his heart to fail.

When Photis had asked about the woman, the policeman had said that there was no one else there, nor any evidence, either in the house or on the yacht, that anyone had been with him. Zacharias assured Photis that he doubted that George would take a girlfriend to the island and his ancestral house. What had probably happened was that they had either fallen out or gone their separate ways over the weekend, and George had decided to make a quick visit to Halia before coming home. He was having renovation work carried out on the house and it would have been logical for him to want to check the progress.

Photis did not sound happy with this but there was no time to consider whether it was a plausible explanation or not. It would be up to the police to investigate it further, if they chose. As George's solicitor and executor, it was now his responsibility to make all the arrangements. George's only close relatives were his son, brother and sister. He had called the brother and sister right away and broken the news, but George had left specific instructions as to how his son was to be told. The two had been estranged for many years. Zacharias's next call had been to book a flight for the next day to London's Heathrow airport.

After a quick visit that afternoon to his office in Piraeus to pick up his friend's file and will, he had made arrangements with the undertakers on the nearby island of Lichas. Normally in Greece a body would need to be buried the next day, but this would not be possible in this case. The undertakers would have to take the ferry across and collect the body and prepare it to be buried next Saturday. Special dispensation would have to be obtained from the local authorities.

Although he had few surviving relatives, George was popular and had many friends. The funeral would be held on Lichas, which was more convenient for people to get to and the cathedral was larger. The coffin would then be taken back to Halia for interment in the family tomb.

It occurred to Zacharias that he would probably have to give a eulogy. There was much he could say that the mourners could relate to. But what about the things he could not say? There was a world of mystery that surrounded George. There were many questions he had about his friend, which he had hoped would one day be answered. Now he feared that these secrets would be buried with him.

He shivered in the dropping temperature and started gathering his papers. Dealing with the son was going to be the difficult part. He could only imagine what resentments the boy would be harbouring. How to explain his father's true feelings and intentions?

Zacharias decided a whisky was needed to help him sleep.

Chapter 4: Jake

Monday, 25ᵗʰ June

Jake put away his papers for the day.

As a sixth form geography teacher, there were always plenty of additional tasks and he could delay his departure considerably. On this particular Monday in June, he locked up the staff room at five fifty-five, walked through the deserted corridors of the two-storey concrete building and was in the car park starting up his Honda Civic just after six.

The drive home to the other end of the attractive market town, nestled in the Chiltern Hills of Buckinghamshire, was short, despite the evening traffic being at its peak. It was a beautiful summer's day.

Jake's red brick and slate-tiled terraced house was on the right-hand side of a quiet and narrow cul-de-sac of similar dwellings. Four properties farther along from his, the row came to an end and the road ran along the towpath of a canal that in turn traversed the valley. There was a footbridge to the opposite bank and an area of woods. The latter was one of his favourite places, which he enjoyed at all times of the year. If there was still light after his return from work, he would go for a walk before supper.

Most of the houses were owned by commuters to London and they did not start returning home until after seven. At this time of day he was guaranteed to find somewhere to park outside his front door. As he approached, however, he was dismayed to find his place taken. The offender was not even one of his neighbour's cars; he would not have minded that.

Parked awkwardly in front of his home was a top-of-the-range, metallic silver Mercedes.

His final resting place was only twenty yards away but he was annoyed just the same. He walked back with his briefcase in one hand and keys ready in the other. As he passed the interloper's car, he saw an overweight, middle-aged man in a white shirt and black tie sitting in the passenger's seat reading a newspaper.

The houses on Jake's side of the street were set back from the pavement by short, front gardens. His boundary was a waist-high brick wall with a black enamelled metal gate. As always he felt a tinge of shame at his neglected front patch. His neighbours' frontages fell into two categories: either a minimalist square of mowed grass with a few potted plants or a vibrant display of gardening prowess. Both shared one feature in common: tidiness. Something he would have to address in the near future.

His front door opened directly into the living room. This was a simple affair with a television in the far corner, bookshelves on both sides of an ornate Victorian tiled fireplace, a settee, a coffee table and some easy chairs.

Once inside, he took off his shoes and left them, together with his briefcase, by the door on the short carpet runner intended to capture any dirt and keep the beech wood flooring clean. Indoors, tidiness of a basic kind prevailed.

Next he removed his jacket and tie and draped them over the back of the nearest chair before picking up the morning's mail from the floor below the letterbox. He sat on the chair to look through it: the phone bill and several items of junk mail, the latter of which would go straight into the recycling bin, but nothing of interest.

He dropped the lot on the table and, looking past the settee, stared at his bay window through the net curtains of which he could see the diffused image of the houses on the opposite side of the road.

This was his predictable routine when he came home in the evening. It all ended with that bay window which Charly had loved. It was the reason she'd decided that they should buy this house, the first and only property they'd owned together.

He'd never ascertained what it was about that feature she'd found so attractive. He much preferred the fireplace and, when there was a blaze in progress, he could spend hours mesmerised by the flames.

In better days, when she was still with him, he would come home, do the housework, light a fire, if needed, and have a meal ready by the time she arrived back from London. Gradually her returns had become later and later and he'd begun to notice the smell of alcohol on her breath. Then the so-called late meetings had started; the ones that lasted till the last train. He'd sensed there was something wrong but had not wanted to believe it. She was a solicitor after all. These days, and in such difficult times, they all had to work late to get on, and did it not make sense to spend a few nights a week in a hotel in London so as to get an early start the next day? He should have confronted her sooner.

His situation now was rather different: twenty-nine years old, career opportunities mediocre, no intimate relationships and the prospects thereof pretty close to zero. At least at work he could focus on his tasks and not think about being lonely.

They had met during their first year at university. He was studying geology and she was reading law. It was their first serious relationship. He still lived at home at the time and she had come down from Yorkshire and was in student digs. When they graduated and started work, they moved in together. At first they rented for a few years whilst saving the money to help buy this place. Jake had wanted to get married then, but Charly always put it off as 'not being the right time'. She was never sure, was she?

Soon after they had moved in, things began to change. He settled into the teacher's life while she joined a leading firm in London. It was not long before she forged ahead of him, both in salary and ambition.

Looking back, he could probably guess when she'd started being interested in the other man. The signs manifested themselves in the bedroom. When they had first met they were both inexperienced. After a while they managed to make it work, but by then the passionate phase had passed and Charly started making excuses: she was too tired, she had a headache, it was the wrong time of the month or she just did not feel like it. But that was not the sign. No, bizarrely, the clue was that she started wanting to have sex more often. Was she making a last attempt to make it work or was she fantasizing about the other man? He would never know, nor did he want to. Anyway, that phase lasted two months and then abruptly stopped and the late returns and the overnight stays in London began.

He actually saw him once. It was at the law firm's Christmas party: a dinner and dance at an expensive hotel. Geoff was one of the partners in the firm; early thirties, tall, fair-haired, immaculately groomed and dressed. This was before their relationship started and Jake remembered thinking that he did not like him and that this was a man who would be ruthless in his quest to get what he wanted. He'd wanted to throw something at him, preferably his fist. Funny thing intuition.

Now, eighteen months after Charly's departure, he knew he should have moved on, but he felt strangely unwilling, lacking any desire for career challenges and intimate relationships. As far as the latter were concerned, he knew he was attractive to women. The way female members of staff and older pupils interacted with him made that clear. Could his reluctance have anything to do with the fact that so far in his life he had lost everyone who was important to him? First his father had left when he was young, then, much later, his mother had died of cancer and, more recently, Charly had betrayed him. What was the point? He had no motivation to discover new ways of losing people he cared for.

He considered going for a walk in the woods or along the canal before making supper. Nature in general, and the woods in particular, energised him, filled him with something that he could not explain. It was the feeling that perhaps life did have a purpose after all. He could also do with collecting more wood for his winter stockpile, which he was still replenishing.

He looked at his watch. It would be a short walk today. It was the last week of the Wimbledon fortnight and tennis was one of the sports he enjoyed watching. He was looking forward to seeing the rest of the day's play and also catching up with the Euro Championships. He balanced watching sport with a degree of participation, so he had been vigorously active all his life. Running, swimming, hockey, badminton and squash; he had tried them all at some point. When he'd moved here he'd also joined a gym and usually dropped in for an hour or so on his way to work.

He was just about to go upstairs to change into more casual clothes when he heard the double squeak and clang his gate made when it was opened and then shut. This was quickly followed by three sharp knuckle-wraps on his front door. He didn't react. Nobody ever visited him. Since Charly had left he'd succeeded in distancing himself from all his friends until even the most persistent had given up trying to call on him. It was probably a hawker wanting to sell him double-glazing or a new kitchen, both of which he already had. Perhaps if he did not answer, whoever it was would push something through the letterbox and go away. He wondered why they had bothered to shut the front gate behind them. Perhaps it was a Jehovah's Witness anticipating a long conversation. They usually came in pairs. God forbid they should look in through the window and see him sitting there.

The sharp three-beat knock was repeated and he forced himself to act, prepared to pour scorn on the transgressor. He opened the door and, to his surprise, it was the man from the Mercedes. He was short, as well as fat, with black curly hair and a round handsome face. He was wearing black-rimmed glasses and a dark blue suit. A gold tiepin fastened his black tie to his shirt and he was carrying an expensive black leather briefcase.

"My name's Chris Zacharias. I'm a solicitor from Greece," he said in perfect English, talking quickly but quietly. He seemed a bit anxious. "I've come to talk to you about your father."

His father! He had not seen or spoken to him for seven years. The bastard had not even bothered to call when Charly had left, something he would have heard about from Jake's grandmother. It would be just like him to communicate through a solicitor. Anything to do with his father brought on a rage in him.

"I haven't seen my father since my mother's funeral seven years ago," Jake said calmly, not betraying any emotion. "Tell him that if there's anything he wants to talk to me about, he can come and do it himself, and I won't promise to speak to him even then." He went to shut the door in the solicitor's face.

"I wish I could," the solicitor replied firmly, putting his hand up to stop the door. "I genuinely wish I could." His voice faltered. "But you're father's dead. Please, may I come in?"

"Dead! Did you say dead?"

"Yes," the solicitor said solemnly. "I'm sorry." Not waiting for a reply or an invitation, he walked past a startled, motionless Jake, and stood in the room. For a few awkward moments they stared at each other. Finally, the solicitor took the initiative and shut the front door. He put down his briefcase and started removing his jacket.

"Please sit," Jake said, signalling with his hand towards the sitting area. The solicitor hung his jacket on a hook behind the door. Jake offered him an armchair while he sat on the settee opposite. He was confused. His father dead? Despite all his anger and frustration, deep within he had hoped that by some miracle the past years were all a misunderstanding and his father really did care and they would be reconciled. "I'm sorry for my rudeness," Jake added, "but my father and I ..."

"You don't need to tell me about your relationship with your father," Zacharias said kindly, raising his hand to stop him. "I have been his solicitor and friend for many years. That is why I came from Athens to see you."

"What happened? How did it happen?"

"He was found yesterday morning on the beach in front of his house on Halia. The doctor who examined him believes he suffered a heart attack either before or after falling down the cliff at the front."

"How could that happen? It's not a dangerous cliff," Jake commented, remembering photographs he had seen.

"There was a thunderstorm at the time; maybe the ground became slippery."

"But what was he doing there at this time of year? He wouldn't normally go until August; end of July at the earliest." Although he had not spoken to his father for years, his paternal grandmother used to call him regularly, until she'd passed away last year.

"We don't know. Nobody knows. Maybe we'll never know," Zacharias said, sounding frustrated. Jake perceived that the solicitor had emotions of his own to deal with. "It seems he left Piraeus with the yacht a few days before to visit some islands and ended up there. He was having renovation work done on the house. Maybe he was curious to see how it had turned out."

"Didn't he have Photis with him?"

"No, he went with a woman."

"Sounds like my father," Jake said, shaking his head from side to side. "What happened to her?"

"No evidence was found of her or her belongings either in the house or on the yacht. She was last seen with him on Thassos. The police are trying to trace her but think that she must've left him to go back home and your father decided to visit Halia before heading back to Piraeus."

"Does Thassos have an airport?"

"No, you have to take the ferry to Kavala on the mainland and catch a flight from there." Unfortunately, this woman's a bit of a mystery. She'd visited your father a few times; the police only have her first name, although the consensus is she's English. I've not been able to find any of her details, either in his house or at the office."

Jake was not at all surprised by the presence of a woman. Over the years he had assumed that his father had left them in order to live the playboy lifestyle in Greece. Then his demeanour changed as he remembered something. "Did the doctor say what time my father died?"

"In the early hours," Zacharias replied, "between three and four."

"You're two hours ahead of us, aren't you?"

"Yes, why?"

"No, nothing," Jake said, looking momentarily distracted. "I'm sorry; I didn't catch your name the first time."

"Chris Zacharias."

"I think I remember you being mentioned by my mother. You came all this way to tell me about my father's death? Why didn't you just call?"

"I wasn't just your father's solicitor. I was also his friend, and in his will he appointed me his executor. He left specific instructions that, in the event of his death, I should meet with you. There's much to talk about but, before I start, I wouldn't mind going to the bathroom and then having something to drink. I was waiting in the car for some time."

"What can I get you?"

"I like English tea, preferably black with lemon if you have it," Zacharias said, standing up. "However hard you try, it never tastes the same in Greece. I'm told it's the water."

"I have a lemon," Jake replied, also standing. "The bathroom's through the kitchen. In fact, why don't you bring your things with you? We'll both be more comfortable sitting at the kitchen table."

The doorway through to the back of the house was opposite the front door and past the staircase to the upper floor on the left. The kitchen consisted of a square room, the width of the house, with an antique pine table in the centre, and there was an archway through to an area Jake used as an office. At the far end of this was a door that led to a small lobby, which in turn had the door to the garden on the left and another to a shower room and toilet. Jake sent Zacharias on through.

Once he was alone he stood for a few moments, one hand on the table, trying to understand what he was feeling. His most predominant emotions were anger and frustration. The long-term anger was directed at his father and the frustration was in knowing that there was now no opportunity of confronting their long-outstanding issues.

He stared out of the window above the kitchen sink to the rear of his garden. It was a gentle slope down and ended in a low hedge with a wooden gate that led to the towpath of the canal. To the right of this was the shed in which he stored his winter wood. The rest of the garden was laid to lawn and had been mowed recently. He could see the magnificent trees of the woods on the opposite bank. At this time of year the canal would start to get busy.

He filled the electric kettle and put it on to boil while he retrieved a teapot, tea bags, cups, saucers, sugar, milk and a lemon from various points in the kitchen.

"You have a nice house, from what I can see of it," Zacharias said after he'd returned. "Victorian, is it?"

"Late Victorian," Jake replied. "These used to be working men's houses. Now they're sought after by young professionals working in London; ironic isn't it?"

"How many bedrooms?"

"Just two. I'm afraid I've no biscuits or cakes to offer," Jake said as he filled the teapot with boiling water and brought it to the table.

"That's fine; I'm on a diet and would rather not be tempted," Zacharias said, feeling his paunch. "I always want to nibble when I'm away on business."

They pulled out chairs at the ends of the table and sat opposite each other. "We'll let the tea brew for a few minutes," Jake said.

"I understand you live alone now?"

"Yes, it's been over a year," Jake replied. He felt a slight resentment being asked such a personal question.

"So where are you staying?"

"I flew in lunch time, hired the car from the airport and drove up. I hope to fly back tonight."

"Okay, so what is it you have taken so much trouble to come and tell me?"

"Are you sure you're ready for this? You need to have a clear head. Do you want more time? I can stay somewhere overnight and come back tomorrow."

"I'm as ready as I'll ever be." As yet Jake felt nothing terribly overpowering.

"As I said, your father left a will of which I'm the executor. What did you know about his financial affairs?"

"Up to the time he abandoned us, he was a property developer in London. After that, my mother never spoke about his business, although I imagine he must've sent her money."

"During his time in London his operation was relatively modest. That was twenty-five years ago. In Greece, however, he expanded the business considerably."

"That surprises me. From what I imagined, my father spent most of his time in nightclubs and on his yacht," Jake said. He had heard as much from his grandmother, who didn't flinch at expressing her disapproval.

"Your father didn't just play hard but worked hard. He only eased up in the last few years. He employed some competent people and the organisation now runs itself on a day-to-day basis. He was proud of what he'd created. He was also particular about what he wanted to happen to his business and possessions after he died. That's where I come in."

"My father must've trusted you," Jake commented, pouring out the tea. He slid the solicitor's cup and saucer towards him.

"I worked with him for many years. Your father's instructions are specific," the solicitor said, acknowledging the compliment with a smile, while pulling the tea closer. "To start with, he separated his business from his personal assets. As you know, there are the two apartments in Kensington, his home in Paleo Psychiko, Athens, and the two houses on Halia. The large house on the island, the one on the cliff, and the other smaller one in the town, he has left to his brother and sister. All the rest of the properties he's passing to you."

Jake fell silent, staring at his folded hands resting on the table in front of him. He was almost as shocked to hear this as he was of his father's death. His thoughts were in turmoil. Zacharias waited a respectful time before asking: "Do you have any questions?"

Jake was having difficulty expressing himself. "I haven't spoken to my father for years," he finally said. "He abandoned my mother and me when I was quite young, you know."

"I know all about that."

"What I mean is I wasn't expecting anything from him. I knew he had two houses on the island, although I've never been."

"He bought the house in the village for his mother. Your grandmother didn't like staying in the big house as it was too far from the town and her friends. After she died, he split it into an upper and lower apartment. The upper one is rented to a local couple. The husband works for the council and the wife's the island's nurse. The lower part was let out to a teacher for most of this winter, but it's vacant now. He only recently got round to sorting out your grandmother's possessions. You did, of course, know your father was adopted?"

"My mother told me some time ago."

"Well, since your aunt and uncle were the natural children of your grandparents, I think he felt obliged to give them the island properties."

"My grandmother was the only one who kept in touch," Jake reflected, appearing not to have heard the last thing Zacharias had said. "She called me every Sunday from Greece. Every Sunday until the end." His voice quivered with emotion. "You mentioned that the business is separate?" he asked, returning to the subject.

"Before I forget, he also owned an orchard on the island, not far from the main house," Zacharias said. "He's left this to a local couple. They looked after it for many years."

"I understand."

"Your father's instructions for the business are rather different. As I told you, the company runs itself on a day-to-day basis, but it still needs someone to head it, to guide it. Your father put it together with you in mind. He always intended you to take over. If you undertake to run the business, you will be given all of it, less a provision in cash he has made for Photis."

"This doesn't make sense to me," Jake said angrily. "On the one hand my father has hardly any contact with me for over twenty years and now you're telling me he's built up this business with me in mind?"

"There's no easy explanation," Zacharias said, looking down at his half-empty cup.

"And what if I can't or don't want to do that?" Jake asked. He would never have imagined himself running a business, especially one he knew nothing about.

"Then the business will be dismantled, the assets sold off and, after Photis's share, you will get sixty per cent and your aunt and uncle the remainder."

"And how much is this business worth?"

"Your father and I calculated its value every year. Even though the property market in Greece has dropped considerably, my estimate of its value today is about twenty million euros."

"What? Did you say twenty million euros?" Jake was astonished. He had read in the press about property at home and abroad and had some basic knowledge of values. He'd assumed his father must have had a few offices and houses mortgaged to the hilt and would have accepted a value of up to a million euros.

"Yes, all of which will be yours if you undertake to run it yourself."

"What would that involve?" Jake said. He was in conflict. On the one hand he wanted to reject this offer outright. On the other, the idea of having a challenge appealed to him.

"Leaving England, going to live in Greece and devoting yourself to his business."

"But I know nothing about it. I'm not sure I remember how to speak any Greek. I certainly would find it difficult to write or read it."

"It will take time, but you will learn. Your father had faith in you. And you're still young. Your aunt and uncle unfortunately are not competent in business."

"What do you mean?" Jake said. Over the years they had made no effort to keep in touch.

"It was your grandfather who was the first in the family to be interested in property development and made a respectable amount from it, particularly on Lichas. He never disguised the fact that he favoured his own children so he turned the management of his wealth over to them. They lost everything. They mortgaged the properties and invested the proceeds on the Athens stock exchange. In the end, your father had to support your grandmother after your grandfather died. It's not surprising he'd rather the business was sold than turned over to them."

"So, in the worst case, I will end up with twelve million euros and the personal properties. Why shouldn't I settle for that? It's more than I'll ever need for the rest of my life. God, it's more than I can imagine."

"More like eight million after taxes but, if you think the money is all you'll ever need, then that's fine, but your father wanted you to have more than that; a new way of life. The life you would have had if he hadn't left you."

"The life I would have had?" His emotions were stirred, the old rage was returning. "That life was a childhood living without a father and with a heartbroken mother. Why didn't my father approach me and tell me this himself?"

"He wanted to but circumstances never permitted him to do so. Also, he didn't intend to die so young."

"Circumstances? What circumstances? Now with both my parents gone I'll never learn the truth. I'll never know why they split up. It doesn't make sense."

"I didn't know your father at the time he left England. I first met him shortly afterwards. He never spoke specifically about the reasons why he left your mother."

"Excuse me, left my mother? My mother did nothing wrong." Jake had raised his voice and pounded the table. "Look, no offence, I'm sure my father was good to you, but I wouldn't be interested in turning into another version of him. The sooner you sell the business and everybody gets their money the better. I'm sure my aunt and uncle will be pleased."

"I'm sorry, I didn't intend to offend you," Zacharias said, looking distressed. "In the end it's your choice. Your father's instructions allow you three months to decide."

"I'm sorry too," Jake said, raising his hand. "I over-reacted, but my answer will still be the same in three months' time."

"Well, if that's the case then, in three months from the date of his death, I will proceed with the dismantling of the business. But there's something you need to do now."

"What's that?"

"It was your father's wish to be buried on the island, on Halia, in the family tomb with his adopted mother. As you know, in Greece burial normally takes place the day after death. I have asked for a special extension in order to give you and his geographically distant friends the chance to attend."

"I can't go to Greece now. I have a job to do and it's the end of term," Jake said. When his grandmother had died, he'd had the same problem.

"I'm sure your employers will understand and, besides, I hardly think you need to worry about job security."

"That's not the point. I have a responsibility to my students and fellow teachers. I can't drop all that for a man who didn't even have the decency to explain why he turned our lives upside down."

"All right, I understand. Although the burial will take place on Halia early on Saturday evening, the funeral will be in the central cathedral of Lichas at midday. You can easily make that and be back over the weekend."

Jake considered this for a moment. He tried to have a sip of tea, but his hands were still shaking from his earlier anger. He felt some empathy for this man and his attempts to paint his father in a favourable light. There was also the possibility that if he did not attend his father's funeral he might regret it afterwards, which is what had happened with his grandmother. Physically saying goodbye to his father might put an end to the bitterness he had been harbouring for years. "That's fine, I can do that, I suppose."

"You can take the night flight to Athens on Friday, the first connection to Lichas on Saturday morning, go to the funeral, stay one night in a local hotel and fly back on Sunday. Do you want me to book the tickets for you? I just need to use the phone."

"I'm sure I can manage that myself."

"There's a direct number where you can arrange connecting flights and get tickets at good prices," Zacharias continued. "I'll write it down. Also, as far as a hotel is concerned, do you want something luxurious with all the facilities or somewhere friendly and interesting?"

"The friendly and interesting sounds more appealing."

"Good, there's one I can recommend which is centrally placed." He took some paper out of his briefcase, together with his address book, and started writing down the details. "The fact is that, apart from attending the funeral, you'll need to come down to Greece in order to complete the legal and tax side of the transfer of the estate and business."

"Can't that be done from here?" Jake said, conscious of the forthcoming Olympics.

"As things are, it takes months to complete all the paperwork and pay the inheritance taxes. If you don't come to Greece at all, it could easily take years. Have you made plans for the holidays?"

"No, I haven't arranged anything."

"Then why don't you come down for the summer so you can be close at hand? I suggest you leave as soon as school finishes in order to get the ball rolling."

"I don't know, I guess I have no choice. My last day is the twentieth of July."

"How soon after that can you be ready?"

"That weekend I expect."

"That's great; I can have the paperwork ready. You'll need to spend a few days in Athens first, then why not go to the island? It'll be the only chance you'll have of staying there before the properties go to your aunt and uncle. You can stay at your grandmother's house."

"I'll think about it," Jake said. He'd never been but was curious as to what it was like. He needed a change. He needed to get away.

"As for this weekend, just give me a call when you have your flight details so I can arrange for you to be picked up from Lichas airport. I'll leave you my card." The solicitor placed this on the table.

"What about my father's place in Athens?"

"His belongings are being sorted out. In the summer you'll be able to use it."

"You mentioned a provision for Photis."

"Your father's giving him one million euros."

"Gosh. He must've thought highly of him."

"Yes and Photis, in turn, is inconsolable."

"What about inheritance tax? I suppose that will take a lot out of the personal estate?"

"There will be tax to pay on the residential properties too. We can square that off by using some of the cash from the company. The tax on the business itself wouldn't be so bad if it was being transferred intact."

"I see you know what you're doing."

"Most of the time," he said smiling. "There's one more thing."

"Yes?"

"Apart from the various bank accounts your father had in Greece, there are also two off-shore company accounts in Guernsey. These are to do with the Kensington flats. I will give you the details of the solicitor associated with us here in London who will be dealing with the matter on your behalf," Zacharias said, beginning to write this down. "You'll also need to go to the International Business branch of the bank here in the City and provide identification and a new mandate. The solicitor will do the rest. I'm sure it won't take long. By the way, you don't happen to have an account in Greece?"

"No, why should I? I've hardly ever been."

"I didn't think so; I've brought you some forms. It's an application to open an account. I've put in all the details; I just need you to sign it." He handed it over to Jake. "I've used the Athens address. When you go to the bank for the off-shore companies you can pop in to the London branch of the National Bank of Greece so they can verify your ID. You can instruct them to send the endorsement to the branch in Piraeus. Then, by the time you come for the summer, your account will be up and running."

"Sounds good," Jake said as he signed the form. "But won't I need to deposit some money?"

"No, that won't be necessary. I'll transfer some from the business. Apart from that, I've covered everything. Your father was meticulous not to leave any loose ends."

"I'd say he left lots of those, but I know what you mean. Would you like some more tea?"

Zacharias looked at his watch. "Thank you, I'll say no. I should take the car back and check into the night flight, but I'll see you at the funeral on Saturday."

"I suppose so."

Zacharias gathered his papers into his briefcase. At the front door he put on his jacket. They shook hands and Jake watched him get into the Mercedes and drive off.

He looked at his watch. It was coming up to seven thirty, too late for a walk in the woods. He went back into the kitchen and switched on the small television sitting on one of the worktops. He would be able to follow the tennis replays while he prepared a meal. He enjoyed cooking and was careful to eat a healthy diet. First though he felt the need to sit down for a few minutes.

He walked through his study area and out the back door into the open air. This part of the garden at the start of the house and before the slope down to the canal was laid out as a patio with stone slabs. There was a green enamelled metal table with four matching chairs. At the boundary, where the patio met the grass, he'd built a square, brick barbeque.

He sat on one of the chairs that faced the canal. He enjoyed this view. If the bay window was Charly's reason for buying this house, the canal and the water were his. He could walk as far as he wanted in either direction and then there were the woods, but there was something about water that was compelling.

As he sat, his mind drifted to other thoughts and then one in particular. When Zacharias had mentioned the day his father had died, he'd recalled a dream he'd had in the early hours of Sunday morning. In it he was looking out of the bedroom window as a fog developed over the canal. This was not unusual in real life as the waterway ran through a valley, but what was abnormal was that it was raining heavily at the same time with high winds, thunder and lightning. In the dream the fog was rising out of the water. As it thickened it began to glow yellow, as if it contained a light source within. Continuing to grow, it started moving up the garden towards the house. He felt in imminent danger but at the same time drawn to the fog. When it had covered the patio and was against the house he thought he heard someone breaking in through the back door. He started to panic, wondering how he was going to escape. He'd woken in a cold sweat.

Was it just a coincidence that he should be having a dream of a thunderstorm at the same time as his father was dying in one? The sceptic would certainly think so.

Yes, now he really was alone in the world. First he'd lost his father, then his mother, then Charly and now his father for the second time. He experienced an upwelling of emotion from within and started to cry.

Chapter 5: Alexander Kephalas

Saturday, 30ᵗʰ June

Alexander Kephalas opened his eyes. The breeze into which he was facing ruffled his dark wavy hair. He looked at his watch and saw that he had dozed for some forty minutes. It was refreshing this wind, as it was on most afternoons. He ran his fingers through his long locks. The roots were damp, indicating that it was time to give his hair its summer cut.

He enjoyed this time on the balcony of his bedroom, looking out on his favourite view while his wife slept inside. On the horizon were the shadows of distant islands, but, apart from that, it was just the sea in its infinitely varying moods; much like him in fact.

He had always wanted to build a house on this spot, on this peninsula, where he could hear the waves and swells break onto the rocks below. His family owned the land so it was inevitable, in his mind at least, that it would happen, as it did, and that was not to mention the other associations with the past. So here it was; another monument to his existence on earth. He thought of the others: the condominium on the Florida coast, also overlooking the sea, the mansion in the most exclusive part of Athens, the townhouse in the Hampstead suburb of London and, of course, the yacht. All that property in his name. All that fame and fortune. Another member of the extended Halian family who had made it big. In the study at his home in Athens he had a shelf full of books dedicated to Halia's businessmen and merchants, their success going back for generations. What unique circumstances could have come together to create such wealth concentrated in such a small population, on such a small island in the middle of nowhere? What circumstances indeed? If the truth be known.

Still, with the help of these 'unique circumstances', he had brought up a family, created a fortune, instigated history-changing events, seduced some of the most desirable women, danced and brawled his way around the world and generally passed the time, such as now. And all of that by following someone else's instructions. How cool was that? This left time for the important things in life, namely women, conflict, dance and alcohol.

He had to admit it was good to be part of the island, part of the community. At first he'd resented having to toe the line, but he had no choice. If he was to have what he wanted he had to follow instructions, and at times it did keep his excesses at bay, he had to concede that much. He may be under the rule of another, but he in turn had power over many. Besides, there had to be discipline. It was difficult being loyal to two opposing sides anyway. Initially he was torn but, through his efforts, he had managed to bring everyone closer together. At least they were now talking. Perhaps in time the others would realise how unrealistic their objective was to achieve and they would all get on much better as a result. In the meantime, he was the protector of the status quo.

As far as the matter in hand was concerned, he was of the opinion that action should have been taken sooner. Better late than never though. The prophecy had to be taken seriously, no matter how far-fetched or ambiguous it was. But everything was back under control. He was glad to see that arsehole George getting his due. He had lived a charmed life, perpetuated by the fact that one side thought it needed him and the other was, for once, too timid to act. He had always been a problem, not willing to cooperate, always wanting to go it alone. Well, okay, so he'd succeeded, but look at him now. Mortally dead and not taking any of it with him. He was on nobody's side, so nobody trusted him. As far as Kephalas knew, he could have been acting on his own account all along.

In his heart Kephalas did recognise his good fortune. Had George cooperated with his master, it would be George the favoured one, and not Kephalas, who would be reaping the rewards of power. Theoretically Jake now posed the same threat to Kephalas's position but, with both George and Anna dead, his life was well and truly fucked up. He lacked the substance to threaten anyone, let alone Kephalas or his boss. On the other hand, the others could easily manipulate him, and it was guaranteed that they would try to do so; he was their last hope after all. It was a good sign that Jake had not come to his father's burial on the island, the reason Kephalas was here today.

The policy now would be one of restraint and gentle persuasion. In this instance manipulation, coercion and corruption were much more constructive and fun. He would make sure that if Jake did come and try to establish himself in Greece, he would be welcomed as part of the community, but encouraged to stay away from Halia itself.

First he would have to find out the boy's intentions, where he stood. He knew his weakness so that part was going to be easy. Like father, like son. He would have to start making arrangements. Time was short.

He looked at his watch. He would wait for the sun to set before leaving. The yacht, moored to the pier below the front of the house, would take him to nearby Lichas, where he would meet friends for a floodlit evening tennis match on their estate, followed by a meal. Then he would travel overnight to Piraeus.

Chapter 6: The Mystery Lady

Monday, 2nd July

In an inn not more than four miles from Jake's house, a woman descended the stairs to the lobby. It was early evening. She approached the reception desk, informed the young man behind it that she would be checking out in the morning, and instructed him to book her a cab to take her to the nearest railway station upon her departure.

She was relieved to be leaving; she did not like hotels. This one was particularly dark and dismal. She passed into the dining room and sat at her usual table. The food at least was adequate, the restaurant being run by separate management.

She focused her attention on her body and what it needed today. It felt good after a prolonged session of yoga and meditation in her room. It was always a problem when travelling to find accommodation with enough space for these most important rituals.

The waiter came and left her the menu. As he walked away, he looked back at her inquisitively. Like most people, he did not know what to make of her, how to class her. Was she old or was she young? Was she attractive or was she plain? Was she easy-going or hard to please? Was she friendly or aloof?

When the waiter returned, she ordered a starter of grilled goat's cheese on a green salad with grated raw beetroot, to be followed by a main course of calf's liver with mashed root vegetables and onion gravy. She chose an additional portion of broccoli and a bottle of mineral water.

As she waited for her food, she reappraised her decision to return home. She was certain that Jake would be safe, for the time being. The moment she foresaw George's demise, she flew out to England to be close to him, just in case. She also wanted to sense his reaction, his feelings and his morale.

As she did so, she enjoyed the setting as well. She was sensitive to the feel of places. She had walked through miles of countryside and visited many towns and villages. There was much past conflict in these hills, but joy and peace as well.

As for Jake, it was as she had expected. There was nothing she could have done for his father, and George would have understood. If she had directly intervened, which was not her way, she would have revealed herself and then all would have been lost. With Jake it was different; she had to protect him at all cost. He was the last chance, the last opportunity for closure.

She had kept her presence hidden, just as she had done with previous generations. She had revealed herself to George as that proved necessary and ultimately fruitful in that they were able to keep Jake and Anna out of immediate harm. Now, with the funeral over and Jake at his most vulnerable, the indoctrination would begin.

It was in her nature to intuit things about Jake that those who would influence him could not. She knew that what they assumed would weaken him, would actually strengthen his resolve, what they thought would subdue his will, she believed would cause him to rebel. Once she had set him upon the right path, he would manifest his true self.

Now, with the course of fate having been set in motion, she had until the summer to prepare. The time for the resolution had come and it was none too soon. She was a tired old soul. The years of vigorous youth were all too brief but the decades of decline were long and tedious. There were only so many different ways you could experience life.

When her food came, she devoured it hungrily. She knew the staff were surprised how a woman her age could eat so much and still stay trim. In the morning she would have a good breakfast as well.

She generally tried to avoid air travel and instead would be making most of the journey by train. She had no shortage of time, no need to rush. She would take the Eurostar to Paris, stay a night in one of her favourite cities, and then continue to Brindisi, from where the overnight ferry would take her to Piraeus. After an evening in Athens, she would take another ferry to the island. There she would wait for events to unfold.

Chapter 7: Athens

Sunday, 22nd July

The new Athens international airport, completed over ten years ago and located outside the boundaries of the city, was a pleasant surprise, with the spacious halls and departure lounges, the air-conditioned passageways, shops, restaurants, cafés and modern conveniences exceeding expectations.

It was therefore all the more unpleasant to leave the cool terminal building for the oppressive outdoor heat, and Jake was grateful for the air-conditioned Mercedes waiting for him.

This, his second transit through the airport, was a lot more civilized than the previous one. The first was on the weekend following his father's death. He had taken the red-eye flight on the Friday evening, landing at three thirty the next morning. The connecting flight to Lichas departed three hours later, and spending most of that time on a plastic bucket-seat was not his idea of comfort.

The funeral on Lichas was a blur. Fortunately, Zacharias was at the entrance of the cathedral, waiting to escort him to the right place. He later gave a eulogy and, although Jake could not understand all of the content, what he did follow was touching. It seemed his father was a wonderful friend to many people; more was the pity then that he could not have extended this to his wife and son. Tellingly there was scant mention of his marriage in the speech.

Afterwards, Zacharias stood by Jake and whispered the names of people as they filed by to offer their condolences. This part lasted nearly an hour and involved a lot of hand-grasping, hugging and cheek-kissing from people he did not know and was not likely to ever meet again. At the end he was exhausted as much from sleeplessness and the heat as from the length of the ordeal.

When it was over, the coffin was taken to the ferry that connected with Halia. Zacharias was to accompany it but first took Jake back to the hotel in his cab. He mentioned that the police had discovered the identity of the woman his father had been with the day before his death. Although there was no record of her leaving Thassos, they were convinced that they had gone their separate ways before his father left for Halia. After that she seemed to have vanished.

Her name was Denise, she was English, divorced, with no children, but had two elderly parents. She worked as a legal secretary and her office colleagues and friends were adamant that she was in love with his father and could not wait to get back to him. The police theory was that they had a falling-out and, having nothing to live for, she took her life, probably by wading into the sea. A very Mediterranean explanation, inspired as much from a lack of public money for lengthy investigations as to cultural assumptions.

This official account must have been accepted because Jake heard nothing more about it in the weeks that followed.

With his luggage in the boot, he eased himself into the back seat and exchanged pleasantries with Dimitris the driver, a scrawny, dark-haired man, who explained in adequate English that he did all the work for Zacharias's law firm. Greek clients liked to see the same face, he took pains to make clear, which meant they left bigger tips. This was followed by a knowing wink.

Before setting off, he handed Jake a brown envelope. It was from Zacharias.

Outside the airport precinct the initial part of the drive was along a newly built highway, through an agricultural area with scattered rural housing. Once they had entered the sprawling and monotonous Athenian suburbs, Jake opened the envelope from the solicitor. Inside were a typed letter and a smaller envelope. The letter started with the usual Greek welcome and wishes for a good summer and rest.

It continued with an itinerary for Monday. It seemed Zacharias intended to get all the paperwork completed in one day, so Jake would be picked up early the next morning. First he would be taken to his father's office and then to the notary public for the signing of documents, for which Zacharias reminded him to take his passport. These were needed for the transfer of the estate and had to be submitted to the courts by Friday as that was the day they would close for the summer, not to reopen until the beginning of September. After the notary, Zacharias would take him out for lunch.

Jake was surprised how he had grown to like this man. During the weeks following the funeral Zacharias had often called to keep Jake updated. His letter continued by giving details of the house: the address, telephone number, and then a surprise. He owned not only a penthouse apartment but the entire building.

Zacharias explained that there was one house on the land when his father bought it. He had demolished this and built a block of four apartments and reserved the penthouse for himself. The one-bedroomed basement unit he had kept for his mother and, since her death, his Filipino girl used it. The middle two units were let at EUR 1,250 a month each, one to an architect and the other to a computer programmer. Both were married with children. Zacharias then gave a breakdown of expenses demonstrating how the rents, after tax, paid for the running and upkeep of the building and left a healthy balance in the repair fund.

In the smaller envelope was a bankbook, a debit card and pin number. He opened the book and saw that his new account had an opening balance of ten thousand euros.

It was a tediously long drive before they turned right off a three-laned main road and into a leafy enclave. Here there was a mixture of detached houses and three- and four-floor apartment blocks. All the properties were of similar height, at or around the tree line, generously spaced in large plots, individually designed and well-maintained.

This wealthy suburb was a maze of streets. Eventually the driver turned down a narrow, tree-lined lane and stopped at number seventy-nine. As Dimitris went to unload the luggage, Jake stepped out onto the grey pavement to survey his building.

The plot was rectangular and roughly twice as deep as it was wide. It was also below the level of the road. Jake guessed that this was in order to add an extra floor without exceeding any local height restrictions. The property was separated from the pavement by a low wall of grey brick and a dark brown painted wooden gate. He stood in front of the latter, from which a concrete ramp ran down the right-hand side to the back, where there was a row of four individual, open-fronted garages. Two contained cars and there was a scattering of children's toy vehicles and bikes. Beside these, along the rear boundary wall, were three well-trimmed mature trees.

The building itself was also rectangular and rendered in an attractive cream colour. The ground floor, first floor and penthouse had balconies that ran the width of the front elevation and each had extended green awnings that shaded them from the sun.

The side of the building he could see had a marble staircase that ran up to the ground floor entrance, with the basement apartment having its own separate door underneath. Each of the top three apartments had a set of glass doors opening onto an oval balcony. On the right side of the entrance, a pattern of transparent bricks ran up the building, and Jake presumed this was to let in light for the internal staircase. The rear of the building also had balconies with awnings on each of the three upper floors, but these were not as deep as those at the front.

The orange rays of the late afternoon sun were bathing the top part of the building and the penthouse. The general impression was that of a well-presented, well-maintained structure. Jake looked at his watch; it was seven thirty.

When Dimitris was ready, he opened the gate and, carrying a suitcase each, they walked down the ramp and up the stairs to the entrance. Taking a set of keys from his pocket, Dimitris opened the imposing wooden door and handed the keys to Jake.

They entered a cool and dark entrance hall decked in white marble with white painted walls. The diffusely-lit, circular staircase was on the right, the door to the ground floor apartment straight ahead with the elevator shaft between the two.

Dimitris helped him put his suitcases in the small, cramped lift. Jake handed him a five euro tip and assured him he would be waiting down on the pavement at nine the next morning. He pressed the second floor button and the lift started with a jolt. There was no internal door and he watched the first floor slide slowly by before the lift stopped on the second floor.

Removing his luggage, he paused outside his solid timber front entrance. He liked wood and he put his hand on it. It felt newly varnished. He was trying to come to terms with the idea that this was his apartment, this was his building. This door marked a threshold to a new life. He inserted the key and turned the lock.

The door swung open onto an entrance lobby. He dragged his suitcases into the dark apartment and shut the door behind him. To his right a corridor led off to the rear of the penthouse, and along the adjacent wall was a simple wooden bureau with a phone on it and next to it a chair. To his left the lobby opened onto a spacious living area, the far side of which consisted of two sets of sliding glass doors and wooden shutters separated by a metre-wide pillar; the former were open, the latter closed.

The right-hand half of this space was laid out as the dining area, having a highly polished dark wood table with six chairs and a matching glass-fronted dresser, set against the wall. The left-hand side consisted of three settees arranged around the sides of a glass-topped table. The floor was white marble tiles with grey veins, but there were rugs under the dining table and in the sitting area. The walls displayed framed watercolour prints of Greek landscapes. Two brass fans with wooden paddles were suspended from the ceiling. His initial reaction was that his father had good taste.

He was just taking in the detail of the upholstery when he heard the soft shuffle of footsteps behind him.

Turning round, he looked up the dimly-lit corridor. Coming towards him was what appeared to be an adolescent girl, barefoot, wearing blue shorts and a loose white tee-shirt. As she approached, he could see her long black hair, which she wore tied back, and her dark oriental eyes.

"Meester Jake, Meester Jake," she called in a tiny, squeaky voice. She had a slight but athletic figure and the top of her head only came up to his chest. She looked about to embrace him but, stopping short, she clasped her hands in front of her and said with a mournful expression on her face, "I so sorry about your father."

"Thank you," he said.

"I so glad to meet you. I'm Tina." She extended her hand.

He had of course realised that this was Christina, his father's Filipino girl. He remembered seeing her at the funeral on Lichas, sitting at the back of the church. At the time she did not come forward to offer her condolences. He took her hand in his and no sooner had she clasped it than she burst into tears. She let go and sat on the nearby chair and started sobbing. "I love your father and grandmother. He like my father," she said looking up at him. Her face was soon smeared with tears. She wore no make-up; she didn't need to, she was pretty just the way she was. "I made promise not behave like this in front of you," she said, composing herself. "But your father, he did much for me." She wiped her eyes with the back of her hand and stood. "Come, I show you room."

Before he could react, she had pounced on one of his suitcases, the heaviest, and was marching up the corridor. Jake took the other and followed. They passed a cloakroom on the right and immediately afterwards, to his left, was the entrance to the kitchen. This was the only room not cloaked in darkness, having a window along the far wall above a double stainless steel sink.

Next door to the cloakroom was a study, and at the end the corridor opened up onto another small lobby. To his immediate right was the bathroom and in front were the two doors leading to the bedrooms. In the right-hand one the double bed had clothes folded on it.

Tina entered the left-hand and larger bedroom. Once inside he saw that the right half of the facing wall was taken up by the sliding doors leading to the balcony at the back of the building. To the left of these was a dressing table with mirror. To the right, and against the internal wall, were floor-to-ceiling, built-in wooden wardrobes. They put down the suitcases in front of these.

Against the wall opposite was a convex-sided double bed, either side of which was a bedside table with a lamp. Tina turned on the light nearest them.

"Why is everything shuttered up?" Jake asked.

"It keep heat out," she said. "Very important at back, because it look south. Your father not like using air-conditioning. I switch on if you want, but must keep everything shut to work."

"Will it cool off at night?"

"Oh yes, much better open everything up and enjoy evening."

Next to the nearest bedside table, and against the wall, was a chest of drawers, which fitted snugly into the corner. Beside it was the entrance to an en suite bathroom and between this door and that of the corridor was a small settee. Above the bed, suspended from the ceiling, was another electric fan.

"Did my father sleep in this room?"

"No, he like other one because it have window and more light. This one for guests. Much cooler."

"And it has its own bathroom."

"Mr Chris say you taller than your father so I take suits and trousers from cupboards and put on bed. Everything else I leave. Maybe you keep? You tell me. Yes?"

"Of course, we can deal with that later. Maybe there are charity shops where I can give what I don't want?"

"You mean for poor people?"

"Yes."

"I find out. Food is ready. When you like to eat?"

"I don't know." He looked at his watch. It was seven forty-five. He wasn't expecting a meal to have been prepared for him "I'm hungry; what about eight?"

"Is good," she said, looking towards the bathroom. "There is hot water and towels." She left him, shutting the door behind her.

Jake lifted one of the suitcases onto the bed, unzipped it and started to unpack. As he did this he reflected on how full of contradictions his father's life was. He seemed to have been wonderful to everyone but his own wife and son. Another mystery was these flats. They were certainly beyond anything he could have previously imagined having and the décor was coordinated and tasteful, but for someone who was worth millions, no tens of millions, they were modest; and he didn't like using the air-conditioning!

He found some fresh clothes and laid them on the bed. Then he undressed and went into the bathroom. It was pleasantly decorated with blue tiling and fittings, although the shower could have had more pressure. After having dressed in a yellow short-sleeved shirt, blue shorts and flip flops, he walked down the corridor to the other end of the apartment. Glancing into the kitchen as he passed, he saw Tina at work over the hob.

The right-hand shutters and curtains were now open and it seemed as though the reception room spilled out onto the balcony. He paused at the sitting area and observed that the central table had a number of oversized books on the shelf beneath the glass. There was an atlas of the world, glossy picture guides of Rhodes, Crete, Corfu and Thessalonica and two architectural volumes covering mainland Greece and the islands. To his right, the dining room table had been laid for him with a place setting and a wooden bowl of Greek salad, covered with cling film.

Stepping outside under the green canopy, he was surprised to see that, apart from the containers of yellow and red geraniums, there was just one square glass-topped table and two chairs. Surely a spacious area like this should have more seating. Didn't his father entertain?

There was a lovely view over the roofs and treetops towards a rocky outcrop, which had turned a dull orange from the sun, and in the distance he could see the mountains that surrounded the city.

You like something to drink? There's beer, wine, ouzo or coke." Tina had come out to him.

"Is the beer cold?"

"Yes, I get you?"

"I can get it."

"No, you sit, I bring."

He sat on the cushion that dressed the black enamelled metal chair and enjoyed the warm but comfortable breeze. Around him he could sense the activity of a city preparing for the evening.

Tina brought his beer in a tall glass, together with a glass bowl of green olives.

"Tina?" he said. "I expected there to be more tables and chairs out here."

"They upstairs."

"Upstairs? What upstairs?" From the street he had not seen anything on the flat roof.

"On roof three more rooms, one store and bedroom with bathroom. That where I stay before your grandmother die."

"Isn't it better than sleeping in the basement?"

"Cooler, not nicer. Basement much bigger with sitting room and kitchen. You come sit at table when ready."

"Tina," he said again just as she was leaving. He wanted to ask her something but was hesitant. "When you said that my father did a lot for you, what did you mean?"

"Oh, too many things. Best was he found me good husband."

"A husband! Tina, how old are you?"

"Twenty-six."

"Twenty-six, you look more like sixteen." Jake was startled.

"You too kind, like your father," she said, blushing.

"Why did he find you a husband?" Jake didn't understand why such an attractive girl needed assistance in that area.

"You know, when my people come here to work, mens and womens, they mostly already married. They come here to make money for to send back home. I come with my married sister to help her and like here very much. I no want to go home for husband. It very hard life. Then I no come back here again for maybe long time. You understand?"

"Not really, why can't you come back after you're married?"

"You know, when you married to husband he want you there all the time. Then after two three children he tired of you and send you to other country to work and give children to mother to keep. You send money home, he give little for children and spend rest for cigarettes. You understand?"

"I understand so far."

"Meester George and his mother, they say I need better husband who look after me too, not only me look after husband."

"I understand that, but a pretty girl like you would have men running after her." Tina blushed again. "Why did my father need to find you a husband?"

"You know, here in Greece, if you girl from other country and go out with man they think you are *gomena*. Your father say he do me *proxenia*."

Jake had no idea what *gomena* meant but guessed it was not something good. He thought *proxenia* was some sort of arranged marriage. "So who did he find?"

"He bring handsomest man he know. He bring him here. I not stop looking at him and he not stop looking at me."

"Love at first sight?"

"Yes, we married two years now."

"But you live in the basement."

"You know, Yianni is chief officer of cargo ship. I live downstairs when he travel and at his home when he rest. You know our house very far. When Yianni home it take one hour for me to get here."

"I wish you every happiness. Tell me, though, how did you learn to speak English so well?"

"You know, when I first come here I work for English family for three years. I learn good English, now Greek good too."

"You're a clever girl, Tina."

"Thank you, Meester Jake. Please another one beer?"

"Yes, I think I will." Tina left and promptly returned with a replacement bottle of Amstel. "Thank you, Tina," he said. The marriage thing still puzzled him. He could understand Tina marrying a Greek man, but wouldn't it be frowned upon for a Greek to marry a Filipino girl?

The beer was refreshingly cold and the olives appetising. He waited until it was dark and Tina had switched on the lights before going to the table. As soon as he had sat, she brought out a steaming bowl of rice and a platter of meatballs in a tomato sauce.

"What about you, Tina, when are you going to eat?"

"When you finish, I take down with me."

"Ah, okay." Tina went back into the kitchen. He felt guilty that he'd waited so long.

The food was so good that he ate more then he should have. After he had finished, Tina cleared it away and brought a clean plate together with a platter of cut-up watermelon, melon and peach.

"You like cheese with fruit?" she asked.

"No, this will be fine."

"You go out tomorrow?"

"Yes, I've got to be downstairs by nine."

"You eat here at night, yes?"

"Yes, please. I've nowhere else to go."

"You like chicken *lemonato*?"

"I'm guessing I will," he said. It sounded familiar. His mother might have made it.

"You want me iron something?"

"Er no, I've hung my clothes up, they don't really crease, but thanks for asking."

"Is basket for dirty clothes in bathroom. You fill and I wash." She left him again for the kitchen. As he was helping himself to fruit, she came back out, holding the rice bowl and the meat platter covered in foil.

"If you not need me I go."

"No, you go ahead and have a good evening. Thanks for everything. Anything planned for tonight?"

"No, just TV. You put plates in bowl in sink and cover with water. I wash tomorrow," she added. "Oh, and if want anything, telephone number downstairs is same but with zero at end instead of one."

"Will I have a problem with mosquitoes?"

"Turn on fan over bed, they not find you."

"Okay, good night. Hey, aren't you going to have any fruit?"

"I have downstairs. Good night."

He could see the apartment door from where he sat and watched her open it, press the landing-light timer and shut it behind her.

He must have sat there for a half hour nibbling on fruit, listening to the sounds of the city, thinking about the day, about Tina and about his dad, before realizing he had finished all of it. He was so full he could hardly move himself to clear the plates. He intended to stay up a while so, taking another bottle of beer with him, he went and sat back out on the balcony.

In the distance he saw the lights of the city and he could feel the energy. He almost wished he could go out and explore, become part of it, but would it be safe?

Much of what he had read in the newspapers back home concerning the political and economic situation was negative.

There was a light for the balcony and he went to get something to read. As he passed the little bureau with the phone, he stopped, sat on the chair and looked through the three drawers. The middle and larger one contained telephone directories for Athens, Rhodes, Corfu, Thessalonica and Crete. There was a block of yellow post-it notes and a few pens and pencils. The two side ones contained an assortment of writing pads, note pads and more pens. There was also a personal phone book. He looked through this, but the entries were handwritten in Greek and he had difficulty discerning the names.

After this, he was distracted by the study. He turned on the light and, from the door, saw that a large settee took up most of the left-hand wall. There were ornamental wooden tables on either side of it with lamps and a low glass-topped table in front. Below the glass was a shelf of magazines, either National Geographic or ones about yachts and power boats. As in the bedrooms, the floor was parquet with an attractive central rug.

The whole of the right-hand side was built-in cabinets below waist level with shelves above. On these were a TV, DVD- and CD-player, video recorder, and loudspeakers.

The books were a mixture of Greek and English. It took too much effort to make out the Greek titles but the English ones were mostly hardbacks covering subjects related to Greek history, ancient Greek plays, archaeology and mythology. This caused him to have a moment of nostalgia. He remembered similar books in his mother's possession. She had taken great pains to relate their contents to him, especially at bedtime when she would narrate the deeds and misdeeds of the Greek Gods. By contrast, the far section consisted of crime fiction written by an assortment of English and American writers.

There were three sets of cabinets below the bookshelves. The first one contained fine glassware, the middle one lit up when opened and held a well-stocked bar and the one at the far end, adjacent to a desk, contained wooden shelves and was stacked with files. This was more interesting and Jake sat on the wood floor and started looking through each one. He was hoping to find something illuminating, but instead they were all to do with either the house or the various cars and boats his father had owned. He seemed to have kept everything from the day he bought the land with the original building through to the present.

He put everything back and sat at the desk, which was positioned so that it faced the door to the corridor. He had his back to the balcony, the wooden slatted shutters of which were closed and the glass ones open; he could feel the draught on his back.

The desk itself was of dark wood with a green leather-inlaid top. There was a phone extension and, beside it, an adjustable table light. To his right and against the external wall was a free-standing bookcase with a metal frame and glass shelves. The books here were all English and comprised several hardbacks and paperbacks on European and Greek history. Surprisingly the bottom shelf contained books related to Atlantis, seemingly contradicting the academic nature of the other publications.

He tried to imagine his father sitting here, doing whatever he did, maybe with the television on or music in the background. He remembered something from his past. When he used to go to school, and later at university, he always found it easier to concentrate sitting in front of the television with either the news or a documentary on. His mother said that his father used to do the same if he was working from home.

He had the idea to look in his father's bedroom. The built-in cupboards had been partly cleared, but there were still drawers full of clothes. They were of high quality and there was also an impressive collection of footwear. He tried on one of his shoes, but sadly it was too small.

The bedside table had another extension for the phone and a half-read crime thriller in the drawer. It was puzzling; there seemed to be nothing personal in the house. No bank statements, no letters, no photographs either in drawers or in frames, no mementoes; nothing. There were no empty drawers to suggest that anything of that nature had been removed, and didn't his father have a computer or laptop?

He looked at his watch; it was nearly midnight, too late to read and he was tired. He went back to the lounge, turned off the balcony light, closed and locked the wooden shutters and got ready for bed.

He reflected that, after cohabitating with someone for many years, it was difficult at first to adjust to being on one's own. In fact, he had gone from living at home with his mother straight into a flat with Charly. This meant that after her departure he was alone for the first time in his life. He was not afraid of an empty house or anything like that. It just required a different frame of mind, a different state of awareness of surroundings. This was particularly necessary in his house in England.

Living by the canal and woods had aesthetic advantages but also some drawbacks. The busy waterway with its constant traffic, particularly in summer, its public towpaths and popular nearby pubs attracted unwelcome visitors to his garden. This was especially so because the bottom end of it was far from the house. Most of the intruders were opportunistic thieves, but there were also drug addicts, drunks and the occasional couple wanting a quick shag.

The back of the house had more than enough security as far as locks and reinforced doors and windows were concerned, and if anyone came too close the motion-sensing flood lights would be activated and that would put an end to any further incursion.

The problem was that he could not stop these people entering the garden in the first place. Whatever locks, padlocks and reinforcing he did to the gate at the towpath end, they would try and break through all the same. He was therefore alert to and aware of any suspicious sounds and, whether still up or in bed, he would switch the security lights on if he heard anything unusual.

Another considerable nuisance, for which he also had no remedy, was those people who thought his garden a good place to sling their trash. At the end of each week there was an assortment of items to dispose of, ranging from McDonald's packaging to used condoms.

That seemed another world now, for here was his first night in a new environment. His new and possibly permanent home.

He undressed and got into bed. Apart from the faint electric sound of the ceiling fan, which he had on low, the only other noise was the hum of the traffic that filtered through the en suite bathroom window from the busy main road. Earlier, when on the balcony, and later whilst eating, he had also heard his neighbours, or rather his tenants, talking from the balcony immediately below.

Although not fitted with alarms, he felt the building and its apartments difficult to break into. It seemed his father had built this block to the highest specifications. Paradoxically, he felt more secure here than in England. He soon relaxed and fell asleep.

Chapter 8: Piraeus

Monday, 23rd July

Dimitris arrived promptly. Jake was waiting outside on the pavement and slipped into the back of the Mercedes. As they drove through the congested streets, he began to nod off. He had slept well last night, but before he knew it, it was seven thirty and time to get up. Afterwards he had walked into the kitchen, wondering what there was to eat and where everything was, to find Tina, sitting on a high stool, reading a Greek gossip magazine.

"Good morning, Meester Jake," she sang, looking at her watch as she dropped to the ground. "What you like for breakfast? Toast or croissants."

"Croissants, please!" he replied enthusiastically. "Where did they come from?"

"From the baker. I get this morning. They in oven. You sit down and I bring you."

The table was set with a glass of orange juice, butter, a pot of honey and an assortment of jams. The balcony doors were open and the cool morning air quivered with the sounds of birds and insects. He could see bees feeding on the flowers in one of the pots. In the distance, the rocky outcrop, rising above the apartment block across the street, made an impressive backdrop.

The croissants were some of the best he had ever had, washed down by filtered coffee. He could still taste them as he dozed in the back of the Mercedes.

He awoke when the sun fell on his eyes. On the left they were passing a cathedral. He guessed they were in Piraeus when on their right he could see the enclosed harbour area. At intervals there were entrances with the names of the various islands that the particular section served.

After a few more junctions, Dimitris pulled over to the left. "We're here," he said, "it's number fifty-one, just back a bit, next to the American Express sign. Go to the fifth floor."

"Will I see you later?"

"Yes, I'm your driver for the day."

The office buildings along Akti Miaouli were a random mixture of old and modern, decrepit and pristine. Number fifty-one was a newer, well-presented version. He pushed through the double doors of the entrance and was confronted by a security guard behind a desk. "Philotimo Properties, please," Jake requested. The guard pointed him in the direction of the lifts.

His father presumably chose Philotimo Properties because it made use of their family name Philo, which in Greek means friend.

On the fifth floor he came out on to a landing. The entrance to Philotimo was on the right. He pressed the intercom, announced his name and, after a brief interval, the door release buzzed and he stepped through.

He welcomed the coolness of the air-conditioning as he entered a reception area. He faced a desk, behind which sat a handsome, middle-aged woman with dyed blonde hair. Apart from a small window on her left and the door to the main office to her right, the rest of the room was lined with filing cabinets.

"Mr Philo, welcome," she said in heavily accented English. She stood up, walked round her desk, took his hand in both of hers and greeted him. "I'm Maria." She was short with large breasts and thighs and an unusually narrow waist. "Mr Zacharias is expecting you; I will take you to him."

He followed her through the double doors into an open plan office. Opposite was the external wall, which was glazed for its whole length from waist-height to the ceiling. Bright sunlight streamed in. There were several desks arranged in the space and facing different directions. Only half were occupied, all with men who, after taking a quick glance at him, resumed their work. Most were on landlines or their mobiles. There was the background drone of subdued chatter.

The left side wall was taken up with filing cabinets. The right had two offices. The first was a glass-partitioned conference room containing a rectangular table for eight. Maria was heading for the next room, in the far corner.

When they reached the door, Chris Zacharias got up from behind a desk to greet him. "Well, I see the Athenian traffic hasn't delayed you too much," he said, as they shook hands across the desk. "Please, sit." He indicated the seat opposite.

The room was surprisingly small with just the desk, a bookcase, filing cabinet and two chairs. The window had a broad vista of the harbour. As he sat, he felt the morning sun warm his back.

"Would you gentlemen like coffee?" Maria asked.

"Certainly," Zacharias said. "What about you?"

"Please."

"How do you take it?" Maria asked Jake.

"Medium, I think." Jake assumed the question referred to the sugar content. He remembered fondly how his mother used to make it in the morning, standing over the hob, holding her *briki* in one hand and stirring the dark brown mixture with the other, waiting for the critical point when the liquid came to the boil and the froth began to fold in on itself.

"Make them doubles," Zacharias added. "I'd like to apologise for making you sit as the guest. This is your business and I hope that before long you'll be sitting here."

"I haven't decided that yet," Jake pointed out. On the desk was a landline phone and an assortment of files stacked either side of an open laptop.

"I know, I know. But do you realise how much of my time I spend here? I come every morning and sometimes it's lunchtime before I go to my own office. I'm a solicitor not a property magnate. The sooner you take over the better."

"I hope you'll be paid for your time."

"When your father and I first met, twenty years ago, I was just getting started in Piraeus. I was working in London before that. He not only employed me as his solicitor, but introduced me to his friends and acquaintances. Whatever I have today I owe to him, but I still had to work for it. My firm will charge for the execution of his will, but the time I've spent here, making sure the business carries on from day to day, is in repayment of his friendship."

"I appreciate what you're doing and I'm sure my father would've done the same for you. It's just that I feel you're pressuring me into a decision when I haven't a clue how to run a property business, or any other venture for that matter."

"I'll give you the benefit of the doubt. I suppose I'm reflecting what your father would've wanted," he said. Then, turning to face the open door, "You see those people out there?"

"Yes."

"Between them and those who are out of the office, they know everything about the work. They will teach you, and most can speak excellent English. They just need a leader; someone to tell them the enterprise will carry on and go forward."

"If they know everything, why do you need to spend so much time here?"

"Because I'm the executor. I have to authorise everything, every payment and every decision." Zacharias looked at his watch.

"Are we okay for time?"

"Yes, before we get on to matters here in Greece, are you happy with how things have proceeded at the London end? You know, the Kensington flats."

"The solicitor there wasn't terribly good at explaining things."

"He's competent and, as a consequence, busy. They're not as laid back in London as we are. Basically, each apartment is owned by an off-shore company. They are on long-term diplomatic lets to the Japanese Embassy and the proceeds of one originally went towards supporting you and your mother. When you turned eighteen, your father made you the sole shareholder and beneficial owner. After your mother died, the rents accumulated for your benefit."

"That's what I don't understand," Jake said. He vaguely remembered signing papers long ago, but wasn't told what they were for. That was surprising enough but, after he had gone to the bank and renewed the mandates, he was given updated statements and found he had £15,000 in the current account and £442,523 on deposit. How was it that he knew nothing about this? The first thing he did was use some of it to pay off the massive mortgage Charly had left him with.

"If it was mine, why not tell me about it, certainly after my mother's death? We were both at the funeral, but my father hardly spoke to me."

Zacharias sat back and sighed. "Your father was a self-made man. Apart from advice and a little support from his father-in-law, nobody did anything for him. He wanted you to have all this but didn't want it to spoil you. He wanted you to have to look after yourself for a while first. He was proud of what you'd achieved and was planning to get around to speaking to you but..." Zacharias stood up, walked round the desk and shut the door before continuing. "It was difficult for your father to get in touch because he knew that things would come round to him having to explain why he'd left. I don't think he was able to do that." He sat back down. "You see, your father had a reason for his behaviour, or thought he had a reason; that much I know. What that reason was, he never confided in me. He came close a few times, I'm certain, but in the end he kept it from me."

"What makes you say this?"

"Just the way things happened over the years. Remember, I knew him a long time. When he first came here from England, you know, to live, he was heartbroken. The first thing we had to do was figure out a way to support you both that was independent of him. That's how the purchase of the other Kensington flat came about. We used some of the funds when he sold his existing portfolio in England."

"It doesn't make sense,"

Zacharias thought for a while, as if he wasn't sure how deeply to delve. "They wrote to each other you know."

"I didn't know that; my mother never told me," Jake said sitting up. "I never saw any letters. Are you sure?"

"At least once a week, maybe twice, right up until she died."

"That's astonishing. It's hard to believe."

"The letters weren't sent directly. Your father would give them to me, I would forward them to our London correspondent office through our weekly courier, and from there they were forwarded to your mother."

"But why? Why would they behave that way?"

"I don't know; but your father was no fantasist, not in any other part of his life. He was down-to-earth. Therefore I believe, and this is where I must warn you, I believe that they believed that you were in some kind of danger and this was the only way to keep you safe."

"But that sounds like complete nonsense," Jake said, becoming agitated. "Besides, I found nothing at the apartment; no photos, no letters, nothing."

"That's because he kept everything here. Come, I want to show you something." Jake got up and stood behind the desk as Zacharias swivelled the chair towards a grey metal, four-drawer filing cabinet. He pulled open the lower drawer. It was full of photo albums. "I won't take any of them out, but they're all pictures of you and your mother, right up to the time her illness started. Your father took pride in showing them to me."

He shut the drawer and Jake went back to his chair. He remembered how his mother was always so meticulous at taking photographs; photographs of birthdays, outings and other occasions.

"The top two drawers contain his personal accounts, including mobile bills and such-like," Zacharias continued. "I've had to go through these in order to make sure his affairs were in order. But the third drawer contains letters. I haven't looked, so I can't be sure, but some, or all of them, could be from your mother."

Just then Maria arrived bearing a tray with the coffees. "I don't understand any of this," Jake said after she had gone.

"I don't either," Zacharias said. "Truly, but once again a warning, your father behaved like a man who believed his family was in danger and was trying to protect them. The danger may not have passed, I don't know. Be careful what you say and to whom you say it." He looked down at his papers and sighed again. "This whole conversation started with the question of the Kensington flats. I take it the matter has been fully explained now."

"Yes," Jake said. The revelation about the letters was making him depressed.

"Unfortunately, matters here in Greece are not so swiftly resolved."

"What does Philotimo mean?" Jake interrupted.

"It means friend of honour or honourable," Zacharias answered quickly. "The transfer of the business is straightforward and everything's in place. We'll have to sell some properties or raise the money to pay the taxes and Photis. I just need your decision and, according to the will, you have eight more weeks."

"What's involved in selling the business, hypothetically?"

"We'd put the properties on the market, pay off some loans and the tax with the proceeds and distribute what's left."

"Can't someone buy it as a whole?"

"It doesn't work like that, certainly not in these times," Zacharias explained. "You see, Philotimo is just the managing agent. Amongst the properties it looks after are your father's, as well as other clients, including myself and some of the employees out there. Your father had a portfolio that reflected his view of what was profitable; mostly new-build shops with apartments above, in small to medium-sized developments; just the type that seem to be holding up in these difficult conditions. To get the best prices we'd have to sell them off individually."

"Where are they?"

"All over Greece, in big cities or towns; a few in Athens, but mainly Thessalonica, Corfu, Crete and Rhodes. Perhaps after the summer holidays we could go for a tour."

"Maybe, I might consider it," Jake said. "So why did he base the office here? Why not closer to home?"

"Because the only exception to the shops and flats is this building. This is his."

"That's amazing!"

"It's by far the most valuable unit, with all the offices let. It's probably worth about two and a half million."

"Okay, say my father's properties are sold, what happens to the office?"

"Your father's portfolio is only about half of the total managed by Philotimo."

"So, will any of these people lose their jobs?" Jake said, looking out at the main office.

"I'd like to say they would if it helped you decide to keep the business but the truth is they're all highly qualified and experienced. They won't have any problem finding jobs either in Greece or abroad, or they might try to run the agency themselves."

"Quite. What about the yacht?" Jake asked, remembering it.

"I got Photis to take it to Lichas, where it was repaired; there was superficial damage to the hull. Now it's back on Halia. It's a lovely boat, but too late in the season to sell at a good price. I was planning to bring it to Piraeus in September, lay it up for the winter and try to sell it next spring. You should look it over; you might like to keep it. It's not that big and we have a permanent berth here."

"I don't think it's my sort of thing," Jake said. To him the yacht represented the most distasteful aspect of his father's lifestyle.

"If you change your mind, the keys are kept at the yacht club."

"What's it called?"

"The *Sevastia III.*"

"Does that mean anything?"

"Sevastos means venerable or respectable. It's occasionally used as a boy's name. Sevastia, I suppose, is the female equivalent, although I've not come across it. It's unusual."

"Maybe he was trying to be different," Jake reflected. "Who's looking after the building in Psychiko?"

"Someone at my office is doing so at the moment, so you needn't worry."

"What will happen with Tina?"

"That's up to you; she's your employee."

"I forgot. How much does she get paid?"

"Five hundred euros a month."

"Doesn't sound like much."

"Believe me, that's good for Greece. Don't forget she gets free food and board."

"Is it true my father found her husband?"

"Yes."

"How did that work?"

"The man concerned is a good deal older. He's an only son with two younger sisters. He came from a poor country family and, as is still common in those parts, was expected to work for his sisters' dowries. By the time he'd finished he was in his forties, set in his ways and put off by the women his parents were presenting to him. He's a chief officer on a cargo ship."

"I know."

"Good career, good money and a nice man."

"I'm sure. But wouldn't such a union be frowned upon?"

"Well, Tina had to convert to Greek Orthodox and, as for what people think, I doubt Yiannis cares."

"I just hope there're no problems if they have children," Jake said as they finished sipping their coffees.

"Before I forget, there's one more item; your father's car, a rather nice Mercedes. I'm keeping it in my garage and take it for a drive once a week. You're free to have it, but I wouldn't advise driving around Athens without some experience first."

"You'd better hold on to it until I decide what to do."

"Okay. I thought we could spend the time, before the notary public, talking about the business. Perhaps it would help in your decision."

"As you know, my knowledge is zero."

"Well, I'm a solicitor not a property developer, but I've picked up a few things. Your father knew what to develop and where, then what to sell or keep."

"That puts me out of the running."

"No, it doesn't. What matters is intuition, worldly knowledge and where you believe economic trends are heading. I think you're qualified in that area."

"I don't know, I'm wary of being dropped in the deep end."

"You won't be, believe me; the people out there will help you. Come and meet them." Zacharias proceeded to take him round the office and introduce each person, explaining what they did.

Finally, they went into the conference room. On the walls were pictures of some of his father's developments. Zacharias explained how large each one was, how many shops and flats, where it was located, how much it cost, what it was now worth and why his father had chosen it. Jake was beginning to relate to his father's logic.

"Why's there nothing on Halia or Lichas?" Jake asked.

"Halia, as you will soon see, is too small. As for Lichas, I don't know. It's the sort of place that would have opportunities and your father would be familiar with it, so I'm assuming he avoided it for a reason."

They sat back in his father's office until twelve, when it was time to leave. Outside the building Dimitris was waiting for them. Fifteen minutes later they arrived at the notary public where Jake showed his passport and signed several documents. Afterwards they drove to the other side of the Piraeus peninsula, the coast of which consisted of yacht harbours and a mixture of residential apartment buildings and offices. They pulled up at the yacht club, where Zacharias had reserved a table on a balcony overlooking a marina. It was a beautiful aspect that included the coast as far eastwards as the eye could see. They sat in the shade and ordered lunch.

"The *Sevastia*'s moorings are down there," Zacharias said, pointing to the maze of berths and yachts.

"One thing that puzzles me about my father is that with all his wealth, why did he live so modestly? The apartment in Psychiko's beautiful, but not what you'd expect."

"The first thing your father did when he came, after taking care of your mother's needs, was to set aside the money for the Psychiko house and then invest the rest. In the beginning he lived in the old dwelling until he could demolish it and build the apartments. He reasoned that if he lost everything else he could live modestly on the rents. He wasn't interested in upgrading, if you like. He used the penthouse to entertain his friends and took his business contacts out to restaurants or for trips on the yacht. The boat was his only luxury."

"I always imagined that my father abandoned us to live the playboy lifestyle, but now, after speaking to you, I'm not sure what his motives were."

"I won't pretend that your father didn't enjoy himself, even whilst your mother was alive, but he would much rather have been with her, I'm sure."

"Maybe."

"You might like to look at the letters. They might tell you more than I can."

"I'd like to do that."

Zacharias reached into his pocket. "I've made you keys for the office, including the filing cabinets."

"I can go any time?"

"It's your building."

"I keep on forgetting. Did he have his mobile with him on Halia?"

"I assume so, but it hasn't turned up."

"What about a laptop?"

"It's in one of the drawers of the desk, but unfortunately it's password protected."

"We can get someone to unlock it, surely."

"Of course, that will be up to you. I should say that he used it for work and often took it out of the office, so it might not contain anything personal."

"I'll think about it then," Jake said. It was still an option.

"The keys for the house on Halia are kept by a man called Panagos Magos. He's looked after both houses for years. He'll meet you at the ferry. I'll write down his landline and mobile numbers."

Jake had thought long and hard about whether he wanted to spend time on the island. Now with these revelations about his father, he was glad he had decided to do so.

Their food came and, while they ate, Jake asked Zacharias about himself and his family. After lunch they returned to the waiting car and Dimitris took Zacharias back to his practice, which was located on a side road off Akti Miaouli.

"When do you leave for Lichas?" Zacharias asked.

"My ticket's for Thursday, so I guess I'll do some sightseeing and visit the office."

"I'd invite you to my house to meet my wife and family but we're out tonight and tomorrow morning I leave for Paris."

"Some other time then. Is it business or pleasure?"

"Business."

"When do you go on holiday?"

"I get back on Thursday. Friday's my last day in the office. I'm taking my family to our holiday house in Halkidiki. Will I be seeing you in September?"

"I'll be back in Athens. I expect to have made up my mind by then."

"When are you back in London?"

"I have an open ticket, I'm in no hurry."

"Well, enjoy your stay on the island and have a good rest," Zacharias said as he got out of the car. "If you need anything at any time, you've got my mobile number. Otherwise, see you in September." He shut the door and Dimitris drove off.

Chapter 9: Teresa

Dimitris drove him home. There was much in what Zacharias had said to think about. Jake held some long-established beliefs about his father, beliefs developed by his early experiences. His mother had rarely spoken about him; she had never criticized him but at the same time had not defended him. Whatever she felt and knew, she'd kept to herself. He had assumed it was resentment; maybe it was frustration at not being with the man she loved and who loved her. Maybe she just could not talk about the reasons for their separation. Maybe Zacharias was trying to give a favourable impression of his friend.

He wanted to have a look at those letters and had half a mind to go back to the office, but he felt uneasy about reading them. What would they reveal? Surely if they'd had a bad separation they would not be writing. Would it not be enough to confirm the letters existed? Was it right to pry into his mother's personal feelings? But maybe the letters contained answers to the questions he had. He knew that in the end he had to know, he would have to read at least some of them. He just was not ready to do so today.

By the time the car pulled up at the house it was nearly four o'clock. He bid Dimitris goodbye and reluctantly got out of the air-conditioned cab. Now the priority was to get inside, strip off, have a cold shower and lie down under his ceiling fan until the worst of the heat went away.

He was just opening the gate when he heard someone calling, "Excuse me, excuse me." He looked up the road towards the sound to see a dark-haired woman, wearing navy shorts, a red short-sleeved blouse, a pair of white trainers and a white baseball cap. Burdened by a sizeable rucksack, she struggled to run up to him.

"Can you help me?" she said stopping in front of him. "Do you speak English?"

"Yes, I do. Take your time," Jake said. She was panting as well as sweating profusely. She was attractive with hazel eyes, fine freckled features and a slim, athletic figure. Her shoulders and arms were red from the sun. "How can I help you?"

"I'm lost, I think; I'm looking for the International Youth Hostel." Although her English was good, she had an accent that Jake thought sounded Dutch.

"I wouldn't think there would be a hostel in this area. But then this is only my second day here."

"Oh dear, I'm sorry, I thought you might be a local."

"I am, sort of, do you have an address?" She handed him a piece of paper. "This address says Psychiko, this is Paleo Psychiko, a different district altogether."

"Oh, no," she said, looking tired, fed up and uncomfortable with the weight on her back. "Is it far?"

"A bit. How did you get here?"

"By bus. Is Athens always this hot?" she said, shifting from one leg to the other. "If I stay in this much longer I'll faint. I could drink a swimming pool of water."

"Look, I live just here," Jake said, pointing towards his door. "Why don't you come up, have a rest and we can discuss your next move."

She thought for a moment. "Do you mind?"

"No, can I take that for you, it looks heavy?"

"It's too much trouble. I'll do it inside."

He led her into the building and to the lift. There was barely enough room for both of them and the rucksack. She had the beginnings of body odour and her breath was stale. By now, he was sweating too.

When he opened the door to the apartment, he expected to find Tina, but it was empty. He shut the door, helped the girl remove her rucksack and placed it on the floor between them. It was indeed heavy.

"What's your name?" he asked.

"Teresa," she said, rubbing her shoulders. "Yours?"

"Jake. You speak English well. Where're you from?"

"I'm English, but I've lived in Holland most of my life. I'm at university."

"Thought so. What are you studying?"

"Chemistry at Bath. Can I have some of that water now?"

"Of course, sorry, follow me."

He led her into the kitchen and got her to sit on Tina's stool. He took a bottle of water from the fridge and a glass from the cupboard and placed them on the worktop beside her. She began drinking steadily. She had taken her cap off and her dark curly hair fell onto her shoulders; it was matted with sweat. He was conscious of staring at her, especially her legs. She had pulled off her trainers; she had nice feet.

"My feet don't smell, do they?" she asked. "They've been in trainers for twenty-four hours."

"No, no, not at all." He looked away, pretending to survey the kitchen. There was a pot on the hob with a note beside it. He went over and picked it up. It was from Tina, written in English block capitals.

DEAR MR JAKE,
I CLEANED HOUSE AND COOKED MEAT AND POTATOES. FRESH SALAD IN FRIDGE, DRESSING IN SMALL BOTTLE. THERE IS FRUIT. I HAVE WHAT I NEED. CLOTHES TO WASH PUT IN BASKET IN BATHROOM. I SEE YOU IN MORNING.
CHRISTINA

He lifted the lid and looked in the pot. He saw three chicken pieces, two leg and thigh joints and one breast, with potatoes in what smelled like a lemon sauce. It was still warm.

He looked back at Teresa. "Feel better?" he enquired. She had already drunk half the bottle.

"Beginning to. Jake doesn't sound Greek."

"It's short for Iacovos. Both my parents were Greek, but I live in England."

"Oh yes, where?"

"Northwest of London, in the country."

"I like the English countryside. It's very different from Holland. Do you know Bath?"

"I've been once. What part of Holland?"

"The Hague. Have you been?"

"Rotterdam, when I was young. I only remember the crossing from Harwich to Hook of Holland because it was so rough. When did you arrive?"

"This morning, so I've been out all day," she said, feeling her shoulders again. Her sunburn was an angry red. "From the airport I took the bus to Piraeus instead of Athens. Then I wandered around the port for ages before I found a bus stop with Psychiko displayed on it, and it still turned out to be the wrong one."

"How did you find yourself in the backstreets?"

"When I got off I tried to hail a taxi but there wasn't one. I just wanted to get away from that smelly road. I was starting to feel sick. I saw the trees and wanted to find someone. You were the first person I saw." She smiled for the first time.

"You won't find many Greeks in the streets at this time," Jake said, smiling back. "Most would've eaten and be having a siesta. That includes taxi drivers, the ones who are still in business that is. Have you had anything to eat?"

"Nothing since the sandwich I bought on the flight."

"Easyjet, I assume?"

"Yes, from Gatwick. I had to get the coach from Bath at ten last night."

"So you can't have slept either," Jake said as he opened the fridge. "There's ham and sliced cheese, what about a sandwich?"

"To be honest, I feel too uncomfortable to eat. I'm hot and sticky, my sunburn's hurting, I'm tired and now I've got a stomach ache from drinking too much water." She put down the glass and pushed it away from her.

"Perhaps a shower would help."

"That would be great, but so rude." She hesitated. "I promise I won't be long."

"Don't worry about that. Have a bath if you prefer."

"No, I'll fall asleep and maybe drown. A shower will be fine."

"Follow me," he said, picking up her rucksack and leading her down the corridor and into his father's bedroom. "Why don't you change in here and use the bathroom next door? I'll get you some towels."

"That's okay, I've got my own."

"Yeah, but then you'll have to put them in your rucksack wet." As he said the words he realised he did not want her to leave. Her presence made him realise how lonely he had been all these months. "You'd better use mine anyway."

He went to the airing cupboard, which was next to the bathroom, and took out a green bath towel and a smaller one for her hair. He brought them to her as she was unpacking some items from the top of her rucksack onto a chair. She now had flip flops on her feet. "I'll go and check the bathroom to make sure there's soap."

"That's okay, I've got my own," she said, holding up her wash bag.

"I'll leave you to it then. Ask if you need anything."

Jake went to his bedroom but was conscious that she might feel uncomfortable if she thought he could see her going in and out of the bathroom so he went into the study.

As the shutters were closed, he turned on the lamp closest to him and sat on the couch. He took one of the National Geographic magazines from the shelf of the coffee table, propped up a cushion against one of the arm rests, kicked off his flip flops, lay down and started to read. In the background he could hear Teresa going to and from the bathroom a few times before shutting the door.

He thought of Charly, who was attractive in a colder, harder sense. Teresa was much sweeter, especially when she smiled. Charly did not do any exercise and also smoked so she was not as athletic and healthy-looking. She also used make-up liberally, whereas Teresa did not seem to wear any. Then he remembered that just before she left him, when she was a few months into her affair, she began to lose weight and looked younger, happier. All because of the other man.

He tried reading, but was only vaguely aware of the contents, all the time conscious of the sounds down the hall.

Eventually, the door to the bathroom opened and he could hear Teresa make a couple of trips into the bedroom and then start down the hall towards him. "I'm in here," he called out, sitting back up.

She came in barefoot, wearing a short jean skirt and blue top, with no bra underneath, and with the small towel wrapped around her head. "I feel a lot better, thank you," she said.

"Would you like to have that sandwich?"

"Love to; show me where everything is, I can do it myself. Can I make you one too?"

"I've already eaten," Jake said. Back in the kitchen he got her a plate before going to the fridge for the bread, cheese and ham. "So did you come to Greece on your own?"

"Yes, but it wasn't the original plan," she said, as she was putting her sandwich together. "I was meant to be coming with my boyfriend, but he dumped me a few days ago."

"Gosh, I'm sorry." Jake could not imagine why anyone would want to dump her. "How long are you staying?"

"Till the beginning of September, if my money lasts. I was planning to sightsee in Athens before going to the islands."

"I was planning to do the same."

"So you've not seen the sights? But isn't this place yours?"

"It will be soon. It used to be my father's, but he recently passed away."

"I'm sorry. So they must be his clothes on the bed," she said. She had finished making the sandwich and was sitting back on the stool to eat it.

"Yes, they are," Jake said. There was no other stool in the kitchen, so he sat on the worktop.

"They didn't seem like yours somehow," she said between mouthfuls. "What about your mum?"

"She passed away some years ago."

"That's sad. I'm lucky to still have both of mine, although dad's health hasn't been too good recently. What do you do in England?"

"I teach geography," Jake replied, "although I'm considering a career change." It was too complicated to explain that he'd already resigned.

"Cool, so you have long holidays too,"

"I also plan to stay till September. Which islands did you want to see?"

"I'd left that to my boyfriend; unfortunately he didn't leave me the itinerary." Another smile.

"What about Athens? Where do you want to visit?"

"You know, the usual places: the Acropolis, Plaka, some museums."

"I've never been to any of those; maybe we could go together, unless you are meeting up with friends or prefer to go alone."

"No, I'd like that; I'd like that very much." She smiled at him again. "Are you attached? You're not married or something like that?"

"No, I'm afraid I've been dumped too."

"Oh, I'm sorry."

"No problem, it was a while ago," he said before yawning. Teresa copied him. "I'm sorry, I had a big lunch with alcohol and that always makes me drowsy, but you must be really tired. I'd offer you the other bed, but it would take ages to move all the clothes. The settee in the study seems comfortable. Perhaps when you've finished you'd like to lie down. I'll get you a pillow and a sheet."

"But shouldn't I leave? I've taken up enough of your time."

"No, not at all. Look it's still hot out there and at this time there won't be any taxis, and I really don't want you to go just yet, unless you want to of course," Jake said clumsily, hoping his plea didn't sound too desperate or pathetic.

"Well, if you put it that way, that's all right then, as long as you want me to stay." There was a twinkle in her eye. "Let me go and finish drying my hair."

"I'll clear up," he said, as she went back up the corridor. Soon he heard the whine of a hairdryer.

Afterwards, he led her back to the study and switched on the ceiling fan. Then he fetched his bedspread and one of the pillows from the other bedroom. Taking them to her, he watched her lie down and cover herself before switching off the light "I'll be in my room having a nap. Do you want me to shut the door?"

"Just pull it to."

"See you later," he said, going back to his bedroom. He decided he was too sweaty to get between his sheets so he had a shower, changed into his pyjama shorts and top, turned on his own ceiling fan and lay on top of the bed.

This was the first time in eighteen months that he had been so close to a woman. Ever since the last days with Charly. There was definitely chemistry between them and he felt excited and nervous at the same time.

He was sure that Charly had cared about him when they had first started out, he had sensed that, but obviously he did not have what it took to keep her. He felt he had been inept in every part of their relationship and that was why he had lost her. Her new lover came along and opened her eyes. After all, he did not have a father as an example, did he? There he was, blaming his father again. He probably had the right idea. One casual relationship after another meant you didn't get hurt and screwed up like Jake.

But what did he know about casual relationships? Here he was fantasising about the girl sleeping within a few metres of him. What an idiot. She must be what? Nineteen, twenty at the most. What would she want with someone nine years older than her? And if she did, she would expect someone experienced and mature.

He could not fall asleep; he could not settle at all, he could not stop thinking of her; her face, her eyes, her lips, her smile, her body. He wondered what her breasts were like; they looked quite full under her tee-shirt. Her legs and feet were fantastic; he loved the way the inside of her thighs touched when she sat. What would she look like naked? What would it be like to be on top of her; inside her, his face buried in her hair while he came. He thought he could smell it.

He got up; this was stupid, he thought angrily. He started pacing the room from his door to the balcony shutters and back again, several times. Eventually, he managed to calm himself. He had turned round to walk back up to the balcony again when there was a soft knock on his door.

"Just a minute," he said in a panic, looking for something more substantial to put on. But it was too late; Teresa walked in. She was barefoot, in her top and shorts. At least they had the same parts uncovered.

They stood there looking at each other for what seemed like ages but was probably only a matter of seconds. Jake felt self-conscious but had no cause to be embarrassed by his physique. At just under six feet tall, he had a classically-proportioned body that was athletic and muscular.

"Is there a problem?" he asked finally.

"I'm tired, but can't seem to sleep," she replied, sitting on the arm of the nearby settee.

"Neither can I. As you can see, I've been pacing the room."

"Me too."

"Maybe the settee isn't comfortable after all. In fact, I was feeling guilty that I'd made you sleep on it," he lied, but he could not think of anything better to say. "I should be on the settee and you should be in here."

"The settee's fine, but my shoulders really hurt. I didn't realise they'd got so burnt."

"Don't you have sun cream?"

"Yes, but I didn't think of applying it when I got off the plane. I came to ask if you have any moisturiser. I couldn't find mine so I must've left it at home."

"Yes, I've got some," he said, going over to the chest of drawers. As he walked past her he brushed her knee with his thigh. It sent a shiver up his spine.

"I've never seen a round bed before."

"Well it's not round exactly; it's sort of got convex rather than straight sides," he said as he opened the top drawer and retrieved a small tub of Nivea.

"Spoken like a teacher." She was teasing. "Is it difficult to get sheets?" she asked, moving over to it and sitting down on the edge. Her thighs did that thing he liked.

"I don't know," Jake said. He was both excited and terrified.

"It does seem more comfortable, the other's too firm."

He sat next to her. "Would you like me to rub some on you?"

She turned her back to him and raised her shirt. He applied a small amount of cream at a time and rubbed it in gently, taking his time. The burnt areas felt hot and taut. The rest of her skin was smooth and cool. He went down the back of her arms as well. He spent some minutes doing this.

"That's so soothing," she said, sighing with pleasure. "I like your technique."

"We'll let that soak up and I'll put more on later," Jake said, realising he had enjoyed it as much as she had.

"I'll take you up on that," she said, pulling down her shirt and turning back towards him. She put her hand down on the bed, right next to his. He sensed it was an invitation, so he put his on top. This made her smile. He leant towards her and she towards him and their lips met, gently, warmly. They embraced, then their hands were all over each other. He caressed her back, her shoulders, her breasts, her thighs. This sudden, mutual outpouring of unrestrained desire was something he had not experienced in years.

He parted lips with Teresa and planted a row of kisses from just below her ear down to the start of her shoulder. She sighed and threw her neck back and took deep breaths. He did it again, she really liked it and now she had her hands under his top. He went further and removed hers before taking his off too.

They kissed again, this time it was more urgent. They briefly stood to remove the rest of their clothes before falling back on the bed.

Jake was the first to wake. It was dark and there was no way of knowing what the time was. He turned onto his back. Teresa was lying on her side facing away from him, towards the door of the bathroom. He could hear the sound of the distant traffic of the main road from the open window. The ceiling fan cooled his face. He wondered what was going to happen in the morning with Tina. What would she think finding two of them emerge from the bedroom? Maybe he should leave her a note. Maybe she was used to it. Like father like son. What was that saying? Don't judge, lest you be judged. It had hardly been twenty-four hours, no, twelve hours since he had condemned his father in front of Zacharias for being a rake and here he was with a woman he hardly knew, doing exactly the same thing.

But he was not married, his father was. He got up and went to the bathroom, pulling the door to, so he would not disturb Teresa. Afterwards he gave his teeth a brush, but getting back into bed woke her. She turned round to him slowly. Would she have a look of regret on her face, or shock or maybe disgust? No, she smiled that lovely, sunny smile.

"What's the time?" she asked.

"I don't know. Why?"

"I'm starving. I'm hoping it's close to a meal time."

"I'll try and find my watch."

"Give me a cuddle first," she said taking him in her arms. To his amazement, they were making love again.

Afterwards, he turned on the bedside light and found his watch on the dresser. It was ten thirty.

"It's so late," Teresa said.

"Yes, but in Greece it's a meal time."

"So I've heard. I could eat a horse."

"What about half of three quarters of a chicken cooked Greek-style with potatoes and salad?"

"You can cook?"

"I can, but I didn't make this. I have someone who does it for me."

"You've got a housekeeper? Wow."

"She sort of came with the apartment."

"Can I have a shower first?"

"Sure, and by the time the food heats up I can have one too."

"Why don't we have one together?" she said, taking him in her arms.

"That would certainly save water. Why don't you bring your stuff in here?"

"Are you asking me to move in with you?" she laughed.

They ate out on the balcony, watching the stars from above the rooftops. They had opened a bottle of red wine that Jake found in a cupboard in the utility room. He was not used to drinking, rarely doing so since Charly had left, but they managed to finish the whole bottle. She got him to tell her everything about himself. He did not intend to reveal so much, but she insisted on knowing everything about someone she continued to sleep with.

Naturally, he wanted to know about her too, but by then it was late and she was not as forthcoming, saying she was tired. They went to bed at two, having decided to devote the next two days to sightseeing.

The next morning they visited the Acropolis and the surrounding ruins. Jake told Teresa what he knew about the Goddess Athena, from her immaculate birth to her various deeds. She was visibly entertained, but he found it too crowded to enjoy the sanctuary itself, and seeing the Parthenon surrounded by scaffolding was off-putting. He loved the views of Athens though, the far-off mountains and the sea. At midday they ambled down through Plaka, the old town at the foot of the citadel, to have a light lunch. Teresa enjoyed walking as much as he did and afterwards they wandered through the streets of Athens to try to get a feel for the city.

They walked all the way to the former Royal Palace and saw the changing of the guard before taking a stroll in a nice cool park. With its ponds and large shady trees it was the best place for the hottest part of the day.

Later in the afternoon, they took a taxi to the foot of pine-shrouded Lycavitos, a limestone hill and the highest point in the city. It was a long walk up, but at the top were an interesting chapel and a café, where they sat and had a soft drink while watching the sunset.

Interwoven between and amongst these sights were the marks of a distressed city, a divided city and a country in suffering; streets lined with deserted offices, boarded-up shops with broken windows, burnt-out tyres and other evidence of strife. There were drunks and drug addicts, down-and-outs and lots of people begging, especially children, and charity-run soup kitchens had queues outside them.

That evening, after stopping back home to change, they went to a fish taverna overlooking a marina, along the coastal road to the west of Athens. After eating and before taking a taxi home, they sauntered along the maze of walkways and piers.

On Wednesday, Jake hired a cab for the day and they visited Delphi. He explained how Apollo, the God of prophecy, came to found the most important oracle in ancient Greece, having to slay the great serpent Python, which protected what was thought to be the navel of the world. It was easy to see how the ancient Greeks came to this conclusion as the setting was awe-inspiring.

On the way back they were dropped off at Omonia Square from where they walked to Plaka again. They passed by bars and restaurants until they found one whose tables were sprawled on both sides of a narrow street and a musician was playing a keyboard. There were no streetlights and they sat at a candle-lit table beneath the stars and the floodlit Acropolis. They ordered their food and, while they waited, shared a carafe of ouzo and a bowl of olives. Jake looked at the lovely face in front of him and realised that today he had hardly seen it smile.

He had thrown caution to the wind and had told her everything about himself, his past history, his present circumstances, his thoughts, his feelings, everything. Yet he still only knew her superficially. Whenever he tried to delve, she moved on to something else or appeared preoccupied. She sometimes stepped away to make calls on her mobile. She did that two or three times a day. The last time was just before they came to the restaurant. He had asked her why she seemed unhappy and she said it was because her father was unwell. She appeared even more distracted now.

"Is everything okay at home?" he asked.

"Oh fine, everything's fine, my dad's much better."

"Then why are you still down?"

"Because you haven't decided what you're going to do.

"About what?"

"About the rest of the summer and then afterwards."

"We're spending it together."

"What about afterwards?"

"I don't have to decide until September."

"Well, that's great, isn't it? You're expecting me to wait until then to find out whether you're intending to stay with me?"

It suddenly dawned on him what her unhappiness was about. All this time he was just thinking about himself. He reached out for her hand. "I didn't realise what I was saying. The truth is, I didn't want you to feel pressured. I didn't want to appear possessive. Of course, I want to be with you. Running a business isn't for me. I'm coming back to England so we can be together."

"Good," she said, sounding relieved. "So, how's tomorrow going to work?"

"Unfortunately, there aren't any seats on my flight," Jake said, releasing her hand to take his drink and have an olive. "We'll have to go by ferry."

"Are you going to get a refund on your ticket?"

"I doubt it. It's a return; we'd have the same problem on the way back."

"That's stupid then. Why can't you take the flight and I'll go by ferry?"

"No reason. I just thought we'd travel together."

"Don't you think I can find Lichas?"

"Of course you can."

"Just because you have the money doesn't mean you should waste it."

"We'll do it your way then."

"What time does the ferry leave?"

"At eight and it takes eight hours," Jake replied. He had looked it up in a timetable he'd found at home. "It stops once or twice, I think. It arrives there at around four. I'll be waiting for you wherever it docks."

"And your flight?"

"It's at one, so we can take a taxi together to Piraeus, drop you off and then I can go on to the office. I'll spend a few hours there before taking the express bus to the airport. We'll need to leave by six."

When their food came, they ate in relative silence. Teresa seemed tense and did not talk much. Jake asked again if anything was wrong, but she said she was just tired.

They took a cab home and Jake ordered the taxi for the next morning from a list that Tina had given him. He was relieved to find that the papers he was expecting had arrived, the ones Zacharias intended him to take to the solicitor in Lichas.

Tina had been wonderful. She had not complained at having to clean up after one more person. She had even offered to do Teresa's washing and ironing. They had said their goodbyes that morning and he had promised to call her while he was away.

When they got to bed, Teresa was warm and affectionate. After they had made love and she had fallen asleep, Jake lay on his back staring at the ceiling fan as it slowly rotated. How things had changed in only a few days. When he had first arrived, he was still in mourning about the end of his previous relationship, not to mention the loss of his father. Now, with the prospect of spending the summer, and maybe beyond, with Teresa, Charly was a distant memory. He fell into a peaceful and contented sleep.

Chapter 10: Lichas

Thursday, 26ᵗʰ July

The check-in hall and departure lounges for flights to the islands are different from those for the other destinations served by the airport. To start with, it is mostly Greeks who use these internal flights, tourists preferring either to fly direct or to use the more iconic ferries. Then there is the nature of the baggage carried by the passengers: fresh produce, large cans of olives or olive oil, whole heads of cheese, televisions, boxes of cakes and pastries and sacks of dried herbs; a security nightmare.

Another difference is that the flights are rarely boarded from the gates. Instead, a bus takes passengers to an area with smaller aircraft that are more suited to landing on the shorter, less accessible runways. The plane for Lichas was a twin-engine turboprop, with the entrance at the tail-end of the aircraft. Inside there was only a single aisle with two seats on each side.

Jake did not arrive at the airport as early as he would have liked and consequently spent time queuing. That morning, after dropping Teresa off at the ferry terminal, he'd had the taxi take him to the office. After being busy with Teresa for three days, this was his last opportunity to look at his mother's letters before going to Lichas and Halia.

Once he was settled in the chair behind his father's desk and had received the coffee he had ordered from Maria, he unlocked the filing cabinet and pulled open the third drawer. He was staggered. Inside was a row of dated, brown envelopes. At the end furthest from him was the one for the year following his father's departure and the nearest, partly-filled envelope was for the year his mother died.

Opening one at random, he counted nearly fifty letters, roughly one a week, chronologically sequenced and handwritten by his mother. It would be slow work trying to read them, but the handwriting was legible and, with the help of a dictionary, he could manage to understand the contents. He did not have any problem with the salutations though. They spoke for themselves. They were all addressed, 'To my beloved husband'. He was so moved by these four words that it was some minutes before he could proceed.

Maybe there would be answers in these letters, if he had enough time to go through them all. He surmised that the initial years were more likely to contain important information. He pulled out the first eight from the first envelope and read as much as he could in the time he had available.

Once in the air, Jake's thoughts drifted back to them. From what he had seen, there was much that could be inferred. The way the letters started indicated a love that was still alive, certainly in the first years. To address her husband in such a way meant that there was no resentment in his mother's heart. She did not hold him responsible for their separation. So, whatever it was that caused it was something they could not overcome. The fact that his father came and settled in Greece seemed to reflect finality, an acceptance of circumstances. Unfortunately there was no indication as to what that reason could be.

He imagined this correspondence containing the history of his early years, if the few he had read were anything to go by. His father would have heard about everything he'd said and done, every meal he'd eaten and every friend he had played with. He wondered what his father would have written in return. After his mother had died and he'd had to sort through her belongings, there was no sign of any correspondence from him. Everything you would expect to find as evidence of a marriage was there up to the separation: photographs, birthday cards, gifts and other mementoes. After that, nothing. She must have destroyed hers. Was he meant to do the same? It appeared he could not bring himself to do so.

Most of the forty minute flight was over water. Once they approached Lichas, it was more interesting as this was one of the larger islands and particularly mountainous. They flew over the lower, flatter part but even this appeared tortuous. The coast was inundated with sand-fringed bays and coves and, where the water shallowed, the dark blue sea turned turquoise. Inland it was semi-arid and sparsely populated.

When the plane reached the eastern coast, it continued a few miles out to sea, banked steeply to the left and landed on the coastal strip to the south of the town, before taxiing to the airport buildings. The only other aircraft on the runway was an army helicopter.

Disembarking, the passengers walked the short distance to the two-storey terminal block as the baggage truck raced past to unload the luggage compartment. It was a nicer temperature here, cooler, with a breeze. To the east was a busy road and beyond that the sea. On the inland side was cultivated land, which in the distance rose to meet the arid and scrubby mountains.

Inside the arrival lounge he found a cart, and within twenty minutes he had lifted his bags from the sole carousel. Out the front he loaded them into the boot of a queuing taxi and was on his way towards the town along the coastal road, which was lined with palms and an inviting pedestrian footpath on the seaward side. The glimpses he had of the shoreline showed it to be rocky, though, and unsuitable for bathing. On the landward side there was a procession of small hotels, restaurants, car showrooms and other retail outlets.

The Meltemi Hotel was not the sort of establishment that provided a porter or doorman to assist with your luggage. This was not a problem on his previous visit, with only a holdall. When Zacharias had asked him if he wanted to stay somewhere luxurious with all the facilities or somewhere friendly and interesting, Jake had chosen the latter. During his first visit he had established that it was also where his father used to stay.

The five-storey structure consisted of two parts. The main building was old, slightly dilapidated, and made of large blocks of limestone. It had a warm, pink glow. The woodwork, including the doors, balcony railings and window frames, was painted a dark brown. The side that fronted the coastal road and overlooked the sea consisted of a raised veranda. The three floors above that had similarly deep terraces. There were smaller balconies on the side he was facing.

On his previous stay, he had learnt from Doros, the proprietor, that this was once the private villa of a rich merchant, and his father had bought it and converted it into a hotel. Unfortunately, it did not have enough rooms to make money, so in the early '60s he had added an annexe at the back, which bore no architectural resemblance to the original. It was basically a concrete block with smaller balconies and windows, and the floor heights did not match.

From the open wooden doors of the entrance, he laboriously heaved his cases up a flight of marble stairs and through another set of glass-panelled doors into the reception area. He reverently looked up at the elaborately corniced ceiling that had impressed him the first time. It was stained and cracked with age but still attractive.

Facing the unmanned reception desk and to his left, through a square doorway, was another large room. In this the ceiling was similarly corniced, but in its centre was a circular display with painted panels depicting important events in Lichan history. This was the dining room and contained a self-service breakfast bar with tables and chairs. At one of these, an older woman sat, reading a book. There were wooden, glass-panelled doors running the length of the far side, which led on to a terrace and more seating. A group of guests at the table nearest a partly-opened door were immersed in a heated argument, with much shouting and arm waving.

To his right was an ornate white marble staircase that curved its way to the upper floors. Under the first arch was a doorway with a step down, leading to the lower floor of the new building and the lift. Above this arch was another landing, which led through to the second floor of the annexe.

Approaching the desk, he considered how he was going to attract attention. He noticed that one of the two doors behind it was ajar. He cleared his throat and a man in his mid-forties, with dark brown hair and eyes, wearing a blue short-sleeved shirt, beige trousers, and sporting a two-day stubble, emerged.

When he saw Jake, he gave him a smile of recognition and a warm greeting, which included asking details of his journey and flights. Meanwhile he messed around his desk, a clutter of three telephones, sheets of paper, ledgers and yellow post-it notes. He eventually found the reservation on a torn-off piece of newspaper.

"The reservation's for two," Doros said.

"Yes, my girlfriend's arriving at four," Jake said, looking at his watch. It would not be long before he would be meeting her.

"I'll need your passport again," Doros continued. "And your friend's when she arrives."

"I know," Jake said. "Where does the Piraeus ferry dock?"

"You can't miss it. You can sit on the terrace and wait for it to enter the harbour. Then it'll dock at the far corner, in front of the entrance to the Old Town. It's a ten minute walk. How long are you staying?"

"Till Saturday."

"Then to Halia?"

"Yes."

Doros handed Jake his key. "It's room fifty-one. Go through the arch under the stairs to the lift, up to the third floor and then to the front."

"Thanks." Jake was about to pick up his suitcases when he remembered something. "Can you recommend somewhere to eat tonight?"

"Well, within walking distance is an Italian restaurant. Didn't you dine there last time?"

"No, you suggested it, but I went somewhere along the harbour."

"They have good pasta and pizzas. A bit farther on is a Greek taverna and, if you want something more continental, there's a nice place on the waterfront. The old town has good places too, but they're small and claustrophobic on hot summer nights. There are a few restaurants out of town. One in particular has good food and a spectacular view. Mrs Charles goes frequently." Doros looked towards the woman in the next room. Jake turned to see her look up from her book.

"Yes, good food," she said, in a mellow voice.

"Should I book?" Jake asked.

"Don't bother," she said. "They can always accommodate one or two."

"By the way, what are they shouting about outside?"

"Haven't you heard?" Doros replied. "One of our track athlete's been banned from the Olympics."

"What did he do?"

"She made racist remarks on Twitter. Anyone that stupid deserves what she got," Doros said with a dismissive wave. "Have you had lunch?"

"No, I hadn't thought about it."

"I've removed most of the breakfast things but there's still ham, cheese and bread," he said, nodding in the direction of the food counter.

"I'll take these upstairs first. Maybe we'll have something when we get back from the ferry."

He picked up his suitcases and headed for the lift. When he came out on the third floor, he walked back into the old building and found number fifty-one to be in the left-hand corner. After fumbling with the key, he entered the dark room.

On the right-hand side, in front of the entrance, was a double bed and, at the other end, a single, each having a bedside table. Between them was the access to the balcony. The glass double-doors were open and latched but the wooden shutters were closed and the only light came through the gaps in the irregular slats. To his immediate left was the door into the bathroom and beyond that was a low table for the TV, a free-standing wardrobe and finally, past the foot of the single bed, a single-width door to a side balcony. None of the furniture or fittings matched, but the room looked clean.

Jake placed both his suitcases on the single bed, leaving enough room for Teresa's rucksack. He then opened the balcony doors to let in the light and had to catch his breath. On his previous visit he had occupied a smaller room on the second floor of the annexe. The balcony there was only large enough for a small table and two chairs and had a view inland. Outside here was a large, marble-decked terrace, four yards deep and the width of the building. It was sectioned into three, for each of the rooms that faced forward, by trough-shaped, stone flowerbeds. Each section had its own set of cane furniture comprising a round glass-topped table and three cushioned chairs.

To the left of the Meltemi was a modern hotel of which Jake overlooked the courtyard and swimming pool. This building blocked the view of the harbour, apart from the breakwaters whose arms extended well out to sea. To the right was a derelict, stone building. Straight ahead, beyond the road, was an uninterrupted, one-hundred-and-eighty degree view of the Aegean. To the right, close to the shore, a solitary yacht with a pale blue hull rode at anchor, facing north and into the breeze.

He sank into one of the chairs and appreciated the view. There was lots of activity out there; there were small ferries, yachts, powerboats, cargo ships and fishing boats. The light brown fluffy cushions were so supportive he could easily have fallen asleep. He couldn't wait for Teresa to be here to enjoy it with him.

He checked the time; it was three thirty. He decided to wait where he was to catch sight of the ferry before going to meet it. They would probably take a taxi back. He wondered whether she had eaten. Maybe they would walk after all and stop off for a snack and coffee along the way. The harbour front, from the little he had seen of it on his previous visit, was packed with suitable places. They could then come back and have a siesta, making love to the sound of the waves caressing the rocky shore below them as the net curtains waved in the cooling breeze. Then they could go out for a meal under the stars. Maybe he would hire a car tomorrow and they could tour the island. He would ask Doros for details. Maybe if they really liked Lichas, they could stay longer.

At the same time as making these plans, he was scanning the sea in all directions. Then, in the distance to his right, he saw it. Rounding the last cape of Lichas, he spotted something big, with a tall pall of smoke trailing behind it.

When the white ferry with a blue funnel was abreast of him but still some distance out, it turned towards the harbour entrance. It was then he decided to go.

He got up, closed the shutters, grabbed the key and ran down the marble stairs. As he walked through the deserted lobby, he noticed the old lady, still sitting in the same place. Through the open doors of the breakfast room to the veranda, he spotted Doros at an outside table, talking to one of the guests.

Once out of the hotel entrance, he turned right, crossed the road and walked along the footpath towards the breakwaters. He saw that the ferry was already much nearer so he quickened his pace. Once he'd rounded the corner, on which was the modern hotel, the view of the harbour opened out. Including the two breakwaters, it was hexagonal in shape.

The first stretch was pedestrianised, paved with the same warm-coloured stone as the Meltemi and with benches and flowerbeds, which meant he could stay close to the water's edge. He passed a small marina on his right, created by an arm off the southern breakwater. Its two piers provided mooring for smaller yachts and fishing boats while on his left and across the road were the buildings that surrounded the waterfront. These were plain and unremarkable except that each had either a bar, gift shop or restaurant at street level, with seating on the pavement under colourful awnings. Farther on and along the quay, the more modest yachts gave way to larger, more luxurious craft, as well as small ferry boats.

After rounding the first proper corner, the pedestrian walkway ended and the road ran along the water's edge. He crossed this and continued along the busy pavement. This ran in front of more cafés and bars whose seating spilled out onto the road and ranged from simple wooden or metal tables and chairs to luxurious settees and expensive glass-topped tables. Each establishment had its own theme, making its own statement.

It was a welcome relief to be under their umbrellas and awnings and out of the hot sun. Now there were also travel agents, newsagents, ice-cream parlours and bookshops.

Looking ahead to the far side, beyond the corner where the ferry was due to dock, a few freighters were moored, their derricks offloading cargoes onto the quay, and looming above this end of the harbour were the imposing walls of the old town with its castellated ramparts and towers.

As he approached, he could see that this was a busy and noisy place, not only because of the imminent arrival of the ferry, but also because it was in front of the entrance to the citadel.

He looked out towards the harbour entrance as the ferry was about to enter. Its deep, guttural horn gave three short blasts, which echoed against the surrounding mountains.

As he neared the corner, he could see scores of trucks, taxis and passengers converging. Opposite the mooring ramp was a double-fronted café with its tables and chairs under umbrellas outside on the pavement. Most of the customers had suitcases at their feet, waiting to board and, at the loading ramp, queues of people, cars and lorries were already forming, held back by a cordon of harbour officials in white uniforms and official peaked hats.

As he milled through the tables of the café, a couple of backpackers got up to join the queue, which freed a seat for Jake to sit on. From there he could see everything that was going on and as soon as Teresa disembarked he could be beside her.

The ferry was well into the harbour now, the prow towering over the dockside as it approached. When it was still about two ship's-lengths away, it started turning to its left. Once it was past starboard on to them, and with the stern now pointing into the corner, it began reversing. As soon as it was close enough, ropes were thrown by the crew from the bow and stern to the shore. As the stern approached the quayside, they started lowering the car ramp. At the side of the ship were three open decks lined with people straining at the railings. He wondered if Teresa was there looking out for him or was she already inside queuing to disembark. He heard a clatter of chains, accompanied by the grinding of metal on cement as the ramp made contact with the quay.

Within minutes cars began pouring out along two lanes and the foot passengers from the doorways on either side. From where he sat, Jake could see every individual clearly. At any rate they were moving slowly because of their luggage, so there was no chance of missing Teresa.

The minutes passed. After a while, the far-side passenger ramp closed and a crew member put a chain across it. The near-side exit still carried on. Next, the cars and trucks stopped. As the last one left the ramp, the ones waiting to board began embarking, flagged on by crew members in blue boiler suits.

Jake was becoming anxious; surely he couldn't have missed her. All sorts of crazy scenarios began going through his mind. Had she boarded the wrong ferry and was lost? Had she been taken ill? Maybe she was tired and had dozed off? It wouldn't surprise him. They hadn't been sleeping much lately. He took his mobile out of his pocket and dialled her number but it went straight to voicemail. Maybe he should board and ask them to make an announcement. If that didn't work, he would search the whole boat if necessary.

But what if she had started talking to a fellow passenger who had a car and had been driven to the hotel? She was most likely there now, unpacking or having a shower, waiting to surprise him. So why did she not call him or answer her phone? Maybe her battery was flat.

Next to the café was a travel agent. He went inside and inquired as to what time the ferry was due to leave. He was told the departure wouldn't be for another half hour. That was long enough to go to the hotel and check if she was there. If not, he would return, buy a ticket and board.

He started back along the quayside at a slow run. Although it was beside the road and in the sun, it would be quicker. By the time he rounded the bend and was on the paved stretch, he was sweating profusely. He crossed the road into the shade and cut through the back streets, slowing to a walk when he saw the hotel.

His top was soaked through, back, front and under his arms, but it had only taken him five minutes. When he reached the entrance, he bounded up the stairs to the reception, which was deserted. Without stopping or bothering to use the lift, he ran up the three flights to his floor. He was panting heavily and his hands were shaking when he unlocked the door to the room. What would Teresa think if she saw him like this?

But the room was empty and just as he'd left it. Right, he would have to get straight back. Something must have happened to her and it was his responsibility to find out what. As he was running down the final flight of stairs, he was conscious of someone standing in the centre of the reception lobby. At the foot of the staircase he looked up to cross over to the exit. A woman in black was blocking his way. It took him a few seconds to recognise her as the one sitting at the table earlier. Now that she was standing, she was much taller than he had expected, nearly his height. He took a moment to acknowledge that she must have been striking when young, and her eyes were such a piercing blue.

"Excuse me," he said, about to walk round her.

"Come and sit with me, Jake," she said. Her voice was mellow and sweet at the same time. He sensed it to be more of a command than a suggestion and he felt a strange compulsion to obey.

"But I've got to go and..."

"Jake, come and sit down," she repeated, more firmly. She didn't take her eyes away from his as she took his arm and led him to one of the tables in the next room. He felt his sense of urgency diminish.

"You don't understand, I'm expecting my girlfriend and I have to find out what's happened to her. I haven't got much time," Jake declared, but his intention was half-hearted.

"She's not coming, Jake," she said, pulling out a chair and sitting down.

"What are you talking about?" he asked with some resurgence of emotion; but within he knew it was true, those eyes were telling him so. He even pulled out a chair and sat opposite her. "What do you know about it? What business is it of yours anyway?" he protested, his voice echoing inside the room. He looked to see if there was anyone else around. It was siesta time, so hopefully they would all be resting.

"There's no easy way to say this, I'm afraid," the woman said, "but the girl, whatever the name she gave you, was not what she made herself out to be. She was a set-up. She's done her job and moved on."

"A set-up? What are you talking about? Teresa's my girlfriend and I've got to find her." He stood up, wanting to get away from this awful woman, willing to say anything to be rid of her.

"You barely know her, you only met her last Monday; now sit down and listen to me," the woman said, all the time maintaining her gaze on him.

He sat down in resignation, feeling a wave of embarrassment. He was sweating even more than before and drips were falling off his brow and nose. "How do you know all this? Who are you?"

"My name is Diana. I was an acquaintance of your father," she said. She momentarily looked away from him, as if to hide an emotion.

"You knew my father?"

"Yes, rather well."

"I've never heard of you and don't remember seeing you at the funeral."

"I was away on business, half way up the Amazon at the time if you must know, and didn't hear of his passing until it was too late. But I probably knew him better than anyone else there. By now you must be wondering whether there wasn't more to your father and his actions than you'd previously believed, eh? Isn't that so?"

"Why, yes," Jake said. She must've been acquainted with him to know that. "But what does that have to do with Teresa?"

"Teresa? Oh yes, I understand. Quite a lot actually. By the way, her name was Amanda."

"Amanda? No, no, she was Dutch."

"Whatever, but we're getting ahead of ourselves." She leaned towards him, still staring into his eyes and put her right hand round his wrist. He felt a tingling all the way up his arm. "What I'm initially leading to is the point that there is much about your father and his life that you don't know."

"That has been suggested to me by someone else," Jake said. He felt such a weight of despair and fatigue that he found it difficult to breathe. He wanted to escape, to run after the ferry and prove this woman wrong, but he was anchored to her, where she was holding him. The tingling sensation had moved up to his shoulder.

"Yes, by Mr Zacharias, I suppose."

"You know him too?"

"I know all about him, but he doesn't know much about me. I suspected that he would have expressed some of his opinions to you." She appeared distracted and glanced at her watch, still maintaining her hold on his wrist. "Look, I've got something important to attend to. Why don't you go up and have a rest. You look like you need it. You'll feel so much better, I promise."

"You're right, I do need it," he heard himself confirming.

"I'll meet you down here at, say, nine thirty. We can go and have something to eat and I'll help you with the answers to some of your questions."

It was true; he was drained and barely managed an acknowledgement of her proposal. All the energy for action that he'd had a few minutes ago had gone. All he could think about was lying down. Diana stood up, gave him a reassuring smile and a comforting squeeze of his forearm before rushing out of the hotel.

He continued to sit for a few minutes. He'd accepted the fact that Teresa, or whatever her name was, wasn't going to show up. He didn't know whether he wanted to cry or break something, but was too emotionally drained to do either. He idly glanced out the front windows at the sea just in time to see the ferry leaving the harbour entrance and start its turn to the north.

He unsuccessfully tried Teresa's mobile before getting up to go to his room.

Chapter 11: Diana

Eight o'clock found him sitting on his balcony staring out to sea. It was sunset and, although the tall inland mountains had put the eastern coast of Lichas in shadow, the ribbons of clouds just above the horizon were still bathed in orange light. The earlier breeze had died down and the sea had turned exceptionally smooth.

After a shower and a sleep Jake felt better. He was anticipating his meeting with Diana and what she had to say.

He tried not to think about Teresa. Were it not for the anger he felt at being so completely deceived, he would be more upset by her loss. He felt the agony of rejection wanting to rise inside him, but he shrugged it off.

When he went down to the lobby sometime later, Diana was sitting on the settee by the entrance at the top of the steps. She was talking to Doros, who was behind the reception desk. He greeted him and thankfully didn't mention anything about Teresa. Jake handed him his passport.

"Do you like Italian?" Diana asked.

"Are you thinking of the one round the corner?" Jake queried.

"I'm quite fond of it; they have a brick pizza oven. Normally, I'd go to the old town. It has some interesting tavernas, but on a warm night like this it's better to go somewhere open." She looked at her watch. "We should go, so we can get a table."

They turned left from the entrance and proceeded along the dark side streets with their narrow pavements. Diana walked at a surprisingly fast pace and before long they emerged at a small square, which had the coastal road on one side. Set in from this was The Stromboli. The outdoor seating was on a raised terrace under a canopy. This had a higher level for smaller tables. They chose one of the latter for two and the waiter gave them menus and asked what they wanted to drink. In the distance Jake could see the glassy sea.

"I'll have an Amstel," Diana requested.

Jake asked for the same and started looking through the menu. Within a few minutes the waiter had brought a basket of warm bread, a plate of olive oil mixed with balsamic vinegar for dipping, two tall frosted glasses and two bottles of Amstel. He also took their order. They both asked for the special starter, which was seafood ravioli. Diana chose a ham pizza to follow and Jake a pepperoni one.

With the food ordered, and after allowing a respectful interval talking about the quirkiness of the Meltemi hotel and its owner, Jake was anxious to get onto the subject of his father. "So, how long had you known my father?" he asked.

"Since before you were born. At that time I lived in London."

The waiter came with their starters and offered them parmesan and grated black pepper before leaving them again.

"I'd like to tell you about when I first met them," she continued. "That was over thirty years ago, when I was doing a research job at a university in London. They rented a flat in a block in St. John's Wood. I lived in the same building. Do you know about those early years?"

"I'm afraid my mother rarely mentioned them."

"Your parents moved in, newly married and very much in love." Diana paused and studied Jake. "You look confused; is this upsetting you?"

"I thought their marriage was arranged, at least that's what my mother told me."

"That was probably the best explanation, but the truth was they met in London at a social function. They fell in love but went through the proper channels. At first both sides of the family were enthusiastic, but your paternal grandfather changed his mind, saying it was because your mother was not from Halia and therefore an outsider." Diana paused to eat some food. "This ravioli's delicious."

"Outstanding," Jake agreed. "But why did he care? My father was adopted anyway?"

"I think he wanted an excuse to favour his own children. Your father defied his parents and married your mother anyway. Your grandfather promptly disowned him and it was only after his death that your grandmother started speaking to him, and you, I believe."

"I know, it was a surprise."

"Well, your aunt and uncle took over their father's investments but were inexperienced. They made some bad decisions in the late eighties and nineties, particularly buying shares on the Athens Stock Exchange, and had such heavy losses that they had to sell up altogether. Do you know why your father didn't want you to have the houses on the island?"

"You know about that?"

"It's a reasonable assumption."

"I assumed it was because my aunt and uncle were my grandparents' natural children," Jake said. "They also have families and I don't."

"There's more to it. When his father died, it passed to them and your grandmother, naturally. Your grandmother didn't want to stay in it after that because it reminded her of the split in the family and the financial misfortunes that followed. That's when your father bought her the other house. In the meantime, his step-brother and sister, desperate for cash, begged him to buy them out, which he did. Despite that they still resented his success."

"It would never have occurred to me to be upset at not having those houses, considering everything else he's left to me."

"I know, I only mention it because I have a feeling they will try to sell the big house again. Your father wouldn't have wanted you to buy it back. He felt it had been tainted."

"I've not had much to do with my so-called aunt and uncle. They've never tried to keep in touch and I don't know what I'd do with a house on the island."

"Needless to say, they also have a vested interest in you selling the business. I'm willing to bet they're going to be very friendly to you."

"I'll bear that in mind, although I don't think they like the island so they might not show up until the memorial service."

"You can understand though why your father won't allow them to run his business."

"So you know about that too,"

"Another educated guess," Diana said. "Did you know that your maternal grandfather was a successful merchant in Southampton and it was he who supported your father by giving him the initial capital and advice to get started? He treated him like a son."

"I vaguely remember being told. When was this?"

"The year your parents wed and six years before you were born, 1976. I got to know your mother first and we started socialising. I would say that from the time they married until shortly after your birth was the happiest time in their lives."

"Until the accident?"

"Yes, that was the turning point."

"My mother hardly spoke of it. Do you remember it?"

"Indeed, it was New Year's Eve, 1983. You were a toddler. Your parents had gone to a hotel they liked, popular with wealthy Greeks, in Torquay, for the celebrations. They arrived a day earlier and your grandparents came from Southampton on the eve. They'd just come off the motorway at Exeter and, as they were driving to Torquay, an overtaking lorry forced them off the road. They went down a bank headlong into a tree. Your grandfather died instantly and your grandmother two days later in hospital. She never regained consciousness."

"And they never found the driver," Jake added.

"There were witnesses, but it was dark and the licence plate was covered in mud."

They had finished their starters and the waiter had come to take their plates. Diana continued, "Your parents were never the same afterwards. They rarely went out. Did you know that before the accident I babysat for you once?"

"No, really?" Jake said. "My father left in 1986, I think."

"Yes, in spring. Those last three years after the accident were very difficult. Your mother drew in on herself. I never spoke to her again."

"I was four at the time. Nothing dramatic happened. No shouting, just the shedding of silent tears. It's hard to believe my mother was ever happy. When she was diagnosed with breast cancer, I had the impression she wanted to die. She waited until I was old enough to look after myself and then she just willed herself to die."

"I'm sure that wasn't so, you must've given her a lot of pleasure."

"I tried, but at the same time I blamed my father for her ill health and death. Now I don't know what to believe." He thought it best to conceal the fact that he'd seen letters from her. That seemed an invasion of his mother's privacy. He had considered taking some of them with him, to study them further, but it somehow seemed sacrilegious to remove them from his father's drawer.

"Soon after your father left, my job also finished and I went back to Greece, but I made frequent visits to Athens. We kept in touch. I watched him throw himself into his work and build the business into what it is today."

"I always imagined him as a rake, not a businessman."

"I'm sure your mother never said any such thing."

"She got upset if I made such comments when I was older."

"That's because she knew they weren't true."

"I thought she was trying to protect my image of him."

"I won't lie to you; your father did start having affairs soon after he moved. That doesn't mean he stopped caring for your mother. It could've meant he'd accepted the inevitability of their separation."

"But why?"

"I'm not able to answer that question fully right now, but..."

"Can't answer or won't?" Jake asked, feeling acute disappointment.

"Listen..."

"No, you listen. I've spent most of my life resenting my father, believing he dumped us. Now, within a few days, I'm being led to believe that this wasn't so, first by Zacharias, who at least admitted that he didn't know the answer but told me everything he did know. Now you're suggesting the same thing. Do you know anything more or are you just playing with me?"

"I know everything, everything," she said, leaning forward. "I cared about your parents; I knew their suffering and could do nothing about it. I care about you too. I not only want you to know everything I know, it's essential you do so and as quickly as possible. There are many layers to this story and you will have to discover them one at a time but I will be there every step of the way."

"Where do I start?" Jake said, suppressing his anger and frustration. If he was to get what he wanted he would have to play whatever game he had to.

"The answers lie two hours away, on the islands of Halia."

"But what do I do? Who do I ask? Who do I speak to? "

"No one, you speak to no one; but you listen to everyone. Your mere presence will act as a catalyst that will start unravelling the facts. There's one person in particular, and those close to him, who will not welcome your arrival, and the longer you stay the more it will irritate him, particularly if he doesn't know your intentions. He would prefer you to sell up your father's business and go back to England and never come back, much like your aunt and uncle would. He's the one who arranged your encounter with Teresa, so that he could discover your plans."

"Why Teresa? Who was she?"

"Amanda Stephenson, second year drama student, lived many years in Amsterdam with her parents when her father worked for a multi-national company. Thus the language and accent. Like many students she's hard up and in debt and was made an offer she couldn't refuse."

"How do you know all this anyway?"

"I had to check up on her to make sure she wasn't going to do you any harm."

"Yes, but how? I only met her on Monday."

"I have my ways," she said. "You'll understand in time."

"Well, I'd say she did a pretty good job. I was completely taken in; thought she was genuine and enjoyed my company." Talking about Teresa was a mistake. It was making him upset.

"What did you tell her?"

"You know, now that you mention it, she did ask a lot of questions about my plans and tried to press me to go back to England. She also kept on disappearing to make calls, pretending her father was ill," Jake reflected. "Basically, I told her I intended to sell up and go back to England, to be with her. Wouldn't it have made more sense if she'd stayed with me and kept me distracted?"

"I think there was no point once she had the basic information."

"I've made such a fool of myself." Jake said bitterly.

"Under the circumstances it's understandable and, umm, I'm sure you enjoyed those three days."

"Of course I did, I just can't stop wondering how much she got paid."

"Look at it this way Jake; you got a free lunch, metaphorically speaking, and she got, I'm assuming, her student debt cleared."

"I suppose. So how long have you been watching me?"

"Watching is a strong term; it's just that I suspected something like this might happen. But I think it's time to move on from Teresa."

The waiter brought them their pizzas and two more beers. They resumed eating.

"You seem to know a lot about my family, but all I know about you is your name."

"I'm the lady in black; a mystery."

"Do you always wear it?"

"No, but I like the fact that in certain countries it gives the impression that I'm widowed."

"Were you married?"

"Once, a long time ago."

"Where do you live?"

"Halkidiki."

"What's your house like?" Jake asked, remembering that Zacharias also had a place in the area.

"It's beautiful. It's in a fishing village on a sloping hillside. It's what you'd call a bungalow in England, surrounded by trees, shrubs and flowers. I have a gardener to look after it when I'm away. I even have a view of the sea."

"Are you going to tell me anything more?"

"I'm a woman of independent means."

"And why do you want to help me?"

"My motives are not altruistic, I'll admit. Let's just say, for now, that I'm on a mission, in which your father played a part. Now that he's gone, you may be able to help. Part of your reward involves your discovering the truth about him. I can't put it more clearly. What are you thinking, Jake? You look sad."

"About Teresa, or Amanda. Someone must've gone to a lot of trouble to get her a fake passport." He remembered seeing it when he'd tried to book their flights.

"We're talking about people with unimaginable resources behind them."

"Sounds intriguing," Jake said. "So, what happens next?"

"When do you leave for the island?"

"Noon on Saturday. What about you?"

"I leave Saturday too, for Thrace."

"Will I see you again?"

"Certainly, on the island."

"Where will you be staying? At the hotel or have you a house?"

"I don't stay on the island, but I will contact you when I arrive."

Jake was startled by the amount of food she was eating. Their starters were filling and the pizzas huge. She was halfway through hers already, with no sign of slowing down, and had nearly drained her second beer. Jake, on the other hand, was struggling. "You mentioned being a woman of independent means. What does that mean?"

"That I don't need to work, although I still do periodically."

"What do you do?"

"I'm a writer."

"A writer! What do you write? I've never heard of you."

"I write under a pen name. I'm a natural history writer."

"Really, what subjects do you cover?"

"I specialize in the sustainability of wilderness areas. I'm also a consultant for various governments and corporations."

"Why would you need a pen name?"

"Some of the areas I cover are in countries that are more interested in exploitation than conservation. I'm a militant conservationist and my life would be in danger if certain people knew who I was and what I was up to."

"I can imagine. So what name do you use?"

"I'm not going to tell you that yet. Why? Are you interested?"

"Well, yes. I taught geography so I often visited such areas on field trips," he said, looking at her in amazement. She looked so youthful. Physically she had no lack of energy and there could be nothing wrong with her metabolism in view of the amount of food she was putting away. "How old are you anyway?"

"Why? Do you think I'm too old to be a militant conservationist?"

"Sorry, I didn't mean it to sound like that."

"I'll forgive you, but I'll have you know that men much younger than me and not much older than you find me attractive."

"I can believe that," he said. He was not flattering. She was still a handsome woman. "So why don't you have a house on the island?"

"I'm a wilderness girl. I love the forests and mountains; they have an impenetrability, a mystery.

Halia's beautiful in its own way, but not exciting for me. Northern Greece; well, that's a different matter. I'm also a hunter."

"I thought you said you were a conservationist."

She put down her knife and fork and looked at him seriously. "You think hunting and conservation are incompatible?"

"I don't know, I've never thought about it."

"Without wilderness, there can be no hunters," she said. "And without hunters, there would be less pressure for wilderness."

They continued talking about conservation until they had finished their pizzas and Jake asked Diana if she wanted dessert.

"I'm still hungry, but I'd better not," she said. "Do you like ouzo?"

"Very much,"

"Let's have a carafe to finish off with," she said and signalled to a waiter.

"Will I have a problem on the island with my rusty Greek?"

"I don't think so," she replied. "Most will know English. I'm more interested in how well you can swim?"

"I've not swum in the sea since the Cyprus years. I've been surfing in Cornwall a few times. Why the interest?"

"Have you ever snorkelled?"

"No."

"It's important that you learn. It's straightforward and just needs a bit of practice."

The waiter came with their carafe, two small glasses and a bucket of ice. "The sea's like a second home to me. I told you I love wilderness. If you think about it, the oceans and seas are the earth's biggest wilderness." She poured them each some ouzo, adding a few cubes of ice and picking up the water bottle. "Do you take water?"

"Yes, fill it up to the lip," Jake said. "Well, I'm up for learning, but have no gear."

"You can get what you need when you do your shopping."

"What shopping?"

"How are you going to eat?"

"I'd not thought of that. I assumed Halia had shops and tavernas."

"I think you're overestimating the sophistication of where you're going. There's a supermarket, but limited supplies of fresh produce like meat, fruit and vegetables. And you can't eat out all the time."

"It's good you told me."

"Can you cook?"

"I'm competent."

"Saturday morning, make sure you leave the hotel by ten and take your suitcases straight to the ferry; it will have arrived by then. Once you've left your things on board, go to the butcher and greengrocer, whose names I will give you, and buy what you think you'll need for a week. Tell them that you're going to Halia and they will deliver everything to the ferry. Also get their phone numbers so that you can order things from the island; they'll allow you to run a tab. They're used to dealing with Halians."

"What about things like bread and cereal?"

"Everything else you can get from the supermarket, except for bread. There's a bakery. Just ask someone and they'll direct you. That reminds me, you won't be able to buy any until Monday, so pick up a loaf here.

After the food shopping, go to the town square. There at the start of the main street is a shop that sells masks, snorkels and fins. You will also need a wetsuit jacket and a speargun."

"Why a speargun?"

"I'll explain some other time. Don't bother with anything fancy, just a basic one will do. It's an expensive place but everything's good quality and the owner's helpful." She had a long drink of ouzo. "Do you like it?"

"Very smooth."

"I suppose Panagos will be picking you up?"

"Yes, do you know him?"

"Yes, he's a local; spent time on the mainland before coming back. He's worked for your father for years, keeping the two houses repaired. He's a nice enough guy, just be careful what you say to him. He's a bit of a gossip." She looked at the time. "It's getting late, we should ask for the bill."

Jake signalled to the waiter. "Do you always eat this much?"

"I have a fast metabolism."

"And you don't gain weight?"

"I've been the same all my adult life. I do a lot of hiking and swimming," she said. "What are your plans for tomorrow?"

"I'm seeing a solicitor at nine, but apart from that, nothing."

"I've a suggestion to make that will pass the time for both of us. Let's go for a tour of Lichas. Let me be your guide."

"Sounds great. Should I hire a car or something?"

"I've hired cars here before," Diana said. "It'll cost at least a hundred and twenty euros for the day, whereas an air-conditioned taxi with driver is only one hundred and fifty."

"A bargain."

"I know; Doros was telling me. He knows the driver. We won't be able to see the whole island, just the south. Shall I book it for ten?"

"Yes, I'm sure I'll be through by then."

When the bill came, she insisted on paying for her half. They then walked back to the hotel, this time along the waterfront. Jake noticed something about her. She seemed to be always on her guard. On their way from the hotel, in the restaurant and now, she was constantly looking around at the passers-by, even up at buildings and into trees.

Once back in the hotel, in the light of the lobby, she did indeed look tired. They walked slowly up the marble stairs and she bade him goodnight on the first floor. Her room faced the front as well. Jake climbed the extra two flights and, once in his room, opened up the balcony and plugged in the mosquito repellent, a square tablet that was inserted into an electric gadget.

He had much to think about and sat outside on one of the wicker chairs. It was too dark to see anything out at sea, apart from the occasional light of a fishing boat swaying in the distance. There was the sound of the waves breaking on the rocks, but this was partly masked by the traffic using the coastal road. Although after midnight, this was still busy, with the motorbikes making the most noise.

He reflected on his conversation with Diana. She had told him a few useful things, but nothing revelatory. And what was this mission she was on that required him to snorkel with a speargun?

She was an enigma; a paradox. She was old but there was a youth and vibrancy about her. There was nothing senile about her intellect and her eyes had an intensity that gave an impression of authority. Her body was slim and athletic.

What information was she withholding? Why was she wary? He could not believe she was afraid of anyone; she seemed too confident and controlled.

He felt drowsy so he went inside, undressed in the dark and lay on top of the bed. When he could not fall asleep he put on his pyjama bottoms and went back outside, sitting on the wicker chair. It was quiet now, with no passing traffic on the road below, and he could hear the waves breaking on the rocks. The stars twinkled and out to sea the lights of the fishing boats bobbed up and down.

But something was wrong. As he sat there staring at the boat lights, they began to dim. They weren't moving, just fading away.

He got up and walked to the balcony railing. He immediately saw the cause. A cloudbank had formed over the water and was thickening before his eyes. He wondered what could cause such a phenomenon; rapidly cooling humid air over a warm sea?

The fog bank continued to thicken and extend on both sides, covering the surface of the water. As soon as all the boat lights had vanished, it began to move inland. So far the top of it was below the level of his balcony.

He watched in awe as the road below him disappeared. Then the streetlights were enveloped and vanished. The cloud seemed to be rising up towards him. It should have turned dark with only the stars and no moon, but he could see what appeared to be a glow in the cloud that was intensifying.

He felt an imminent threat. He turned to run inside, but as soon as he was halfway to the balcony doors, he slowed, as if a magnetic force was pulling him from behind. When he managed to get to the wooden shutters, he took hold of them and tried to pull himself the rest of the way, but the force drawing him back became stronger until he lost his grip and fell backwards into the glowing cloud, into the sea, into unknown depths. He felt a cold wetness all around him…

… He opened his eyes. He was lying on top of the bed, as he had fallen on it, covered in sweat and shivering. The sheets underneath him were soaked through.

How could he have got so wet? He had only been asleep a few minutes, but his distended bladder told him otherwise. After going to the bathroom he looked at the time. It was three; he had slept for two and a half hours.

He decided to change beds. Why that same dream again?

Chapter 12: The Tour

Friday, 27th July

The next morning, after a good sleep and breakfast, Jake found Doros at the reception desk and showed him the address of the solicitor. It was in the middle of the commercial part of town, behind the harbour front; at worst a ten-minute walk. He arrived there in plenty of time, handed over the papers that Zacharias had given him, signed a few, showed his passport, and within ten minutes was on his way again.

He was back at the hotel by nine thirty. As he entered the reception area and looked into the dining room, he saw that Doros had just finished clearing the remains of breakfast from some of the tables and had put out clean cutlery. He had started replenishing the breakfast bar.

"You mentioned that my father used to stay here," Jake said, walking over and pouring himself a coffee.

"Oh yes, several times a year," Doros said, pausing what he was doing. "In summer he would moor the yacht in the nearby marina. At other times he flew in."

"But I thought he only went to Halia in summer," Jake said. From what he had heard from his grandmother, his father would go by yacht to Halia but stop in Lichas for a few nights, mainly for supplies.

"That may be so, but he would come and stay here six or seven times a year, just for the weekend."

"That's curious; why would he do that? Did he come with someone?"

"No, always alone. He was visiting."

"Visiting who?"

"I don't know. Sometimes, at about nine in the evening, I would drive home for a meal before coming back to the hotel. If he didn't feel like walking, he would ask me for a lift. I would drop him at the entrance to the old town, the one by the ferry landing. He would continue on foot."

"Did you ever talk?"

"Often he would come back at one or two in the morning. We would sit outside on the veranda if it was warm enough, or in here, and have a brandy."

"What did you talk about?"

"The usual things; politics, sports, music and women," Doros said, with a knowing smile. "He was easy to talk to. I miss him."

"Thanks," Jake said. He decided not to finish the coffee. It tasted awful and was barely lukewarm. He left it at the counter and, going up to his room, changed into denim shorts, tee-shirt and sandals. He packed his beach towel, swimming shorts and digital camera into his rucksack, went back downstairs and sat on the veranda with his book. The sun had moved and he was in the shade. He turned to the first page of *Riddle in the Sands*, a rather apt title he thought.

He felt a slight movement of air on his face. Looking up, he saw the first ripples forming on an otherwise calm sea. He was considering calling Panagos, to remind him of his arrival, when Diana appeared before him. She was wearing black trousers, a black tee-shirt, a broad-brimmed straw hat and had a woven straw beach bag hung over her left shoulder. She wore oversized impenetrable sunglasses that obscured a large proportion of her face, and her white hair was tied back.

"How are you this morning, Jake? How did it go with the solicitor?"

"Fine, I was in and out of there in ten minutes." He had got up and pulled out a chair.

"No need, the taxi's here."

It was a yellow Mercedes. The driver was a round-bodied, round-faced, dark-haired man. When they'd got into the back, Diana had a brief conversation with him in Greek and he set off.

"We have to drive through the town, so the first part will be slow and tedious."

Jake looked out the window as he watched the busy commercial part give way to its own version of suburbia; street after street of detached villas with gardens. As they did so, they started climbing and heading for a pass in the inland mountains. Meanwhile, Diana started talking about the history of Lichas, but Jake was not paying attention, his mind being on the conversation he'd had that morning with Doros.

Once they were out of the town, they started ascending even more steeply, zigzagging up the mountainside. Their first stop was a monastery. It was located at the head of the pass and had far-reaching views over the town and Aegean. Afterwards the taxi took them southwest to a spectacular but deserted hill-top fortress town. They continued towards the coast, before heading south, passing several pristine beaches, their headlands embracing calm turquoise waters.

They came to a picturesque cove with a quaint village, which was overlooked by a small acropolis on one of the headlands. It had steep narrow streets with gift shops, various studios, boutiques and artists' galleries. Some of the items for sale were displayed out in the streets, which gave the settlement a pleasing intimacy.

They walked up the dusty path to the ruins of what was once a temple to the Goddess Hestia. From there, there were spectacular views of the rooftops and the sea. The cove was semi-circular with pale yellow sand and there were tidy rows of beach umbrellas, strung like the beads of a necklace, from one end to the other. A dozen or more boats and yachts lay at anchor just offshore.

"This is where the wealthy have their villas," Diana informed him. "Not just Greeks, but also Italians and Germans."

"I'm familiar with Greek mythology," Jake said, "but this is the first temple to Hestia I've heard of."

"She was the Goddess of the Hearth," Diana explained. "She didn't delve in the affairs of Men, preferring to be a recluse."

"So you couldn't expect any favours from her," Jake commented as they began their descent.

Their next stop was a fortified town. From a distance this wasn't obvious, except that it was built on raised ground and the buildings formed an oval shape rather than being sprawled along the road as one would normally expect. Diana explained that an unbroken ring of houses, whose entrances faced inwards, formed the outer wall. They were dropped off at one of the three entrances as no cars were allowed inside.

They walked through a maze of narrow, covered alleys and lanes, passing brightly painted houses until they came to a square, in the middle of which was an attractive church. Diana was particularly interested in this and spent some time inside while Jake sat outside on a bench that overlooked an ornamental flower bed.

He had not bothered much about religion. He knew he had been baptised Greek Orthodox but was non-practising. His mother had made him go to church on Sundays when still at home but since then he had only been to weddings, baptisms and funerals.

Off the main square was a smaller plaza, shaded by large old trees. Beneath their canopy was a taverna. In contrast to the rest of the town, this was bustling.

"Let's have lunch," Diana said on coming out of the church.

"What about the driver?"

"He knows we're stopping," she said, leading him to one of the few tables available. "He'll do his own thing and meet us at a café at one of the other exits." They had to wait a while for a waiter. "What would you like to eat?"

"The *pastitsio* looks nice," he said looking at the tables, "but, as it has meat, I think I'll steer clear of it."

"Why's that? You ate meat last night."

"Because it attracts hornets." He could see that the other tables were plagued by them, as well as wasps and flies. This was also the problem in Cyprus, whether lunch was at home or out. As soon as the food came to the table, so did the pests.

"Don't worry about that," she asserted confidently. "I can promise you they won't bother us; besides, I'm having it."

He was sceptical, but ordered it anyway. They continued to speak generally of the history of the places they were visiting. It was obvious that Lichas was unusual in many respects and he was warming to the subject. When the food came he braced himself for the invasion of insects, but not a single one came near them. This curious thing distracted him to such an extent that he was still thinking about it long after they had left.

After lunch, their next stop was an underground cavern. It was interesting, although Jake had visited others in Europe that were more impressive. Diana explained that there were many such caves throughout the island and more were being discovered.

"Does Halia have caves?" Jake asked.

"Not really," Diana replied. "The geology's different."

They then visited another town, which was famous for its pottery, before hitting the eastern coast and starting to work their way back north.

Their next stop was a surprise. The varying landscape they had been travelling through was at first mountainous and now more gentle, but it was what Jake would describe as semi-arid, typical for the Mediterranean. They now stopped at the foot of what appeared to be a steep and narrow valley going up the side of a mountain that was at the edge of the central range. They parked in a car park beside a café and went for a walk. The path was stony, but from the start the surroundings were lush with vegetation: trees, plants and wildflowers. The quantity of birdsong was overwhelming and every tree they passed offered up a chorus of its own, seemingly just for them. There were butterflies everywhere and, as they walked up the slope and then back down again, they were swarmed by them. They were the only walkers to whom this was happening. Diana appeared to be in a trance and did not say a word. It was the only time during their tour that she removed her sunglasses. Meanwhile, in the background was the sound of a gurgling stream that they would cross every now and again on wooden bridges. Eventually they came to the head of the valley and the top of the mountain from which there were views in all directions.

Diana left reluctantly and their final stop, just south of Lichas Town, was at a sandy public beach.

"Would you like to swim?" Diana asked.

"I wouldn't mind," Jake replied.

"You go ahead, the driver will take me for a drive and we'll be back in an hour or so."

"You're not swimming?"

"I don't like public beaches."

"I'm not going on my own," he replied. He could see that Diana was uncomfortable parked where they were. There were lots of passers-by and she was looking at each one as if wary of someone recognising her. "I'm happy to go back and relax at the hotel."

"Are you sure?"

"No problem." No sooner had he said this, she instructed the driver and they were on their way again. She visibly relaxed.

They arrived back at five, got out and paid the driver. "Shall we eat together again?" he asked after the taxi had driven off.

"I'd like that and I have a treat in mind," she said. "Shall we meet in the lobby at the same time? I'll arrange the taxi."

"Great, see you then."

When he entered his room, he had a nasty surprise. Inside his house Jake was a tidy person, having taken after his mother. This was not to the extent of an obsession but for the sake of efficiency. He liked to know where everything was, which meant that he remembered where he had put it. It was therefore obvious to him, although maybe not to someone else, that his room had been searched. It was clear that the intruder had intended to leave things as they had been found but hadn't quite managed it. It was definitely not the hotel cleaner because she had already been while he was at the solicitors.

After establishing that nothing had been taken - his passport was still with Doros and he had kept his other valuables with him - he dismissed the incident and opened the shutters, stepping outside. A place like this, with no security, would be open to people coming in off the street, looking for easy pickings.

It was blowing a decent breeze now with white horses racing down from the north. Next door, in the swimming pool area of the hotel, he saw that the clear plastic tarpaulin they were using as a windbreak was flapping noisily and shaking its wooden frame. They had laid out tables around the pool. Perhaps they were having some sort of event tonight. He was drowsy and contemplated sitting on one of the chairs and having a nap, but decided to go back inside.

Kicking off his sandals, he lay on the bed and relaxed, listening to the tarpaulin and the waves breaking on the rocks. He thought of Diana in a room a few floors below him. He was wary of her, although he readily believed her when she said that Teresa would not be coming. Perhaps he knew intuitively that she was right. Still, he wondered what he felt about being the focus of her attention and, by implication, that of the other, whoever that other was. It was important that Diana believe he was bonding with her. He had a feeling that, whatever her agenda, she had the information that he wanted to learn. The aura of mystery he felt surrounded her had been enhanced today by the incident at lunchtime with the insects and in the valley with the butterflies.

Tomorrow he would be on his way to Halia and, if Diana was right, the answers to his questions would begin to reveal themselves. He took his mobile out of his pocket and for the last time dialled Teresa's number. The response was the same. He switched it off and placed it on the bedside table.

He chided himself at having so gullibly fallen for her and willed himself to get over it. He promptly fell asleep.

The taxi took them southwest into what Diana explained was the old Genoese quarter; a different historic period from the walled town, and much older. The roads were narrow with high stone walls that separated the detached mansions and their orchards. Most of the estates were dilapidated, but restoration work had begun. They started climbing into the hills until the road opened onto a square. They stopped outside the entrance to a taverna. Once out of the cab, Jake saw that the restaurant was laid out on three levels, carved into the hillside. Perhaps this was once a vineyard or orchard.

They entered via the highest terrace, where there was a red-tiled, stone-built structure which had had its window panes removed. There were some tables and chairs here, but none made up. They walked through this and down some stairs to the centre of the next open terrace, which was bigger and densely packed with tables. Although it was nearly nine thirty, a third were still empty. The first waiter who approached seemed to know Diana and showed them to a table for two at the far end. From there Jake could see the lower terrace, which was an ornamental garden lit by coloured floodlights.

Beyond that the view was spectacular. In the distance was the sea. To the left were the lights of Lichas town from where they had just come and, below them, only a few miles away, was the airport. With the addition of the stars sparkling above and the moon past its first quarter to the west, the setting was magical.

A waiter brought them a bottle of cold water and the menus. When Jake opened his, he saw that it was in Greek. Diana noticed his puzzled expression. "The menu here is traditionally Lichan. Why don't you let me order for both of us? Let's see if I can guess what you like."

Jake nodded his acceptance, smiling at her. He had few culinary dislikes. She smiled back, holding his stare, leaving him with a feeling of intrusiveness. It was as if she were trying to bore into his head; to read his thoughts and feelings. At the same time he felt reassurance, the desire to open up to her, to tell her everything. Something within him resisted. He noticed her eyes and mouth harden in determination. Feeling uncomfortable, he turned away. When he looked back she had returned to reading the menu.

In no time they were helping themselves to meatballs, stuffed vine leaves, dips and an assortment of dishes he'd never tried before.

"This food's the best I've had in years," he said. "And the ouzo's so smooth."

"Tomorrow night, your first on Halia, I want you to eat at the Paralia taverna at the far end of the harbour; it's below a small church. That way you can make sure everybody knows you've arrived."

"Is it that busy?"

"Not terribly, but you need to walk through most of the town to get to it. For good measure, on your way back drop into the yacht club for a drink or an ice cream."

"If I don't speak to anyone, how will they know who I am?"

"Don't worry, a small community has an uncanny way of knowing. You'll even find that some of the older people might approach you."

The waiter came and brought some more dishes. They topped up their ouzos.

"When you want to go for a swim, I can recommend somewhere nearby," she said.

"Where's that?"

"Where the ferry docks, behind a wall at the start of the breakwater, there's a cove. It's frequented by families and older couples."

At ten thirty Jake was surprised to see a lot of people leaving. "Greeks usually come at this time, not leave," he commented.

"It's the opening ceremony of the Olympics," Diana said. "We should make a move, I don't want to miss it either."

"I'd completely forgotten about that. I'm not sure about the TV in my room. It looks like it's from the Stone Age."

"Doros will have it on his big screen in the dining room."

So, after a satisfying meal, they called a cab and returned to the hotel. Doros did indeed have his wide screen television on and there were several people already gathered to watch. He offered them coffee, beer or ouzo and each section of the ceremony ignited a lively debate. Was this opening in London as good as the one in Athens eight years ago? When the Olympic flame was lit, Doros offered everyone a complimentary brandy.

It was well after two when Jake went to his room and he was too intoxicated to worry about the earlier intruder. He quickly undressed, plugged in the mosquito repellent, opened up the shutters and got into bed.

Chapter 13: The Crossing

Saturday, 28th July

It was eleven thirty and the sun burned. There was no wind and the air was thick with the dust thrown up by passing trucks, cars and scooters. It got into Jake's eyes, his hair, on his skin and up his nose. He was back at the café where only two days previously he'd anticipated the arrival of Teresa, this time waiting for the departure of the Halian ferry.

He looked over at the entrance to the old town. Perhaps during a future visit he could explore behind the walls, and possibly discover where his father used to go.

On board the ferry were his suitcases, which he had transferred earlier that morning. At his feet were several plastic bags and his rucksack, containing his newly bought fins, mask, wetsuit, snorkel, a loaf of bread and an assortment of other things. A separate box contained the speargun. He now waited for the butcher and greengrocer to deliver his purchases.

He bought himself a coffee and, sitting back down under the awnings, watched as various pick-ups, vans and other vehicles came with food, supplies, crates of water, flowers, building materials and a variety of other items, all destined for Halia.

At eleven forty-five, the greengrocer turned up in his van and delivered several orders, which hopefully included his own. By now the passengers were also arriving. Some seemed to be going to sit on the open deck that was aft of the wheelhouse. It had a canvas awning on a metal frame and looked well shaded. At ten to, it was the butcher's turn. He came on a scooter with bags hanging from the handlebars. After he had left, Jake decided to board.

Picking up his shopping, he walked up the stern ramp onto the car deck, crammed to capacity with vehicles and supplies. He squeezed through the gaps between them towards a door at the far right-hand corner. Through it was the lower passenger compartment, which was full of luggage, passengers, bags of groceries and boxes. It was hot and airless and the sound and vibrations of the engine idling somewhere below were intrusive. Carrying just his rucksack, he went up the staircase into another lounge that was situated behind the wheelhouse. All the seating here was occupied so he continued aft and found the open space under the awning. Before finding a seat, he calculated where the sun would be during their outward voyage and thought it best to occupy one of the middle rows. He chose the one facing to port.

With minutes to go before departure, there was a stampede of passengers boarding and, impressively, exactly on the hour, the electric winch raised the ramp and the mooring ropes were loosened and cast off. He heard the sound of the anchor being raised forward, drawing them away from the quay. Once it was weighed, the engine sounds increased in volume and they surged ahead. The ferry proceeded across the harbour to its entrance and then picked up speed as it passed the breakwaters and turned northeast. Jake now faced Lichas and would do so for the first part of the journey. The breeze buffeted him and the boat rocked as it cut diagonally across the oncoming weather.

The journey was a tedious two hours. Jake tried reading, but the lateral rocking was such as to make him feel nauseous. He tried listening to the conversations of those around him, but the sounds of the ferry's engine and the buffeting wind made that impossible, as was trying to listen to his MP3 player.

As they ran up the coast of Lichas, they were also pulling away from it, until it became a smudge on the horizon. Ahead of them, Halia would be emerging, hidden from view by the forward accommodation space. As they approached, the island spread and its western extremity became visible. He looked behind him and saw the other end also emerging. In contrast to Lichas, the landscape was gentler and less arid.

The rocking subsided as they entered the lee of their destination. Some of the passengers, mostly children, got up and went forward. He decided to do the same. They collected on the narrow, curved section of deck in front of the wheelhouse. Jake just managed to find some standing room.

The brilliant sun, the clear blue sky and dark sea were a heady mixture. The bows were slicing through the oncoming waves and the spray was being lifted by the prevailing wind. The angle of the sun, over his left shoulder, caused this fine mist of water to display the colours of the rainbow in front of their eyes before dowsing them with an exhilarating salty shower. The children shrieked with delight.

Ahead the island loomed. It was hilly and a patchwork of green and brown. They appeared to be heading for a cliff, on top of which were houses, with no signs of a harbour. As they approached, though, it was clear they were nearing a headland, past which was a bay. On rounding this, they began to turn to port and, as the gulf opened up, the entrance to the harbour, with its breakwaters, revealed itself.

As they passed these, the ferry cut speed. A third of the way into the oblong haven, a fraction of the size of the one on Lichas, it turned round one hundred and eighty degrees to starboard and started coming back on itself. It kept turning another ninety degrees and then started reversing so that the stern went into the corner with the breakwater on its port side. As it neared the pier, Jake heard the rattling of the anchor chain running free. On the quay were dozens of waiting cars and people. Protecting the landing point were two harbour officials, dressed in white. Passengers were standing and queuing to go downstairs.

When the ferry docked and the ramp was dropped, there was a rush to disembark and an equal surge of landsmen to get on board to meet acquaintances or collect deliveries. The officials held them back with outstretched arms. The first cars went ashore and it was only after the last one of these had come off that the landsmen were allowed to board. Jake remained seated, reasoning that if everybody had to negotiate the single passenger door down below, there was going to be a bottleneck for some time. There was lots of mayhem and shouting but after a while the foot traffic eased and some of the cars on the quay started departing, having collected what or whom they came for.

He was the only one left on the upper deck, when a short, stocky man with jet black curly hair and stubble approached him. "Meester Jake?" he asked.

"Panagos?" Jake assumed, extending his hand and receiving one that was as rough as sandpaper and covered in black and white smears. He was wearing dirty jeans, a grey tee-shirt and looked like he had just emerged from under the bonnet of a car. He started speaking in Greek and gesticulating, wondering what on earth Jake was doing sitting up there by himself.

Down below, with the shared burden of his suitcases and shopping, they disembarked and Panagos led the way towards an old pick-up. Most likely once white, it was now daubed with different coloured paints, cement and dirt. Everything was thrown into the back, together with other deliveries. The inside of the cab was in an even worse condition with torn seats and the detritus of used plastic cups, empty cigarette cartons and spent matches. Panagos lit up before turning the ignition.

Miraculously the car started and they inched their way through the remaining crowds. After a hundred yards, these eased and they continued along the harbour front. Turning inland, they meandered their way past the town square, a taverna, the museum, a bank and several imposing residences surrounded by walled gardens before starting to climb uphill, where the villas gave way to smaller, more modest houses.

They took a left fork and the pick-up struggled in first gear to make headway. This caused the dash to shake so much that it looked in danger of coming away from the car and falling on their laps.

At a bend to the right, Panagos drove into the first alley to the left and up to a point where it narrowed. Getting out, they picked up his belongings and started walking. It was hot work, but the road was level, hugging the contour of the hill. They passed several houses before coming to a cream coloured one with red shutters on their left. Like the others on that side, it was built into the descending slope on two floors. The upper apartment had level access with the road, while the other one had its entrance down a steep flight of steps. Panagos went down these and stopped under the red tiled canopy of the front door, taking the keys out of his pocket.

They entered the living room area, which was more or less square with a range of cheap-looking furniture. Jake had to remember that, ever since his grandmother's death, this flat had been rented out to a teacher of the local school and any decent furnishings would have been removed. There was a table covered with a green and white flowered plastic tablecloth and three chairs against the wall on the right. Beyond that was an unusual corner unit with shelves, drawers and a mirror. To the left of the entrance was a small table for a TV, and beyond, an open fireplace that looked as though it had received good winter use but which now contained a vase. Against the left-hand wall were two wooden, cushioned armchairs with a matching circular table between them. In the far corner a corridor led to the left.

"Izz good?" Panagos asked as they put down the suitcases and carrier bags. He indicated that he had other deliveries to make, handed over the keys and left, shutting the door behind him. This plunged Jake into near darkness with the only light coming from wherever the corridor led. He sat on a chair at the near end of the table and removed his dusty sandals, leaving them by the front door. His feet welcomed the coolness of the marble floor.

Leaving things where they were, he went to explore. From the start of the corridor he saw that it led to a set of patio doors, but first, opposite each other, were the two bedrooms. Both contained a double bed, wardrobe, chest of drawers and a bedside table. The one on the right was the larger of the two. It was also darker and, upon opening the window and shutters, Jake saw that on this side of the house was a narrow alley, level with the sill and barely wide enough for a man. It was covered in rubble, dried leaves and animal droppings. Opposite was a derelict house.

From the window of the smaller bedroom was an unobstructed view over the roofs of the houses towards the sea. Unfortunately, as he now experienced, the room was much warmer as it received the afternoon sun. This side also caught the breeze, but for now he closed the shutters.

At the end of the corridor and to the right was the bathroom. This was roomy, all in white and fully tiled. The basin had built-in units underneath as well as above. There was a corner bath with shower, toilet and a top-loading washing machine between the wash basin and the door.

To the left was a narrow kitchen with beech-coloured wooden floor and wall units on both sides, a fridge-freezer on the left and an electric oven and hob near to the patio doors on the right. The white marble worktop ran from the oven all along the right-hand side to the end of the kitchen, where there was a double stainless steel sink. Above this was a window, which looked similar to the one in the bathroom and different to those in the rest of the house. Walking over, he saw that it was double-glazed with an insect mesh. It had the same view as the bedroom but was closer to a large tree that gave it shade. He opened it to let in the breeze.

The last thing was the patio. There were two sets of doors here. First the wooden-framed glass ones; these opened inwards and were rickety and barely secured themselves into the frame. The others were wooden-slatted, more substantial and folded up as they opened outwards.

The courtyard was a surprise; a concrete square washed in a greyish blue, surrounded by a waist-high wall of patterned cement blocks. There was a foot-wide gap between t concrete and the wall for a flowerbed but, apart from a small pear tree in the right-hand corner, the rest had gone to weeds. On the left, between the side of the house and a concrete pillar, was a white metal gate with three steps that led down to the alleyway. This descended steeply to a wilderness of short trees and undergrowth.

Contrasting the plainness of the patio was the view. To the left, the plane tree that shaded the kitchen window also sheltered the patio. It was tall with a thick trunk and the lower branches had been trimmed away leaving an uninterrupted view to the sea. Every time the breeze gusted, there was a pleasing rustling of leaves and creaking of branches.

On the other side of the patio was the unsightly derelict house, but from this, back round to the plane tree and above the vegetation below, was an open view of the surrounding hills, uniformly brown with a scattering of green shrubs and dwarf trees.

On the patio, to the left of the doors, was a circular, white-enamelled metal table around which were four matching chairs with red cushions on the seats. Overlooking the patio was the terrace of the upper apartment.

Stepping back inside, he put his groceries away first before unpacking his belongings, choosing the darker, larger bedroom.

It was three thirty by the time he had finished and he was hungry and thirsty. Fortunately there were two bottles of water in the fridge and that would do for now. He still had shopping to do before he could prepare a meal and should have asked Panagos where the supermarket was. He did not see it along the route they had taken and thought it unlikely to be open in the middle of the day. Usually shops in Greece closed for lunch and siesta time. He decided to go out to find somewhere to eat.

He remembered passing a taverna and so made his way back down to the harbour front. Here, sheltered from the breeze, the heat was oppressive.

When he reached the junction with the bank, he turned left. Opposite the museum was a house on the right and beyond it the town square. On its east side, his left, was the taverna, on a raised patio area. Here there were several short trees, with tables taking advantage of their shade. Otherwise the rest of the seating was under the awning that ran the length of the building.

In contrast to the empty streets, here it was busy. Jake chose a spot to the right of the entrance. Inside and to the right was the kitchen and to the left an empty space with chairs and a large TV, which sat in a bracket secured to the wall. It was turned on to a Greek sports channel. A reporter was discussing the order of the day at the Olympics.

The table was laid with a paper tablecloth and cutlery but no menu. There was subdued and lazy chatter coming from the other diners, who were nearing the end of their meals, and there was no waiter in sight.

After a few minutes, Jake went into the kitchen. This was vast, all stainless steel, with several extractor fans spinning at the same time from the ceiling. He stood at a counter and waited. At the far end, by the back door, two men sat on chairs talking. One of them saw him and came over, wiping his hands on a pair of baggy jeans. He had an uncombed mop of black hair, thick stubble and a cigarette hanging out of the corner of his mouth with a length of ash ready to fall off.

"What is there to eat?" Jake said putting his hand up to his mouth.

"Plenty good," the man shouted over the noise. This agitated the cigarette and the ash fell to the ground. Going over to the ranges, he started opening pot lids and oven doors and each time turned to him and shouted "pork" or "beef" or "macaroni" and so on. The dishes he was referring to were more sophisticated than the single ingredient description he was giving, but in the end Jake ordered the stuffed tomatoes and peppers, and a bottle each of beer and water.

A younger man, who was at least clean-shaven, brought these out, together with a basket of bread. Jake relished every mouthful between swigs of beer. By the time he had finished he felt drowsy. He went back inside, paid and went home, struggling uphill in the searing heat.

Entering his front room was a relief, especially when he took off his sandals and walked on the marble floor. It was five o'clock and all he could think of was bed. He opened the glass doors of the patio, leaving the slatted ones closed. This, together with the open kitchen and bathroom windows, created a good circulation of air. He lay on top of the bed and fell asleep to the sound of the wind rustling the branches of the surrounding trees.

Chapter 14: The Yacht Club

An urgent pounding on the front door woke him. He got up, stiff and groggy, hurrying to open it. It was Panagos. In his hand was a telephone with a length of lead coiled round it. "Telephono," he said holding it up.

Jake stepped aside while Panagos unwound the wire, positioned the phone on the table between the two armchairs, then plugged the end into a socket on the left side of the fireplace, next to the one for the television aerial.

"Very good, Panagos, thank you, but you needn't have bothered, I have my mobile."

"Mobile? No mobile," Panagos said, making an action as if slitting his throat. "Up here no good."

"In that case I'm glad you did," Jake said, as Panagos was about to rush off again, before remembering, "Where's the supermarket?"

"Supermarket? Up, up, you go up," Panagos replied, gesturing towards the heavens.

Jake nodded and Panagos left. Obviously a busy man.

Hoping the shop would still be open at this hour, he put on his sandals, picked up his keys and wallet and went to find it. He surmised Panagos meant the upper town, so when he reached the main road he turned right and started up the hill.

The day had cooled off considerably and the setting sun was bathing everything in orange. The houses of the upper village were different from the villas and manicured gardens of the lower town. They ranged from the well-maintained to the completely derelict with only four outer walls standing, or sometimes even less than that. He estimated that a third of the properties were uninhabitable. No two buildings looked the same either in shape or colour. On both sides there were alleyways that followed the contours of the hill.

At one point the road levelled out and came to a square. It skirted round a raised terrace that had tables and chairs laid out amongst short manicured trees. Where the road narrowed again there was a taverna on his left, to which the tables perhaps belonged.

The road continued to climb past terraced houses, then levelled out again, narrowed, twisted to the right and passed beneath the church before opening out onto another square. To his left, on the side from which he emerged, were marble steps up to the entrance of the church. Farther along was the supermarket, occupying the ground floor of a three-storeyed building; thankfully it was still open.

In front of the entrance was a raised area shaded by vines, growing on a wooden frame, under which were freezers with ice creams and cold drinks at one end and refuse bins at the other. The latter were infested with wasps and flies.

Inside, the air-conditioned store was cramped with only enough width in the aisles for one person. It did, however, contain a broad variety of provisions. By the entrance, a short and stout, stern-looking man with curly greying hair and dark-rimmed glasses stood behind the till. He was shouting down the telephone and from the content of the conversation it was evident that he was the owner.

Jake picked up two green plastic baskets and filled them with most of his requirements. A fat lady served him feta cheese and olives from a small delicatessen counter. A separate section had an assortment of syrupy pastries, which had attracted a handful of wasps. As he joined the queue for the till, he wondered how he was going to carry all this home, let alone the other things he needed.

When it was his turn, he asked about mosquito repellent and was given what he needed. He enquired about bottled water, whereupon the owner said that whatever he wanted could be delivered, free of charge. He asked for two twelve-packs of this and another of beer and paid for everything. When it came to describing where he lived, all he had to do was give his name and say it was his grandmother's house and the man knew exactly where it was.

Walking back, with dusk fast approaching, there were now children playing out in the square and the surrounding houses had opened their windows and shutters. The pleasant smells of cooking added themselves to the not-so-welcome ones of refuse and drains. The sounds of televisions and dozens of conversations also spilt out onto the streets.

At the square with the tables, a waitress from the taverna was setting these with tablecloths and cutlery for their expected customers. When he arrived home, he rushed through to the patio. As he'd hoped, below the branches of the plane tree he could see the horizon and the sun beginning to set. He sat watching the egg yolk-coloured orb slowly vanish and the hues of the surrounding sky fade from orange to red and finally purple before he was interrupted by another knock on his door. His delivery had come.

After stowing his groceries, he prepared himself for the evening and went back out. It was a different village now. Two houses away from his, on the right, three ladies were sitting out in a yard on a rickety wooden bench under a dim light, chatting away, seemingly all at the same time, while gesticulating in typical Mediterranean fashion. The next house he passed on the left had a paved yard under an extensive vine. This was also lit, a table had been laid and a family was preparing to have their evening meal. It was the same all along his route, houses opening up to the night and people spilling on to patios and balconies to chat and eat.

Back at the junction with the bank, he turned right, assuming this would take him to the other end of the harbour. There was a lot happening along here. The first house on the right, which earlier in the day had been shuttered up, had opened its ground floor to reveal a café for young people, also providing two snooker tables and two table-football tables. Directly opposite it was an open-air cinema. A wall enclosed it and, although the doors were shut, the top of the screen was visible from the street and he could hear English being spoken. Going up to the notice board, he read that a performance of one of the Harry Potter films had started at nine and, following that, there would be an update on the day's events at the London Olympics.

Farther on there were people either walking or standing in groups. A long queue waited beside a telephone kiosk. Behind the cinema, between it and the harbour front, were blue plastic tables and chairs beside a van selling kebabs. Next to a derelict house on the right was a playground where, despite the lateness of the hour, there were lots of small children, attended by Filipino nannies.

Beyond this was the main throng of people he had seen in the distance. On the left was a confectioner's and between it and the road was a walled, seated area with wooden chairs and tables. Here children and teenagers were having ice creams, soft drinks and sticky pastries, whilst texting on their mobiles with their free hands. Opposite, and on the corner of a road bearing right, was a busy café with metal tables and chairs outside. All were occupied and there was recorded Greek music coming from within, which added to the sound of many conversations.

On the left, a group of youths were sitting on marble benches under a row of trees, on the other side of which was a car park. This led on to a pier where yachts and powerboats of various sizes were moored. Opposite this, on Jake's right, was a flight of marble steps that led up to a low building on a terrace, from which could be heard the sound of music and people talking. This must be the yacht club.

He paused here remembering his father's yacht, the *Sevastia III*, and wondered whether to go and look for it, but was reluctant to do so, especially with so many people around. He continued on his way.

After this, the scene changed. The road came to the water's edge and there were no buildings on the right, just a hillside with open scrub that led up to a clump of trees at the crown of a hill. The sounds of music and conversation gave way to that of cicadas, and he was aware of the smells of unfamiliar plants and herbs. It was darker here with only a few dim streetlights.

People on their own or in groups continued to pass him. The breeze barely ruffled the smooth water. Above him was the vastness of the sky with its breathtaking concentration of stars and the moon one day from full. At intervals there were stone benches, many occupied.

The road came to a square, at the far end of which was the Paralia taverna. He had spotted this from the ferry when he had arrived. In the square, which was separated from the water by a low wall, tables and chairs were laid out. Sheltering half this space, on the side of the restaurant building, was a wooden frame supporting a thatched roof. A handful of bulbs hanging from the cross-beams provided the only light. Jake chose a table along the water's edge and sat facing back towards the town.

From here he could appreciate the topography beneath the rising moon. A young waiter came and left him a menu. There was a good selection and he decided to try the kebabs.

An hour later he stood at the foot of the steps that led up to the yacht club. He felt awkward but forced himself to climb. At the top, by the entrance, he saw that the terrace was split into two. The left-hand side was where the music and most of the noise was coming from. It ran back down the side of the building, which for its full length was a bar. All the tables and chairs were occupied by young people up to his age. Many more were standing in groups surrounding the bar.

The other side was smaller with only six tables: three large ones near the edge of the terrace and three smaller ones against the front of the building. Again all were occupied, but the people here were of mixed ages and the conversations more sedate.

Seeing nowhere to sit, he was about to leave when he heard his name being called. Turning to where the sound came from, he saw someone waving from the table in the far front corner. When he approached, he recognised the man from behind the till of the supermarket. He was sitting in the shadows with three others. He introduced his wife, Assimina, and his sons, Michael and Andreas. They greeted Jake warmly and wished him an enjoyable stay on the island.

"Sit with us, unless you have somewhere else to go," the man said, still standing.

"I don't want to intrude."

"No, no, you sit down. My wife and the boys are leaving for the bouzouki."

"The bouzouki? Where's that?"

"At the Town taverna," he replied, turning and pointing behind him. "We have it most Saturday nights in summer."

Jake took him to mean the place where he'd had lunch. He had seen no evidence at the time that a band was going to be playing. He sat down on the cushioned metal seat. "I'm sorry, I don't know your name."

"I'm Savvas," he replied. He turned to the others and had a brief exchange, whereupon they left. "They say you should join them."

"Aren't you going?"

"Not me. I'm not interested in watching old men dance, though I might drop in later. When did you arrive?"

"Today," Jake replied. "Do you often come here in the evenings?"

"Oh no, only Saturday nights. We open after church on Sundays and so we don't have to get up early."

"Where did you learn English?" Jake asked. It was good and had a familiar accent.

"I studied in Sunderland, before going on to become a chief engineer."

"You mean at sea?"

"That's right."

"So when did you get the shop?"

"Three years ago; the previous owner was retiring. It was an opportunity, so we bought it."

"Does it include the whole building?"

"Yes, it used to be the old hotel, but we've converted it into our home."

A young girl came up and asked them whether they wanted anything. Jake asked for a beer. "I'll have an ouzo," Savvas said.

"I don't know much about shipping, but chief engineer sounds good."

"It is."

"So why did you give it up?"

"My wife wanted us to run a business." Savvas replied, his expression even more stern than usual. "I'd go back tomorrow if I could."

"It must be difficult to work through the summer and miss the good weather though."

"The boys find it so because it means they can't stay up until dawn with their friends, but I prefer the winter myself."

"I thought it was cold and damp."

"By Greek standards, but for someone accustomed to an English winter, like you, it would be rather pleasant by comparison. I certainly thought that after Sunderland."

"But still, there must be few people to talk to."

"Yes and no," Savvas said. "Look at it this way, you look around you now and you see all these people. One week ago there were only half as many. After the twenty-fifth of August it will again be only half as many. By the end of November, when the weather changes, there'll be very few, around a hundred widows, another hundred retired couples, and a hundred working people. To us that is normal and this time abnormal."

"But what about your sons? They can't have many friends here in winter?"

"Oh, they leave by the beginning of September. We don't need them then. My wife and I can manage."

"Where do they go?"

"Back to Athens, they're civil servants."

Jake wondered how they got such long holidays but didn't ask. "So what do these hundred working people do? It seems a lot for a small island."

"You'd be surprised, it soon mounts up. Two work in the bank, another two in the post office, there's the curator of the museum and his wife, who's the head of the local council, and her personal assistant. Three work in the town taverna, which stays open all year, there's the two of us, the baker and his wife, the policeman and his assistant; the yacht club employs two, three run the hotel, there are the teachers of the school, three dustbin men, three who maintain the water supply, one of whom lives above you and is married to the nurse; there's a doctor, three run the electric generator and maintain the grid, and another six run the ferry. Then there's the harbour master and his assistant. There are several goat, sheep, pig and turkey farms and half a dozen fishermen. Some of the bigger villas have caretakers living in them all year. For the rest, there are half a dozen builders who make their living maintaining houses. There are also at least eighteen soldiers stationed at various camps. So you see, it isn't difficult to reach a hundred."

"Do you see them though?"

"Most end up in the taverna in the evening to eat, have a drink, watch TV or just play backgammon. It's surprisingly sociable, if you want it to be."

"I've obviously had the wrong impression," Jake said, as the waitress brought their drinks.

"Look, I don't want you to believe it's a paradise. It's not for everybody. From December to March it can be pretty grim. The gales can last for weeks and if it's that bad the ferry doesn't run. Also our electricity gets cut."

"But I thought the island had its own supply."

"It does, but if the tanker that brings the diesel can't deliver, we get rationed and, in extreme cases, cut off. On top of that we often get wires down from the wind."

"What happens to your freezers?"

"We've got an emergency generator. We'd go out of business otherwise."

"You stay open all year?"

"Yes, we have to; it's a condition of the permit from the council. But from October to Easter it's only from three until six to coincide with the ferry bringing fresh supplies. It's a nice time. Most of the residents come into the shop every day."

"So you have the rest of the time off."

"Not as much as I'd like. We have to do our maintenance in the winter. Our building isn't in the best condition, as you may have noticed."

No amount of work will make it look more attractive, Jake thought. "So what do you do when you're free?" he asked.

"I'm a photographer; I spend as much time as possible taking and editing photographs."

"That's interesting." Jake knew next to nothing about photography, apart from pointing and shooting. "Where do you take your photos?"

"All over the island," he replied enthusiastically, with something resembling a smile on his face.

"But there can't be that much to photograph." Jake said. Savvas appeared too pale-skinned to be spending that much time outdoors.

"Ah, you don't understand. To start with, even a small group of islands like this has many places, especially along the coasts. You just need a good boat. It's true that in summer there's rarely a cloud in the sky and the light's the same from one day to the next. But winter...." He wrung his hands as if he was about to describe an amazing sports car. He took a long sip of his ouzo. "In winter," he continued, "the sea and the weather come alive."

"That's hard to imagine," Jake said. From where he sat he could see most of the harbour. The wind had dropped and the sea was like a lake.

"Let me explain something," he continued, leaning towards him. "Where we are now, this road from the kiosk to the taverna is under water most of the winter."

"Under water?" But how's that possible? There must be continuous storms."

"Not necessarily; from Christmas to Easter the weather comes from the south and the sea seems to swell. When there are southerly storms, the waves break onto the steps down there. But that's not all; in winter there are also racing clouds, fog banks and dramatic sunsets. Every day's different."

"So what do you actually photograph?"

"Landscapes mainly," Savvas said. "It depends on the weather, but I always start in the morning, before sunrise. If it's calm and the weather's from the south, I'll go to the other side of the island and catch the dawn and the early morning light. It's dramatic round there, particularly the northwest, you know, cliffs, inaccessible coves, unreachable ravines and dramatic rock formations."

"What if the sea's rough?"

"I keep my boat in the harbour at the other end. It's called Paleo Limani. It's a bay surrounded by smaller islands, so if the sea or wind is too strong I can go to one of them. Unfortunately little of interest is accessible from the roads apart from in spring."

"What happens then?"

"Something remarkable; this brown landscape explodes into colour. Every square metre is covered in flowers. You wouldn't believe how many varieties there are."

"That's also hard to imagine."

"There are varieties of plants here which I'm convinced are unique. I'm thinking of taking samples and having them identified by the botanical centre in Athens."

"So, when you take your photographs, do you also edit them?"

"Yes, I download everything onto my computer and work on them there."

"Do you have a favourite place?"

"Oh yes, where I have my boat, Paleo Limani, that whole area. You know, the bay was an ancient harbour, no one's sure why. It's a haunting place."

"I'm here until the beginning of September. I'm going to try and do as much exploring as possible."

"If you're going to go walking, do so in the early morning or late afternoon, otherwise it's too hot."

"How do I find out about local history?"

"Best place is the museum, the curator's friendly, but he'll only know about relatively recent times. Little is known about the distant past."

"So, what are you going to do with your photos?"

"I'll probably have an exhibition. It won't be for a few years though."

"If I'm here I'll look forward to seeing them."

"You don't have to wait that long. After the twenty-eighth, when it gets quieter, I'll show them to you. If in the meantime you go for a few walks and learn where everything is, you'll appreciate them more."

"I'll look forward to that." Jake had been infected by Savvas's enthusiasm. His host signalled to the waitress to bring him the bill.

"Let me take this," Jake said, when it arrived.

"No, I'll pay. It also contains our ice creams and drinks. You pay next time."

"That's very kind," Jake said. Savvas settled the bill and got up to leave. Jake stood and said goodnight, but sat back down as he'd not finished. He'd enjoyed this conversation. It was twelve thirty and there were just as many people about as before; maybe even more. He wanted to enjoy the atmosphere a little while longer as well as the background music from the bouzouki.

By the time he'd climbed the hill, he was perspiring. Indoors it was stuffy and, even after he'd opened the patio doors, there was no movement of air. He got undressed and thought of having a cold shower before going to bed but instead had some water. He feared he wouldn't be able to sleep, not only on account of the heat but because he could still hear the music and singing from the taverna. In spite of his reservations, though, he was out as soon as his head touched the pillow.

The next thing he knew he was swimming in the sea. The water was hot, like a bath. In the distance he could hear a whining. He knew it was the sound of a small boat with an outboard motor. Then he woke, it was a dream, but the whining continued and came closer to his ear. He swatted with his hand. It was a mosquito; he had forgotten to plug in the repellent. He got up and turned on the bedside light. It was two thirty. He went and found the box of capsules and put one in the device and plugged it in beside the bed. He also plugged another one in the wall socket in the corridor outside his room. He then went back to bed and had no more trouble.

Chapter 15: The Cemetery

Sunday, 29th July

Jake slept well and woke to the sound of church bells. It was nine thirty. Eager to get out, he put together a breakfast of cornflakes and toast, followed by a mug of tea. He ate this sitting outside in the cool morning air of the patio.

He left at eleven with his towel and beach mat. He would not snorkel today, just a quick swim. He walked through the hot dusty streets towards the ferry landing, passing the taverna in the square, where the tables and chairs were still in disarray from the night before. The loudspeakers and other musical equipment were stacked in one corner. A few individuals were enjoying a coffee in the shade.

Before the ferry pier, he took the road that went up to the other end of town. After a short but steep climb, he passed through a gap in a stone wall. He walked down a rocky path through an overgrown field to the deserted beach. It consisted of coarse pebbles of varying shades of grey. In the middle of the strand was a wooden changing hut. It had lost its door and the concrete base to which it was secured had subsided forward making it close to toppling onto its front. To its right was some temporary shade, where Jake laid his mat and towel. Taking off his trainers he sat, staring out to sea.

At first he speculated idly as to the cause of the subsidence of the beach hut. If Savvas was right about the winter weather, then the sea here would easily come up to the concrete base and, as it compromised the ground underneath, it would sink in the way that it had.

But today the sea was a picture of calm. The sloping land behind him blocked the breeze, so the water near to the shore was completely smooth. A hundred yards farther out, though, the surface was being ruffled, causing ripples to fan out away from him. In the distance, to the right, he could see the headland that he had rounded on the ferry. To the left was a shorter bluff, and beyond that the island continued to its end. He now knew that this was where the big bay surrounded by smaller islands was.

Apart from the sounds of passing insects, it was peaceful. It was twenty past eleven and he wondered where everybody was until he realised that they were probably still at church.

He watched the shade receding, first exposing his feet and then his legs to the sun. He was getting hot, so he decided to test the water. He removed his top and, after applying sun cream, walked down to the water's edge. The pebbles were angular so he had to tread gingerly. His first step into the water surprised him. It was icy; not what he had expected of the Mediterranean. He went in up to the middle of his thighs and paused. He was seriously considering going back out when his attention was caught by lots of little fish chasing around the pebbles at his feet.

After a few minutes he grew used to the cold and went in a bit deeper. Once up to his groin the next step was to dive in. His willpower faltered but, as he turned to go back, he saw two women coming down the path. They were middle-aged, one slim and blonde, the other full-bodied and dark-haired; both were wearing beach gowns. When they reached the pebbles, they walked past the changing hut and laid themselves out near the shoreline.

Although he had never seen them before, he was now too embarrassed to walk out having obviously not swum. The women took off their gowns; both wore bikinis and were deeply tanned. As they started oiling themselves, he turned seawards and launched himself. He swam vigorously until he was short of breath. It was enough, he was comfortable and so he stopped and trod water. Below him, through the smooth surface, he could see the bottom. It was a mixture of reefs, weeds and sand.

He turned round to face the beach. He had swum out a sufficient distance in order to observe this end of the village. The arrival on the ferry was too quick to take in any details. Now he could appreciate the detached, brightly coloured houses as they rose up the hill. The first of these, which overlooked the beach, had obviously had its foundations eroded away because its cellars were now open to the elements; the rest of the building was still intact and occupied.

Past the headland to his right was a bay surrounded by a cliff, on top of which were more houses. Beyond that again was a headland protecting another inlet, which was hidden from view but appeared to mark the end of the village. Here the houses were smaller and built in terraced rows.

Looking back to the beach, the ladies were preparing to swim and the dark-haired one was carrying fins. To their left was the start of the breakwater, which ran for about a hundred yards to the harbour entrance, after which was the other, smaller breakwater, which ran out from the headland.

As the ladies entered the water, an older couple arrived and greeted them. He was amazed at how well he could make out their voices from such a distance.

His attention was drawn to the sound of an outboard motor that came from within the harbour. Soon a rigid hull inflatable emerged. Once clear of the breakwater, it picked up speed and headed for the far end of the island. There were several people sitting in it. Meanwhile the two ladies had passed him and were heading towards the adjacent bay.

When he began to feel the cold, he drifted back to the cove. He walked out onto the beach, his skin tingling pleasantly. He moved his towel and mat away from the remaining shadow. He would do a front and back until he was dry and that would be enough for the first day. He did his back first, but after he had turned over, he began to doze. He woke when he began to feel sore from the pebbles prodding from underneath. He sat up slowly and stiffly and saw that, in addition to the two original couples, there were now two families with children. He looked at his watch; he had slept for twenty-five minutes. His skin felt dry and he knew he had to leave. He pulled on his top and trainers and gathered his things.

It was a relief to get back inside the house. He opened the patio doors and let in the breeze. The table and chairs were still in shadow but he could see that in another hour they would be in the sun. He looked at his watch; it was one thirty. He decided to have a salad. His mother had showed him how to make them, that was simple enough, but she had also told him that they never tasted as good as they did in Greece or Cyprus. It was the ingredients.

He went into the kitchen, took out a bowl, cut up two tomatoes, one small cucumber, a quarter of a red onion, a green pepper and then added six Kalamata olives, a large chunk of feta cheese, a dusting of mixed mountain herbs and a drenching of olive oil. He cut himself two slices of bread and took a can of beer out of the fridge.

His mother was right, so right. He sat back outside and savoured every mouthful as he breathed in the pure air and enjoyed the unspoilt surroundings. He had another slice of bread, more feta and another beer before he was through. By the time the sun was upon him, he was satisfied. He washed up, closed the wooden shutters and went to lie down.

He had intended to go for a walk in the afternoon but, after he had woken from his siesta, he could feel the first signs of sunburn, particularly on his back and shoulders. He therefore delayed his outing until seven, when the sun was weaker.

He headed back towards the pebbly beach beside the harbour breakwater, where he had been that morning, but walked past this and continued to ascend. He passed three houses on the right and then came out along the edge of the cliff that overlooked the adjacent inlet. The view from here was magnificent and, with the bay in shade and the sea calm, he could see through to the sandy bottom. The orange of the setting sun had turned the landscape a warm chocolate brown with rich patches of evergreen. In the sky flocks of dark birds flew silently northwest, towards the sunset.

At the highest point of the cliff, the road split into two. To the right it continued along the coast. The left fork, which he now took, carried on up the hill and through the village. The road narrowed and snaked erratically between terraced cottages, passing many side lanes and alleys. Again, he was taken aback by the sharp contrast between the well-maintained properties and the complete wrecks, sometimes next door to each other.

There were the sounds of many voices and activities coming from open windows, not to mention the smells he had experienced the day before. It was all very intimate; this was not a place to keep secrets. Occasionally he passed someone who greeted him politely.

After the supermarket and church, he continued back down the other side, past the alley to his house and towards the harbour again. From his patio he had seen, rising on the other side of town, a wooded hillock. Within the trees was a small church. He assumed that this was the cemetery. He was going to try to find it.

He walked towards the yacht club, where the crowds were only just beginning to gather, but took the right turning beforehand, beside the café on the corner. Once he had distanced himself from the chatter and music, his attention was claimed by the sound of the most exquisite melody coming from someone playing what he recognised was a mandolin. This brought back memories of festivals he had been to with his mother in Cyprus.

After a hundred yards, he came to a crossroads at each corner of which were detached houses surrounded by lush gardens. The turning right led back home and straight ahead was a dead end. The left seemed the right direction. He started climbing and, after passing between two houses, the right-hand one of which was the source of the mandolin-playing, the road turned sharply right and ran along the foot of the pine-clad hill.

Up the slope, through the dense pines, was a stone wall. He followed a paved drive that led through the trees to an iron-gated entrance within a stone arch.

Inside, on the flat crown of the hill, was the cemetery. The tree cover was thick, especially outside the surrounding wall, and the orange rays of the sun sent shafts of light through as it approached the horizon.

Having passed the gate, he observed that the cemetery had three sections. To the left, surrounding the small church, were ornate tombs and walk-in mausoleums. To the right were more modest monuments and, at the far right end, simple graves with headstones. Where would his father be? From what he knew of his background, his descendants were of respectable but modest means, mostly merchants. His father was the first to make a fortune and certainly, from the evidence, not one to flaunt it. On the other hand, if it was a family tomb, it could be large.

He started from the chapel end and picked his way through the larger monuments first. They were all different, ranging from the minimalist to the elaborate, with stained-glass panelled windows and doors. As the light faded, he noticed that some had lamps burning within, signifying they were attended frequently.

Towards the middle of the cemetery, the less fancy, more uniform structures consisted of raised marble monuments, roughly chest height, with steps that led down to metal gates, through which one could enter a partly-buried chamber. Looking into some of these, he found they housed two tombs separated by a narrow aisle. Most contained icons, oil lamps, framed photographs of the deceased and wooden boxes.

Jake walked the paths, carefully reading inscriptions. The light was fading and he began to despair about finding the right one when at last he came to a plot against the north western wall. The monument was a simple rectangular shape, like the others, in blue-veined, white marble. At the front of it were three steps that led down to the padlocked, black-enamelled iron gate. At its head was a marble cross on which the words, carved in Greek, identified it as belonging to the Philo family. On the top of the tomb were the individual names, one below the other, with the date of birth and death. He ran his fingers over the recently engraved letters and numbers of his father's inscription.

He had a look inside, not expecting to find anything, but was surprised to see the solitary flame of an oil lamp burning on top of the left-hand tomb. Beside it, to the left, was an icon and, on the right, a small photograph. It must have been recent because his father looked very grey. Behind these three items, in a squat vase, was a spray of fresh flowers. Someone must have attended the tomb today. But who?

On the right-hand tomb across the narrow aisle, there was just an icon, a yellowing photo of his grandmother and the inevitable wooden box.

With a sigh he walked up to the wall. This was only waist-high and, from the other side, the hill sloped down to where he had walked the previous night, between the yacht club and the Paralia taverna. He sat down and, with the sun setting behind him, looked upon his father's final resting place.

He had no idea how long he was there but when he stood to leave there was only just sufficient twilight for him to see his way out. He had a last look back and saw the light of the oil lamp flickering inside the tomb. Once out of the cemetery and away from the trees, he heard the beating of wings above him; darting in all directions were dozens of bats. In the distance, the mournful melody of the mandolin resonated with his mood.

Supper was roast potatoes and a pork chop, all cooked in the oven as he showered and changed. After clearing up, he put out the mosquito repellent and went out. He walked up and down the promenade twice. It was thronging with people, as the night before. He went up to the yacht club, looking for a table, but none was available. He was hoping to find someone to talk to. He was hungry for knowledge. He could not get his father's grave and the questions it raised out of his mind. He needed to acquire the keys to the padlock; he was sure Panagos would have them. More importantly, he wanted to know who was attending the tomb. Neither Photis nor any relatives were on the island. He made his way home and to bed.

He dreamt again. He was back in the cemetery. It was dark but he could see everything. This time he had a key, so he went to the tomb, unlocked the padlock and went inside. But instead of the small cramped chamber, what he entered was a cavern full of coffins, each having on top of it an oil lamp and someone's picture. He felt disorientated, the photos were of strangers and there were no inscriptions. He had to find his father. He tried to lift the lid of one of the sarcophagi, but it was too heavy. He felt a wave of despair before waking up.

He was cold. The wind had picked up during the night and he could hear it buffeting the tree and rattling the wooden shutters of the patio and the other windows. The breeze flowed easily through the house.

He pulled the sheet over himself and went back to sleep.

Much later, in the early hours, something woke him. He was lying on his side facing the shuttered window and he slowly rolled to face the open bedroom door. He lay still, listening.

He heard nothing; maybe it was nothing. Usually waking up naturally was gradual. But this time he had gone from sleep to full awareness in a second, so he must have heard a sound that his subconscious had interpreted as being suspicious. Back home he knew exactly when this happened. It usually meant an intruder in his garden.

He thought of reasons why he should dismiss it. The breeze was strong and every few seconds would gust and shake the plane tree. Anything could have moved in such a wind: a shutter, a window, a branch. There were also nocturnal animals around. There were the bats, of course, and during the night he had heard the shooting of an owl. It was similar to the calls from the woods opposite his house in England. But there were other animal sounds he could not identify. There was also evidence of goats prowling the side paths. Did they move around at night? In the courtyard he'd found rat droppings, not to mention the hundreds of insects that must also be foraging about.

He closed his eyes and began to doze, but was now needing to relieve himself. Being unaccustomed to the heat, he had been drinking a lot of water. He got up, having forgotten his earlier worry. He walked out of the bedroom, turning right towards the patio doors, then right again into the bathroom. He passed the open window on his left and poised over the toilet.

It was then he realised there was something wrong. Turning his head he saw that the wire-meshed insect screen was missing. Instantly he whirled round 180 degrees just in time to see the bathroom door, which opened inwards, swinging shut and a dark shadow lunging at him from behind it, holding something over its head.

Instinctively and without any forethought at all, he dived head first out of the open window. The threshold was high and he glanced one knee painfully on the sill. He fell roughly on the concrete, doing a forward roll and getting to his feet again. Looking back, he saw the intruder stepping out after him. He had an impression of someone slim and taller than himself, dressed in black, wearing a balaclava. The hands and eyes were the only parts exposed and the latter looked insane and murderous.

He squared himself for another attack with whatever the intruder held and was considering leaping over the low wall to his left and into the narrow passage between the houses when he saw something white fall from above and on top of the attacker. The latter shouted in pain and dropped to one knee, the object clanging onto the concrete of the patio. He quickly got up, but another chair followed accompanied by shouting. It was then that the attacker himself leapt over the wall.

Jake rushed to the alley and just glimpsed him running downhill into the undergrowth. There was a frenzy of rustling of bushes and then silence.

"Are you all right?" the voice called from above. His neighbour, or rather his father's tenant, stood in the shadow of the balcony in his pyjama shorts.

"I'm fine, I think," Jake replied, rubbing his grazed knee, remembering he was naked. "What happened?"

"I heard a scraping sound while I was lying in bed," his neighbour said. "We sleep with the balcony doors open. I came to investigate but saw no one. Then I noticed the insect screen down there. It was leaning against the house. I thought 'why would he take the screen off at this time of night?' So I waited. Lucky for you, my wife's away."

"Thank you very much, but who could it have been?" Jake said. He had wrapped his arms around his body and was shivering.

"Let me come down and put the screen back," the man said. "I've got tools."

Jake moved his neighbour's chairs out of the way, stepped back inside, turned on the lights and pulled on a pair of shorts. He did not have long to wait before there was a knock on his door. When he opened it, his neighbour was carrying his tool kit in one hand and a tumbler with an amber liquid in the other. He wore a short-sleeved shirt, trousers and sandals. He was thick-set and brawny with short black hair and a bushy moustache.

"I thought you might need a brandy," the man said, handing him the glass.

"I think you're right," Jake said, his hand shaking as he took it. He showed his neighbour out onto the patio and watched him as he started putting the screen back. "Who could it have been?" he asked again, taking a sip.

"Before I came down, I called the policeman," the man said. "He'll be over as soon as he gets dressed, but he's wondering if it's not gypsies."

"Gypsies? Where do they come from and what would they want with me?"

"We sometimes get them in winter," the man said. "They come in boats and land in a deserted cove somewhere. They prowl at night and break into people's summer houses. They know they'll be unoccupied and can take everything: televisions, cutlery, clothes; anything they can carry. That's why the wealthy have live-in caretakers. These nomads move from island to island. When they have enough, they go to the mainland and sell it."

"But it's not winter now."

"These are desperate times. There's a world recession and the result is that people will do anything to feed themselves."

"Yes, but breaking into a house with someone in it?"

"He was probably looking for cash and your passport. He may have got away with it were it not for the wind. I think that when he took off the window and put it down a gust moved it and caused the scraping I heard."

"I thought I heard something too, so I was already awake," Jake remembered. "But he looked like he meant to kill me."

"He was carrying a cosh, so he probably would've tried to frighten you into giving him your valuables," the man said thoughtfully. He had nearly finished screwing in the screen. "I think once you leapt outside he was just trying to make sure you weren't going to follow him."

"There wouldn't be much I could do naked," Jake said, remembering something. "You said it was lucky your wife's away."

"Oh, yes," the man said, smiling. "She's accompanying a sick patient to Lichas. She's the nurse, you know. But when she sleeps, she snores so badly I wouldn't hear a Turkish invasion."

The policeman came a few minutes afterwards. He offered his condolences about his father, had a look around and repeated his earlier suspicion that it was more than likely a gypsy. He also confirmed that he was the one who was called to the scene of his father's death, together with the local doctor, but could add nothing to what Jake already knew.

After they had both left, Jake went back to bed, this time with the bathroom window closed. The kitchen one he left open as it seemed inaccessible without a ladder and the wooden patio doors would make considerable noise if they were forced open. It was first light before he felt secure and relaxed enough to fall asleep.

Chapter 16: Paleo Limani

Monday, 30th July

Jake was woken by the sounds of building work. It was only eight o'clock and, after the events of the night, he was not ready to start the day. Fortunately, he found that closing the bedroom window cut out most of the noise. He slept again until nine, when he got up, pulled on his swimming shorts, a top and sandals and went in search of bread.

Once outside, he found the source of the commotion. On the other side of the path, uphill from him, builders were renovating a ruin. On his way to the upper town, he found other workers painting houses, women putting out washing or hosing down balconies and patios, and people walking by with bags of shopping.

The baker was down the steps of the ally opposite the supermarket. His shop was located in the corner of a building of rough stone, which was once rendered in cement that had, with time, fallen away. In places the rusting reinforcing steel was now visible.

Outside the entrance there was a queue that consisted entirely of old women in black. Most were short and fat and, because he towered above them, he could see over their heads into the shop. Inside it looked like something out of a third world country and consisted of a square room with a single small window, with half its glass missing, high up on the right-hand wall. A bulb dangled at the end of a twisted wire attached to the ceiling. Also against the right side wall was a wooden trestle table with a deeply grooved top covered in flour and bits of broken crust. The queue ran along the side of this and out the door.

At the far end of the room was the oven, the door of which had a rectangular slit. Through this Jake could see flames licking up the sides of a surface arranged with loaves. Beside the opening was a skinny, dark-haired, moustachioed man, wearing a white string vest and dark trousers that were, like the table, caked in flour. Dangling from his mouth was a cigarette, the end of which glowed with each intake of breath. His right hand rested on his hip and his left held a long wooden implement that looked like an oar. He stood motionless, staring at a wrist watch that lay on the table in front of him. The air held the smell of wood smoke and the fragrance of bread baking.

Meanwhile the ladies stood in line, amiably chatting and gesticulating to each other. Occasionally one would give him a suspicious glance. Looking behind him, he saw that the queue had grown considerably. He also noticed that everyone carried a small towel. It had never occurred to him that he would be buying bread straight from the oven and he must have looked stupid coming empty handed. He decided he would solve the problem by taking off his tee-shirt and using that instead.

Suddenly the queue fell silent, as if in reverence of the approach of a solemn occasion. Looking ahead he saw that the baker was looking into the oven. Satisfied with what he saw, he opened the metal door. Taking his implement, with an astounding speed he started removing loaves, two at a time, and throwing them on the table. As he did this they skidded to the end along the grooves that years of use had created.

At the same time there was a change in the mood of the queue. Whereas at the start they were placidly standing and talking, as soon as the first pair of loaves hit the trestle table top, they surged forward. Jake was jostled from behind and women pushed past, elbowing him and grabbing loaves, sometimes three or four at a time. At this rate there would be nothing left for him. He decided to set politeness aside and use his advantage of height and reach. He pushed forward through the throng, reached the edge of the table, grabbed two loaves as they were sliding along and wrapped them in his top.

At the head of the table a mound of coins and notes was accumulating. As customers collected their bread, they dropped the money on the pile and left. It was obvious that they all had the right amount with them in order to save time. He had to wait until the baker had finished removing loaves before asking how much he had to pay.

Back home, the smell of the fresh bread filled the apartment. He cut thick slices, spread them with butter and honey, and went to sit outside. It was when he was opening the wooden shutters to the patio that he was startled to find an envelope wedged underneath them. He sat at the table with his breakfast and opened it. There was a note inside.

> Dear Jake, I hope you've settled in. Come to Paleo Limani for eight thirty. It's a one-and-a-half hour walk. Bring me some salad ingredients, feta and bread. Diana.

Paleo Limani, the Old Athenian Harbour, the far end of the island; what was she doing there? He had not expected to hear from her so soon, and when had she delivered the note? How had she got onto the patio?

The gate was locked so she would have had to scale the wall from the side path, just like last night's intruder had done. He found it disturbing that people seemed to be able to come and go whenever they wished.

He went and examined the front door. It would have been impossible to slip a note underneath it as it had an overhanging lip and there was no letterbox; the patio was the only option. She must have come when he was buying the bread, he was sure he would have heard her otherwise. He was glad he'd bought the two loaves; he wasn't going to go up there and have another battle with those women again.

He planned to go to the beach, but first needed to withdraw some cash. After breakfast, with his bank book, wallet and passport in hand, he walked down towards the harbour. He had already been a couple of times to the cash till in Athens, and once in Lichas, and had still only managed to spend seven hundred and fifty of the ten thousand euros Zacharias had deposited.

The bank consisted of an entrance hall and two rooms. The one on the left was what he assumed to be the administrator's office. It was open, and the manager, a short, fat, balding man in a white open-necked, short-sleeved shirt, was sitting behind his desk, talking on the phone. Opposite him, in front of the desk and turned so that he faced the entrance, was a broad-shouldered, mature man with short grey hair and a trimmed beard. He wore an open-necked, light blue shirt and navy trousers. He had the tanned and weathered skin of a yachtsman and was examining Jake as he entered. The other room was the public part with two glass-screened serving counters; a young girl was behind the farthest one. He approached her, handed in his bank book and passport and asked for five hundred euros. She entered the details on her computer and then went into the manager's office through a door behind him. She waited for him to finish his call, exchanged a few words with him and then came back out and showed Jake in.

The manager stood up and introduced himself, extending a hand. He seemed somewhat nervous and his handshake was clammy. The other man also stood. In contrast, he looked calm and confident. Upright, he was an imposing figure: tall, well-built, with muscular arms and neck.

"Mr Philo, I'd like to introduce you to Yiannis Vassilliades, our mayor," the manager said.

"It's a pleasure," Jake said, taking his hand, which was dry and hard. He noticed that behind the manager, to his right, was the safe. It was open with bundles of notes, sacks of coins and papers for all to see.

"Welcome to the island, and my condolences about your father," the mayor said. He had a deep voice.

"Thank you."

"We'd always socialise whenever he was here," the mayor said. The manager meanwhile had gone to the safe, taken out a bundle of notes and was counting them. "So, have you come to stay for a while?"

"Probably till the end of August."

"When did you arrive?"

"Just yesterday."

"So what do you think of our island?"

"Beautiful and peaceful, most of the time."

"Here you are, Mr Philo," the manager said handing him a wad of notes. "Could you please count it and sign the receipt?"

"I'm sure it's correct, thank you," Jake said, putting his signature on the confirmation slip.

"Only half an hour ago I heard about the incident last night," the mayor said.

"It was a bit of a shock," Jake confessed.

"I'm sure the policeman's explanation was correct," the mayor said, "although such incidents rarely happen in summer." He looked towards the bank manager, who nodded in agreement, beads of sweat on his brow.

"I'm sure he's right too," Jake said.

"We're a close community," the mayor continued. "I hope you will want to be part of it, so if there's any way that I can help, please feel free to ask."

"I'll bear that in mind."

"Enjoy your stay, and I'm sure we'll meet again," the mayor added finally.

The bank manager showed him out, and Jake went back home to put his valuables away, taking greater care in hiding them, before going back out to the pebbly beach.

He restricted his time to a quick swim, came back early, had a salad with a beer, sat and read on the patio until he lost the shade, and then had a siesta. Afterwards he showered and dressed in shorts and a top. It would be too hot to walk so far in trousers; he would have to risk the mosquitoes once the sun had set.

He left at seven, having packed what Diana had asked for in his rucksack.

He retraced his route of the evening before, up the hill from the pebbly beach to where the road split. This time he took the right-hand fork and the road continued along the top of the cliff with its sheer drop on the right into the bay and a steeply rising slope on the left with detached, mostly derelict houses. In the fading light, the sea was nearly black. After a couple of hundred yards, the road snaked inland, and now there were houses on the right-hand side as well, built onto the rocky cliffs and overlooking the sea.

When he came to the next inlet, the road bore left and started to descend. From his vantage point, he could see that there were rows of terraced houses hugging the headland below, and a third of the way up the inlet, on the near side, was a small harbour with a handful of fishing boats. The breakwater consisted of a length of neatly piled boulders. Opposite, on the other side of the inlet, was a sandy cove between low rocky cliffs and backed by a grove of trees, amongst which was the ruin of a homestead.

The road followed a steady descent inland, taking him to the head of the inlet, a narrow silty beach with a single square stone structure, before turning right and crossing the floor of the valley, through a patch of dense, head-high vegetation. Before the road climbed again, there was a petrol station on the right. A sign gave the hours of business as 7 p.m. – 9 p.m., but it didn't appear to be attended. He wondered how the petrol was delivered as the ferry was not big enough for even the smallest tanker.

After this, the road turned sharply left and began a series of zigzags as it mounted the next hill. It turned back on itself three times before reaching the summit, by which time he was breathless; he saw that he was near to one of the highest points of the island. There was more of the hill to climb to the east, so he could not see in that direction but, to the west, in the face of the breeze and sun, he looked over to an equally high peak that was beyond the village. The island was roughly circular with a hilly landscape and irregular coastline. In places were derelict homesteads and much disused terracing enclosed in ruined stone walls. The sea to the south and west was a shimmering gold from the setting sun. To the north it was a milky blue.

The path then swung right, across the top of the hill. It went past a smelly, untidy and noisy sheep and turkey farm before coming to a fork. There was no signpost, but the road to the left seemed to turn back along the northern side of the island. He turned right and continued along the top of the hill until, quite unexpectedly, the view to the southeast, the direction he was heading, opened out to him.

Below was a long winding valley into which the road descended. The tarmac was newer here and he could see the ivory ribbon meander into the distance and up and over two ridges before disappearing. Beyond that Paleo Limani was visible, the bay surrounded by islands, and beyond that again was the open sea with a strip of cloud on the horizon, which was now acquiring an orange tint.

There was still a distance to go. As he descended into the shadows, the topography changed and, with it, the mood. Whereas before the scrub was low, perhaps knee-height, here the vegetation was head-height, with a lot more trees, which in places formed impenetrable groves. In addition there was much more abandoned terracing and ruined stone huts. On the other side of the mountain, from where he had just come, the terrain was open and transparent. Here it was closed, mysterious and somewhat threatening.

Before the next ridge, the valley widened into a flat plain and the road passed between two farmsteads. Wire fences, enclosing areas given to growing a mixture of crops, surrounded them. Passing one of these he saw corn on the cob and sunflowers. He picked up the scent of mint and other herbs. There was no one to be seen, but from one building came the sound of a dog barking. At the top of the next ridge was a miniature white chapel, just high enough to catch the sun's last rays. On the other side was a long finger of water from the sea, like a fjord, but without the steep sides. This was a surprise as it was not visible from the mountain. The road ran a long way inland around the edge before reaching the other side and the next ridge, which was just opposite him across the silky water. He could have swum across in a few minutes.

As he continued, he saw another reason why he wished he could have avoided the road. At the head of the inlet, the whole of the scrubby slope was crowded with goats. At first he could not make them out because they were hidden in the vegetation, their predominantly brown skins blending with the surroundings. He was first alerted to their presence by the sound of the bells they had around their necks. They seemed to be migrating en masse towards the road so that when he came to this part it was blocked. As he approached, they stopped whatever they were doing, grazing or walking, and just watched him. It was eerie; he did not pause in his stride but walked straight through the midst of them, while they followed him with their soulless eyes.

When Jake looked back, after a comfortable distance, the goats had started moving away from the road and back up the slope, the sound of their bells echoing throughout the length of the inlet.

By the time he reached the opposite bank and the ridge, the sun had set. He looked at his watch; it was twenty minutes past eight. On the other side was the bay. It was impressive; large and circular and surrounded by the smaller islands. These appeared entirely devoid of trees, being covered only by the prevailing scrub, apart from the island to his left. Here a copse of evergreens surrounded what appeared to be a white-washed chapel. This was half-way up the facing slope and was connected to a rickety old pier by a steep path.

Below him was a narrow shingly shore with a few beached boats. Did one of these belong to Savvas? In the middle of the bay a solitary, single-masted yacht rode at anchor. He saw no houses, people or cars. He had no idea where he was meant to go, but the road continued south eastwards, along the edge of the bay towards the next headland, so he followed it. It led to another, larger strip of beach, this one silty. Here the road ran along the water's edge, and there were more small boats. Inland there was an odd assortment of houses and parked cars dotted around, seemingly at random. As he neared them, he saw that most of the dwellings were single, square concrete structures with an entrance, a few windows and a raised veranda in front. Others were constructed of reclaimed materials such as parts of cars. All had an oil barrel, which would be used for storing water, on their flat roofs.

As with the farmsteads he had passed earlier, these buildings were surrounded by some sort of fencing and enclosed flower and vegetable gardens. There were washing lines strung with clothes, swimwear and the occasional wetsuit. The cars were all sorts from rusting wrecks to a modern four-wheel drive. There was no sign of people though, but he felt he was being watched.

Where was Diana? He'd thought he might find a café or a taverna en route, but there was nothing. He regretted not remembering to ask for her mobile number. As long as the road continued, he would carry on along the bay. He would have a problem getting back home though, as there were no street lamps and he did not have a torch.

At the next headland, the tarmaced road ended and turned to dirt, proceeding along the top of a low cliff. In the distance, to his left, was another single-storey structure, but this one was more substantial and was surrounded by small fields, partitioned by stone walls. It looked more like a farmstead, like the two he had passed earlier on, but without the wire fencing. As he approached, and for the first time, he saw someone. They were hanging something on a line underneath a nearby tree. It appeared to be a rug or a blanket but, when he reached the nearest point from the road, he realised it was a woman dismembering a goat. He forced himself not to stare.

As darkness approached, so the sounds of the goats' bells become more audible. They came from the hills around him and yet there were no animals to be seen. He probably should have turned back long ago. He rounded one smaller headland and saw that he was near to the end of the road and the northern entrance to the bay. Ahead, the path descended to a low sandy causeway that led to an outcrop. Beyond was an isthmus that connected the bay to the open sea. On the other side of this channel, the off-shore island with the chapel rose steeply out of the water.

The causeway, with its north side facing the breeze and catching a steady procession of wind waves, was composed of coarse sand. It made a crunching noise as he walked across it. To the west, the rugged northern side of the island faded into the distance, beyond which the horizon was now crimson. The southern side of the causeway had finer grains and faced the bay. The outcrop attracted his attention. It consisted of near horizontal layers of tan-coloured sedimentary rocks. They were crumbly and broke off in his hand.

Looking around in the approaching gloom, he noticed a strange mound in the centre of the causeway, midway between the two beaches. As he approached, he saw that it was the remains of a cow, half buried in the sand. Somehow it must have been swept onto the beach, maybe during a storm last winter. All that was left was the skull and skeleton covered with hide. On closer examination, it had a gaping hole in its side. What was a cow doing in the sea in the first place and how did it lose such a big chunk of itself? A shiver went through him.

He had been on edge since last night's incident but this was a strange place; he could feel it. Not just the causeway, but the whole bay. He kept on wanting to look over his shoulder, as if someone was watching him. At first he thought it was the people in the houses he passed, but now it was the hills themselves. They seemed to be pressing in on him; and where were all these goats he was hearing?

As he looked up at the slope that rose above the dirt track that brought him here, he saw them emerging over the crest of the hill and climbing down towards the path. Were they intending to block his way again? Had they followed him here from their last encounter?

He walked back to the inner beach and, close to where the dirt road ended, there was a smooth boulder to sit on. He would have a short rest before starting back, goats or no goats. Surely the available star and moonlight would be enough to see him home.

As he faced into the bay, in the distance across the water he saw the blue hull of the anchored yacht. There were lights on board, one at the top of the mast and one at either end. It was then he noticed a disturbance in the inky water. It was a wake. Coming towards him, from the yacht, was a small, dark-hulled inflatable. Soon he could hear the buzzing of the engine echoing from the surrounding hills.

At the same time he was perplexed to see the goats retreating. Were they troubled by the sound of the outboard?

As the launch approached, he recognised her. So this was what she meant when she said that she never stayed on the island.

She wore white trousers and a long-sleeved navy top, and had her white mane of hair tied back. He saw her smile and he could hardly suppress his. She turned off the outboard and raised it as the launch neared the shore.

"Take off your shoes and wade in," she called. He did this, walked in up to his knees in the cold water and caught the prow as it approached. "Give me a push back out, and jump in."

After doing this, he threw in the rucksack and lunged head first into the boat. He righted himself and sat on the bench amidships. Meanwhile, Diana had put the engine back in the water and, with one gentle pull of the starter, had it running again. She went a short distance in reverse to turn round and was soon heading back towards the yacht.

"How are you?" she said sitting back down, facing him. "I hoped you'd find your way to this beach. I purposely waited until you got here before coming to get you. It's the most convenient for a launch. The rest of the shoreline is either too silty or rocky."

"I didn't know what to expect or where you'd be. Certainly not on a yacht."

"I would never stand you up."

They glided across the water in silence until: "So you must've taken the launch to deliver the note?" Jake asked.

"Actually, I arrived at the main harbour from Lichas this morning. I went to your house and as you weren't there I left the note for you. I left straight after and anchored here."

"But how did you get onto the patio?"

"I have my ways," she said, with a smile. "You'd better get ready to grab hold," she continued, cutting the power and letting the launch glide the rest of the way.

As they approached the rear of the yacht, he saw the name '*Pelagos*' written in forward-leaning white letters against the blue of the hull. The stern end was flat with a stainless steel ladder, to which Jake, having grabbed hold of it, tied the bowline. Although the boat was generally in immaculate condition, there was a faint patch of scratches and rust stains just above the water line, between the tiller and rudder.

Diana turned off the engine. "You first," she said.

He climbed the ladder and stepped down into the steering well. The companionway hatch was open and there were lights on below. She jumped down beside him.

"Come down below," she said, "but mind the step and watch your head."

He followed her down. Apart from the head height, it was surprisingly spacious in a cosy sort of way. The first area was the desk and chartroom section with an array of electronic instruments, which had no meaning to him. Beyond that were two settees facing each other with a half-folded table between them. It could comfortably seat four. Beyond that again was the galley, which ran up to a bulkhead and a closed door. The walls and most of the fittings were finished in beech.

"Welcome to my home-away-from-home," she said. "Let me show you the rest of it before we sit." She walked on ahead. "This, of course, is the galley. It may be small, but you'll be amazed what I can do in it." It was neat and tidy. The work surface opposite the oven had a roasting tin covered with foil on it. "I hope you like seafood?"

"Love it."

"Through this door," she said, opening it, "is the main cabin." He was looking along a short corridor to a double bed set into the bow. "On the port side is the toilet and to starboard the shower room. Feel free to use whichever you need, although I would appreciate it if you peed from the deck, as you're a man. It would save a lot of water and trouble. But promise me that when you do go in here you'll not look into my cabin; it's the only part that's a mess."

"I promise."

"Now, hand over the food, sit down at the table and make yourself at home. I'm sorry to have asked you for these, but I didn't feel like shopping when I arrived."

"That's fine." He gave her the rucksack and went and sat at the table.

Meanwhile, Diana turned on the oven. "The main course will take forty-five minutes, so we'll have the starter. Are you hungry?" she asked.

"After that walk?" Jake said, getting a whiff of gas.

"Good. Now, the only problem with my galley is that it doesn't have a big enough fridge, so I have to sling things over the side in a net; so, be a darling, and go to the port side, where you'll find a bottle of ouzo and one of water. Meanwhile, I'll get the salad ready."

He climbed back out into the steering well and, over the side, found the rope netting suspended from a bollard. Inside were the bottles. By the time he got back down, Diana had extended the table and was putting out plates, glasses, a small jar of vinegar, cutlery, the bread and a tub of ice. Remembering how she liked her ouzo, he prepared two with water and ice. "What shall we drink to?" he asked.

"To our continued good health and a good summer," she replied, taking a sip. She picked up the tin and placed it in the middle of the table. When she took the foil off, Jake could not at first understand what he saw. "They're sea urchins; have you not had them before?"

"No, I can see what they are now, but they seem to have been cut in half."

"They've not been cut in half but have had the bottom part of the shell removed to expose the eggs. They're the coral coloured strands."

"I hope I like them, there seem to be quite a few."

"There's little to eat in each, but they're a delicacy in many other parts of the world. This is what you do." She took one of the black spiky things out and put it on her plate and, with a teaspoon, scooped out the contents in one and ate them. "Go on, try it."

Jake did the same. "It's delicious. I've never tasted anything like it. It's both salty and sweet with a taste of the sea. And it goes so well with ouzo and bread."

"I'm glad you agree. It's the caviar of the Aegean. Some people prefer to sprinkle vinegar on them. Personally, I don't."

"I'm not that keen on vinegar. But where did you get them, there are no shops around and they look like they've just come out of the water."

"They were caught just three hours ago," she said, looking pleased with herself. "They're fresh. If you look carefully you'll see that the spines are still moving."

"You're right," Jake exclaimed, after studying them. "And you caught them? But that's amazing. There must be at least fifty."

"Fifty-four actually and, before you become too in awe of me, they're easy to catch. Firstly it needs to be early morning or evening so that the sun's at an angle to enable you to see the bottom better. Then you need a boat, a long pole with three prongs, a hand-held glass-bottomed barrel to see the seabed with, and the right scissors to cut them open once you've landed them. There're some large beds just outside the islands."

"I think you're amazing, just the same. What do I do with the empties? My plate's filling up fast." Diana went to fetch a plastic bowl and checked the oven at the same time. "And you sail this boat all by yourself?"

"I've had many boats in my time. But I don't sail that much anymore. These days it's much easier to switch on the engine. So, tell me about your first two days."

Jake told her everything that had happened since he'd arrived while they finished the sea urchins. When he described the events of the previous night, she was concerned at first but agreed with the explanation.

After they'd finished, Diana cleared up and Jake went and threw the empty shells over the side. By the time he came back, she'd put out fresh plates and was assembling a salad from the ingredients he had brought. Finally, out of the oven came the baking dish. In it was a large silver-grey fish, cooked in tomatoes, oil, onions and garlic.

"Help yourself to salad," she said as she served him some of the white flaky flesh."

"What's this?"

"Sea bass."

"Don't tell me."

"Yes, I admit it, I caught it myself, just this morning, with a speargun," she said, noticing the amazement on Jake's face. "When I'm with the yacht, my food comes from the sea, whenever possible."

"No wonder you're so good for your age."

"It's not only the food, but the exercise. I just love the thrill of the hunt on both land and sea. I was in the water for over an hour before I found this one, and it's no big deal. A lot of the locals catch their food in this way."

"And where did you find this?"

"Beyond the smaller islands there are some submerged reefs. They're good for fish. So, changing the subject, I gather you met our mayor?"

"Yes, but I can't imagine he would have much to do."

"It's more of an honorary role, a hobby for him. He lives in Athens."

"How does he manage that?"

"It's hardly like running London, and Niki, who heads the local council, is competent. It also helps that he flies his own plane. There's a private airstrip on Lichas."

"I visited the cemetery yesterday."

"Did you find your father's grave?"

"Yes. I noticed that the tombs are padlocked. Before last night, I wouldn't have thought it would be necessary."

"It's done mainly to keep out children and pranksters."

"I also saw wooden boxes."

"Those contain bones," Diana explained. "After a number of years, they're dug up and put in the boxes in order to make way for the next occupant."

They ate and drank heartily, taking seconds and thirds of fish and salad until there was nothing left but the skin and bones. Finally they mopped up the juices with bread.

"Do you visit here often?" he asked.

"Being from the island, I've always come. I've visited many places over the years, but it's special here. It has an atmosphere. You probably didn't feel it because you were anxious about meeting me."

"That reminds me, I saw something strange on the beach. The remains of a cow, half buried in the sand. Just the skeleton and skin."

"I expect it was washed up in bad weather."

"That's what I thought, but what was a cow doing in the sea anyway?"

"Probably fell off a ferry. They often transport livestock between islands and along the coast of Turkey."

"That would explain it, but it had a gash in its side, like it had had a bite taken out of it."

"Great White."

"Great White?"

"Yes, you know, the shark."

"I know what you mean, but here in the Aegean?"

"I thought you were a geography teacher. There has long been a controversy whether Great Whites bred in the Mediterranean or strayed in through the Strait of Gibraltar. Within the last thirty years, marine biologists have proved that there's an indigenous population. The coast of Turkey and the North Aegean are a hot spot."

"But why here, surely there's not enough prey?"

"The islands used to have breeding populations of monk seals, one of their staples. They're endangered now, but the sharks are certainly still around. What were we talking about before?"

"About the strange atmosphere. Savvas said the same thing. He seemed to think something happened here."

"He may be right. Why don't you go up and see if you can feel it for yourself? I'll clear up a bit. If you get cold, there're blankets in the lockers under the seats."

Up in the steering well, he opened the lid of one of the seats, took out a blanket and wrapped it round his bare legs before sitting down. Although the breeze had died down, there was a chill, being so close to the water. After a while his eyes grew accustomed to the dark and, from the twilight of the stars, he could make out the outlines of the dark islands around him. The yacht was anchored pointing northeast into what was left of the breeze, and he was facing starboard. Forward he could also make out a few lights from the dwellings he had passed along the shore. On the last ridge, before he'd descended to the bay, a lone street lamp stood sentinel. But on the island facing him, the largest in the encircling group, he spotted a solitary light. It was down near the shore and didn't coincide with the chapel he'd seen earlier.

He laid his head back and stared at the sky. It felt so close, and was crowded with stars. It was still, and in the distance he could hear the tinkling of goat bells. It was not true what Diana had said. He had felt the atmosphere as soon as he had crossed the last ridge.

Diana appeared at the hatchway. She handed him a tray containing a plate with a selection of sticky Greek pastries and two glasses of brandy before coming to sit beside him. She was wearing a jumper.

"How am I getting back?"

"I could run you to the harbour, or you can sleep on the spare bunk. It's very comfortable."

"With all I've had to eat and drink, I don't think I can move," Jake said. The truth was, he didn't relish going back to sleep alone.

"I can't say I want to move much myself."

"So, whatever happened here in the past must've had something to do with the Athenian Harbour. Maybe a battle of some sort?"

"The Athenian Harbour's only mentioned once in the ancient historical texts. No reason's given for its existence. There were plenty of remains once, but they've been removed by trophy hunters since the Second World War." She picked up her glass and drank the rest of the brandy in one. "I'm going to bed now. Give me about fifteen minutes to turn out your bunk and use the bathroom."

"Okay, if you're sure you want me to stay?"

"Definitely, I'll leave a light on and a bottle of water with a glass on the kitchen worktop. See you in the morning, and leave the hatch open for ventilation."

"By the way, what's that light over on that island?"

"Probably the army encampment."

"Why there, of all places?"

"They're mainly looking out for drug smugglers and illegal immigrants. They're not likely to turn up in the middle of town."

"I see what you mean. Goodnight then," he said as she went down the hatch. He sipped the brandy while he looked back up at the stars.

When he went down, he found that the lights had been dimmed and the table folded away. One of the settees had by magic become a bunk. After a visit to the cramped bathroom to rinse his mouth, he undressed down to his underwear and slipped under the sheet and blanket. The bed was narrow and short but, once he got the hang of lying on his side in the foetal position, he fell into a deep and restful sleep.

He slept straight through until morning, which surprised him. After all he'd had to drink, he'd expected to be in and out of the bathroom, or on the deck as Diana preferred. He had been woken by the sounds coming from her cabin. She came out dressed in jeans and a blouse.

"Good morning," he said, propping himself up on his elbow.

"Good morning; I hope you slept okay."

"I did, surprisingly, for a strange bed."

"It's the sea air. There's no rush getting up, it's early," she said, looking at her watch. "I'm just going to pop out for an hour or so. See you when I get back."

He heard the launch start up and fade into the distance. He visited the bathroom. Blow going on deck, he was still half asleep. He lay back down and slept until he heard the launch returning. It was an hour and a half later. He pulled on his clothes and was dressed by the time Diana came down the hatch. She was carrying two buckets, one overflowing with figs, the other with grapes.

"You're a born scavenger," he said.

"A hunter actually, but I do all right."

She put the produce in bowls and they ate in the morning sunlight while sitting in the steering well. They peeled the figs and dipped them in the sea.

"Who are the people who live in those makeshift shacks?" he asked.

"Islanders, they live in the main village most of the year but come out here in July and August to escape the crowds. These are summer places."

"The crowds? What crowds?"

"You're used to England. These people see those who come for the summer as invaders. They can't stand them or the noise they make. I agree with them. I prefer the sounds of nature and the sea. This is where I feel at home. Now, do you want me to run you back in the launch or would you rather walk?"

"I think I'll walk."

"Then you'd better start before it gets too hot." She went back down and brought up his rucksack. "I've put some of the figs and grapes in here and also a bottle of water." She took him back to the beach.

"When will I see you again?" he asked as they made landfall.

"Tomorrow; go to the pebbly beach by the breakwater and swim out along the coast towards the little harbour you saw from the road on your way here. You'll find me with the inflatable in the vicinity. You'll need to start at about twelve, and use your mask, snorkel and fins; don't worry about the other stuff."

"So, what are you doing today?"

"I'm making a quick trip to Lichas for more supplies and fuel. See you tomorrow."

Chapter 17: The Sea

Wednesday, 1ˢᵗ August

The following morning Jake unrolled his mat and towel, in which he had his fins, and sat in the shade, his shade. He was struggling to acclimatise. Yesterday morning it had taken him an hour and a half to walk back. As a result, his arms, the back of his legs and neck were red and sore. When he'd arrived home, and not realising the damage, he had changed and gone to the pebbly beach for a swim.

Today would be the first time he would be going for a proper snorkel. How difficult could it be? He was a strong swimmer, so he was going to allow thirty minutes to cover the distance to the little harbour. In the meantime, he was warming up nicely. There was no breeze and the sea was flat, the only waves being created were by the two children playing in the shallows to his right. They belonged to a couple sitting a few yards away.

He was acknowledging to himself that he had come to an important conclusion yesterday morning on the road back home. He'd started thinking about his father and seeing him in a different light. Here was a man he'd believed he'd hated but in reality loved and whose love he had longed for. He'd realised that actually his father was a good man and a new determination had gelled inside him. He'd made a decision, two in fact. He would do whatever it took to find out the truth about his father. The truth was here, around him, on this island. Secondly, he was going to put on the mantle his father had passed on to him. As soon as he had arrived home, he had picked up the phone and given Zacharias a call on his mobile and told him. There was nothing he could do about it until September, but he was pleased and supportive. They agreed that it would be best if nobody knew of his decision for the time being.

He checked on the time; he would have to get ready to go and meet Diana. Now there was a mystery woman. He had never met anybody who could say so much and yet reveal so little. She was either an eccentric or genuinely knew something. If the latter, then he was certain he would have to earn that knowledge. There was something she wanted from him and he would have to go along with whatever it was.

It was time to be on his way. He tiptoed across the hot pebbles to the water's edge and sat on a boulder to put on his fins. Positioning the mask over his eyes and nose and the snorkel in his mouth, he waded waist deep and pushed off with hardly a thought about the cold.

It was the first time he had seen an underwater landscape, other than on television. The first thing he noticed, after he had got used to swimming and not having to breathe bilaterally, was the clearness of the water and the bright colours of the pebbles in the shallows: mostly yellows, reds and browns. As he swam into deeper water, the bottom became rocky and the colours faded to a monochrome greyish-blue.

He turned left towards the adjacent bay and encountered a reef, which came within inches of the surface and was impossible to cross. He had to follow it out for a while before finding a channel deep enough to swim through. As he did so, he saw crevasses and hollows in which small fish and sea urchins lurked. Some of the fish had irregular black stripes, like zebras, others were a silver colour. The rocks were cloaked with strange growths and weeds. As he entered the bay, the bottom changed to sand.

He decided to swim into the bay and shallower water before turning right and following the coast. As he did so, he realised that what at first had seemed a featureless landscape had lots of individual fish grazing, and an occasional flat fish would betray its position by disturbing the sand under which it was hiding. As he approached the cliff, he bore right and swam along the coast again. Here the bottom was strewn with irregular rocks and boulders.

He continued past a low headland and a featureless cove, where there were two fishing boats tied either side of a decrepit wooden pier, on to a stretch of sheer cliff. Here there was a lot more life. The rocks were covered with red starfish, pink sea anemones and dark sea urchins. Large schools of black fish patrolled the rocks in deeper water. Beyond that the bottom dropped away to an inky darkness.

When he reached the end of the cliff and the entrance, he had a rest. This was the first of the two large inlets he had passed on foot. It did not penetrate inland as far as the second, but it was wider. He knew that the small harbour was just a few hundred yards farther on this side. He carried on swimming until he saw the boulders that made up the breakwater. There was no sign of Diana so he stopped at the entrance, pulled up his mask and had a look around, while treading water.

He saw no one either in the harbour or nearby. On the opposite side of the inlet was the sandy cove he had seen on his walk. On it was a blue tent and a beached inflatable. It was too much of a coincidence, so he decided to swim across. It was a long haul and most of the time he could not see the bottom, just spooky shafts of sunlight disappearing into the depths. Eventually it became shallower and a pebbly shelf became visible. He approached a school of finger-length silvery fish that parted to let him through.

When the water was waist deep, he stood up and started to remove his fins.

"I wouldn't do that quite yet if I were you." It was Diana's voice coming from the tent. "There are sea urchins, or worse, amongst the pebbles."

Although the entrance to the tent wasn't facing towards him, he could see two feet, covered by a towel, poking out.

"What's worse?" he asked walking out of the water backwards.

"A stone fish," came the reply. "They're hard to spot and have poisonous spines."

Once on the beach he removed his fins, mask and snorkel and made his way to the tent. The sand was coarse and hot. When he reached it, he saw that it was open to the front and back. Diana sat on a straw mat under the canvas. She was wearing a black bathing suit, her legs covered by the towel. Her wet hair fell to her shoulders and had a yellowish tinge. Beside the tent, on a rock, was a pair of yellow fins and a matching mask and snorkel. When she saw him, she smiled, moved over to the left side and patted the mat beside her.

Leaving his gear next to hers, he got on his hands and knees and crawled in. They were perfectly angled to catch the breeze.

Diana reached behind her and handed him a towel. "I can see you're cold," she said smiling.

Not for the first time, Jake wondered what this woman had looked like in her youth. She must have been very attractive, but there was something cool and remote about her too. She gave the impression of someone trying to be warm and friendly without really understanding these feelings.

"I thought we were going to have a swim," he said.

"I've already had mine," she replied looking out to sea. "I didn't want to leave it too late. The sun gets too strong at this time for old skin like mine, but I wanted to see how you would cope for the first time. There's not much of interest around here anyway. Tomorrow will be different. There are some things I want to show you and time is pressing." There was a sense of urgency in her voice. "But for now, I'm starving, what about you?"

"Me too."

"Lunch is in the basket under the prow and the drinks are in the water beside it."

Jake sprung up and retrieved these. Diana set everything out between them: salad, cheese and bread, and fruit juice. They ate in silence for a while, content just to look at the view.

"After lunch I'll leave you," she said. "I have arrangements to make. If all goes well, I'll have something important to tell you." She started giving him directions as to where he was to walk tomorrow, where he was to swim from and where he was to meet her. They finished eating and he helped her dismantle the tent and load the boat. "I'm sorry our time was short." They hugged. "We'll have longer tomorrow."

He watched her as she sailed off towards the mouth of the inlet and then left towards Paleo Limani. He sat on a rock to warm up. His shoulders were feeling raw. He put on his gear and began the swim back.

The pebbly beach was full of people and his patch was now in the sun. It was coming up to two, the hottest part of the day, so he sat down on the steps just long enough to dry before going home. He had a quick shower, drank some water and collapsed onto the bed.

Half an hour after leaving Jake and twenty-five minutes from the time of her return to Paleo Limani, a rigid hull inflatable entered the bay and came alongside the *Pelagos*. Three passengers clambered aboard and descended into the cabin. Some minutes later they were sitting round the table drinking freshly brewed coffee.

"This time you've gone too far," Mina said.

"That's surprising coming from you," Diana retorted.

"Our circumstances are rather different now, or haven't you noticed?" Mina said, turning to Yiannis. "I also speak for the others."

"I didn't think anyone else knew," Diana said, sounding slightly alarmed.

"They don't, but you can be sure there would be universal condemnation."

"That's easy for them," Diana exclaimed. "They're not charged with producing results."

"Which is why they're not here," Yiannis pointed out.

"How do you propose keeping this secret?" Mina asked.

"By staying calm and unaffected," Phivos said.

"That's easy for you, you've got no feelings," Mina cried.

"Of course I have. You're being emotional, as usual."

"And you lack remorse."

"Unfortunately, it's these feelings that have kept us from achieving our goal," Diana said. "There's no margin for error. That's why Phivos and I have been left with the dirty work."

"If you want me to be 'unaffected', just leave me out," Mina pronounced.

"You know we can't do that," Phivos said. "You're the one who insists on knowing everything."

"I prefer being told before the event, not afterwards."

"Stop squabbling," Yiannis said, glaring at Mina. "Diana and Phivos are right, they had no choice; but it's not true to suggest we could've done things differently."

"Do you realise how much trouble we could get into?" Mina challenged.

"If we get things right, it won't matter," Yiannis pointed out.

"If Alexander and Basil get wind of this, we're all screwed," Mina said.

"That's why it's just going to be the four of us from now on," Yiannis stated.

"If Joanna is so irresistible, why did you have to do it anyway?" Mina asked.

"She's not infallible, not yet at least," Diana replied. "Besides, she wouldn't cooperate otherwise."

"Wouldn't cooperate? Has she no grasp of reality?" Mina raised her voice. "She's probably afraid of the competition. That brat needs a good hiding."

"When it's over, you can give it to her with my blessing," said Diana.

"Stop it," Yiannis said with authority. "Don't forget what we have to gain. Besides, a bit of extra insurance could prove useful. Diana and Phivos will share the security and Mina will give them anything else they need. I'll take over from Diana when she's away."

"And what about the others?" Mina asked.

"You'll have to make sure no one suspects," Yiannis replied.

"Have you forgotten who we're dealing with? How can I lie to them?"

"You'll have to find a way," Yiannis retorted.

"I can manage as long as they think their opinions are valued," Mina said.

"They all have their parts to play making Jake feel at home," Yiannis acknowledged.

"And it'll take all of us to keep Joanna under control," Diana added. "So we'll have to tell them something, especially when she turns up."

"I think therefore we should be meeting every day or so in order to keep things on track, especially now Jake's here," Yiannis said.

"I agree," Phivos concurred. "We must be all eyes and ears and share our intelligence."

"So, we decide and pass on our orders," Diana confirmed.

"Most will be happy with that, but I'm not sure about Stephanos and Niki," Mina said.

"Niki's the problem," Diana acknowledged. "She's too inflexible."

"The word you're looking for is principled," Mina said. "Like Natalya."

"I'll deal with Niki," Yiannis said. "And Natalya's rarely here."

"And Stephanos will just go along with it?" Phivos asked.

"Trust me," Yiannis replied.

"I still fear we're too reliant on Joanna," Mina said. "She could easily jump in with Alexander or Basil, or both at the same time."

"That's why I've kept her away all these years," Diana said.

"Do we really need her?" Mina asked. "Jake may not be as stubborn as his father. Could we not persuade him in some other way?"

"George wasn't stubborn," Diana declared. "He simply had no choice after Basil had finished with him. Jake's something different."

"Yes, he doesn't have anyone to protect," Yiannis remarked.

"But he lacks his father's courage," Diana said. "He doesn't have the guts to do what we want him to do, whatever the reward. Only Joanna can motivate him."

"Turn him into a brainless idiot, more like," Mina said.

"As long as the result's the same, who cares?" Phivos exclaimed.

"When are you going to tell him?" Yiannis asked.

"As soon as I return, after Joanna has had time with him," Diana replied.

"That's one job she'll make easy for you," Mina said. "He'll believe whatever you say."

"So, we're agreed on the way forward?" Yiannis asked, waiting for them all to assent. "Then let's meet again tomorrow."

"It'll have to be late afternoon," Diana said. "I'll be leaving for Piraeus soon afterwards."

"I suppose your departure was her idea too," Mina ventured.

"She wanted me to step aside before she came and while she got settled."

"There's no end to her vanity," Mina said.

"I'll use the time keeping track of Basil."

"He's still in Piraeus?" Mina asked.

"For the time being, but I'll be in daily contact with Joanna."

"Just keep reminding her what's at stake," Yiannis said. "In the meantime we must keep close to Jake."

"That's the other danger," Phivos exclaimed. "Basil could simply decide to get rid of him."

"I doubt that," said Yiannis. "He has no cause."

"He didn't with George," Phivos said.

"That we know of," Mina mooted.

"We're assuming that was his doing," Yiannis said. "There's no evidence."

"But plenty of suspicion," Phivos proffered. "George didn't have any other enemies."

"But lots of women in the background," Yiannis reasoned. "Any one of them could've…"

"I wonder whose example he was following," Mina said, glaring at Yiannis.

"And what happens when they start poking around here?" Phivos asked.

"Let's find it first and we'll deal with that problem when it comes," Yiannis said, looking at his watch. "We've got to go. I have a meeting."

That evening, before sunset and preparing his meal, Jake went back to the cemetery. Arriving at the gate of the tomb, he looked inside. The small oil lamp was still burning but had moved position. Also, yesterday's flowers had been replaced with fresh ones and the fallen petals had been swept away, leaving faint stains on the marble top.

Having seen what he wanted to see, he went back home. As the light faded, he decided not to go out again that evening. He was hesitant to eat outside on the patio, as he usually did. He had not recovered his confidence after the break-in. Fortunately his neighbours upstairs were sitting on their balcony with guests, so he felt it was safe to do the same.

After clearing up, he read for a few hours until he was tired and then went to bed. The night passed without incident.

Chapter 18: Yacht Bay

Thursday, 2nd August

Jake set out earlier than he needed to the next day. He wanted to visit the cemetery again. He surmised that whoever was attending his father's grave was doing so in the morning. His evidence for this was that the oil in the lamp was low on both evenings and the flowers had wilted. When he arrived at the tomb, he saw that he was right. The oil had been topped up, what looked like a new wick had been inserted in the lamp, and the flowers had been replaced. These looked freshly cut. They could not have been brought from Lichas because the ferry did not arrive until the afternoon. It was as if they had come from someone's garden.

Leaving the mystery for now, he went back down to the main road and continued his way out of town. He had not been this way before. The pines of the cemetery hill provided some initial shade, but after that he was exposed to the sun.

His skin was sunburnt, even more so after yesterday for now he could add his shoulders and back to the affected parts.

There were a few detached houses within gardens on the right and, after the cemetery, he could see down a slope of rough ground towards the harbour on the left. As he climbed towards the brow of the hill, he thought of this morning and his second encounter at the bread oven. The black-clad widows treated him with a bit more respect. This time he came away with three loaves.

From the top of the hill, the road went down into a semi-circular bay, which was fringed by smaller beaches and coves. Apart from a handful of houses in the distance, the surrounding hills had the usual mix of derelict stone buildings and overgrown terracing. At one time a lot of growing had taken place on the island, he thought. Now it was brown scrub with the occasional dab of green. Contrasting this was the dark blue sea. It was a breathtaking panorama.

He began his descent, remembering his instructions. He was to go to the beach with the café. There he would deposit his things and swim out past the far headland. From where he stood now, that was quite a distance past another smaller bay. It was much further than his swim yesterday, maybe twice as much. After the headland was a secluded inlet, where Diana would be waiting for him.

He passed a small beach below, where there was a family under an umbrella. As he neared the bottom of the first valley, he came upon a strand of flat round stones. If there ever was an international spooning competition, this was where it should be held. Bending down and choosing a fine specimen, which fitted snugly between his forefinger and thumb, he flicked it along the calm surface of the water and watched it perform eleven skims before submerging.

Climbing up to the next headland, he looked down upon a larger beach which, at the end nearest the road, had a covered seated area for which refreshments were served from a trailer parked alongside. From it emanated the whine of a generator and Greek music.

The cove was sheltered from the northerly wind and the water was subsequently calm. A rope with red coloured floats enclosed it. From his vantage point, he could see that the bottom was shallow and sandy. There were two boys playing with a beach ball in knee-deep water. The strand itself was a narrow crescent of coarse sand backed by the wall of a derelict house. There was shading from a row of three short trees and three permanently fixed umbrellas. As it was still early, there were only a few bathers. A couple had taken up residence under one of the trees and, from the assortment of stuff they had, Jake assumed that the two boys belonged to them.

Farther on, under the umbrella nearest the café, a young girl was lying on her front, reading a book, with her bikini top undone. Jake laid out his things under the middle umbrella. He calculated he had a good twenty minutes before he had to leave, so he went to buy himself a drink.

The seated area was a rectangular platform with wooden floorboards. There was a wooden frame supporting a rush-matting roof, but otherwise it was open on all sides. Only half the tables were taken, with people chatting away. At the hatch of the trailer, Jake bought himself a mixed fruit juice and also asked for a cup of water. He went to sit down at the table furthest away from anyone else but from where he could observe the whole scene.

He intended to relax and take his time but his drink soon attracted the attention of several wasps. This caused him to recall the *pastitsio* lunch with Diana in Lichas and to wish he possessed her knack of repelling pests. He finished promptly and disposed of the plastic cups in a nearby bin, also infested with wasps. As he walked back along the beach, he noticed many more. Two were inspecting the feet of the girl in the bikini.

Back at his umbrella, he dabbed on the sun cream as best he could and waded into the water. The first few yards were stony but after that it turned to fine sand. At the far end of the beach was a small concrete quay with steps into the water. He sat on one of these and put on his fins, mask and snorkel. He walked in a bit further until he was waist deep and, at eleven forty by his watch, he started swimming.

The bottom continued sandy and shallow. He soon ducked under the floated rope and passed a small cove with a concrete jetty on the right. As he approached the first headland, it became deeper and the sand gave way to reef where the bottom of the cliff extended into the sea. He swam round the fringe and could see a similar selection of fish and sea urchins as yesterday, except that here there were more shells, particularly ones that had shiny insides when overturned. In places there were clumps of seagrass that swayed to and fro in unison as if to the beat of some oceanic heart.

As he passed over one patch, he noticed some movement and stopped to observe. After a few seconds the brown patterned head of an eel emerged and disappeared again. From what he knew about eels, they ate fish and had sharp teeth. This particular one was deep, but in future he would have to take care when swimming over similar hiding places.

At the end of the reef and the headland, the bottom became sandy again as he entered the bay he had seen from the road. It had rocky cliff on both sides, and at the end was a deserted beach. He paused for a moment trying to decide whether to swim straight to the main headland or go in shallower and then cross over. It was a long stretch of open water and it was not because the sea was rough that he was hesitant to attempt it. It was calm with only a few wind ripples. No, he was loath because he found it unnerving to snorkel and not be able to see the bottom. He realised it was an irrational fear of the unknown, for which he had Diana and her talk of Great White sharks to thank. He forced himself to do it anyway, distracting himself by concentrating on his breathing and watching the endlessly shifting shafts of light piercing the gloomy depths.

Once on the other side, he turned left along the cliff edge towards the headland. Here the underwater landscape changed as he approached the point. It became deeper and sheerer and there were more large fish. This scene continued when he started rounding the point, but, at the same time, the water was rougher and colder. As he continued round, he realised that this was more of a peninsula than a headland and he now faced into the wind and current.

He was making slower progress and kept getting water in his snorkel, from the waves, but ahead he saw the entrance to the cove. It was a long narrow inlet, and in the distance were the inflatable and the blue tent. In the shelter of the cove, the water calmed and became warmer. Underwater meanwhile there were boulders and crevasses. As the water shallowed, the seabed turned pebbly, and he saw small fish foraging about. There were also sea urchins and he would have to be careful coming out of the water.

While he was still in the shallows, he saw Diana approaching, wearing a black costume and carrying her mask and snorkel. "Stay where you are," she called out. "Let's go for our swim. Did you find it all right?"

"Oh yes, no problem," he said, having a look around while she prepared herself. The surrounding cliffs were sheer and inaccessible. The strand itself consisted of gritty sand and pebbles, but the latter were of varied colours. The exposed outcrops were also colourful and Jake guessed that this must be an area that had seen some igneous volcanic activity in the past. Diana was soon at his side.

"Shall we go? Just follow me," she said as she waded in. He was soon in the wake of her yellow fins, following her out of the inlet and turning right into the wind and current.

The sea became choppy and he had to stop frequently to clear his snorkel. This was a nuisance for, even without this problem, it was an effort keeping up with her. Despite her age, she cut through the water effortlessly. Her legs were kicking to a rhythm that came from years of practice. To make matters worse, the bottom was strewn with large boulders close to the surface and Diana was picking her way through the different channels, while the constant twisting and turning were sapping his strength.

The barren stretch of rock-strewn cliff, interspersed with rocky coves, seemed to go on forever. They eventually came to a cove with an ageing pier, weathered round its edges and exposing the reinforcing steel, which had rusted and stained the surrounding concrete. A crack through the middle of it was causing the dismembered half to start tipping into the sea. There was a villa standing above it on the cliff. He knew it was his father's and he would not have chosen to come to this place. He followed her in, past the jetty and towards the beach, where she stopped when it was shallow enough to stand.

"Do you know where we are?" she asked.

"I do," he replied. The place gave him the creeps.

"Your father was found at the foot of the cliff, on the beach," she said in a matter-of-fact way. "The police say he had a heart attack as he was standing at the top, and fell."

"In the middle of the night?"

"They say there was a storm and he was concerned about his yacht."

"I'm not surprised," Jake said. With the end of the pier tipping forward as it did, he was probably worried it would damage his stern. Looking at it now, he saw that the protruding edge had spines of rusting metal sticking out from it.

"Did you notice anything about the bottom as we came in?" she asked.

The question interrupted his train of thought. "It changed from those boulders we were swimming through to a smooth surface."

"Come out with me now and have another look."

He followed her out. As he passed the pier again, he thought it strange that his father had not repaired it. After the stony slope of the cove there was an area of flat shelf. He did not notice it before because it was so featureless. On closer inspection, he saw crevasses and gaps, like the caramel top of a crème brulée after it had been cracked.

"Is it artificial?" he asked, after they had resurfaced.

"There was a harbour here."

"When and why?"

"History has no answers to those questions," she replied. "Come, let's go back."

"Wait, didn't my father's house overlook a beach?"

"Yes, on the other side of the headland. Come and have a look."

They went along just far enough to view a long sandy beach. At the top of the next headland was another house and below it a short breakwater protecting two piers. On the beach there were only a handful of bathers.

"This beach has the best sand on the island," Diana said. "Do you remember our conversation about seals and sharks?"

"I do."

"Well, past the next headland is a smaller bay, not as sandy, but its Greek name is Seal beach. I believe there's still the occasional sighting, especially in winter. Come, let's go back."

The return swim was easier. The wind and current were behind them and he did not have to keep clearing his snorkel. By the time they reached the inlet, Jake was feeling the cold and the tips of his fingers were numb. He had been in the water for over an hour and was glad to get a towel round him and sit in the tent.

"This is a beautiful cove," he observed.

"It's only accessible from the sea and has a history of being a meeting place for lovers."

"Really?" He could not picture any of the locals frequenting it. "Do you know anything about my father's death?" he asked Diana as she sat down next to him.

"When we warm up and are dry, I'll get lunch. It's the same as yesterday, I'm afraid."

"You're not answering my question."

"I could speculate, but it would be better if I told you some other things first, which I can't do yet." She got up and went to the boat. "There's just one more thing I need to do and, given the right outcome, you will know everything." She was bringing the picnic basket over, together with some bottles. "To that end, I'll be sailing after I return to the yacht."

"How long will you be gone?"

"I don't know, but it's now that your work begins," she said, sitting back down.

"My work? What work?"

"While I'm gone, you'll be looking for something, something important."

"What?"

"It's underwater. It's a structure that's recently been uncovered by an earthquake, so initially you'll be looking for an underwater landslide."

"What does it look like?"

"You'll know it when you see it because it doesn't belong."

"But where do I look?"

"In and around Paleo Limani," she said. "I've already looked in a few places over the last few days, but nothing systematic."

"That's a large area. Besides, if you've never seen it, how do you know it's been uncovered?"

"Half a kilometre south of the entrance to the bay, there's an ancient wreck. It was discovered about three summers ago and is being studied by the Underwater Archaeological Institute of Athens. Their reports are on the internet. They've dived and mapped the wreck for two seasons and they came back at the beginning of June to continue their work. When they reached the sight, they found a layer of silt covering it. The wreck's at a depth of forty metres; so bad weather or shifting currents wouldn't be responsible. Their only explanation was that a landslide in shallower waters caused an avalanche of silt to move down into those depths. Needless to say, they've had to abandon their expedition for now. There was a significant earthquake here last Easter."

"So? What's so special about a landslide?" Jake asked.

"It's special because the geology of the area precludes them," Diana replied, "according to my sources, that is. Therefore, the implication is that the landslide was caused by the collapse of something artificial."

"I see."

"This information's confidential. The team are worried that trophy hunters might take advantage of the sight being abandoned for the season, so you must keep this to yourself."

"How did you find this out then?"

"I have a friend and an occasional diving buddy who works for the team. I can't tell you more, but don't worry, I'm sending you help; she arrives on Tuesday."

"She?"

"My granddaughter, Joanna."

"Your granddaughter? You never mentioned you had children."

"I had one daughter."

"You said had."

"She died when my granddaughter was young."

"I'm sorry you had to go through something like that. I can't imagine the horror of losing a child."

"It happened twenty years ago, but at times it feels like yesterday."

"What happened?"

"A car accident; a simple, stupid car accident. It took both her parents."

"And Joanna?"

"I was looking after her at the time, at my house in northern Greece. I had to bring her up."

"So where will she be staying?"

"At the hotel. You're to meet her when the ferry arrives."

"What do we do if and when we find this structure?" Jake asked as Diana began distributing the food.

"Nothing, until I return."

"But how will we manage? Paleo Limani is a one and a half hour walk away and then…"

"I'm leaving you the boat."

"It must be important then. Is it easy to manoeuvre?"

"Dead easy. But there's one thing you must promise me."

"What's that?"

"After today, on no account must you go to Paleo Limani alone, or anywhere else outside the town. Do you promise?"

"Are you going to tell me why?"

"Not yet, but it's critical you do as I say."

"Okay, I promise, but reluctantly."

"Thank you, Jake."

They finished lunch and packed everything in the boat. Then she showed him how to start and sail it while they did the run to the *Pelagos*. After they'd arrived and unpacked Diana's belongings, she topped up the two-gallon tank from a plastic container and gave him another full spare.

"Keep the spare tank at home," she said. "There should be enough for a while. If you need more, ask Panagos."

"Where do I moor?"

"Tie up in the first basin next to where the ferry's docked. None of those moorings are reserved."

"I've got to go back to the beach and get my stuff first."

"Not with the boat; that's why they have the rope barrier. The best you can do is anchor just outside it and swim the rest of the way."

"But then my clothes and sandals will get wet when I swim back. Can't I tie up at the adjacent cove? It has a jetty."

"But then you'd have to clamber over the headland barefoot; there's no path so I wouldn't recommend it. An assortment of scorpions and other nasties live in the undergrowth. Of course, if you were a real hero, you'd swim the whole way."

"That's miles!"

"One and a half from the pebbly beach actually. It's good training. You'd better get on with it then; I have to get under way." Diana cast him off.

"Your granddaughter, how will I recognise her?"

"You can't miss her."

Can't miss her? He started up the engine and made his way back. He went as fast as he could into the wind until he aquaplaned. As he approached the harbour a rigid hull inflatable passed him with two men and a woman on board. He was sure it was the same one he had seen the other day, and he now recognised one of the men as the mayor and the woman was Assimina, Savvas's wife.

Once in the harbour and in the first basin, he found plenty of places to moor the boat and he chose the one closest to the pebbly beach. He dropped anchor and tied up, like Diana had showed him, and covered up the tanks with the tarpaulin.

Putting on the mask, snorkel and fins he slipped into the water and started swimming through the harbour to its entrance. He felt cold at first and his sunburnt skin stung, but there was no way he was going to let Diana believe he was not up for it. He distracted himself by observing his surroundings. It was pretty dismal at first. The rocky bottom was mossy and strewn with rubbish, plastic bottles and rusty cans, as one would expect.

When he had swum past the moored ferry and along the breakwater, it improved. The latter was made of concrete blocks and, as he approached the end, the water became deeper and the blocks larger.

The breakwater ended in a great pillar that went straight down to the bottom with an ever-widening girth. He could not guess how deep it was, but it was near the limit of visibility. Looking across the harbour entrance, the next breakwater appeared a long way away. He checked for passing boat traffic and, with the coast clear, he set off. When he reached the other pillar, he stopped and trod water for a few minutes to catch his breath before continuing.

He had to swim out a distance in order to round the headland before he could turn towards his destination. The stretch to the point was easy as the water was calm, shallow and warm. He saw his highest concentration of sea urchins here and ahead, on the cliff above the point, was the automated light that warned local shipping.

Things changed dramatically after this. The water became deeper with large boulders that seemed to go down to unknown depths. It also became colder and, as he gradually turned into the oncoming wind, rougher. In what seemed at an impossible distance, he could see his destination. When he was with Diana, he only had a few hundred yards of these conditions to swim through. Now it was over a mile. This end was particularly exposed, sheer cliffs on his right and open sea to the left, with a steep, bare and rocky slope underneath. In the distance, out to sea, were large, solitary fish and he wondered if they were not being stalked by something larger still.

For what seemed an interminable length of time, he swam against the waves, which at times would break over his snorkel and cause him to get mouthfuls of seawater. He seemed to progress only a few feet at a time. Eventually, as he penetrated the bay and came to the first beach, which he had seen below him from the road that morning, the sea became calmer and the water warmer. Knowing he had somewhere to land if he had to, and seeing people nearby, made him feel safer.

As he approached his beach, and before he reached the barrier wire, there were several small powerboats anchored. Inside people sat under the shade of canopies and conversed with others treading water nearby. Farther out there were two much larger power yachts with associated tenders and another two yachts were anchored deep in the bay Jake first crossed when he was going to meet Diana. In the calm waters, a speedboat pulled a water skier, and two jet skiers performed extreme twists and turns. This was a scene more associated with the south of France.

He made it back to the beach at five o'clock, over five hours after he had left. Had anybody noticed him leave, they would have seen him swim in one direction and come back from the other. The thought made him smile. After he had ducked under the wire, he swam to the point where he could touch down and stand. He removed his fins and walked the rest of the way. His feet were sore with raw abrasions on both heels and at the sides of his feet by the toes. This sandy part became gradually shallower and there was an area where the water was only thigh-high. Here children and teenagers were playing a variety of games. Amongst them, groups of adults stood in circles, chatting.

Jake had several close encounters with balls on his way through the crowds. The beach was just as busy, with the shoreline being taken up by people playing tennis with wooden paddles. Farther up there was a greater covering of towels than exposed sand. Greek music coming from the trailer competed with pop music from the thronging quay, which was crowded with teenagers wearing baggy swimming shorts, baseball caps and oversized trainers. In front of the café, four men had put a white plastic table and chairs into the shallows and were seated up to their waists in water, with drinks and nibbles, playing cards.

Where he had left his things the shade from the umbrella had gone and a young couple were now beneath it. There was no way he could stay out in this heat and it would be equal folly to walk back now. He put the towel over his shoulders, gathered everything up and, walking along the water's edge, made a dash across the hot sand to the shelter of the platform. Right at the back was a free table and two chairs He settled there with a bottle of water and his book as he waited for the day to cool.

He did not start back until six thirty. His progress was intentionally slow. His feet felt raw in several places, a result of the rhythmic rubbing of the fins on his unaccustomed skin, and his muscles were tightening. It would be worse tomorrow and worse still the day after. He would have to think of things to do before Tuesday to accelerate the recovery process. His discomfort was only relieved, temporarily, by hearing the mandolin as he passed the house near the cemetery.

When he arrived home, he dropped everything off and went to the boat to retrieve the spare petrol can. The village was quiet, with most people seemingly still at the beach or having a siesta. Afterwards, he sat on the patio with his book until sunset.

That night he had the last of his food and decided that tomorrow would be a good time to replenish. He would make a list, buy what he could locally and order the rest from Lichas. The question was, did he buy for one or two, or would they be eating at the taverna together? He decided to double up just in case as there was plenty of room in his fridge and freezer.

He'd intended to go out that evening, for a walk at least. The wind had dropped, as it often did after sunset, and tonight it felt particularly clammy. Unfortunately, his sunburn felt too raw for clothes, his muscles had tightened up even more and his feet were impossible to walk on in any footwear. He stayed in, prepared his shopping list and tried to watch the Olympics on the television. The reception was terrible and he only managed to catch up with events on a Greek news channel. He was relieved that Britain had managed to win its first gold medals.

He went to bed after midnight, convinced that he would be too uncomfortable to sleep.

Chapter 19: The Beach Bar

Friday, 3rd August

The supermarket was busy that morning and Jake had to queue to pay, but he could have stayed in the air-conditioned shop all day. He had woken with a bad headache, probably from too much sun, and the sunburn itself was easily the worst he had ever had. On top of that, his feet were covered in raw patches and he'd had to put on two pairs of socks in order to tolerate wearing trainers. In addition, every muscle in his body ached.

The weather did not help. Something had changed. When it was his turn to pay, he asked Savvas about this.

"It's the south wind," the grocer said. "It makes it humid and the beaches dirty."

"How so the beaches?"

"Well, whenever the prevailing wind's from the south, it deposits all the trash floating around in the sea from the islands of the southern Aegean onto our beaches. It also brings jellyfish, so take care. Go to Perivoli for the next few days."

"I'll remember that." Jake had no intention of swimming anywhere today, but he knew Perivoli was the beach he had glimpsed with Diana. "You'll deliver?"

"Of course, but it will take a bit longer; as you can see we have a backlog. Will we see you at the yacht club tomorrow night?"

"Sure, see you then."

He was relieved to get back home and take his shoes and socks off. He rang the butcher and greengrocer with his order, had a bowl of cereal, drank plenty of water, put away the groceries when they came, and generally tried to pass the time before the ferry arrived at two. After a few hours reading, he was bored.

He decided to go to the museum. He applied considerable amounts of sun cream, put his socks and trainers back on, and set off, walking slowly and keeping to the shade as much as possible.

The museum had two floors. The upper one had no windows, just decorative recesses painted a cream colour, whereas the rest of the building was white. The ground floor consisted of the entrance to the museum and, beside it, a glassed-in hall, which, from a displayed list of forthcoming events, looked as though it was used for town meetings and exhibitions.

A slim, intelligent-looking, fresh-faced man with greying hair welcomed him from a small office just inside the entrance and sold him an English version of the guidebook. His first favourable impression, when he went upstairs, was the air-conditioning, but he was subsequently disappointed to find that the exhibits only dealt with the permanent habitation of Halia since the 1880s and nothing earlier. There were some interesting turn-of-the-century photos and models of fishing boats, but there was nothing to occupy him for more than half an hour.

He was almost finished with the galleries and about to go downstairs when the man who met him at the door approached. "We close at one to new arrivals. You may stay until half past if you like, but you must inform me when you leave so I can let you out." He spoke excellent English.

"Actually I'm leaving now," Jake said. He saw a hint of disappointment on the man's face, as if his museum didn't warrant a longer stay.

"Excuse me if I ask, but are you a tourist or a guest?"

"Neither actually. My father was from the island."

"And who was he?"

"George Philo.

"Oh, dear me, Mr Philo, my condolences, but you weren't at the interment."

"I only came as far as Lichas for the funeral, but not here for the burial. I had to return to England."

"And I couldn't come to the funeral, but was here for the burial," the man said, shrugging his shoulders. "Are you in business?"

"No, I'm a teacher."

"A teacher? So am I, well, sort of," he replied with enthusiasm. "I'm the curator, and I also do a bit of teaching at the local school. Have you come with your family?"

"I have no family. I'm staying on my own."

"At the big house at Perivoli?"

"No, just up the road from here, where my grandmother used to stay."

"Ah yes, I know where that is."

"It's not terribly busy." Jake hadn't seen anybody else during his visit.

"It's different when the tourist boats come on Saturdays and Sundays. There are many visitors then and we collect lots of money, which reminds me, I must give you the five euros back."

"Give it back? Why?"

"We only charge the tourists. Technically you're an islander."

"Keep it anyway," Jake said. "You must know about the local history?"

"That's what I teach at the school but I've only lived here four years. Are you interested, because you didn't seem to spend much time just now?"

"That's because I'm more interested in what happened before this."

"Ah, excellent. I wish I could talk to you about it now, but I've got work to do. What do you do in the evenings? You must eat out?"

"Sometimes."

"When my wife and I dine out we usually go to the Town taverna. They do a selection of cooked dishes every day."

"I know, I've been there once."

"But tonight, with this weather, it's best to eat at Paralia. Why don't you meet us? We'll have something to eat and I'll tell you what little I know about our mysterious island."

"Sounds excellent, I'd like that. By the way, what's your name?"

"Stephanos. Meet us at ten." He escorted Jake downstairs to the door and let him out into the heat.

It was just after one. He had planned on spending longer in the museum. He did not want to walk back home and then back out for the two o'clock ferry so he went to the café, the one attached to the taverna. He sat at an outside table in the shade of a tree and ordered a fruit juice. Those sitting at the surrounding tables were groups of old men doing what Greek men did, talking loudly whilst waving their arms. He imagined what it would have been like to be sitting here with his father, having a drink or a coffee together. What would they have talked about? He felt tears welling up at the thought of what he had missed. It's what should have been.

Going to the ferry landing afterwards through the searing heat was like walking through molasses. At least when he reached the harbour front he was able to feel the south wind. The pier was already crowded with people and cars. It seemed like everybody on the island had some business here.

He had a look over the wall to the pebbly beach. There were foot high waves thrusting onto the stones. There were no bathers, but neither was there any rubbish. There was also no shade and his headache was getting worse. He sat on a low wall and waited.

Doubling up on food meant a heavy load to carry back. He was glad to be eating out that night, feeling lethargic and not motivated to do any cooking.

He was not hungry and skipped lunch, but his headache worsened, so he took a couple of paracetamol and lay down. His sleep was fitful and sweaty, but at least his headache eased. By the time he got up the light was going and he just managed to witness the sunset. The humidity and the wispy clouds made it an angry red, which turned to crimson and then purple. It was riveting.

Afterwards, he made himself a cup of tea and sat down to read for a bit before getting ready for the evening.

He sauntered down to the harbour after nine thirty, taking his time. He felt a lot better and his headache had gone. His sunburn and aching muscles had also improved. The itching from the mosquito bites he had just received from sitting out on the patio didn't help, but he could bear that.

Maybe he should go to the beach tomorrow. Perivoli seemed promising, especially if the weather stayed like this. When he'd seen it with Diana, he'd spotted some of those permanent umbrellas. If he left early enough, he could miss the worst of the heat and get there before anyone else. He would take fruit and water so he could stay a while. Maybe he would walk up to his father's house afterwards and have a look. The thought made him shiver. On second thoughts, maybe not.

He caught the breeze again when he reached the harbour, this time on his back. It was busy with even more people milling around. Children on bikes wove in an out of them at crazy speeds, risking injury to themselves and others. The yacht club had placed tables at the foot of the stairs to cater for any overflow, although no one was sitting there yet. When he arrived at the Paralia, he saw that most of the tables were taken but he spotted his host sitting at one under the awning. He was reading a pink newspaper in the dim light.

"Good evening," Jake said.

"Good evening, come and sit down," Stephanos said. "I've just arrived myself. My wife should be along shortly."

"Thank you," Jake said as he pulled out a chair. "Any interesting news? I've tried to look at the television but my Greek isn't good. The reporters talk very fast."

"Just the usual reports about the global credit crunch and our disgraceful domestic situation. You must've heard enough about it in England?"

"I have," Jake replied. "I'm more interested in the Olympics."

"Very wise. Greek politics would bore and perplex you, although you mustn't say that to anyone around here. This is a European business paper I have sent to me. It arrives three days late but it allows me to keep in touch." Stephanos folded it up and placed it on the seat beside him.

"Are you interested in business?"

"In a way. I've been, at various times, an investment banker and financial journalist."

"So why did you come here?"

"Well, my wife was head of the legal department of another bank and decided she wanted to enter local politics. When this posting came up she went for it, so I retired as well and we moved here. I am interested in history and archaeology so I volunteered to look after the museum while my wife runs the local council."

"You must've retired early?"

"You're very flattering but no, I'm sixty-five." Stephanos looked at his watch. "I'm sorry my wife's late, but on her way here, she'll probably get stopped by everyone in the village who has any complaint."

The waiter came and covered the table with a paper tablecloth and secured it with plastic clips. There was an odd combination here. The taverna and the wooden tables looked old and traditional, but the chairs were of cheap white plastic.

"Is there anything you want? I know pretty much what my wife likes," Stephanos said.

"No, I don't mind. I've eaten here before. If you want to order a selection, it's fine with me."

Stephanos gave the waiter a list of dishes. "What do you drink?"

"What are you having?"

"I like ouzo and my wife drinks wine."

"Actually I think I'll have beer tonight."

Stephanos completed the order. "I hear you're selling the house on Perivoli," he said after the waiter had left.

"Is it for sale? That's not me. My father's given it to his siblings." Jake hadn't heard of this development, but it made sense.

"So, he just gave you the place in town?"

"Not that either; just the house in Athens."

"So, do you live in London?"

"Just outside, in the countryside."

"Very nice, I've been to England. What do you teach?"

"Geography, at a local school. You teach history, you said?"

"Local history, it's a small school of thirty-five pupils, but history's my interest, particularly of the Aegean."

"What about Halia?"

"Many people ask about it and, unfortunately, the answer is that little is known."

"Are there no records?"

"That's partly the answer. What you have to understand is that Greece is a country with a complicated mainland, hundreds of islands and thousands of archaeological sites. We have limited resources, especially now. Halia's small and off the tourist radar. We've never had a proper geological, geographical or biological survey. You can't even get an accurate map."

"I heard that an ancient wreck was discovered nearby."

"Indeed, from the classical period, which meant some attention."

"I can't believe that's it."

"Yes, but even finding records requires research. The little that's known comes from accounts that are easy to get hold of." The waiter came over with their drinks, cutlery and bread. "The first place to go would be Athens. I would look through the archives there. A lot of these were destroyed through the ages, you know; wars, natural disasters and foreign occupations. After that, if I had time, I would maybe go to London and look through the collection of the British Library, although there I would encounter my first problem."

"Which is?"

"Well, I'd only be able to look at publications written in Greek, Ancient Greek and English. If there was a book written in Arabic, for example, about an explorer who had visited, I would never know."

"I understand."

"And that's only the British Library. What about the French archives, or those of the Egyptians, or the Turks? The list goes on. To your health." They clinked glasses. "So, to start with, there could be a lot we don't know about."

"Have you done any research?"

"I've been to Athens and the British Library, but only spent a few days in each. You would need months. Once I've got the museum on a steady course, I might do more."

"Doesn't the museum make enough money to pay for research?"

"It doesn't, no. It doesn't entirely pay its costs."

"Who pays for it? The government?"

"Oh no, this is a private museum. The funding comes from the Association of Friends of Halia."

"I've never heard of it."

"You should have; your father was a member at one time, as am I."

"My parents, although married, hadn't lived together since I was four. I knew little about my father's dealings."

"I did hear something along those lines; I'm sorry."

"Tell me about this association."

"Well basically, without it, this island would be deserted. Throughout the decades its members have paid for the major projects. The harbour's an example. This used to be a beach. The association paid for the breakwaters, the jetties, the squares and the promenades. The yacht quay and club were also built from donations. It's only in the last few years that the EU has funded the recent improvements."

"Did they also pay for the roads?"

"No, the government pays for those, but the association built the reservoir, the police station, the clinic, the hotel, the town taverna, the children's playgrounds and, most important of all, it bought the ferry."

"The ferry?"

"That's right. The government pays a subsidy towards the running costs, but the ferry itself is owned by the association."

"So, where does the money come from?"

"Donations from rich inhabitants; and there are lots of them."

"So, the members are those who make donations."

"Technically all islanders are members but, in practice, it's a closed club; they elect officials and can influence much that happens."

"I thought there was a mayor."

"There is, but his budget from local and central government was, until recently, small compared to the association. My wife's the permanent civil servant." Something caught Stephanos' eye. "Talk of the devil."

Jake turned to look. In the distance a tall, slim, handsome, grey-haired lady was approaching. She was dressed in a dark skirt and blouse and looked business-like. She stopped at the first table and started talking to the occupants, who stood up to greet her. "It will be a while before she gets to us," Stephanos said.

"If they've got all that money," Jake said, continuing the conversation, "why don't they spend some of it on research?"

"Because their priority is to the inhabitants. So, they will pay for things that maintain the quality of life and keep the islanders here, but they will avoid anything that attracts tourists." The waiter brought them Greek salad, meatballs, kebabs, cheese balls, squid, sausage and chips. "Can you imagine if archaeologists found the remains of a temple? Think of the attention that would bring."

"So, what is known?" Jake asked.

"The furthest back we can go is to what was written by the ancient Greeks. The island was famous for its forest and being the home of the mares of the Gods, which fed on the abundance of acorns."

"Well, there's little of that now."

"Quite, only a few pockets. Since then there's superficial evidence that these islands were inhabited and deserted several times. Other sources mention wine production of such high quality it was, again, reserved for the Gods. Then there's the ancient Athenian naval base at Paleo Limani. It was extensive."

"What was its purpose?"

"That's a mystery. Usually, in ancient texts, if they mentioned the building of a fortification or the taking of military action, they would also state the purpose; for example, if it was protecting a trade route or something."

"Could that've been the reason?"

"Probably, especially as there's evidence of harbours in other places."

"Could they have been protecting the island from invasion?"

"Yes, but what's so important about it? Why allocate so many resources to a volcanic rock? And there's more. When the present inhabitants came, they found fortifications where the village is built, also at Perivoli. So, the three places on the island that were vulnerable were reinforced."

Jake remembered Diana showing him the underwater remains the other day. "So, can't any assumptions be made?"

"No, because there's not enough left. Whatever could be physically removed has been taken, either by treasure hunters or locals. Whatever's left would be underwater or underground. But that's not all; pirates, the Turks, and who knows who else, have inhabited the island over the centuries. All other mentions are sporadic and there are long gaps in the timeline."

"What about the terracing I see everywhere?"

"I don't believe that's terribly old, I'm afraid. Sometime before the present inhabitants came there was cultivation; that's when the forests were cut down."

"It's intriguing."

Just then Stephanos's wife arrived. They stood up to greet her. "This is my wife, Niki," Stephanos said.

"I'm pleased to meet you," Jake responded, taking her hand. Close up she looked youthful and intelligent. Jake imagined her being extremely competent at her job.

"I'm hungry," Niki said. "Please let's start. Mr Philo, I'm pleased you've joined us tonight. We knew your father well. We would meet in Athens. I was sorry he passed away, and so young. But I believe you live near London?"

She asked about his life in England and what his future plans were. Jake was selective with what he revealed, being at the same time careful not to seem so. Every now and again, someone would come to the table and speak with her.

"So, it must be a busy time for you?" Jake observed, moving the focus of the conversation away from him.

"It is," Niki said.

"So what does the local council do?"

"Well, to start with, don't get the idea that we're big. Basically it's me, my secretary and the mayor, when he chooses to be here," Niki said with a cynical undertone. "But we supervise the local services: the water supply, the rubbish collection; things like that. As you can probably guess, if a place has three hundred people most of the year and for one month has three thousand, there are going to be problems. But these are mundane things that I used to complain about myself. The really interesting part is trying to get money for improvements. It's frustrating most of the time, with occasional moments of satisfaction."

"I can imagine," Jake said. They'd finished their food and drinks. "Can I buy you both a drink at the yacht club?"

"Oh no, I don't like it there. It's too noisy and you have to be either young or very old," Stephanos said.

"Where else is there?" Jake asked.

"There's the beach café," Stephanos replied.

"I was there this morning. I thought they only served coffee and soft drinks."

"Well, at night it becomes a bar."

"How do we get there?"

"The moon's practically full," Stephanos said as he dipped into his trouser pocket and retrieved a torch. "This will also help," he added getting up. "I'll go and pay."

"No, please let me."

"I'll pay this one; you take the tab at the bar," Stephanos said. They got up and Jake waited with Niki outside the taverna as Stephanos went in to settle the bill. When he re-joined them, they started walking back towards the town.

"I hope you don't mind, but I'll go home," Niki said at the turning for the beach bar. "I have work to do, and I don't think these heels are suitable."

Five minutes later they had passed the cemetery and were heading out of town, following the pool of light made by the torch whilst under the pines. Once in the open they did not need it, the moon was so bright. Jake ignored his painful feet, grateful that Stephanos was not a fast walker.

"When walking around the island I've seen a lot of goats," Jake said.

"Too many goats. They were introduced during the last hundred and fifty years to provide milk and meat. If it weren't for them, the inhabitants would've starved during the war. But they're also destructive. They eat everything and anything. Some of the worst feuds between islanders have occurred because of them. For example, the man who runs the taverna hasn't spoken to his cousin, a local handyman, since Easter because the latter's goat managed to get into his garden and eat his vegetables. He accuses him of doing it deliberately."

"That's hilarious. I suppose the goat could be a better instrument of revenge than a knife or gun. But what about wildlife?"

"I'm no expert, but there are plenty of bats, birds, including owls, lizards, insects and snakes; oh, and some recent introductions: rabbits and quail."

"Rabbits?" Jake said. "Surely they need running water."

"You'd think, but Halia's overrun with them. The islanders go out at night to hunt them."

As they walked along, the occasional car or motorcycle passed them.

"It seems popular this bar," Jake said.

"It is, but not all these cars are going to it. There's another taverna farther along, beyond Perivoli. The bar's popular because it represents a rebellion on the part of the locals."

"In what way?"

"The mayor decided that, apart from Saturdays and certain special dates, places in the town have to close by two or, to be more precise, they have to stop playing music, so that people can sleep. So, one of the locals opened the bar for those who don't want to sleep."

"I bet he's popular."

"He is, by everybody except the mayor and his supporters. That's why Niki won't come; she doesn't want to be seen there. Come two, three o'clock, the bar and the beach will be heaving."

"But why would they object? What possible harm could it do?"

"Nothing, absolutely nothing. All that happens is that people drink, dance on the beach and have fun. Then, at sunrise, they go home. That's all, but objectors say they pee on the beach, or worse. Personally, I haven't seen anything like that."

"So, there's another taverna farther out. I've not heard of it."

"It's a bit basic. A family, as at Paralia, runs it. The husband and his daughter are fishermen. Together with his wife they prepare the day's catch."

"Sounds great," Jake said, wondering if they were the ones who'd found his father.

"They also own the land around them and grow their own produce. Sometimes they serve quail and rabbit."

They had rounded the last headland and were making their descent to the beach. They could already hear the music. There were extra tables and chairs in front of the permanent seated area and even more cars parked along the road than during the day. There was a mixture of all ages and most people had chosen to sit at the tables on the beach around an area that had been reserved for dancing.

They chose a free table on the raised part and Jake went to the hatch to buy drinks. The same people were serving as during the day. Back at the table he asked Stephanos about it.

"These people work all day and night from mid-July to the beginning of September," Stephanos said. "The rest of the time they have nothing to do except look for treasure."

"Treasure?"

"Yes, remember I told you that this was the haunt of pirates?"

"You did."

"Well, there's rumoured to be buried treasure. Two people have actually found some."

"Tell me about it."

"The first was a shepherd; he came across a pile of rocks that had been dislodged by an earthquake and found a chest of gold coins underneath it."

"What type of coins were they?"

"Nobody knows, he didn't exactly go to the authorities. He suddenly became rich and that was his explanation."

"And the other?"

"The second find took place during the last war. Some of the terracing you see was created at the time of the occupation or brought back into use to feed the population. The owner of one such allotment was walking round his land when he fell down an old well, broke his leg, but also found a horde of gold. People wondered how he managed to come into such wealth. He admitted the reason on his death bed."

"Has anybody tried looking with metal detectors?"

"Not that I know of."

"I wonder why?"

"I don't think they would work in this terrain; it's too hilly, the ground's rocky and uneven and the undergrowth impenetrable."

"I suppose." Jake wondered about the structure he was going to be looking for and what it signified. "What about underwater, could there be more ancient wrecks?"

"There could. Just think of the thousands of years that the Aegean has been the centre of civilization and the crossroads between the Med and the Black Sea, east and west, north and south. There could be wrecks anywhere and everywhere. There probably are. You know that, apart from some designated tourist areas, it's illegal to dive in the Aegean without a special licence?"

"I didn't know that."

"It's to prevent the pilfering of artefacts that took place in the past. In fact, if they catch you leaving the country with anything like that in your luggage, they'll throw you in jail."

"I approve of that," Jake said. He noticed that the south wind had picked up while they were sitting. "The air has a smell of stale seaweed."

"The beach piles up with it during this weather. It dries and discolours during the day and it looks like shredded paper."

As it neared one o'clock the beach and bar started filling up and people resorted to sitting on the platform edge facing the beach. The proprietors turned the music up.

Jake saw a man approaching their table. He was tall and slim, elegantly dressed in dark trousers and an open silk shirt. He was tanned with flowing dark hair and a trimmed beard. He wore jewellery around his neck, a bold gold ring and a gold Rolex watch. He was carrying a drink in one hand and a cigarette in the other. At first Jake thought he had come for the spare chair, and then he noticed Panagos trailing behind with two attractive, scantily dressed women.

"Hey, Nicos," Stephanos said when he saw him.

"Hey, man; how's my favourite scholar?" Nicos said in a deep gravelly voice, which had the hint of an American accent.

"I'd like to introduce you to someone," Stephanos said. "This is Jake, George's son."

"Gosh, I'm sorry about your dad," Nicos said. He shook hands with Jake.

"Why don't you join us?" Stephanos asked.

"Seeing how you've got the only spare chair in the whole place, I don't know how I can refuse. Here, I'll let one of the girls sit," Nicos said. The two girls, one fair and the other dark-haired, could not agree who was to take it. "I think I'll give it to Panagos then as he's the only one who works during the summer."

"What do you mean? I look after the museum."

"You don't count because you're doing what you enjoy and, being a teacher, well, all those impressionable young girls." He was looking at Jake as if expecting a response. He took a drag of his cigarette and a sip of what looked like a whisky with ice. Panagos had an ouzo and ice. "I hear you might be taking over your dad's business," he continued.

"I might," Jake said.

"Yeah, it's a shame about him. He was really cool."

"I think it's time for me to go and make room for the serious revellers," Stephanos said.

"Why don't you stay?" Nicos said to Jake after seeing him get up as well. "The old fart won't mind."

"No, I'll walk back with him in case he gets lost. Maybe next time," Jake said. He was tempted to stay, but he was still recovering from fatigue and sunburn and didn't think his feet were up to any revelling. Some people had already started dancing barefoot on the sand.

"What about tomorrow night?" Nicos said. "We're going with the yacht to Lichas for some night life. If you want to come, we leave at eleven."

"I'll think about it. Which yacht is it?"

"The *Bacchus*."

They left it at that and went on their way "So, who's Nicos?" Jake asked once they were away from the music.

"He's the local playboy. Couldn't you tell? His father's rich and he's already inherited a fortune from his uncle, who died childless."

"So what does he do?"

"His life revolves around drinking, clubbing and women."

"Did my father spend much time with him? Nicos seems to know him."

"Your father only basically went to one or two clubs in Athens. Nicos would sometimes join him. I think he admired your father because he could play hard and work hard and knew where to draw the line. Something Nicos finds impossible to do."

"I suppose I'd better stay away from him?"

"Not at all. He's not a bad sort. Going out with him will be a scream; just remember; don't try and drink as much as him. It's easy to fall under his spell."

"I don't know. I think I'll feel out of place, which makes me wonder what Panagos is doing with him."

"They're friends, surprisingly. Panagos tends to get depressed, so Nicos gets him to lighten up."

"If he needs the nightlife, why does he come to Halia?"

"It's his father who insists he's here for August. Have you ever been to a Greek club?"

"No."

"Go then, you'll like it. You might not get much sleep, but the yacht will be back in the morning."

"I'll see," Jake said.

When they got back to town he was surprised at how busy it still was, even at two in the morning. They parted company at the alley where Jake lived, with Stephanos continuing uphill.

Their evening together had helped him forget about his physical discomforts and the beer had numbed them. This was just as well as the wind had dropped and it felt even more humid.

Indoors it was airless and his reluctance to open the bathroom window did not help. After undressing, he lay on his back on top of the bed in his pyjama shorts. His skin burned and he could feel it oozing perspiration that made it itchy. He tried not to scratch. When he had taken his shoes off he'd seen that his socks had blood stains in several places and the abrasions stung badly. He tried to distract himself by listening to the sound of the cicadas, but that didn't help.

He concentrated on his breathing; this was not difficult in the thick stagnant air. His mind began to wander and he was dozing. Blissful sleep seemed minutes away. But then the sound of the cicadas abruptly stopped. The resultant silence was so intense that he could hear his heart beating. He tried to open his eyes, but could not raise his lids. He tried to move, but could not do that either. Was he asleep after all? Was he dreaming?

Then he felt a movement in the air, like the wake of something or someone passing. He redoubled his efforts to move, to open his eyes, but to no avail. As his terror grew, so did his efforts to stir himself.

Then he heard the voice. It was a whisper, heavily laden with breath, ending with a long hiss. "Open your eyes," it said.

His eyes opened without effort, although the rest of his body remained inert. What he saw at that moment made him go cold to his core, so much so that he feared his blood might turn to ice and stop his heart.

From the left there was a glow of yellow light originating from outside the shutters, the beams escaping through the gaps in the slats. From the right there was another glow that appeared to be coming from the open bedroom door. Between the two, past the foot of the bed, was a black, formless mass. Its height was greater than its width and the top of it was just below the ceiling light. Otherwise its shape was amorphous and opaque.

Nothing happened for some seconds and then he heard the voice again, but it did not come from the dark object. It was inside his head. "Do not oppose me, Jake, or I will strike you down. Make no mistake, I will be watching and listening."

As he heard these words, he was overcome by a crushing sense of helplessness, a feeling of powerlessness and vulnerability. Then his lids felt heavy. He tried to keep them open but he could not stop them closing. He sensed movement in the room and knew that whatever had been present had now gone. He could hear the cicadas again.

His body moved freely and he opened his eyes. Everything was as it should be, except he felt cold and was shivering as if his core body heat had been extracted. He got up and walked around to get warm. Was it a dream? There was no evidence that anyone or anything had been inside the house, and yet he felt so cold.

He opened the wooden shutters to the patio and stepped outside. There was no wind or condensation due to a sudden drop in temperature, so he had to assume that the weather had not changed and it was still sultry.

After he had closed the shutters and calmed down, he felt a great fatigue. That would explain it. He was suffering from an overexposure to heat. And the dream? Nothing more than a reaction to this, and his concerns about the future.

He got back into bed under the sheet, and a blanket from the linen cupboard, and fell into a deep sleep.

Chapter 20: The Fisherman's Wife

Saturday, 4th August

Jake woke feeling a lot better and, after breakfast, left for Perivoli. He wore just one pair of socks with his sandals, having put plasters on the worst abrasions.

As he walked through the quiet, sun-drenched lanes of the village, he reflected on his decision to break his promise to Diana. He reasoned that he was playing this game for the sake of his own aims, not hers. Was she restricting him through concerns for his safety or was she trying to prevent him finding things out for himself; of forming his own opinion? He was not going to uncover the truth about his father by timidly following orders.

Twenty minutes later, as he passed the beach café, he saw little evidence of the partying of the night before, just a few people enjoying a coffee.

What was different from his visit two days previously was seeing the wind waves rolling in from the south. On the fringe, above where they broke, were bundles of seaweed strands, which varied in colour from dark brown to white, depending on how long they had been dried and bleached by the sun.

From there he continued up the next hill.

According to Stephanos, there were three routes to Perivoli, all starting at the top of the road. The first, the longest and most scenic, started just behind the wall of the derelict house that was behind the beach, and ran along the coast. The second, and least attractive, was the next tarmaced turning to the left, which was for cars. Just before it reached the beach, it was joined by the first path and, soon after, it passed a rough track on the left, which led to his father's house on the headland. The third, and shortest, route started at the same point as the road, but was through fields in which there were groves of fig trees.

Aware of his sunburn, he chose the quickest route, so he took the steep path down from the road into the first field. In the distance was the open sea, in the middle of which were the Green Isles. These were two small rocks that were roughly a mile offshore.

The first fields were a strange place. They were bare except for the occasional barren fig tree; not even a single blade of grass, yet the boundaries and hedges that separated them were green, consisting of bushes and stunted trees. After walking through a few like this, he entered more of a grove, which had a higher density of fig trees, from which he was able to pick fruit that felt soft and ripe. He saw an abundance of goat and rabbit droppings. Maybe this explained the lack of grass. As he left the grove and neared the beach, the bush thickened, until he passed through a gap in a sand dune.

Perivoli was, as claimed, a crescent of proper, yellow powdery sand. Behind the beach was a single dune held together by a thick growth of vegetation, backed by a row of mature trees. Farther inland were a few well-spaced, single-storey dwellings. At the top of the headland to the left, the back of his father's house poised forlornly, with a similar, less-imposing villa at the top of the right-hand bluff. The latter also had its own pier at the bottom of a flight of concrete steps. A short rocky breakwater, jutting out from the foot of the cliff, protected it.

There were three permanent umbrellas along the beach. The only other occupant had already taken the first, so Jake walked over to and laid out his things under the second. He peeled his figs, washed them in the sea and sat down in the shade to eat. He savoured the intense flavours.

His sunburn and soreness were better and he would try and go for a swim. He needed to keep up the training for when Joanna came. He did not want to embarrass himself. He hoped that the salt water would help the healing of his feet. If he had a long swim today, tomorrow and Monday, he could ease back on Tuesday and be fully recovered by Wednesday.

He had come just in time. He could see people arriving from both ends of the beach, groups of teenagers playing football, beach tennis or volleyball, families with buckets and spades, couples and, occasionally, people on their own. Quite a few had gathered on the pier and were taking turns jumping or diving into the sea, either individually or en masse. The air was full of chatter, laughter and music.

Being sheltered from the south wind, the sea was calm. Even in the shade he began to feel hot. A nice long swim, the type that made the tips of his fingers go numb, would cool him off for hours. He decided to start right away.

The water here was the clearest he had seen so far, with sand all the way in and without the stony barrier of the other beach. As he entered, he saw that it also deepened more quickly. He gingerly put on his fins, over a thin pair of socks, then his mask and snorkel, before swimming off. For once the cold water was welcome.

He decided he would check out Seal Beach today, so he headed for the tip of the breakwater. Underneath it was sandy, with the occasional tuft of seagrass, a few shells and flat fish.

Outside the breakwater, it changed. The bottom became rocky with more life and proper schools of fish. The headland that separated the two bays was narrow and he was soon within the shelter of Seal Beach. It was similar to Perivoli in size and shape but backed by a dense grove of trees, with no dwellings. At the far headland though, was an imposing residence, below which was a pier protected, on the seaward side, by a breakwater. To this a yacht was fastened stern first, its anchored prow facing out to sea. To the right of this, no more than thirty yards away, was another smaller jetty, moored to which was a wooden fishing boat in which two people were sitting.

He swam farther into the bay, towards the gap between the two piers, to where the water was shallower. The bottom here was also sandy and he wondered what the beach was like as there were no bathers using it. As he approached he saw that a concrete wall, crowned with barbed wire, surrounded the house. He could also see that there was a road that came through the grove and ran past both piers to a metal gate in the concrete wall. The house itself was a cubist design over three floors. It was a cream colour with balconies and verandas. The grounds within had ornamental trees and flowering shrubs. Despite the fact that there was no one to be seen, apart from the two in the boat, he felt uncomfortable, as if he were trespassing and should not be there. He was deciding whether to turn back when cramp seized his left calf muscle.

He tried to relieve it by holding the fin tip up while treading water. It would go away but, as soon as he let go, it came back. He needed to reach shallower water, so he made his way towards the shore, while holding his leg. He approached the beach to the right of the pier that had the fishing boat tied to it. Once it was shallow enough to stand, he removed his left fin, lifted his mask and looked around.

The fishing boat was painted white and blue; it had a small engine house amidships and a metal hand winch on the prow. Inside and in front of the engine housing was an old man with a grey handlebar moustache and brown leathery skin. He had a thick head of grey hair and was wearing a blue denim top. Next to him was a much younger woman with dark hair and complexion, wearing a yellow bikini. They were sorting something out inside the boat. It suddenly occurred to him that they were the fisherman and his daughter bringing in the day's catch for the evening meal at the nearby taverna. Were they also the two who'd found his father? They ignored him as they went about their business.

Looking at the beach, he saw that it was not as nice as Perivoli after all. The sand was plentiful enough and the grove of trees behind it attractive, but this was fenced off and there was a thick band of pebbles to walk across before entering the sea. There were also no beach umbrellas or other shade; so why come here?

Once his leg was better, he put the fin back on and started to swim back, hoping there would be no recurrence. By the time he was back in Perivoli bay, he felt fine and wanted to carry on. Just off-shore three yachts had anchored in his absence. He decided to follow the route he had taken with Diana, but in reverse. As he swam across the bay, he passed groups of people shouting and laughing in the water around the yachts.

He crossed his father's cove and continued along the long stretch of cliff. The weather was coming the other way, head on, but it was only slightly choppy and did not have the swell he had experienced before. He carried on until he reached the mouth of the inlet in which he had met Diana. He rested a few minutes and then started back. He had been swimming for forty minutes already; another twenty to get back would take him to the hour. That would be sufficient. He was beginning to feel the cold.

He was about to turn round and put his head down when something caught his eye in the direction of the headland to the south. He saw it again; it was unmistakeable. Two black fins surfaced and submerged. He felt a surge of adrenaline similar to the feeling he'd had the other night with the intruder. He started swimming back as fast as he could. He kept as shallow as possible, winding through gaps in the rocks and waters, occasionally scraping his stomach or knee. As he swam he would take quick glances around him. His speed and endurance were fuelled by apprehension. All he could think of were the Great Whites Diana had told him about. He did not stop until he reached the shallows of Perivoli and was standing amongst the children and adults playing and swimming in the shallows.

He was breathless and stood there recovering. He soon became aware of people on the beach standing and pointing. He turned round and looked. There they were, two dark fins disappearing and reappearing as they transited left to right. Around him he could hear talking in Greek. He made out one recurring word: '*Delfini, Delfini*'. It was only a pair of dolphins. How silly of him. Maybe he could have had a closer look if he had not been so spooked. By the time he was out of the water and back to his belongings, the dolphins and the excitement had passed.

He'd intended to stay on the beach until late afternoon. His rucksack contained water and his book. The lack of any breeze, though, and the abundance of nearby undergrowth meant a plague of insects. There were pinching sand flies and overly curious wasps. The other people did not seem to notice, or were used to it, but Jake found them irritating and decided to leave.

He took the tarmaced road back as he had intended. It started at the southern end of the beach, behind the sand dune and in an area where several cars were parked. After a hundred yards, he took the turning to the right, which led to the headland. The dusty earth had several recent tyre impressions on it.

His father's villa was located where the headland narrowed sufficiently to allow a dual aspect. The front of the house faced the cove and the back Perivoli. It was a two-storey, simple rectangular dwelling, with nothing fancy about it. The front, facing the cove, had a balcony, supported by pillars, running the full length of the upper floor. The shutters of the windows, a bright coloured blue, were closed. Above them, the awnings were tidily wrapped and enclosed in plastic covers. It looked recently repainted and renovated.

After walking round, he stood at the front, outside the dark varnished wooden door. This was where his father would have come out that fateful night in June. What had happened then? He looked down the slope, trying to guess the trajectory he would have taken when he fell, but saw no disturbance. He looked at the ancient, broken pier and tried to imagine the yacht, straining at its moorings in the inclement weather.

Looking down at his feet, he noticed something else. The ground and earth were dusty, as you would expect from such a dry climate. But there were signs of recent footprints. So, were potential buyers looking at the house already, as Stephanos had suggested? It puzzled him that his aunt and uncle would put it up for sale before it had been passed on to them. Were they that desperate? But if that were so, why did the lower wooden shutters have cobwebs on them indicating they had not been opened in weeks? Perhaps the promontory attracted the idly curious.

Anyway, the house was attractive and the location stunning, although there was a sadness about the place which made him want to leave and not spend time speculating. Even if he had a key, which he had made no attempt to ask for, he would have no desire to explore inside.

That evening he could not decide whether to take up Nicos's invitation, so he dressed for the occasion, which he imagined would be smart casual, just in case. At seven he wandered into the yacht club for a drink and to watch the sunset. He did not expect to find anyone so early and was surprised to see Savvas.

"Are you here on your own?" Jake asked.

"No, the others wanted to go for a walk, I'm being lazy. They'll be back to eat."

"They serve food?"

"Just pizzas. Would you like to eat with us?"

"No, it's too early for me," Jake said. He had made a salad when he had returned from the beach and was not hungry. "You must be busy at the shop."

"We close at six on Saturday. That's why I didn't want to walk. I've been on the move all day. How was your first week?"

"I've seen a lot. On Monday I walked to Paleo Limani. It's beautiful. I can see why you like it. It has an atmosphere."

"From the past, and there's a legend that one of the islands is haunted."

"Really? Which one?"

"The one with the flat top," Savvas said as the waiter arrived. "What will you drink? I won't join you if you don't mind."

"A fruit juice would be nice," Jake said, as Savvas instructed the waiter. "On another day I went to the beach with the café. It was quite pleasant."

"I don't like it, it's too noisy."

"I've also been to Perivoli."

"There's a gem."

"I agree, although today it had lots of people, and dolphins, not to mention annoying insects."

"It's the south wind. It's the source of all our problems," Savvas said. "But it sometimes brings dolphins from the north side."

"From Perivoli I swam round to the next bay, you know, Seal Beach. Have you ever seen seals there?"

"I've never seen them anywhere, but the fishermen claim to have."

"Whose is the big house?"

"You mean Kephalas, Alexander Kephalas."

"It's like a prison, with a wall and barbed wire."

"He does it to keep people out."

"Isn't that a bit paranoid?"

"Vain yes, not paranoid. You see, he's rich. He invites people there during the summer: celebrities, politicians. Some wouldn't go if there wasn't security. The wall's for his guests, not him."

"That would explain it," Jake said. "Yesterday I went to the museum. I spoke to the curator. Nice man."

"Nice, and informative."

"I know, he told me all about pirates, buried treasure and shipwrecks."

"Very entertaining; our Stephanos does tend to embellish the facts a bit."

"It sounded quite plausible to me."

"We all wish we could find buried treasure, don't we?" Savvas said, looking at him with raised eyebrows.

"Sure," Jake said, wondering what was behind the expression.

Savvas's wife and two sons returned. They greeted Jake and asked him how he was. Then Assimina spoke in Greek to her husband, while still standing. Meeting her again caused Jake to remember that she was the woman he had seen in the launch with the mayor, speeding out of the harbour, when he was returning with Diana's inflatable from Paleo Limani the other day. He thought of mentioning it but they soon left. Finally, Savvas turned back to him.

"They don't want to eat here tonight. We're going to the taverna," he said.

"You're eating early."

"We've got an early start."

"But it's Sunday."

"You don't know? The church service is taking place at St Theodore's on Panagia Island. It's the biggest one at Paleo Limani. The service is at ten; you should attend. Everyone will be going."

"How do I get there?" Jake remembered seeing it when he had gone to meet Diana.

"By boat; they'll start taxiing people from the harbour from eight thirty. There will be a shuttle service from the pier in front of the council offices."

"Are you taking your boat?"

"I can't unfortunately, otherwise we wouldn't need to go so early, but there's only one pier at the other end and no space to moor." He was standing up to go. "If you go, you'll need to arrive early or you won't find a seat in the church."

"Maybe I'll see you there."

Jake sat on his own, drinking his juice and wondering whether he should go. The thought that everybody would be there made him nervous, but maybe it was what he should do. And then there was Nicos's invitation. He wondered whether he could stay up all night and be okay in the morning. Sometimes his thinking was that of an old man. Going with Nicos might be fun or a waste of time, but he might learn something about his father. What worried him was the thought of not being able to leave if he didn't like it and was bored.

He decided to go. He couldn't go back home to eat because he hadn't taken anything out of the freezer, but he couldn't hang around here either. He decided to go to the taverna beyond Perivoli. The thought of eating fresh fish was appealing. He estimated that there was probably enough light and time to make the journey there, eat and be back for eleven.

The walk was uncomfortable at first, until his muscles warmed up. He came close to turning back when he started up the first hill by the cemetery. There was that mandolin music again and he was tempted to find somewhere to sit and pass the time there.

Once at the top though, with the breeze on his back, it became easier. He was facing the setting sun and the beauty of it, as it hovered above the sea, drew him forward.

Hardly a car or motorcycle passed him. Even the beach café was quiet, caught between the daytime traffic and the evening nightlife.

After the turning for Perivoli, the road became level and straight and he was soon past the road that led to the house on the right-hand headland. After this the land was walled and contained orchards. There were pear, peach, pomegranate and fig trees that he could identify, but others that he could not. The air was full of exotic and unfamiliar scents. On the landward side the rising hills were turning orange from the sun, which was now blocked from view by the trees of the groves.

The wall gave way to fence and here the fruit trees were not as well-tended and were more widely spaced, with thick undergrowth. He guessed he was behind Seal Beach and this was confirmed when he came to the access road which cut through the greenery towards the jetty with the fishing boat. In the distance, through the gap, he could see the headland and the fortified house. The fenced land to his left continued as far as he could see, but on the right, not much further away, was another smaller, enclosed plot with an open, double gate. In here was a cultivated allotment of vegetables, herbs and flowers. There was an approach that led to a single-storey building in front of which was a seated area under thatch, supported by a metal frame. This was the taverna he was looking for, but it did not appear to be open. There were lights on in the building, but the seated part was dark. Deciding to investigate, he walked up the drive.

As he approached, he heard the sound of voices and music. Someone must have spotted him for as soon as he stepped under the thatched canopy a woman came out of the door and switched on the lights. "Can I help you?" she asked in Greek from a raised area in front of the building. She was short and slight with black hair streaked with white, tied up in a bun. Her skin was dark and wrinkled.

"What time do you open?" Jake asked in Greek.

"We're open now, but we won't serve any fish for an hour. You can sit and have a drink with some meze."

"Do you have fruit juice?"

"Peach or orange?" she asked, showing him to a table on the raised part, close to the door.

"Peach, please," he replied, climbing the three steps and sitting down facing the sun, which was about to touch the horizon. His table was separated from the rest of the restaurant, which was on bare ground, by a white painted wooden divide.

The woman came back with the juice and put it on the table. She studied him. "There's something about you I recognise," she said. "You belong to this island."

"Why do you say that?"

"I've lived with these people for a long time. I can see their characteristics in their offspring. What confuses me is your accent."

"My accent?"

"It's Cypriot."

"My mother was from Cyprus and that's where I learnt Greek."

"Of course, how stupid of me; you're George Philo's son, Jake. My condolences. I'm Maria. Your father was a few years younger than me; my mother was your grandparents' housekeeper and cook. She worked at their house during the summer. She would take me along with her and I would play with your father on the beach. But recently I looked after his orchard."

"His orchard?" So this was the family his father had left it to.

"Yes, it's a few hundred metres inland from the house, in the fields behind Perivoli."

"I know about it, but I've never seen it. My father gave the house to his brother and sister."

"I know," she said with sadness. "I looked after the orchard, maintained the walls and fences, and your father let me keep most of the fruit, except for the little I supplied him and his mother with when they were here. I also provided them with vegetables from my land." She made a sweeping gesture of the surrounding area. "I told Mr Zacharias that I don't want the orchard, it belongs to you. I understand why you're not getting the house, but the orchard? It didn't belong to your grandfather; your father bought it himself. It should be yours."

"It was my father's wish that you should have it."

"It was my husband and daughter who found him," she said, solemnly.

"It must've been a shock for them."

"It was; we were very fond of him." She pulled out the chair in front of him and sat. "Whenever I brought him fish and fruit, he would invite me in and we would sit and have coffee on the veranda. He liked talking to me because I knew all the gossip."

"Unfortunately, I didn't know him that well."

"I know, and I felt he had many regrets when it came to you."

"How so?"

"He would talk about you and your mother, but in a superficial way. I felt he wanted to say more, but couldn't. Whenever I tried to talk about it myself, he would change the subject. Your father was a troubled man."

"Yes, but what troubled him?"

"I wish I knew what to tell you," she said, lowering her head. She seemed to reflect on something before continuing. "My family, and my husband's, have been here for many generations. Mine were farmers and my husband's fishermen. We have lived off the land and sea for as long as we can remember. We never leave; we are here all the time. My two sons have left, but my daughter stayed to become a fisherman too and to help with the restaurant. What I'm trying to say is that we see, hear and know a lot. There's more here than what you see."

"I don't understand," Jake said. The truth was he'd had strange feelings in certain places and at certain times. But were they not products of his imagination?

"At this time of year, when there are many people and you are busy and distracted, you sense little. But when it's quiet, when you may see no one for days, you feel it; a presence, much more on the other side than here. Don't ask me to tell you more because I can't. Ask my husband and daughter, they often go to Paleo Limani fishing and it affects them; especially my husband. He says he gets thoughts and feelings that are not his own; as if something or someone was trying to get into his head. Sometimes he's had to come back. Some people are more affected than others."

"What do you think it could be?"

"I don't know, but it feels like something happened here, something forgotten, and it wasn't good."

"So, it's like a haunting?"

"No, it's more potent than that. As I've said, it seems to affect some people more than others. But I think that it also possesses some."

"Possession? That's pretty strong stuff." Jake was disappointed, as the discussion seemed to drift into the realm of superstition.

"I've seen people I've known since they were children change. Some have been residents; some frequent visitors. I've seen them change into different personalities. Other people I know will tell you the same thing."

"But people often change as they're growing up, some quite dramatically. It doesn't mean they've been possessed by spirits."

"Yes, people change. They change their beliefs and their behaviour, not their personalities. It's only if you've lived in a closed community like this that you appreciate how much of personality is inherited."

"Do you think it affected my father?" Jake asked, trying to draw the conversation back to him.

"No, not him. It didn't affect him in that way. But the others, the ones it did affect, they wanted something from him."

"Who are these others?"

"I don't know all of them. Just the ones I've had contact with over the years or those I've heard about. One of them is that woman with the yacht. The one called Diana."

"Diana? But I thought she was my father's friend."

"Oh no, she was always pestering him; he hated it when she turned up."

"Who else?" Jake asked. This was a revelation.

"Kephalas, the owner of the big house," she replied nodding in its direction. Jake looked too and saw that the outside was now floodlit. "They hardly ever spoke. I could see it in church or at other gatherings. Your father could not look at him. But there were others as well. He had few friends here."

"So why did he come? Why not stay away?"

"At first I thought it was because of your grandmother. But then he continued after she died. Your father was stubborn, defiant. Maybe he had to come; maybe he came because he could. I don't know."

"You said there are others?"

"The ones I know are Diana, the mayor, that doctor who comes every summer and Assimina or Mina, the grocer's wife. They wanted something from him, but with Kephalas it was different. Kephalas and his boss had a different relationship with him."

"Kephalas has a boss? Who?"

"Basil Protopapas. He usually turns up in the second week of August, in a week or so. Always stays on his yacht, the *Trident*."

"And you're telling me that they had some sort of influence over my father?"

"I'm certain of it, but couldn't tell you what. What I can say is that your father was a good man. He loved you and your mother; especially you. You are so much like him."

"Really? How?"

"You're just like he used to be when he was younger. I can see it in your face. You have his intelligence and spirit, although I can see you've suffered," she said, having a quick look at her watch. "We've talked too long. I must go back to my daughter and husband. Our customers will be coming soon and we can't talk like this in front of them. But come again; at the same time. You're always welcome here. Are you staying at your grandmother's?"

"Yes."

"Then I will come to you sometimes, when I'm in town. I will bring you fruit from your father's orchard. It'll have some nice figs in a few days and later on grapes."

"I'd like that."

"Would you like something else to drink?"

"Another fruit juice would be nice."

"What about food?"

"I have to leave by ten," he said, looking at his watch. "Just bring me some meze. Surprise me."

"I will. Your father and Photis came here often and sat where you're sitting."

She brought him the juice with a bowl of olives. He did not have long to wait before the first customers came. People he hadn't seen before. He didn't notice the time go by. His head was full of what she had told him. Eventually she brought him some starters: small dishes of freshly fried squid, whitebait and charcoal-grilled octopus tentacles, together with a basket of bread. He ate slowly, savouring the atmosphere and the moment.

He wondered why the people he knew did not come here. They just didn't belong. The dirt floor, the simple wooden tables, the white plastic chairs. None of those here were bankers or businessmen. Here were fishermen, farmers and shop owners. He saw how this was the ideal refuge for his father.

The starters were followed by a Greek salad, but not like ones he'd had at home. It contained herbs and other unusual ingredients. He asked Maria about them.

"We have many herbs around here that are unique," she replied. "The ones I use for the salad grow near the shore and have a certain saltiness. They are good for the digestion."

He did not want to leave. He considered changing his mind about going with Nicos. He enjoyed the atmosphere so much that he hoped to stay until after the last customer had left, but Maria came to him and said: "The people at that table aren't staying to eat, they're leaving soon. They live in the upper town; they will give you a lift."

He saw the sense in the suggestion. It was dark and he could not see himself walking back all that way. "How much do I owe you?"

"This was on the house, in memory of your father and grandmother. I loved them both."

"Thank you, Maria. There's one thing I'm curious about. Someone is going to my father's grave and taking flowers. Do you know anything about this?"

"I do," she said. "But you must go now. I will tell you about it next time."

He left with the older couple, who dropped him off at the harbour front, just near to the museum and bank. It was after ten thirty and he started walking slowly towards the yacht pier.

As he approached the yacht club it occurred to him that by going to the yacht pier for the first time he would either pass or come close to the *Sevastia*. He tried to understand why he was avoiding it. Did he think it represented a side of his father's nature of which he disapproved? Surely he knew better now, or did he still have doubts?

At the bottom of the steps to the yacht club he paused briefly before going up to ask for the keys.

There would not be time to see it now, but he would be free to go at a time of his choosing.

Chapter 21: The *Bacchus*

Jake made it to the *Bacchus* as it was departing. After giving his name to a deckhand and replacing his shoes with slippers, he went into the lounge to find Nicos and the two girls sitting on armchairs round a low table. A waiter dressed in white was hovering.

"Hey, man, take a seat. I'm glad you could make it," Nicos said. "You've met Vicky and Emma?" Vicky looked glum and bored, but Emma was smiling.

"I imagined there would be more of us," Jake said.

"For some reason the others backed out," Nicos said. "So, we'll be sharing the fun four ways. Sit down." He indicated the chair opposite and next to Emma. "What are you drinking?"

"A beer will be fine," Jake said to the waiter. "So where are we going?"

"To Lichas, but not the town," Nicos replied. "On the north coast there's a harbour well known for its fish tavernas, and also a club, which is in a cave."

"Really?" Jake said. "I've seen a cave on Lichas."

"That one's in the south," Nicos said. "This one's smaller. Wait till you see it."

The waiter brought Jake his drink.

"Since we're only four, let's go and sit on the bridge deck," Nicos said.

They went up a flight of steps and came to a dark room surrounded by windows. The aft end had two settees either side of a table like the one they were sitting at below, while at the forward end were all the controls and navigational equipment. Two men dressed in white, with epaulettes on their shirts, sat at the two swivel seats.

They sat as before. In the background was the squawking of the radio and the voices of the officers talking between themselves. Apart from the stars and the waning moon behind them, there was nothing to see outside.

"Is it safe travelling at night?" Jake asked.

"The captain doesn't like it unless there's a moon," Nicos replied. "We have excellent radar, so the risk comes in hitting something low in the water, something made of wood or fibreglass, like a log, or a fishing boat. We have two men forward with the spotlight and we're going slowly."

Vicky turned and whispered something in Nicos's ear. "Will you excuse us for a few minutes?" he said as they got up and went back downstairs.

Emma looked distracted and serious. She was attractive, with wavy shoulder-length dark hair, large brown eyes, prominent cheekbones and a generous mouth. She had a well-proportioned figure, although looked slightly underweight. Her suntan was a milk chocolate colour. She wore a simple denim skirt and a black short-sleeved top. She picked up her handbag, opened it, retrieved her mobile and checked the display. Then she took out a packet of Marlboro Lights. "Do you mind if I smoke?"

"No," he said. His mother used to smoke, until her cancer was diagnosed. "As long as you don't blow it in my face."

"I'll try not to," she said, lighting up with a disposable lighter. "So, do you have a yacht of your own?" She was smiling again.

"Technically yes, but in practice no."

"What does that mean?"

"Well, my father died recently and I inherited his yacht, but I've not done anything with it. Actually, it's not a yacht at all, more a powerboat."

"Don't you like it?"

"No, it's not that," Jake said. After collecting the keys, he'd stood outside the *Sevastia III* for several minutes. It was, as he expected, nothing flashy, but modern and well-maintained. "It's not my sort of thing."

"So what are you into then?"

"What am I into?" Jake repeated. "Well, I'm a teacher, if that's what you mean."

"A teacher?" Emma exclaimed. "Okay, what do you teach?"

"Sixth form geography."

"Are you kidding me?"

"No, why are you treating it like a joke?"

"I'm sorry but you're the first person I've met on this yacht who actually works, apart from the crew."

"You're talking about Nicos and his friends, I suppose?"

"Yeah, and you'd be amazed what they say they do," she said, drawing on the cigarette and inhaling deeply. She exhaled at the side of her mouth, away from him. "From brain surgeons to plumbers. In reality, they have trust funds or get an allowance to do nothing."

"Why would they claim to work?"

"You soon discover it's part of some chat-up line."

"I see. And you, what do you do?"

"Vicky and I are interns."

"Where?"

"The Royal Free hospital."

"Where's that?"

"Hampstead, London."

"I know. That's hard work."

"It is. That's why it's so weird to meet people who do nothing. They just drink, take drugs and are totally bored."

"So how did you come to be here?"

"Well, Nicos has a pad in Hampstead, or should I say a penthouse, next to the Heath. One of the consultants at the hospital, who's also Greek, is a friend of his. Through him we were invited to a do that Nicos was having at the end of June," she said, taking a final drag before extinguishing her cigarette in the ashtray. "It was awful."

"In what way?"

"Well, the flat was fabulous, the food fantastic and you could have whatever drugs you wanted, but there were only seven men and eighteen women. The purpose of the party was to find women they could lay, but Vicky and Nicos hit it off, so we were invited to the yacht for our holidays."

"A bit short notice; you had no other plans?"

"We'd arranged to go cycling in northern France, so the invitation to come on a luxury yacht and tour the Mediterranean was too good to turn down."

"You don't seem so sure."

"Well, without Vicky, I probably would've gone to stay with my parents at their cottage in Wales for the hundredth time; besides, someone has to look after her."

"Does she need looking after?"

"Unfortunately she tends to overdo the drugs and alcohol. I bet that's where they've gone. She seems to think she can keep up with Nicos and his crowd. She doesn't realise they're hard core."

"So, it's been disappointing."

"It's not been too bad. We've been to Mykonos and Rhodes and that was great. It's the company that's been a bit iffy. Anyway, it's coming to an end."

"When do you go back?"

"We leave the island Monday, with the yacht; arrive in Athens in the morning and the flight's in the afternoon."

"Nicos must really like Vicky to give such good service."

"Vicky thinks so but, between you and me, I bet he'll have a replacement on board the next day."

Nicos and Vicky came back upstairs. Vicky sat down while Nicos went to speak to the captain. After a brief exchange, he came and sat opposite Jake.

"Everything all right?" Jake asked.

"Captain says we'll be in port in half an hour," Nicos replied.

They arrived at a harbour much smaller than that of Halia. The left side had three jetties and was where the yachts and larger boats moored. The right-hand side comprised a waterfront dedicated to restaurants, whose tables and chairs, under extended awnings, came right up to the water's edge. There was music and the sound of many voices. Here only fishing boats were moored. Between the two ends was a pebbly strand.

Owing to its size and draft, the yacht was moored at the end of the middle pier. There were only two other yachts. When they disembarked a taxi was waiting for them on the main road.

"Is it far?" Jake asked, as he got in the back next to Vicky. She looked strangely blank and Emma, sitting next to her, was looking concerned.

"Just the top of the hill," Nicos said, sitting in front with the driver.

They were there in a minute; probably a distance of half a mile. Nothing indicated anything unusual, just a car park with a square concrete structure in a corner.

After getting out of the cab, they entered the building and approached a young woman sitting behind a wooden counter. Nicos gave his name for the reservation and, after she produced their passes, she directed them through a steel door. This led to a carpeted landing and the cloakrooms. Beyond this was a ramp, which they descended for about twenty metres before coming back on themselves for another twenty metres and then doing the same again. Throughout there were metal ducts and the sound of forced air ventilation. It was not until the start of the final ramp that they could hear music.

On the lower landing was another metal entrance fronted by a doorman. Here there were customers standing in small groups smoking. A sign beside the door, written in English and Greek, said that no smoking was allowed in the club.

The doorman took their tickets and let them in. Immediately the full strength of the music hit them. They stepped onto a steel walkway which led to a large oval structure, suspended and supported by scaffolding. There were spotlights everywhere, above and below, showing coloured rock walls, stalactites and stalagmites. Railings protected all the public areas.

The far end of the platform had a raised stage, with the dance floor at the front, and was surrounded by tables and chairs. The stage had band equipment set out, promising live music to come.

Apart from the walkway by which they had entered, there were two others that came off the central platform. One went to the left on to another narrow platform attached to the side of the cave, and supported a bar with stools. The other went off to the right and led to an entrance in the rock wall.

As soon as they had stepped onto the walkway, Jake could feel the movement made by the dancers. A waitress, who seemed to know Nicos, greeted them. She led them towards the dance floor. They skirted round it to the right and crossed the walkway that led to the entrance in the wall. As soon as they entered, the music subsided considerably. Here inside a cavern no bigger than a large room were individual tables and benches, alcoved off for privacy. They sat at a table with a reserved sign. Nicos spoke to the waitress again and gave her a folded banknote.

"What do you think of this?" Nicos said.

They muttered their approval, and even Vicky seemed impressed.

"I've never seen anything like it," Jake said. "Did my father ever come here?"

"Oh, yes," Nicos said. "Together a few times."

Jake wanted to ask more, but did not feel he could in front of the girls.

"I've ordered a bottle of champagne," Nicos said. "If you two want anything different, just asks the waitress; I've got a tab."

"What about food?" Vicky asked.

"They're bringing some cold meze," Nicos replied. "They can't do anything hot."

"I've had something already," Jake said.

"So have we," Nicos said. "But it's a long night and we might get hungry."

The waitress brought a stainless steel stand and bucket. The latter was loaded with ice. After a few minutes she returned with the champagne, fluted glasses, plates and forks.

"Whenever we get to the bottom I want you to replace it," Nicos told her after she had filled their glasses. He passed her another note. "Here's to our health," he said, raising his glass. They all drank. "So, are we going to see more of you in the months ahead?"

"Maybe," Jake replied.

"You keep your cards close," Nicos observed.

"I like being mysterious," Jake said.

"Hun, maybe we can go for a cigarette and then I'd like to dance," Vicky interrupted.

"Of course," Nicos said, getting up. "And I'll be expecting to see you two on the dance-floor."

"Do you dance?" Emma said, after they'd gone.

"I haven't done much of it recently, but I'm sure I could manage when I'm in the mood," Jake said, not sure about his feet. "Is it an invitation?"

"Not just yet. I need to drink a bit first. I get embarrassed, especially in front of Nicos."

"Why? Is he good?"

"I'd say," she said, sipping her champagne. She looked nervous. "Let's just chat, for now. Why did you ask Nicos about your father?"

"It's a long story."

"I'd like to hear it."

Jake told her as much as he felt able to. In the meantime, the waitress had brought the cold meze and they began to nibble as well as drink.

"What about you? Tell me about yourself," he said.

"My life's pretty ordinary compared to yours. I'm from Kent; both my parents are doctors, which says a lot about my career choice, and my younger sister's studying to be a dentist."

"What about friends and relationships?"

"I had a major break-up last summer with someone I was really serious about. Since then nothing's happened on that front."

"I broke up with someone I was living with a couple of years ago," he said. "It's not easy, is it?"

"But what about friends?"

"I've sort of neglected them."

"You seem to be getting on all right here."

"Well, Nicos is friendly and he knew my dad. Otherwise, I've not been around that long."

"What have they been like?" she asked. "I bet they're not the sort you are used to back home."

"I'd say." Jake began telling her about his experiences. He told her about Diana and the others he had met. After a few glasses of champagne it became easier and easier to talk. Eventually it dawned on him that he was being interrogated.

"Why are you so interested in these people?" he asked.

"No reason. Just passing the time," she replied, turning away from him. "Listen, I'm dying for a cigarette. I'll be back in ten and maybe we can dance."

"Okay, I'll wait for you," Jake said, letting her out.

He brooded over his suspicions, but not for long as Nicos came and sat next to him. He was sweating from his exertions.

"The girls went for a cigarette," Nicos said. He emptied the bottle and waved it at the waitress. "You look pissed off; not enjoying yourself?"

"Everything's fine. I'm just not used to the champagne."

"You should burn it off, like I do."

"You're right; I'll get Emma on the dance floor when she returns."

"You ought to. I think she likes you and she's not had much luck with my other friends."

"I wouldn't mind some water though. It helps me cope with the alcohol."

"No problem." The waitress came back with the new bottle of champagne and Nicos ordered two bottles of mineral water. A few minutes later the girls returned. Jake and Nicos moved over to let them sit just as the waitress came back with the water and glasses.

"Sorry we were so long," Vicky said, "but Emma was ages in the ladies."

"Shut up," Emma said. "You can talk."

"Should we go for this dance?" Jake said, after having some water.

"Let's," Emma said, getting up to let him out and taking her handbag.

"You won't be able to put that down on the dance floor," Nicos said.

"But I always do."

"Not in places like this you don't. What's in it that's valuable?"

"Just my mobile."

"Are you expecting any calls?" Vicky asked. "I left mine on the yacht."

"No, I guess I took it out of habit," Emma said.

"Let Jake put it in his pocket, then you can leave your bag," Nicos said.

She took it out of her bag and handed it to Jake. She seemed hesitant for some reason. The mobile was a Nokia, a slightly newer version than his. He pocketed it.

Nicos and Vicky followed them out. The band was in full swing, the music energising and the atmosphere great. Nicos was amazingly elegant and agile. It was hard not to stare at him. He was the centre of attention and he knew it. Emma, meanwhile, kept on looking at Jake, smiling, flirting provocatively; he wondered what she was thinking. He knew she was up to something; he was certain of it. He had an intuition and an idea. He just needed an opportunity to carry it through.

His chance came when the dance floor became particularly crowded at the start of a popular tune. Just when Emma was trying to whisper something in Vicky's ear, he slipped away. He headed for the entrance. As he went through, he looked back and saw that he was not being followed. He ran up the ramps to the top level and went into the gents. He locked himself in one of the cubicles and took out Emma's mobile. Luckily the layout was the same as his and it had no password protection. He went to recent calls and found what he was looking for. He brought up the most recent number and called it. After a few seconds he shut the phone and went back.

On the dance floor he found Vicky, Emma and Nicos dancing together. Emma came over and asked him where he'd gone and he explained that he'd had to go to the gents.

Later the music slowed, the lights were dimmed and the dancing became more intimate. Emma was holding him close, rubbing gently against him and bringing her face close to his. He was not falling for that a second time.

"Let's sit down for a while," Jake said. "I'm thirsty again."

Leaving Nicos and Vicky behind, they returned to their seats, and Jake had a long drink of water. Looking at Emma, he perceived that she looked content and satisfied with herself. He'd soon put an end to that. "So what about you? What friends have you made here these last few days?" he asked.

"I haven't made any," she replied. "I told you, I've met a few people, but made no friends."

"I thought you must've done in order to bring your mobile. The rest of us have left ours behind."

"No, as I said, it's just habit."

"It's just that when we were sitting on the yacht you checked your phone."

"Well, I was just checking to see if I'd had any texts from my sister."

"So, you're telling me you've not received or made any calls?"

"No, just texts, but what business is it of yours? I don't belong to you."

"I wouldn't want you anyway. When I told you about the people I'd met, I didn't mention the fact that I'd been set up before."

"So? What does that have to do with me?"

"All this pretending to be nice just to milk me for information."

"God, you're weird."

"And you couldn't wait to go back and relay the information as soon as you could."

"You're paranoid. You need help."

"It's all here," he said, taking the phone out of his pocket. "The call you made to a Greek mobile when you went for a smoke. Judging by the time of the call, I guess you made it while in the loo."

"Fuck off," she said angrily. "What right have you got to delve into my privacy?"

"You can keep your privacy. I hope you enjoy whatever you got paid to delve into mine."

He did not wait to hear her reply but walked out of the lounge, past the dance floor and out of the entrance. Fortunately it was too dark and crowded for Nicos and Vicky to notice him. He went up the ramps, out into the car park and started walking briskly down to the port.

When he reached level ground, he slowed. The harbour was deserted; the restaurants all shut and dark, the water silky smooth and the air still. All he could hear were his own footfalls as he walked to the yacht. He would ask the crew to let him into one of the cabins so he could get some sleep tonight. He crossed the part of the waterfront that fronted the pebbly beach.

He was approaching the first pier when he heard someone running towards him from behind. He turned round just in time to see two men wearing dark hoods. Before he could react, they were upon him; each grabbed one of his arms as they dragged him backwards down the beach and into the water. One had his hand over his mouth and he could not call for help. Both were much bigger and bulkier than him and, despite his efforts, he could not break free from their grip.

When they were waist deep, they immersed him in the cold sea and held him down. As much as he struggled he could make no impression on them. After what seemed like an eternity, they raised his head out of the water. One of the men, the one with his hand over his mouth, hissed in his ear. "You will leave Greece. Do you understand? Tomorrow morning at the latest."

"You have the wrong guy," Jake mumbled in vain, trying to take in enough breath through his nose.

They plunged him back under for another spell. "Leave tomorrow," the same man hissed again. "Do you understand?"

"Why?" Jake tried to ask. "I don't understand why."

They plunged his head back under; this time for longer. He felt the panic rise in him. Then the pain started in his lungs. He was struggling to stop himself breathing in water when abruptly one man loosened his grip. The other quickly spun round and immediately loosened his as well. Jake stood up and frantically gulped air.

He barely had the strength to stand but was able to see what had happened. Both men were staggering out of the water. One was holding his head, with blood streaming down his hands, groaning, the other was holding his face, also with blood over his hands. Standing over them was Emma, holding a wooden oar.

She had moved to place herself between Jake and the men and was keeping her eyes on them with an expression that said she was ready to strike again, but they were now running away as best they could. Close to the beach, on the tarmac, they fell into a waiting car, started the engine and drove off.

Meanwhile, Jake had waded out of the water and was on his hands and knees, on the pebbles. Unfortunately, he was not close enough to the car to read the license number. He was also certain that neither of these two was the man who'd attacked him last Sunday night.

As soon as the car was out of sight, Emma dropped the oar and ran to him. "My God, Jake, are you all right?" she said.

"I'm not injured. They were just trying to scare me, I'm sure," he said, shivering. "What are you doing here?"

"Don't talk now, let me take you back. Did you breathe in any water?"

"No. What happened to your shoes?"

"I left them by the fishing boat, with the lady."

"What lady?" Jake said, looking over to that side of the harbour. It was deserted.

"She was there just a minute ago," Emma said, looking in the same direction.

"Well, you'd better go and get them. I'll be all right for a minute. And don't forget the oar."

She picked it up from where she'd dropped it.

"You hit them pretty good," Jake said. "You'd better get that blood off it."

She rinsed it in the sea, put it back in the fishing boat, and retrieved her shoes. When she returned to him, he was shaking violently.

"It's the wet as well as the shock," she said, helping him to his feet.

They walked back to the yacht and told the man on watch that he had fallen in the sea. He smiled knowingly back at them. She took him down to her cabin.

"Come on, get your kit off and into the shower," she said. "Don't be shy, I'm a doctor, remember."

He took off everything but his underwear, went into the bathroom, removed his briefs and stood under the hot stream. After a few minutes, Emma came in and sat on the loo seat holding a towel.

"Are you going to tell me why you followed me, what you were doing on the beach?" Jake asked.

"I came after you," she said. He could see from the cubicle that she had lowered her head. "I came to tell you that you were right."

"Who was it?"

"It happened soon after you left the beach on Friday night," Emma began. "Nicos went off for a few minutes to take a call on his mobile. I could see him from a distance. He was arguing with whoever had called. When he came back he said he'd just received a call from someone inviting us to their house, pretending it was a fortunate invitation. I suspect now that it was his weird friend, the builder, who made the original contact."

"You mean Panagos?" Jake asked.

"That's his name," Emma said, shivering. "Whenever he goes near anyone with a skirt he's got his hands all over them. Anyway, a car came and collected us, a Land Rover as a matter of fact, and took us to this house, just up the road. It was huge and floodlit and we had to go through a steel gate and wall with barbed wire on it."

Jake turned off the shower and when he opened the cubicle Emma handed him the towel and he started drying himself.

"We met this man and his wife. His name was Alexander. I can't remember her name; she was foreign and didn't stay long. They put on music and we started drinking and chatting. He was asking everything about Vicky and me, but mostly me. After a while Alexander took us for a walk around the grounds. When we got to the cliff's edge, Nicos and Vicky sort of edged away and he got me on my own. He got more or less to the point then."

"What did he say?" Jake asked. Emma had stopped and was looking upset. She was rocking slightly back and forth.

"Well, I don't know how it happened, but he started telling me that the opportunity had arisen for me to do something really important and that I would get a big reward for it. He said, just talk to this person and get some simple information. That's all I had to do." She had stopped again and looked as though she was about to cry. "I was bored and thought it all sounded exciting and harmless."

Jake had dried and wrapped the towel round his waist. They went into the cabin and Emma sat on the bed.

"Where are my clothes?" he asked, looking around the room.

"They were soaked," she said. "I gave them to the cabin boy. They'll wash and dry them. I've put the stuff in your pockets on the table."

"Okay, we'll work something out in a minute. What happened next?"

"He gave me the names of some people I was to listen out for and his mobile number and that was it. I just didn't realise," she said and then started sobbing.

"Didn't realise what?" Jake said, sitting next to her and putting his arm around her. She rested her head on his shoulder. It was soon wet with her tears.

"I thought you'd be like the others, but you were different. I meet someone I really like after so long and I screw it up."

"What names did he give you?"

"There was a Diana, Savvas, Stephanos, Yiannis, Assimina, Maria and Niki. He made me repeat them over and over until I remembered. I actually felt sorry for Nicos."

"Nicos? Why?" Jake asked.

"He was livid. He had to put off the others who were meant to be coming with us tonight. When we were driven back to the beach and got out of the car, Nicos told Panagos to fuck off and keep on going."

"So he didn't approve then."

"No, but this Alexander obviously has something on Nicos."

"And Panagos," Jake observed. "So what did you tell Alexander when you called?"

"I just told him what you told me, as best I could remember. That's why I went right away, so I wouldn't forget," she said between sobs. "He said it was good, but not enough; it was too superficial. He said I should do whatever it took to get more and he would increase the reward accordingly."

"You mentioned a woman on the beach."

"Yes, well, when I got down to the harbour and saw what was happening, I didn't know what to do. I just froze. I couldn't even cry out for help. Then this woman was just there beside me. She appeared out of nowhere. She handed me the oar and told me what to do and I just did it."

"You're a brave girl, Emma, I'll give you that."

"I'm a coward really. It's just that when that woman spoke to me, I forgot myself. I only realised what I'd done after I'd done it."

"What did she look like?"

"She was tall, had dark shoulder-length hair, fair complexion, early forties, nice shape, a good-looking woman."

"Look, I'd better go. Maybe you could get me a cabin."

"No, don't go, please," she said, holding him tightly. "Don't leave me; let me make it up to you." She was showering him with kisses and her face was salty with her tears. "I'll do anything you want."

"I'm not taking advantage of your guilt," he said. But he could not be angry with her, even after what she had done. She was warm and attractive and he needed that right now. After what had happened on the beach, he was scared and did not want to be alone.

"No, you're not," she said, holding him even tighter and kissing him more passionately. "I've not been with someone I really liked for so long."

"I suppose it would give the impression that you succeeded in your mission," Jake said with a wink.

"I don't want to take the money, not now. It's you I want."

"No, I want you to take the bastard's money. I want him to think you've succeeded and maybe later we can discuss what else you're going to tell him."

Chapter 22: Panagia Island

Sunday, 5th August

At nine in the morning, dressed in smart trousers and a light blue short-sleeved shirt, Jake stood in the hazy sunshine with the group waiting on the quayside for the next shuttle. The boats used were large wooden all-weather craft that could carry fifteen at a time. There was a forward housing for the pilot and the passengers sat in an aft cabin.

He did not have to wait long, which was just as well. The humid south wind continued and he was tired. He overheard someone saying that normal weather conditions were due to resume tomorrow. It was none too soon.

He got on to the next boat and they were soon powering down to the far end of the island. As he watched through the salt-smeared windows, they first passed the familiar places he had swum and then those he had walked. The sea was slightly choppy, but no problem for the boat, whose bows occasionally threw up spray.

Inside Paleo Limani, the sea was calm as they crossed the bay to reach their destination. Panagia Island was basically two hills extruding out of the sea and covered with vegetation. The only man-made structures were the pier, the church, which was on flat ground on the lowest hill, and the concrete path that ascended up to it. In addition, on top of the highest hill was a permanent army camp and lookout.

Following the other pilgrims, Jake came to the simple white-washed chapel within a circular low wall. This barrier had gaps at equal intervals for the occasional short stumpy tree. Behind the church was a small copse of more sturdy pines. People were entering the church but, when he passed the entrance, he could see that it was standing room only, with women furiously airing themselves with fans. What seemed wiser was copying those who were sitting on the surrounding wall. He found a place underneath one of the trees. This was perfect. He was in the shade, could hear what was happening and, at the same time, look over his shoulder at the spectacular view of the bay with the three smaller islands. They all looked pretty much the same, apart from one which was flat and seemed to have a mesh of low stone walls. What were they for? The island did not look large enough to be worth growing crops on or pen animals. Was this the haunted islet that Savvas had referred to?

In a few days he would be exploring this area with his new assistant. What did Diana mean when she said he could not miss her? Was she really fat? He doubted it. Was she unusually tall? Maybe, Diana was, for a woman. Or was she beautiful? Judging by Diana, that was possible too.

The procession of the faithful continued up the path as the water taxis kept arriving. Soon the wall filled up and then the patio. Some worshippers, who had obviously done this before, had brought their own fold-up chairs. At ten o'clock sharp the service began. There was no organ music, just chanting, and this could be heard outside, together with catching the occasional whiff of incense. It was mesmerising for the one and a half hours it lasted. During that time Jake was immersed in thought.

He had no regrets about last night and looked forward to being with Emma again. He liked her and it just seemed right, for both of them, to have these two days together. There was the other advantage too and, before Jake left the yacht in the morning, they had agreed what she was going to say to Kephalas.

At the same time as having these thoughts, he was studying an industrious colony of ants that was marching in long lines over the round concrete plate of the patio. They were coming out of a series of oddly arranged cracks in the centre of it, outside the door of the chapel.

Abruptly, the service came to an end and the church emptied. Some people stood outside talking while others immediately made their way down to the pier to board the waiting taxis. As he began walking through the crowd towards the start of the path, he heard someone call out his name. He turned in the direction of the voice.

A slim, wiry individual, slightly shorter than him, was approaching. He was clean-shaven with short greying hair. He was wearing a white short-sleeved shirt tucked into black trousers. He extended his hand. "Mr Philo," he said, "I'm Alexander Kephalas, a friend of your father." His hand was cool and dry with a testing grip. The tightly knotted muscles of his exposed forearm flexed menacingly.

So this was the owner of the fortress on Seal Beach, the powerful, influential person Savvas and Diana talked about. The one who had been setting him up. Was he also the individual responsible for the violence directed against him? He had an intelligent face and searching eyes.

"I would like to extend the condolences of my family for your loss. George was a good friend and compatriot." The sentence was well delivered, but there was no emotion in the brown eyes to back it up. Perfect English, must have been educated in England.

"Thank you."

"When did you arrive?" Kephalas asked.

"A week yesterday," Jake replied. As if he didn't know.

"I wish I'd known sooner. Come, I would like to introduce you to my family," he said. He led the way through the crowd to a group just outside the church. First he introduced Jake to his wife, an impossibly glamorous woman who looked almost Persian, but whose strained English betrayed Italian origins; then to his three children, two boys and a daughter, all perfectly dressed and manicured. At the end of this, he exchanged some words with his wife. "My wife and I are having a buffet party this evening. Perhaps you'd like to join us? If I'd known you were here, I would've already have extended an invitation. What do you say?"

"It would be a pleasure," Jake lied, "although, I don't have clothes for anything formal."

"Come as you're dressed now, I will be."

"I'd be pleased to then."

"Excellent," Kephalas said. "I noticed that your father's house isn't occupied. You're staying in the town?"

"Yes, where my grandmother lived."

"I understand. There are other guests coming from the village. I'm sending a car to pick them up from outside the museum at nine. Would that be convenient or would you prefer some other arrangement?"

"That would be perfect."

"I'll look forward to seeing you then and having a chat," he said, turning abruptly to look out to sea. Jake followed his gaze and saw a white launch approaching the pier. There was a white-uniformed man at the helm. "I believe we shall be leaving now," he said.

He rounded up his family and left. A few minutes later Jake did too.

He arrived back at the town square at one o'clock and met Emma outside the café. They went back to his house and, after showing her round, he prepared a salad, which they ate with bread out on the patio.

Afterwards they had a much needed sleep, and in the late afternoon he took her for a walk around the town before she returned to the yacht. They had agreed that Jake would text her after he had left the party and they would meet up again later for their last night.

At nine he arrived outside the museum and was pleasantly surprised to find Stephanos waiting there too. "You didn't tell me you were going to the buffet tonight," he said.

"My excuse is that I wasn't invited until this morning," Jake said.

"Ah, let me guess, you went to the service at Paleo Limani."

"That's right, but you weren't there."

"It was tourist day today. I had to open the museum."

"Why are you getting a lift? I thought you had a car; and where's Niki?"

"Niki drove as she had to take dignitaries from Lichas. Besides, I've only just finished here."

"At least you're one person who's going that I know."

"I always get invited to these things because of Niki."

"Who will be there?"

"All sorts, the mayor, locals like us. There are usually some outsiders and houseguests. There could be a Greek celebrity or two."

"I thought there'd be others waiting?"

"I think we're the only ones."

A brand new black Range Rover arrived, driven by a Filipino man. It was registered in England and the license plate began with KEF. It was only two nights ago that Emma was in this car, Jake reflected.

"Where does Kephalas live when he's not here?" Jake asked.

"He has houses in Athens and Florida, but he lives mainly in Hampstead, London."

They drove slowly through the streets of the town before picking up speed on the main road. He could see the house from a distance; it was lit up, much like the Acropolis in Athens. The car stopped outside the now open steel doors he had seen the day before from the sea. The path that led to the entrance of the mansion was well lit. On the left-hand side of the house, the one that faced the sea, was a raised veranda, from which the sound of guests' conversations and soft music drifted down to them.

Stephanos and Jake walked up together and came into an entrance hall with others who had newly arrived. From there they entered a large reception room with settees, armchairs and side tables. There were people sitting and standing in groups talking. The left-hand side of the room opened out on to the veranda, with even more guests. A waiter came up to them, speaking in Greek, and offered them a flute of champagne.

"What did he say?" Jake asked. It was too fast for him to follow.

"He said that the starters are on the table in the next room and the main buffet will begin when the doors on the right open."

As they made their way past the guests, he noticed they were carrying small plates with food, but he did not expect what he saw on the table. At one end there were the plates, cutlery and serviettes. In the middle were platters of Parma ham, smoked salmon and some salamis. The centrepiece, though, was a trough of ice inside which was a row of three silver bowls of caviar. Jake was astonished. He estimated that each bowl held a half kilo and must have contained several thousand pounds worth of the stuff. There were people spooning heaps of it onto their plates. As soon as one of the bowls ran low, a waiter came and replenished it. He was so transfixed he did not notice that Stephanos had left his side. He looked around and found him a few yards away with a middle-aged couple, signalling to him to go over. He recognised the man.

"Have you spoken to your neighbours yet?" Stephanos said as Jake approached. "This is Polys and Stavroulla Stephanou."

"I'm glad to meet you," Jake said, taking the woman's hand. She was a large, dark-haired lady with a round, happy face. He recalled what Polys had said about her snoring. She was holding a plate of food, as was her husband. "Polys and I have met."

"Of course, your unfortunate incident with the burglar," Stephanos said. "They told me that they always miss you because they're both out early in the morning. She's the nurse, you know."

"I know. What do you do?" Jake asked Polys. He was sure someone had told him, but he had forgotten.

"I work for the council," he said. "We see you outside on your patio in the evening but you're either eating or reading, so we don't like to disturb you."

"I can hear you chatting and it's comforting, after what happened," Jake said.

"We've bought a house in the upper village. We're renovating it and we anticipate that by spring we'll be moving out," Stavroulla said.

"The house is being left to my aunt and uncle and it's them you should speak to," Jake said. "I'm just going for some food. Looking at you eating is making me jealous."

He went over to the buffet table, took a plate and put on it thin slices of toasted and buttered brown bread, some smoked salmon and Parma ham and just a spoonful of the caviar. He had never had it before and wanted to taste it first before having any more. Taking his plate and glass, he moved out onto the veranda.

It was a large space, with cushioned, cane furniture and glass-topped tables. The night was mild. The moon, a few days past full, was bright enough to subdue the normal abundance of stars. Owing to the brightness of the lamps dotted around the garden, he could not see the sea but could hear it lapping the rocks below. In the distance, to the northwest, the warning light on top of the Green Isles flashed at regular intervals.

He placed some caviar on a piece of toast and put it in his mouth. It was the most delicious thing he had ever tasted. The experience reached unbelievable heights as each individual egg burst in his mouth. The smoked salmon and Parma ham were also undoubtedly the best. He went back to the buffet table to replenish. The caviar bowls had been topped up, so he spooned generous amounts onto his plate.

Next to him an attractive young woman was also helping herself. She turned to face him and smiled. She was around five foot seven with fair hair, blue eyes, perfect teeth and a pale complexion. She wore a black dress with a modest neckline and a hem that came half way down her thigh. "It's divine food, do you not think?" she said in English with a Russian or Eastern European accent. He noticed she had another plate that she was filling.

"Delicious," Jake replied. "One never tires of it."

"I'm Natalya," she said, putting down a plate and extending her hand. She had the most beautiful smile. "And your name please?"

"I'm Jake." He juggled his plate and offered his. Her hand was warm and soft, but the grip was firm. He held it longer than he should have.

"I know, you're Jake Philo. You're one of the London Greeks."

"You could say that," Jake replied.

"Do you work? Are you in business?"

"You could say that too. What about you? Where do you live?"

"My father's Russian, he came to Greece to live because he wanted to be in business here. He met and married my Greek mother, so we live in Athens. Do you have a family?" Jake watched her mouth move as she spoke. It was very expressive, as were her eyes.

"No, both my parents have died and I'm not married."

"That's right and your father quite recently. I was sorry to hear of it," she said, giving a mournful expression before continuing. "So, you must feel honoured to be here."

"I don't think so. My father was an acquaintance of Mr Kephalas."

"You're more important than you might think," she said knowingly, raising an eyebrow. "Will you excuse me a moment?" she continued, holding up one of the plates, "I must take this back to my mother."

He looked at her as she walked off. She had a lovely voluptuous figure and walked with a natural ease and grace, no doubt about that. He went back to the balcony to enjoy the caviar, eating it slowly. When he had finished he was about to get some more when Natalya returned. He had not expected to see her again and was pleasantly surprised. "I'm sorry to have left you," she said. "I can see you don't know many people."

"I'm afraid I'm new to the scene."

"Do you have a house in Athens?"

"An apartment in Paleo Psychiko."

"I know the area," she said, nodding approvingly. "Very nice, we have a house much farther out, in the suburbs."

"Where do you stay on the island?" he asked, as they moved towards the railing of the veranda that overlooked the garden.

"On our yacht. What about you?"

"I have a house here."

"The one on the cliff?" She turned her head to look in the direction of Perivoli.

"No, somewhere in town."

"I thought so," she said, looking preoccupied. "Also very nice, but far too quiet, don't you think?"

"Well, it depends on what you're looking for. I've come from near London, so this makes a nice change."

"The beautiful beaches and the sea are good, but there's nothing else to do. There are no shops, few restaurants and no clubs; isn't this important to you?"

"To be honest, this is new to me," Jake said, looking around. "I'm far from being bored just yet."

"Well, Jake, you're not like these other men. All they do is moan and complain."

"So I've heard," he said, remembering what Emma had told him. "What about the women though?"

"They're worse," she emphasized. "They complain about how they are part of high society and that nothing is good enough for them here; that there's no hairdresser or somewhere for their nails and feet."

"Can't they just sail over to Lichas?"

"That's what they do, but it's all such an effort," Natalya said in an exaggerated way, raising her hand to her head and pretending to swoon.

It made Jake laugh. "Well, your hair looks beautiful as it is." It was true and it looked natural. "You're lucky, you don't have to do much to yourself. But the others, if they hate it so much, why do they come?"

"You're very flattering," she said, smiling appreciatively. "I can see that I'll have to explain this to you. The ones who like being here are the fathers and mothers and they force their sons and daughters to come."

"But why?"

"So that they will make friends and marry within this society. They don't like people from the outside."

"I don't understand this closed attitude."

"Don't you?" Natalya said with surprise. "I believe all men are the same, so I'll test you. Think about what it is you want from a wife. If you're a rich man, who is high up in society, you want a wife who's pure, strongly religious and virtuous, who believes in the family. She shows this with her appearance to the world. She must have the highest standards of presentation. Don't you have a fiancée or girlfriend?"

"No, I haven't at the moment, and as far as I'm concerned there's more to a woman than her presentation or her breeding."

"Who are you going to marry then? Your *gomena*?"

"Probably not." That word again. He must find out what it meant. He wondered what having one would be like. Maybe that was what Emma was.

"So this whole society here," she continued, "is to protect the virtue of the young girls and to make sure the men want to marry them."

"Sounds awful, for the women," Jake remarked. They heard the announcement that the main banquet had opened. The doors to the next room were folded back and people started advancing to the buffet table. "Shall we make our way?"

"Let's."

"Will you be staying long?" Jake asked as they walked to the other room.

"I don't know. We came last Tuesday. My father hasn't said when we're leaving. He tends to decide at the last minute."

"Makes life less mundane, I suppose. So what do you do, just stay on the yacht?"

"No, we go swimming during the day and go to the yacht club in the evening."

"How do you get to the beach?"

"The yacht takes us."

Of course, theirs must have been one of the boats that turned up off-shore from Perivoli. She must think him ignorant about the workings of privileged society. "You must've seen the dolphins then?"

"We did, and we got out of the water quickly," she said, her beautiful eyes widening.

"You didn't need to, they're not dangerous," Jake said, remembering how much he had panicked.

"No, but they're dirty, we might have caught a disease."

"I don't think so," he said. This was turning into an interesting conversation.

"You're probably right," she said, looking embarrassed. "Tell me about yourself," she said. "I know of your father, but not you."

Why not? And so he did. He tried to make it as short as possible. She looked interested and, while he spoke, her eyes flitted between his eyes and mouth. She smiled at the right time, looked sad when she should and occasionally asked questions. By the time he had finished, they had gone through the queue, collected their food, the choice and quality of which was staggering, and were sitting back outside at a table. He took care in what he revealed though, conscious of the fact that this Russian beauty could be another interrogator.

"Your history explains a lot about you," she said, after he'd finished. "It has made you strong and serious. How old are you?"

"Well, I'm twenty-nine. What about you?"

"I'm twenty-one."

"Just twenty-one! Gosh, I would never have guessed." She seemed more mature. Twenty-five seemed more like it.

"You look surprised? Is this a problem?"

"No, not at all. It's just that you look younger than your years, but speak like someone older."

"That's good, isn't it? Don't men like women who look youthful and are at same time knowledgeable? I can speak four languages: Russian, Greek, English and French."

"Impressive, but I've told you my story. I'd like to hear yours."

"Mine is short and simple as I've done little, because of living a sheltered life," she said, before starting. But she spoke four times as long as he did. Had she not been so sweetly endearing, he would have fallen asleep. She started with her great-grandparents, placing great emphasis on how God-fearing and virtuous each one was, especially the women, as if expounding her pedigree. She spent the most time on her father though. How he had struggled and suffered to make the money so they could have a privileged life. And how, too, her parents had taught her and her sisters 'to love and respect their family'.

When she had finished, Jake did not quite know what to say, so he snatched at the first thing that came into his mind. "You're such an attractive woman, Natalya. Don't you have a boyfriend?"

"Another compliment? You must like me," she said, looking pleased with herself. "No, never. I've already explained this to you, my father would never allow it."

"So, you can't to go out with a man?"

"No, not without a chaperone. Only if a man intends to become my husband can we go alone. Otherwise I must have one of my sisters with me."

"How can you live with that? It's like being in prison."

"It's a choice, Jake," Natalya said seriously. "I'm not a prisoner, I could live my own life, if I wished. It just wouldn't be under my father's roof. Besides, to date I've not met anyone worth the effort."

"But you said you've been in this country for many years. You must've met some nice men?"

"I've gone to many parties like this, but have met few good men."

"I don't understand. There must be several here, just like me."

"No, not like you," she said with a smile. "Not the slightest bit like you."

"There's nothing special about me," Jake said, laughing. Flattery wasn't going to get him to lower his guard.

"I think you're special and a wonderful man. I could see that right away. I'm good at judging people. It's the others that are no good."

"How so?"

"I'll explain so that you can understand. They're born to rich parents. They have everything done for them. They don't have to think what to do next because they're told what to do. They don't have to fight for anything, work for something; they are weak."

"What a waste."

"It's not their fault. Their parents have made them this way. They're like the alcoholic, they are addicted to being supported and they don't believe they can live without that support. They don't believe they are capable of doing things for themselves. They're afraid to cut themselves loose and the parents are scared to let them go. They are not independent, so therefore they are not men."

"But what about the women, the daughters, they're the same too. You're all the same. You shouldn't criticize, Natalya, you belong with them." Jake saw that the comment prickled her; she looked hurt by it.

"What you say is true, and I'm not proud of it. I'm in the trap as well," she said, leaning forward and lowering her voice. "And there's more to it than you know." She was about to say more when Kephalas approached them.

"Natalya, my dear, I hope you're enjoying yourself?" he said.

"I am, thank you."

"I wonder if I may ask you a favour. Could I borrow Jake for a bit? I haven't had time to speak with him yet and it's getting late."

"Yes, of course. I will be with my family," she said looking at Jake. "Will you come to find me before you leave?"

"Maybe," Jake said, looking at his watch. It was already midnight. Although intrigued by the last thing Natalya had said, he was conscious that Emma was waiting for him. He watched her as she walked back into the room and disappeared into the crowd.

"Let's walk and talk," Kephalas said. Jake followed him to the end of the veranda, down some stone steps and into the grounds. These were crisscrossed with paths lit by ground level lights. There was the scent of flowers in the humid air. "I see you've been introduced to our Russian friends."

"Many have settled in London. I didn't know they'd come to Greece as well."

"I assume they go all over Europe. But they mainly come here because of business. They bring lots of money, probably earned by dubious means, and then look to us to legitimise it, by investing in shipping mostly."

"So what? They're looking for partners?" Jake asked. They were walking downhill and away from the house.

"That's right; don't forget, they have little tradition or experience in free enterprise."

"From what I've read, I imagine they'd be dangerous to deal with."

"Most of the people I know would never entertain such a relationship. But others are willing to take the risk in order to expand."

"And Natalya's father?"

"His approach is different. He seems to have his own money. Again, no one knows where from. My guess is that he made it through dealings with commodities in Russia. All perfectly legal, but maybe not ethical. I think he left before a potential backlash. But he doesn't just want to be associated with anybody, so he's constantly networking. He has three daughters, as beautiful as each other, and he's trying to get them advantageously married off."

"An unenviable task."

"I'm not saying they're not nice girls, but be careful or before you know it you might be engaged with a shotgun pointing at the back of your skull."

He could imagine worse fates than being married to Natalya. For the first time he saw Kephalas smile, although it was more of a smirk. They stopped walking when they came to a wall. They were overlooking the sea. Below Jake could see the white, foamy water as it washed onto the rocks. This must be his favourite place for dubious conversations.

"Once again, I'm sorry about the loss of your father. By now you must've realised he was a troubled man."

"Yes, indeed. Can you shed any light on it?"

"I wish I could," Kephalas replied, looking away from him. "The concern is that whatever it was will not spill over on to you."

"How can anyone know that?"

"They can't, but there are certain precautions one can take."

"Such as?"

"It's natural to want to discover the truth about your father, but I think that could lead you into the same danger he was in."

"To be honest, I've no idea what my father was involved in. It could've been one of these Russians for all I know." Jake wondered whether this wasn't the same sort of pressure his father was put under. The pressure that forced him to abandon his family. "I don't even know where to start looking."

"I believe you, Jake, but it's not me who wants to harm you or whom you have to convince."

"So what are these precautions I should be taking?"

"The community that we have on this island is far-reaching and works well together. It has power through mutual collaboration. If you want to be part of it then you must, well, cooperate. It's give and take. You give a little to us and we will give a lot back to you. That's how everyone got to where they are. On the other hand, if you don't intend to work with us, then I think you're at the greatest risk on this island and significantly so in Greece. There's a world out there. Just think what you could do and see with the money your father's left you. Best to sell up and cut all contact with this country."

"Sounds like a threat."

"It's not a threat," Kephalas said, turning to square up to him. "There is a threat, but I'm not the one behind it."

"Well, who then?" Jake demanded, trying to control his anger.

"I can't tell you that," Kephalas replied smugly.

"So that I don't get it wrong as well, what was the mistake my father made?" Jake said, studying Kephalas's face. He appeared pleased to have invoked anger in Jake, almost as if he welcomed a confrontation. Jake calmed himself.

"I don't know, but he seemed to sit on the fence. Not to make his intentions clear."

"You mean he managed to succeed without any help?"

"I told you, I don't know what your father was involved in," Kephalas said, turning back towards the sea.

"How can you not know anything? And if you're telling the truth, you who have been coming here all your life, who has all this wealth and influence, if you don't know anything, how can I?"

"I can understand your frustration. But you don't want to be influenced by those on the island who wish to upset the status quo."

"You've lost me now."

"There are those who want to destroy what we have here. They will put out false and sometimes ridiculous information to influence those gullible enough. Maybe that's what your father was experiencing, I don't know."

"Are you suggesting that my father's death wasn't natural?"

"I know nothing different from the official explanation. I wasn't referring to his death. Your father's life was messed up by something. He also upset certain people here on the island. Don't let that happen to you." Kephalas turned to walk away. "Enjoy the rest of your evening and remember, you have been warned," he added, not looking back.

Jake stayed there and stared down at the foaming rocks. He lost track of time meditating on what Kephalas had told him. The anger and frustration choked him. He felt movement beside him.

"Why didn't you come back to me?" It was Natalya.

"I'm sorry but I had things on my mind," he said. She looked so sweet it almost calmed his emotions.

"I know, I could see. I was watching from the balcony above," she said, looking behind her. "I couldn't hear any words, but could see you had a difficult discussion with Kephalas."

"I thought you were going to your family."

"I did at first. I had a short discussion with my father. I told him about you and he asked what you were like."

"Why did he do that?"

"Because I told him you're the nicest man I've met in my life."

"You're pulling my leg."

"I'm serious."

"Natalya, I like you, but we've only known each other a couple of hours."

"I know you don't think much of me," she said sadly. "Anyway, my father says we're going to the yacht soon."

"What, now?"

"He's decided that we're leaving in the morning."

"That's a shame, I enjoyed your company," Jake said and he meant it, in spite of his reservations.

"We'll be back on the nineteenth. It's an important week. I hope you'll be here too."

"I should be. Why, what's happening?"

"Lots of important events and parties," Natalya said, but she had that distracted look again. "You know, I like you very much. These feelings were unexpected." She looked out at the sea. "I could fall in love with you," she added, lowering her head, as if voicing a thought.

"You can't predict how you're going to feel about someone," Jake said, wondering if this charming girl wasn't a bit nuts after all. "Besides, I doubt we're suited," he added cynically.

"No, you don't think I'm right for you, I know. I'm telling you this because there's not much time, but sometimes a woman knows when she has met the right man."

"What? After one evening?"

"Yes, maybe after a few minutes."

"Tell me, I'm curious," Jake said, "do you have these weird conversations with everyone you meet?"

"No, just you." she said, looking at her watch. "I have to leave now; my father gave me ten minutes. Come with me."

He followed her. She took him a different way back to the house, one that went through an area that was not lit and obscured by trees. When they were in the dark she took his hands in hers.

"You know, much goes on here in secret," she said with a lowered voice. "I'm afraid for you, that's why I've revealed my feelings."

"What do you know about it?" Jake, said looking around him.

"Behind all this socialising and posturing, there's a struggle for power. There's much that is dark."

"But what do you know about it?" Jake asked, frustrated.

"I cannot say," she said mournfully, regret in her eyes

"Can't say or won't say," Jake said, trying to control his renewed anger. Was this girl genuine or just trying to get at him in a different way? "At least tell me who's involved? Who's behind it?"

She stared into his eyes. "I am one of them," she confessed.

"What? How? I don't understand," he said, pulling his hands away.

She hesitated and looked at her watch. "I must go, this is dangerous."

Before he could say anything, she put a hand on each of his cheeks and drew him towards her lips. The kiss was loving and gentle. All too soon she pulled away. "I wish things were different, simple and not complicated." She left him, without waiting for a reply.

He did not go back into the house, but went back to the cliff's edge. Maybe he had underestimated her or she was a bit crazy. The warning light, flashing across the water, mesmerised him. Soon other concerns crowded out thoughts of Natalya.

When he arrived back at the house, it was one o'clock and many of the guests had already left. He could not see Stephanos or any of his hosts, so he walked back out to the gate, where he asked a couple who were also leaving whether they would give him a lift in their car.

He asked to be dropped off outside the yacht club. The town was as busy as ever. As soon as he was alone, he took out his mobile and sent a text to Emma; then he sat on a nearby bench to wait for her.

Chapter 23: The Green Isles

Monday, 6th August

He was swimming below the waves, breathing without a snorkel. He was surprised he'd not realised he could do this before. The visibility was crystal clear and the colours were as vibrant as those on land. He was able to swim any distance and to any depth without effort.

The sea was teaming with life, full of shoals of colourful fish. Then, out of the shadows, the dolphins appeared. He knew they were the two he'd sighted the other day. He was surprised how dark they were, black even. They swam by, eyeing him suspiciously.

He forgot about them, at ease with their presence, and swam around the rocks and crevasses, looking for something he knew was important. He thought it might be some sort of treasure.

Suddenly he felt a shock wave in the water, coming from behind. He swivelled round to see two Great Whites within seconds of being upon him. In his mind he realised that the dolphins he'd seen earlier were really these sharks capable of disguising themselves to fool their prey.

He tried to swim away, moving into shallower water. Just when he thought he was safe, he realised that what at first had appeared to be rocks below him where actually stonefish, hundreds of them, all with poisonous spines. He tried to avoid being stung, but inevitably the spine of one brushed his chest and he became paralysed. As a consequence he started drifting back into deeper water. He struggled to move his limbs, but to no avail; it was too late. As the Great Whites were about to devour him, he woke.

He turned on the light and looked at his watch. It was four thirty. He saw and felt movement. It was Emma stirring, but not quite awake. He switched the light back off. He felt cold, but was not sweaty. He got up and realised something was different. He could hear the rustling of the tree. The wind had turned back to the north and the air was much fresher.

He went back to bed and fell into a deep sleep, the best since he'd arrived on the island. They both slept straight on through to ten; even the builders working nearby didn't wake them.

He had an idea for the day. It came to him while having breakfast and involved using the boat. He wanted to familiarize himself with it before Joanna came and this was an opportunity. He also needed to revisit Maria. The question of the flowers remained unanswered and, once Joanna arrived, he might not have another chance.

He walked Emma back to the *Bacchus*, which was due to leave at midday. They had agreed, in view of the previous night's events, that she should tell Kephalas that, after his stay on Halia, Jake had every intention of selling his father's business and going back to England. They expressed their wish to see each other again, but Jake knew it was unlikely to happen. It wouldn't be the same and he felt she knew it too. There were no regrets.

He reached the other end of the harbour and found the boat just as he'd left it. He got in and sat, watching the *Bacchus* as it left.

It took a dozen pulls to start the engine, but soon he had weighed anchor and was heading out through the breakwaters, following in the wake of the much larger boat. At the point, he turned right and went across the next bay to the headland. The wind was not too strong, even when he was heading down towards Perivoli.

When he reached the headland separating the small cove with Perivoli, where his father's house was, he turned away from the shore and headed for the Green Isles. As he approached, the wind waves became bigger and the current stronger. He saw that these so-called islands comprised two rocky outcrops with a cap of sparse vegetation. The one on the right was the largest and accommodated the warning beacon. It was crescent-shaped, with the ends pointing south. The smaller outcrop was circular and positioned just twenty yards away. The two together formed a circular, sheltered enclosure, especially now when the north wind blew. When he reached the little bay, he saw that the water was shallow, and the inside of the crescent had a narrow pebbly shore. He anchored the boat and drew it close to the beach before stepping out and tying up on an irregular boulder. This was an ideal, secluded spot. He doubted that anyone, apart from a passing boat, could see him.

He put on his mask, snorkel and fins and started exploring the surrounding sea. It had occurred to him that an obvious place to look for shipwrecks was around these reefs. After all, in the past there would not have been a light here. He was not expecting to make an earth-shattering find, but even something minor would be exciting.

He circumnavigated the smaller rock first and made a discovery. Immediately south of it was a trail of debris consisting of twisted metal. He followed this deeper and found the scattered parts of a small steel coastal ship, coated with a layer of weed. He could tell from the corrosion and thinning of its hull that it had lain there for a few decades at least. The excitement spurred him on to explore the north side of the larger island. Here there was an extensive area of underwater reef, surrounded by beds of weed.

He had swum quite a distance, crisscrossing these rocks and seeing nothing, when, as he was coming back from his furthest extent, he noticed a pattern. Up to now he was focussing on details, looking for something unusual. Once he had given up and was just looking at the whole scene, he spotted it. Parts of the reef were a different colour and texture. He swam to a point that was shallower and dived down for a closer look. The parts that looked different were mounds of debris. Debris consisting of shards of pottery.

From what he remembered of his history, goods used to be transported in the Mediterranean in wooden sailing ships. The liquid cargoes, like oil and wine, were carried in amphora. It was a ship such as this that must have come to grief here. The wooden hull would soon have rotted and dissolved leaving the broken containers. In time they would have become encrusted with underwater growth and fused together. He dived down a few more times, trying to pick up a piece, but it was not possible.

Still, with more detailed exploration he found the mouths and necks of jars, bases, and fragmented sides. All were identifiable even though fused to the rock.

The sea in this exposed part was noticeably colder than nearer the shore so he soon had to swim back. He found a flat rock that had been smoothed by the waves and, after spreading his towel, he lay on it to warm up.

He had acclimatised well to the sun. His skin had recovered during the last few days and he felt that he could cope with anything. He thought about tomorrow and meeting Joanna, he reflected on what Kephalas had said to him the night before and on his own search for the truth. He realised that, just as he'd seen a pattern while he was swimming back and forth over the reef, believing there was nothing there of interest, the same was happening on shore. The longer he stayed the more he learnt, the more he learnt the more likely he would see something, a correlation. He was damned if he was going to let Kephalas threaten him. Maybe that was his father's attitude too. He was puzzled by the two attacks on him though. Why would Kephalas try and get information out of him on the one hand, using first Teresa, then Emma, and maybe this Russian girl, and at the same time send thugs to threaten him? It did not add up. His thoughts dwelled on Natalya. Something about her had touched him. He acknowledged that this was an emotion he could not afford.

Who was Kephalas talking about when he said that it was not him he had to convince? Was it this Basil Protopapas? In how much danger was he? Surely Diana would not let him get himself killed if she wanted something from him? Maybe that was why she did not want him to venture out of town alone. So much for his promise not to do so. And who was the mystery woman on the beach with Emma? He looked back at the shore. The most distinguished landmark was where he was the night before, Kephalas's mansion.

It was then he realised that the wind had picked up. It was noticeably fresher and the occasional white horse was visible. It would be prudent to go back to the harbour straightaway. He quickly stowed his mask, snorkel, fins and towel under the bow, before unlashing the boat.

The engine started on the first pull but, as he began to cross the strait to the southern headland of Perivoli, the nearest landfall, the force of the wind picked up even more. The white horses increased in number and, as he was sailing across the weather, the waves, combined with the gusting wind, appeared to be trying to overturn him. He quickly moved and sat on the port side, using his weight to keep the boat from flipping over.

This helped for a time, but the wind continued to increase and the waves became steeper. It was then he realised that this turbulence was confined to a circular area only a few hundred yards wide. He appeared to be in the centre of it, so he continued heading for shore as best he could.

Was he above a shallow reef that was causing the sea to behave in this way? Were the waves and currents somehow being exaggerated by some kind of underwater feature?

He had little time to speculate as the waves continued to steepen, dangerously so. He began to panic. He turned the boat south, so that he could outrun them, but then they started coming at him from random directions. He twisted and turned, but it was only a matter of time before he would be engulfed or, at worst, overturned. The inflatable wouldn't sink, but he would lose the engine and all the contents.

He wished he had kept his mask, fins and snorkel near him as he had made little headway across the strait and subsequently faced the prospect of a long swim, assuming he could survive in such a sea. He experienced an overwhelming sense of despondency, of complete discouragement. What was the point of fighting?

Then, just as he thought his situation was futile, it stopped. The sea calmed itself and the wind returned to what it had been earlier. As he looked around, perplexed, he spotted a powerboat behind him, heading in his direction. It had come from behind the island and was closing fast. As it approached, he saw several people on board and one waved a greeting. He allowed them to overtake him, before falling in behind and following in their wake as the boat made its way into the harbour.

After he had moored the inflatable and gathered his things, he walked slowly back home. He was badly shaken and could not think of an explanation for what had happened.

That afternoon, after lunch and a siesta, he set out for the taverna. He'd noticed from his porch that there was an upper road that led to the north end of the island. Perhaps, if he could find it, he could walk to this point and come back along the coast and be at Seal Beach by the time it got dark. At least he would remain on dry land.

He left at six thirty and climbed up to the top of the town. From there he found the track heading north along what looked like the spine of the island, from which he could see the sea on both sides. The wind had either picked up or, from this height, had more unimpeded force. He walked through a landscape that was starker and more dramatic than that of his walk to the south. There was less terracing and fewer deserted buildings, which reflected the fact that farming would have been more difficult. On both sides there were deep, wild valleys.

As he continued towards the north eastern corner, the island narrowed and, on his left, was a deserted cove, semi-circular in shape, facing north and now in shadow. From the steepness of the terrain, it could only be accessible by boat and, judging by the briskness of the wind, one a lot more substantial than his inflatable.

The road, as he had hoped, turned to the left and descended to the coast, where it turned back towards the town. From here there was a rough track that continued northward and he could see that he was close to the end. The island kept on narrowing and he came to a point where the path ended. The sea was on both sides and even behind him and, in the distance, he could see Paleo Limani. Ahead, though, the land was dissected by deep ravines which ran parallel from one shore to the other. The geological action that would cause this must have been extreme. He had never seen anything like it.

The sun was now close to setting. In the distance, to the southwest, the mountains of the nearest island, Lichas, were low dark silhouettes. He watched as the sun first touched the horizon and then disappeared beneath it. Darkness began to fall.

He walked back to the main track. As he reached it and continued along, he could see where he was in relation to the coast. He was now descending to a small cove. After that there was a much larger bay, longer than Perivoli, at the far headland of which he could see the north side of Kephalas's house, probably the closest habitation.

Once on the coast, the road was level and snaked its way through a dark, wooded glade. It must have been fertile here once because on the landward side was the most concentrated terracing he had seen so far, with many derelict buildings. It was also greener than anywhere else. Through the trees on the right he caught occasional glimpses of a sandy fringe and the sea, and through one break he saw the beached and bleached skeletal remains of an old wooden boat.

He was puzzled, though, as to why a mist should be forming on the water with such a brisk breeze. In fact it seemed to be noticeably denser every time he came to a gap in the trees. Something was not right. He felt a sense of urgency and walked faster. Surely there could not be much farther to go and he was walking as quickly as he dared without stumbling in the dark and falling on his face. Yet the fog was thickening and the next time he looked it had obscured the sea, sky and coastal strip and was beginning to invade the tunnel of trees.

Looking forward and back he could see wisps of it filtering through the gaps; it was then he realised it was glowing. Panic was invading his senses and reasoning. He knew he had to flee, while at the same time he felt his will weakening from within. Going forward or back was hopeless. The only way was through the fields and back up the slope of the mountain. Crossing to the other side of the road and looking between the trees, with the little light still available he saw that the bush was nearly waist high and far too thick to move through with sufficient speed.

Just when despair was about to overcome him, he saw something. He moved along to where a stone wall met the road and ran straight up the mountain. Before mounting it, he quickly looked about him. The glowing mist had blocked both ends of the tunnel of trees and covered the road. In the direction from which he had come, a dark formless shape, within the glowing cloud, was approaching. For an instant he felt compelled to stop and allow it to overtake. Instead he looked forward and climbed the wall.

With care and only the occasional stumble, he made good progress. Looking back, he saw that the fog or mist, or whatever it was, did not follow. It illuminated the trees from within, forward and back along their full length. He climbed and looked back, climbed and looked back and, at some point, the glow began to fade, and by the time he was half way up the slope, it had been blown away altogether.

He felt temporarily safe and eventually found a wall that followed a contour in the direction he wanted to go. When he had bypassed the grove of trees and was walking parallel to the open road, he descended down another wall. At this point the road was a good distance from the coast. It seemed that these phenomena needed the proximity of water, although that did not explain the appearance of the fog at the house. Or was that a dream? He had no time to evaluate events now. He had to remain on his guard and fully alert. Other dangers could emerge at any time, from anywhere, as was the case this morning.

By the time he was abreast of Kephalas's house, it was already lit up. Just before the road to the right that led to it, and in the middle of the field on the left, was the taverna owned by the fisherman and his family. This time there were lights on outside the building as well as within, and he could hear voices and Greek music filtering down to the road.

He walked up the drive and, by the time he'd reached the seated area, Maria had come out to greet him, warmly embracing and kissing him. He sat at a table and minutes later she brought out two fruit juices and sat opposite him.

He started by telling her what he had done since he last saw her. She wanted to know about everywhere he had been and everyone he had seen, so he told her about Stephanos, Savvas, Natalya, Nicos and Kephalas. He felt he could trust her, but nonetheless he left out the details of the two attacks on him and the incident on the coastal road; at least for now.

"I thought so," she said. "You see, I was right. This is what they did with your father. Jake, you must get away. Take Kephalas's advice. Your father would want you to."

"He may have wanted me to, but it's not what he would've done."

"His circumstances may not have been the same. Putting yourself in danger for nothing is pointless."

"There's a reason for this, so it can't be pointless. I just don't know it yet. But there's something we didn't finish talking about."

"I don't remember."

"I asked you about the flowers on my father's grave."

"Ah yes, well, I put them there."

"Okay, so they come from your garden?"

"They're sent to me from Lichas."

"Yes, but why don't you use your own?" Jake asked. He looked over at the bed of blooms in front of the taverna. He could sense Maria was hiding something.

"Because they're not the right type."

"Maria, you're not telling me something. What is it?"

"Your father always told me I was a terrible liar," she said, reaching across the table and putting her hand on his. "I'm supposed to keep it a secret. Someone sends them."

"Who?"

"I'll tell you the story." Maria settled herself. "It was at your father's burial; at the cemetery. Photis approached me. You know who I mean?"

"Of course I know him, though we met for the first time at the funeral on Lichas."

"He took me to one side and told me that he would be sending flowers for the grave every day for the forty days."

"The forty days of mourning?"

"Exactly."

"And he told you not to tell anyone?"

"Yes."

"But why? Everyone knew Photis was fond of my father. Why the secrecy?"

"I don't know. But I told him that if no one else supplied flowers and looked after the grave, I would do it myself, but he insisted that there should be no others. He arranged there and then that I should have the key to the tomb from Panagos."

"So he must have the flowers delivered to the ferry every day before it leaves Lichas. I certainly didn't see him when I came. Does he have a place there?"

"No, his home's in Piraeus. He's always lived aboard your father's boat the rest of the time."

"Do you know how to contact him?"

"No, he's got my numbers but, since the funeral, I've not spoken to him. Every day one of us goes to the ferry to pick up our supplies and the flowers. We bring them back and I prepare them. I don't have time to go to the cemetery in the afternoon or evening so I go each morning."

"I see," Jake said, having in mind his father's nocturnal visits to the old town. Maybe Photis was staying in the same place.

"Photis even offered to pay me for doing it, but I refused."

"When the flowers come are they wrapped in anything that could indicate the name of the florist?"

"Oh, they don't come from a florist. They're from a garden; they're freshly picked; I can tell. They're always wrapped in nice tissue paper."

"It doesn't sound like something Photis would do himself. So maybe there's someone else involved. The one who doesn't want to be known. Who would Photis know in Lichas who has a garden?"

"I didn't think he knew anyone. The only people he was acquainted with were here; the people you saw the other night."

"Damn, it's too late," Jake muttered to himself.

"Too late for what?"

"If it's forty days, it means the last delivery will be on Thursday."

"Yes, and there will be a memorial service the following day at the cemetery. So?"

"What I mean is that there can't be many people delivering flowers from a garden and wrapped in expensive paper. Wouldn't most flowers come from florists?"

"Exactly, what are you thinking?"

"If I watched the ferry I could possibly spot the delivery and follow Photis, or whoever, back to where they came from."

"It's only Monday, you could go tomorrow."

"That's the problem, I can't. I'm expecting someone."

"May I ask who?"

"Joanna, Diana's granddaughter."

"Her granddaughter?" Maria said, looking concerned. "You will be careful?"

"Don't worry, I will, I've had too many people con me to fall for it again. What do you know about her?"

"Just that her parents were killed in a car accident when she was little. Diana raised her. She brought her here every summer until her teens. I saw her a few times, very pretty and bright, but also precocious and spoilt. Diana, to her credit, was strict, but I don't know whether it had the right effect. She hasn't been recently."

"What about this memorial service? Who's organising it?"

"Your aunt and uncle."

"But they're not here."

"They're coming tomorrow and staying until the sixteenth."

"At the house?"

"I've heard they're staying at the hotel. They wouldn't be bothering to open it up just for a few days." A car came up the drive. The first customer had arrived. She had a quick look at her watch. "I must get back to my kitchen."

"I understand."

"Are you staying to eat?"

"Of course," he said, "but I would also appreciate it if one of your customers could give me a lift back afterwards."

"I'll bring a menu. You will come and see me again?"

"Certainly."

He took his time ordering and eating, feeling safe here. At the end of the evening, Maria found someone to drive him back

"Please be careful, Jake. I'll be praying for you," she said, kissing him on the cheek.

He was dropped off outside the cinema. He felt secure with people around so he spent time wandering amongst them. Outside the yacht club, he looked towards the pier and saw two gaps where Natalya's and Nicos's yachts had been. At this point anyone's company would do.

In the end he plucked up the courage and walked home, wary of every derelict house, dark alley and secluded doorway. Recalling what Diana had told him about not leaving the town alone, he assumed that he must be somehow protected within its bounds. As he had reasoned earlier, perhaps the presence he had experienced the other night was a dream induced from without and only capable of scaring him but not able to do him any physical harm, unlike today's encounters.

He remembered the dream he'd had at home in England at the time his father died. He had no doubt that this was what his father had experienced and succumbed to.

Chapter 24: Joanna

Tuesday, 7th August

There was a point on the road, before it split in two, from which it was possible to see over the headland that protected the harbour and out to sea, and thereby watch the approach of the ferry. It was at this spot that Jake sat, under a tree, on the stone wall that separated the road from the cliff edge. As he waited, he watched tiny lizards in the undergrowth scampering from the shelter of one stone to that of another.

He was nervous about this meeting. He did not know why, but he had felt the tension building since the morning. In addition to that, he had slept badly. It had taken a considerable amount of effort to enter his house, let alone get undressed and go to bed. He was alert to every noise, every creak. He'd even considered moving to the hotel, but then he'd thought that for these things to be happening it meant he must be getting close, close to the truth. The choice was clear; either he gave in, packed up and left, or he stood his ground and accepted the worst, should it occur. In a strange way, by facing what his father had had to face, he felt closer to him, was able to accept him, was able to love him. Once he had made that decision, he'd relaxed sufficiently to sleep for a few hours.

Apart from a bowl of cereal, he had not eaten. He was not particularly hungry, but also did not know what to expect. Would Joanna have already eaten or would he have to provide her with lunch?

For a while, as the ferry approached, it disappeared behind the cliff. It reappeared as it rounded the point and started heading towards the harbour entrance.

When it had passed between the breakwaters and slowed, he got up and started to walk down.

The quayside, as usual, was full of cars, pick-ups, scooters, motorcycles and people. This was the start of the peak time. The next two weeks would be the busiest.

As the ferry reversed towards its mooring, he scanned those who were standing on deck, but saw no one who stood out. When it was secured and the ramp lowered, there was the usual fifteen minutes of chaos when the passengers and cars were trying to come off while fighting the tide of people going on to retrieve their shopping. To make matters worse, those passengers disembarking and meeting friends or relatives would stall just in front of the ramp and delay others from leaving. He spotted the fisherman and his daughter sitting in the cab of their white pick-up as they waited for the jam to clear.

Jake went and sat on the wall enclosing the flowerbed. Once the cars had come off and freed the car deck, there was an orderly two-way flow. Amongst the first wave of disembarking passengers he saw his aunt and uncle. Unsurprisingly they looked nothing like his father. They were both short and rather fat with grey hair. His uncle had a moustache, and both wore black as a sign of mourning. He thought of getting up and greeting them, but Panagos quickly came forward, took their luggage and led them to his pick-up, presumably to take them up to the hotel.

When Joanna stepped off the ferry, he knew it was her. Quite simply, she was the most striking woman he had ever seen. Her hair was the richest gold and flowed in wavy locks that were tied and bunched back with clips and combs. She wore blue denim shorts that reached down to her knees, a pair of denim pumps and a white blouse. Her skin was a golden olive colour, her eyes a piercing blue, like Diana's. Her curvaceous limbs and figure were perfectly proportioned and exuded both a robust athleticism and a soft femininity. Many heads turned and the boisterous chatter of the throng lulled for several seconds.

She stood in the sunlight, at the foot of the ramp, expectant, looking from side to side, waiting for someone to approach her. Jake rose and weaved his way through the crowd towards her. When she saw him she gave an enticing smile and her eyes widened in recognition. Her brows and lashes were a slightly lighter gold than her hair. Her face had a faint covering of freckles that reminded Jake of his mother's rice pudding, which she would dust with cinnamon powder.

She spoke first with an inquisitive "Jake?"

"Joanna?" he replied, putting out his hand. She took it briefly in a warm but limp grip. He felt awkward and did not know what to say; he was overwhelmed. "How was your journey?" he asked.

"It was okay," she said with a forced smile.

"Shall we go?"

"Actually, I didn't come with just a rucksack. I have a couple of suitcases. I just couldn't bring anything out with all these people."

"Of course, I wasn't thinking," he said, feeling pretty stupid. Had his brain stopped? "Are they easy to identify?"

"They're upright on wheels, all green canvas with leather trim. They have green ribbons tied to the handles."

"I'll get them, wait here." She didn't offer to help, but he was glad to get away from her. He needed to catch his breath; she was making him feel awkward. What was the matter with him? He found the suitcases easily and, as they were quite compact, he was able to bring both out in one trip. She had not moved from where he had left her. "Shall we go?"

"Where's the hotel?" she asked.

"Half way up the hill," he said, realising he should have arranged for transport. It would take them ages to wheel these up. He looked around him. Panagos had already left. Then he saw Savvas with his pick-up. He had backed on to the ramp and was loading up supplies for the supermarket. "One minute," he said to Joanna, and went over to Savvas and asked him if he could take the suitcases up. Of course he could, he said. It was more or less on his way. Going back to Joanna, he took the suitcases and left them in Savvas's care. "He'll drop them off on his way to the supermarket. Do you want me to carry the rucksack?"

"No, I'm perfectly capable," she said, sounding irritated.

What a start. They began walking and he felt it was probably better not to say anything, but then the silence itself felt awkward. Looking at her, he could see tiny beads of sweat, like pearls of nectar, forming on her forehead, and her cheeks had a pink blush.

"Down that end of the island is Paleo Limani," he said when they reached the top of the hill from where he'd watched the ferry arrive.

"I have been here before," she pointed out, putting an end to further conversation.

Taking the inland fork, they walked through the town, where it was cool in the shadows. They turned left back down the hill and there was the hotel. Immediately inside the entrance was the reception desk.

They rang the bell and sat to wait for attention. A fat, old man arrived, probably having just seen his aunt and uncle to their room. Joanna spoke fluent Greek so she handled all the arrangements and collected her key.

"So, we just have to wait for the suitcases," she said.

"They shouldn't be long," he replied. "Have you eaten?"

"Not since breakfast. Lichas town doesn't have anywhere decent. Besides, my flight was late."

"I haven't had lunch either. Are you hungry? Would you like to eat something?"

"The hotel doesn't do food. Is there somewhere I can go?"

"There are tavernas, and two will be open now, but I can make us something at home."

"I don't want to trouble you."

"You won't. I need to eat too." They heard Savvas's pick-up pull up and went out to retrieve the suitcases. Jake helped her take them into the reception.

"Give me a few minutes," she said picking them up and mounting the stairs.

He went and sat out on the terrace. It was shaded by the balcony above and caught the breeze. It allowed him to cool off. He tried to understand what it was about Joanna that was making him go to pieces. He had the nerves of a teenager who was going on his first date with some impossibly attractive woman. He had to put things in perspective; this was Diana's granddaughter. So far he was behaving like a fool. On the other hand, why was she so prickly?

She came back down and they walked across the village to his place. They said nothing. Once there, he sat her outside on the patio with a fruit juice while he prepared a salad. He took everything out and they started eating.

"How long will you be staying?" he asked.

"I don't know. I was meant to be going to France, but Gran insisted this was important."

"You were going for a holiday?"

"Sort of. I was going to meet my boyfriend's parents."

"I see." That would explain her mood. "How long have you known each other?"

"Eighteen months; since I started my job in Brussels."

"What do you do there?"

"I'm an interpreter for the European Commission."

"What languages do you speak?"

"French, German, Italian, Greek and English."

"Wow. That's impressive."

"Not that impressive really. I learnt English and Greek as I grew up anyway. Do you speak any languages?"

"Just English and some Greek."

"What do you do for a living?"

"Well, I used to be a geography teacher. But that looks like it's going to change."

"After languages, geography was my favourite subject."

"Anyway, you must be disappointed you're not going to meet your boyfriend's parents."

"I'm not actually. I don't know what they're like, but I do wish I was with my boyfriend."

"I understand."

"Do you? Gran tells me you once lived with someone and are now separated."

"I am, but that was a while ago."

"Look, thanks for the salad, but I'm going back to the hotel for a nap. I'm tired."

"I wouldn't mind one myself." He walked her to the door.

"Where's the boat?"

"It's down by the ferry, in the first harbour with all the fishing boats. It has '*Pelagos*' on the prow."

"I know what my Gran's boat is called," she said impatiently. "What time shall we meet tomorrow?"

"I don't know, whenever you like. Actually, I think ten thirty would be a good time."

"I'll see you then. Oh, and don't forget your wetsuit and speargun."

"What's the speargun for?"

"To make it look like we're spearfishing. Isn't it obvious?" She looked at him incredulously.

"Wait. What about tonight? Don't you want to meet for a meal?"

"No, I can look after myself. No offence, but let's just keep things to the basics. I owe Gran everything. I'm here as a favour to her. Let's keep any other contact to a minimum. Is that okay?"

"No problem. See you tomorrow." He shut the door on her. Her last comment stung him. What did he expect anyway? A woman with her looks would have men salivating over her. No wonder she sees everyone as coming on to her.

He went to the freezer and took out a pork chop to have later that evening, and then went to lie down.

Wednesday, 8th August:

He was the first at the boat. When Joanna arrived, she dropped her rucksack and the speargun holder into the prow before gracefully stepping in. She was wearing navy shorts and a tee-shirt and had her hair tied back.

"How are you this morning?" he asked.

"I'm fine," she replied mechanically.

"Did you sleep okay?"

"Not bad for the first night in a strange bed. It's an awful hotel." She untied the boat while he pulled it out along the chain from the stern. When he had stowed the anchor on board, he lowered the engine and started it on the third pull.

"Did you get a meal?" he asked, as he navigated his way out of the basin and into the main harbour.

"I went to the taverna in the square. I've seen better places. Is that the only one?"

"No, there are two others in the town and one outside. Two of the others are much better, in my opinion, but I've not tried the fourth. What about breakfast?"

"The hotel provided that, but it looked so awful I ended up going to the shop and getting fruit and yogurt. What do people do around here? This place is the pits."

"They obviously don't come for the nightlife. They come to see people they know and enjoy nature."

"How boring."

In spite of her looks, he was beginning to not like this girl. He found himself feeling defensive about the island. "I took the liberty of packing lunch. I assume we'll be out most of the day."

"That's the idea," she said, avoiding looking at him. "I called Gran last night. She sends her regards."

"Thanks. So where do we go?" he asked when they had left the harbour entrance.

"Just head for Paleo Limani. I'll tell you more when we get there."

He powered up as she sat on the prow to keep the front of the boat down. They were soon aquaplaning. Within minutes they had reached the south western entrance and Jake slowed.

"Go in and stop in the middle," she said.

When he got there, he powered down to idle. Joanna stood up and surveyed the scene. To the northeast was the other entrance and, clockwise from that, the other four islands, with the biggest, Panagia, first. There were irregular gaps and narrows between them. "According to my grandmother, what we're looking for could be anywhere along the seaward side of these islands, starting from one entrance right round to the other."

"That's a large area. Why those places specifically?"

"Along these coasts, the depth is relatively sheer from the shore line. Those within the bay are shallow and couldn't contain the feature we're looking for. If we don't find it there, we may have to start along the north coast of the main island, the first five hundred metres or so. The south coast is also too shallow."

"Okay, what sort of depth are we talking about?"

"Between five and ten metres."

"Great, look, I know I may be inexperienced, but diving down to five metres would be a struggle at the best of times. I certainly wouldn't then be able to spend time exploring at that depth."

"The best I can do is ten and I can hold my breath for two and a half minutes."

"That's impressive. How do you manage to get that deep, even with fins?"

"Lots of practice."

"So what sort of structure is this?"

"An entrance."

"What? A cave?"

"No; a sealed entrance."

"Like a door?"

"Sort of. It'll be of stone and probably circular."

"How long has it been there?"

"A long time," she replied vaguely.

"So, whatever it is, it will be covered in marine growth. Given that we're just snorkelling, even with your superior skills, it will take a miracle to spot it."

"I agree, except we're looking for more than just an entrance. This was once hidden under a scree of boulders or debris, which in the beginning would have looked artificial until it too was covered in marine life. But now that has been dislodged by an earthquake, so what we're looking for is a rockslide. If we can find that, we'll find the entrance."

"Your Gran's already told me some of this," Jake said. "I don't suppose it matters where we begin. Let's start from the most likely place." He pointed over to the island by the entrance they'd just come through. It was the nearest point to where the ancient shipwreck had been found.

"Whatever," she said indifferently.

He powered up and made his way southwest. As he approached, he noticed the seaward side of the island had a small cove. "Perhaps there's a beach to land the boat on," he said. Leaving the boat with enough momentum, he switched off the engine and raised it. At the last moment before running aground, he stepped out into thigh deep water and walked the boat the rest of the way. Joanna also jumped out and they ran the inflatable aground. "Should be able to get some idea how much ground we can cover each day," Jake commented.

"The more the better, as far as I'm concerned," Joanna said, putting her wetsuit top on and taking her speargun out of the holder. "Then I can get back to my other plans."

Her insolence was getting on his nerves. "So, what's the best way to do this? You're better in the water, but I'm more qualified to recognise underwater features."

"That should be true, depending on how competent you are, although I'm sure I can tell a rock slide when I see one. Since we've grounded the boat, we can each take an end of the island to explore for now. At other times we might just take turns. Whichever's the most efficient."

"One more thing," he said, as he slipped on his wetsuit jacket.

"What?"

"Where's your grandmother at the moment?"

"Piraeus, I think."

"We could do with a hydrological map of the area. The British Admiralty does them. She can find them in any yacht chandlers."

"I'll call her tonight. I'll take the right-hand side, you the left. Take your time and be thorough. Go right into the bay. I'll meet you back on the beach."

A few minutes later he was in the water, holding the uncocked speargun in one hand. He had no intention of shooting anything anyway. He swam in a zigzag pattern along the coast, first going deeper, as far as he could see the bottom, and then coming back in. He was glad to get away from her and was trying to understand why she was so rude and disrespectful. As he swam, he realised that the search could take even longer than expected, especially if the hydrological map showed offshore reefs. Judging by how much progress he was making, it could take days. He wondered whether he could stand Joanna's company for another hour.

His part of the search lasted for an hour and forty-five minutes, and by the time he returned to the beach, he was frozen and exhausted, in spite of the thermal protection. Joanna was already back, lying on her towel. She was dry.

"Good, you're back," she said. "Let's move on."

"Wait a minute."

"Why? Is there something wrong?"

"Yeah, I'll say. I've been swimming for nearly two hours and I'm frozen."

"You should've got a full-length wetsuit."

"Well, nobody told me."

"Do you have to be told everything?"

"What's the problem?"

"The problem is that I want to get this project over with as soon as possible, so I can get on with my life."

"But this is something your grandmother's been waiting for all of her life, from what I understand."

"That's right, that's why I'm here. But I believe that there's also something in it for you."

"There is, but I'm trying to understand your attitude."

"Look, it's just that we don't get on. You're upset because you're not going to get what you want from me. Don't get fixated about it."

"Fixated?" That was the last straw. He threw his stuff in the boat and started dragging it into the sea.

"What are you doing?" she asked.

"Don't worry, I've got the perfect solution to the problem. Just get in." He started the engine and powered up.

"Why are you heading back into the town?"

"You'll see," he said as he got up to aquaplaning speed. Joanna sat on the prow. They were travelling into the wind and the waves were causing the boat to rise and slap the sea. He entered the harbour and cruised straight to the berth. He dropped anchor and brought the boat alongside. There he threw his things on to the quay and climbed out. "There," he said. "If you need more fuel, I've got the other can."

"Where do you think you're going?" she said standing up in the boat, hands on her hips.

"Home probably, although I might go to the yacht club for a beer first."

"But we have work to do. This is no time for a tantrum."

"Fine, you go and do what you have to do and I'll go and do what I want to do."

"You're letting my grandmother down."

"No, you're letting her down. I've no responsibility for finding whatever it is she's searching for. I'm responsible for what I'm looking for."

"I've come to help you. Let's talk about this."

"I don't need or want your help; I'm going now." He walked off, ignoring her continuing pleas.

Maria was right about her. She was still a spoilt brat. Despite his anger, he could see the opportunity this argument presented. As he walked along the harbour front, he noticed that the two sea taxis that ferried the worshippers to the church last Sunday morning were moored to the pier. On the inside of the windows of each wheelhouse were the names of the owners and their contact details. As he walked by, he took his mobile from his rucksack. After Panagos's comments on the day of his arrival regarding mobiles, he had established that the only reception available was along certain parts of the south eastern coast. The upper town, where the house was, had none. He dialled the first number on his mobile and asked the man who answered how much it would cost to take him to Lichas. It was one hundred euros. He agreed to be ready to depart at two; in an hour.

He hurried back home and started throwing a few items into his rucksack. It was important to track Photis down and he had to leave immediately. He could guess what would happen. Joanna would call her grandmother. Diana would insist they patch things up and get on with the agenda. Whatever Diana and the others wanted from him was more important than spoilt little Joanna, so why send her?

He had little time and did not want to be distracted so he switched off his mobile and left. The boatman was already there and they set off as soon as Jake was on board.

Chapter 25: The Old Town

The trip took one and a half hours, and when they arrived at Lichas harbour, he paid the boatman and disembarked. Regrettably he could not stay at the Meltemi as Doros knew Diana and she might try to contact him. Or, for all he knew, Joanna could be lying and Diana could be staying there.

He had an idea. When he was last here and doing the shopping, he'd come across a bed and breakfast above a café. It was in the first street behind the harbour front and in close proximity to the ferry. It also looked recently renovated.

He walked a short distance along before turning right into a pedestrianised, triangular space with a flowerbed enclosed by metal railings. There, in the apex of the triangle was the place he had seen. There were tables and chairs outside and within was a bar area.

A waiter came out carrying *frappés* for a couple seated at one of the tables and Jake asked him whether there were any rooms available. The waiter told him to wait and went back inside. Minutes later a slim, middle-aged woman with dyed-blonde hair came out.

"Can I help you?" she asked.

"Have you any rooms?"

"How many?"

"Just the one, for tonight."

"I don't have a single till tomorrow night, but I do have a vacant double."

"How much?"

"It's just been renovated and has a new en suite shower and air-conditioning," she said, whilst appearing to be assessing him. "I have a restaurant as well, so for sixty euros you can have breakfast included."

"Sounds good. Can I see it?"

He followed her inside as she fetched a key from behind the bar. The room was perfect. It was on the second floor; clean and tidy.

"This will be fine," he said. "Do you have any food?"

"I have some moussaka."

"Great."

"I'd like to close at five."

"I'll be right down."

Wednesday, 6th August

Next morning at ten he was sitting by the quayside café watching the ferry dock. He had checked out of the bed and breakfast and informed the owner that he might be back that night. He hoped that would not be necessary, but realised that anyone delivering flowers might do so as late as possible in order to prevent them from wilting.

He had slept better than expected. After the late lunch, he'd gone to the shops and bought himself an underwater torch, a navy baseball cap and sunglasses. He'd then read until it was suppertime. He'd eaten at the restaurant downstairs and found the food adequate. After that he'd walked up and down the quayside so many times he'd lost count. The bars and restaurants were overflowing but he was not tempted by any of them. He was too wrapped up in his thoughts, trying to make head or tail of all that had happened so far.

He had walked until his feet ached and the fatigue of the last few days overcame him. He had gone back to the room, shut the windows, turned on the air-conditioning and gone to bed.

Now here he was with a potential wait of up to two hours. He sat just within the open-fronted café, wearing the sunglasses and cap. Even if it was Photis who brought the flowers, he would have to be unlucky to be recognised. If someone else delivered, it would be the flowers and their distinctive wrapping Jake would be looking for.

Then, just after eleven, he saw a familiar-looking man approach the ferry from the entrance of the old town. He noticed him early because he was dressed in black and carrying a bouquet of flowers wrapped in off-white tissue paper. There was a nametag hanging from it. He had to assume this was it.

He watched as the man boarded, and confirmed that it was Photis. The crew acknowledged him and a few minutes later he came back out and headed back to the entrance of the old town. Jake, rucksack on his back, followed.

As soon as he had passed the arched entrance, he entered a different world. The road surface turned to cobbles and started going uphill. There were turnings to the right and left, but his subject went straight ahead. They walked through interlocking squares with restaurants, through archways and along narrow streets. They passed shops on both sides, mostly boutiques, small cafés, tavernas and patisseries. Jake worried that Photis would go into one of these or have reason to look back. Worse still, he could stop off and have a coffee somewhere. As they continued to ascend, the shops turned to residential houses. This was a rabbit's warren of lanes.

Before reaching the crown of the hill, he turned down a street which was too narrow for cars and which headed back towards the sea and curved slightly round to the left. This lane had stone walls on both sides, with entrances at intervals. The few that were open revealed houses set in gardens. Every now and again there was another alley. There were fewer people walking here and it would have been difficult to avoid notice if Photis looked behind him.

Finally his quarry turned down a narrow alleyway to the left and Jake reached it just in time to see a doorway at the end closing. There was neither a number nor a name.

On his way back to the harbour, Jake wrote down in his notebook directions and the names of all the streets and squares to enable him to find the door again. He arrived just in time to board the ferry back to Halia.

When he arrived home, it had gone three. On his way he had stopped at the taverna and had a plateful of fried squid with chips. He thought of having a siesta but chose to read instead, so he sat out in the shade of the patio.

He had barely started when he heard a knock on the door. He did not move. Half a minute later he heard it again. Still he did not react. A few minutes after that he became aware of someone standing on the other side of the gate to the patio. "I'm not going to change my mind," he said, not looking up from his book.

"I just want to talk; to explain." Joanna's voice was gentle, sweet and pleading. "Where have you been anyway? I've been looking everywhere. Don't you answer your mobile?"

"I'm not going to change my mind, so I don't want you to waste your time, knowing how precious it is." He hadn't switched on his mobile since before leaving Halia yesterday afternoon.

"I still want to talk, please let me in." She seemed determined to have her say, and probably would not go away easily.

"All right, come to the front door. I don't have the key to the gate." He went to let her in, taking his time.

"It's nice and cool in here," she said, once she had entered and he had shut the door.

"I know, it's like a cave. Come on through to the patio."

"I think I'd prefer to sit here. I won't stay long."

He indicated one of the armchairs either side of the coffee table. She sat on the one on the left. "Can I get you something? Have you eaten?"

"No, I've only been back to the hotel briefly. I'm not hungry, but wouldn't mind a drink."

"What would you like?" Jake asked. He wanted this to be as brief as possible.

"Have you got any juice?"

"I have."

I'll have that and a glass of water," she said, taking off her sandals. Her feet were perfect, with the toenails painted pink. "This floor's lovely and cool," she said. "You don't mind, do you? I've been walking all over looking for you. Where have you been?"

He did not reply. There was something in her voice, which indicated she had already got her way. He would show her otherwise. He went to the kitchen and took out a tray, put four glasses on it, filled two with fruit juice from the fridge, and the others with bottled water. He brought it back and put it on the table. Joanna had most of the juice and the glass of water before she spoke.

"I'm not going to excuse my behaviour, just try to explain it." Her attitude had completely changed. Whereas before she did not look at him and spoke dismissively, now she stared into his eyes and engaged him. She was flirting. "Well, it's sort of a misunderstanding really," she said, looking embarrassed.

"What misunderstanding?" Jake said. He caught himself staring at her bare feet and legs. He forced himself to look at her face.

"Before I came, Gran told me about you, your father, your mother, your ex-partner. Things like that."

"Okay."

"And then she said that we're actually related."

"Related? How?"

"Well, quite, it's a bit silly really. You see, I called her yesterday, told her about the Admiralty map. I didn't mention anything about our little misunderstanding, by the way. I asked her what she meant about being related. She said she was sorry that she gave me the wrong impression. What she meant was that we probably came from the same family tree, one that went back many generations."

"How can she know that?" Jake said. What a pathetic excuse and besides, if she didn't tell Diana about their bust up, how did she get his mobile number? Diana didn't have it either. They must have got it from Doros."

"She does seem to know certain things."

"I know what you mean, but say we were related. What does that have to do with your attitude?"

"Well, from the moment we met, I felt that your thoughts and intentions towards me were inappropriate," she said, tipping her head and smiling.

"Why? Are you a mind reader? You thought I was coming on to you? And, because you thought I was your cousin or something, you treated me like a pervert?" Jake was being defensive, but he knew it was true. How could anyone not be interested in someone so attractive, so appealing?

"No, not at all," she said, looking dismayed and hurt. "There's more to it than that." She looked down at her lap.

"Well, what?" he asked, impatiently. She said nothing, but looked at him with a knowing smile. He looked at her beautiful face; her perfect locks. Her blue eyes were large and moist and seemed to grow larger as he stared; he could see the pupils dilating. Suddenly he felt drawn to her in a way he could not resist. He felt an intense, insane desire to be closer to her. Nothing else in his life mattered, past, present or future. All his other intentions evaporated.

"You're too far away from me," she said, as if reading his thoughts. "Come closer."

He got up and knelt down in front of her. Her hands were on her bare legs and he took her right one in his left. She squeezed it firmly. He took it to his lips and kissed the palm. It was slightly salty. She sat up and slid forward until she was sitting at the edge of the chair. They embraced and she gripped him with her thighs.

"Have you been swimming? I can taste the salt on you," he said.

"I've been to all the beaches I could walk to, looking for you," she said. Her eyes bore into him and he felt complete abandon. "I was so upset that I'd let Gran down, but even more unhappy at the thought that I'd pushed you away from me."

She embraced him and pulled his lips to hers. For a while they just kissed. Everything around Jake went misty. He lost all track of time and place. All his attention was on her. He kissed her face, her neck and her ears and then she did the same to him, all the time giggling with delight. Then she gently took his head in her hands and said, "Do you want to make love?"

"Yes, very much," he said, feeling an indescribable thrill and excitement.

"Me too," she said kissing him on the lips again. "Let's just concentrate on enjoying each other." She started to take off her top. Underneath she wore her bikini. She turned round for him to undo it. Her breasts were faultless. She was kissing him at the same time as taking his top off.

"What about your boyfriend?" Jake said, vaguely remembering some mention of someone else.

"I can't answer that. All I know is that from the moment I set eyes on you, I've wanted you." She stood up, undid her shorts and let them drop to the floor. She was only in her briefs now. "I've never felt such intense desire and feelings."

He knew what she meant. He felt it too. He knew he could not resist her. Why would he want to? She stood up, took his hand and led him into the bedroom.

When Jake opened his eyes it was dark; too dark to see. Well past sunset he thought. He was lying on his back. His mouth was dry and his lips sore from kissing. Was there any part of her body he had missed? He had never made love or been made love to like that. Joanna was beside him still asleep. He felt the warmth of her body and could hear her breathing.

She began to stir. A hand explored towards him. "Are you awake, my love?"

"Yes."

She slid over and embraced him, kissing him on the cheek. "I'm starving."

"So am I. I've no idea of the time, but we should get up. Shall we eat out?"

"Let's, but I have to go to the hotel first."

"I know, I could meet you down at the taverna later."

"It's best if I come back here first, isn't it? I'm assuming you want me to spend the night with you."

"Of course I do."

"Well, I can bring what I need."

"Sounds perfect."

She returned with some overnight things in her rucksack. They decided to avoid the crowds and walked uphill to the taverna in the square, where they sat at a table under a tree.

"I wonder how long this search is going to take," she said after they had ordered food, a carafe of ouzo and water.

"Why? Are you still in a hurry to go?" Jake said, having quite forgotten about it.

"Not any more, but we still have to keep our minds focused on the task ahead."

"I don't know how you felt after your swim, but after that hour and forty-five minutes, I needed some time to recover before doing more. It took me ages to get warm."

"I know, I wasn't in as long as you, but I still felt it," she said. They were holding hands across the table and leaning as close to each other as they could. "How long could you be in the water without getting cold?"

"Certainly forty-five minutes. I don't begin to feel it until after the hour."

"Okay, what if we start by doing forty-five minutes each in the morning, then have a rest and some food and afterwards swim to exhaustion. That way we could probably get two and a half hours of search time per day."

"Sounds good. Any idea how long we've got? When does your Gran come back?"

"She was vague, but mentioned Tuesday. She asked me to call her again tomorrow."

"What are we going to tell her about us?"

"It depends on what you think is happening. Maybe we should talk about it again nearer the time," she said. They moved away from each other when the waitress brought them their drinks, some bread and a plate of *tzatziki*.

"How long have you known about your Gran's quest?"

"I've been aware of her preoccupation with it for as long as I can remember. I still couldn't tell you what it is."

"Is this the first time you've been involved?"

"Yes, and she's promised to tell us everything when she returns."

Chapter 26: The Memorial Service

Friday, 10th August

They left home at nine thirty that morning. Joanna headed up to the hotel to check out and bring the rest of her belongings to the house while Jake, dressed in a short-sleeved white shirt, black trousers and tie, headed for the cemetery. It was the morning of his father's memorial service; forty days after his death.

This would be expected to be a sombre moment, a time of reflection upon his new found knowledge of his father. The memorial service would also be an opportunity to advance his quest for the truth. Who would be there? How would they interact? What would they say?

But Jake's mind was not on this at all. His thoughts were on Joanna. He had forgotten about the service. It was Joanna who reminded him that he had to go, and even then he was reluctant. She had said it was her grandmother who had instructed her to prompt him.

As he walked through the hot and airless lanes, he tried to focus his thoughts. He had an inkling that he was somehow not himself. It was as if his mind had somehow become diffuse and transparent. No sooner had he latched on to one thought, it floated away. It took so much effort to concentrate on the same thing for more than a few seconds that in the end he just gave up. Thinking about Joanna, on the other hand, was easy and so much more pleasant. He relived every moment they had spent together, every word they had said, every touch, every kiss.

He was half aware of climbing the path to the cemetery. He vaguely noticed the presence of others around him. On the forecourt in front of the church there was a small crowd. Instead of joining it, he went over to the wall overlooking the town. There he stopped and stared away from the church towards the sea. He thought of the two dolphins, swimming together somewhere out there, just like Joanna and he would be doing later.

There was a persistent and annoying tug on his arm. He turned angrily at the transgressor. It was Maria.

"Jake, are you all right?" she said, softly so that no one else could hear.

Somehow, in some way, his head cleared slightly. It was as if the sound of her voice blew the mist in his head away. "Yes, Maria, I'm fine."

"You must come inside now. Everyone's waiting."

"I don't know what to do."

"Don't worry, follow me."

The inside of the chapel was tiny; circular in shape, with recesses in the front wall for a few icons. Apart from the open door, the only natural light came from four small windows, equally spaced above head height. In front there were two stands for candles either side of a table. The latter contained an upright crucifix, two framed icons and an oblong silver tray containing the *koliva*. This was a mixture of boiled wheat kernels, nuts, vine fruits, sugar and spices. It was meant to be the colour of earth and shaped like a grave and was covered in powdered sugar. On its surface Jake could see his father's initials and in the middle stood a solitary candle.

Beside the left-hand candle holder stood a priest dressed in black. He had a dark beard and his hair was tied back. With both hands he held the thurible, a gold censer suspended from chains, which contained charcoal and aromatic herbs. A wisp of smoke rose vertically and there was a pleasant smell of incense.

Jake remembered all this from his mother's memorials, held on the third and ninth days after her death. Doubtless this would have occurred, in his absence, for his father as well.

There was no seating and only enough room for a small group of people either side of an imaginary aisle. He went and stood in front of his aunt and uncle, while Maria remained at the back. He looked around him. His aunt and uncle nodded a strained acknowledgement. Behind them were their spouses, their children and their respective spouses. On the other side of the chapel, in front of Maria, were the mayor, Kephalas, Stephanos, Niki and a handful of strangers.

When everyone was in place, the priest started swinging the thurible and, to the backdrop of tinkling chains, he chanted the service.

His aunt and uncle had arranged all this and he was grateful for that. However, he suspected that they'd resented his father throughout his life and no doubt felt the same way about Jake. It would be an uncomfortable few hours.

The brief service in the chapel ended when the priest led the congregation out and to the graveside, where he said a few more prayers. Everyone then collected their small paper bag of *koliva* and, after paying their respects to Jake and the other relatives, walked to the yacht club for coffee.

Jake stayed behind with Maria, who let him inside the tomb. He could see how lovingly she had tidied up that morning before everyone had arrived; fresh flowers, a new wick and replenished oil for the flame.

"Maria."

"Yes, Jake."

"I'm surprised Photis didn't come."

"I am too," Maria said. "But maybe he didn't want to stand next to these people."

"That would be it," Jake said. His mind had cleared and he had remembered everything again. "I wish I could believe enough to hope that my father, wherever he is now, could know that I've forgiven him."

"Oh, Jake, maybe he can. He deserved your forgiveness."

"I want to do what's right by him. Not necessarily what he would want me to do, but what he would respect me doing."

"I have no doubt you will."

"What you say is well-intentioned, but misguided. I fear I don't have the inner strength." He was recalling his earlier confusion as he walked to the cemetery. "I seem to be easily distracted."

"I don't know what you mean. You seem fine to me," Maria said. Then, after she had thought about it, she added, "You mustn't let them influence you. Maybe you should leave now."

"Running away will solve nothing. My father stood up to them. I have to know whether I can too."

Maria took him in her arms as he broke down and cried. After he had composed himself again, she locked up and they left the cemetery.

"I'm not going for the coffee," she said at the bottom of the path where it met the road.

"I wish you would, I could do with your company."

"I don't really belong, and your aunt and uncle certainly don't like me."

"I'm not relishing having to speak to them either."

"You'll come and see me again?"

"Of course," he said, as they kissed and embraced.

The reception at the yacht club was held inside. People sat at the tables and chairs brought in from the terrace. The three electric fans that hung from the ceiling offered minimal relief from the heat. His aunt and uncle had kept a place for him at the head of their table and, taking his jacket off, he sat. The waiter brought him a coffee and a glass of brandy and he helped himself to a couple of biscuits.

He was introduced to his aunt's and uncle's spouses and children and used up as much time as he could asking about them, but inevitably the conversation turned to the subject he was trying to avoid.

"Mr Zacharias tells us he can't start to sell the business until the fifteenth of September," his Aunt Roulla said.

"That's a minor point," Uncle Charis said to his wife, but loud enough for all at the table to hear. "The worst part is that we're only getting forty per cent. Look at all these children and grandchildren; and there's only one of Jake."

"It's terribly unfair, after all that our father did for George," Aunt Roulla continued. "Without him George would be nothing."

Jake looked at them blankly. What should he do? What should he say? Should he defend his father? Argue with them in front of all these people? He could not just sit there and say nothing.

He looked round at the other tables. Nobody had paid any attention to them so far. He drained the rest of his brandy, calmly got up, took his jacket and left.

Chapter 27: The Sea People

Thursday, 16ᵗʰ August

Diana had arranged to meet them at the yacht club by sunset and the sun had dipped below the horizon as Joanna and Jake sat at a table on its terrace, enjoying a drink. The town was as busy as ever, having just celebrated the feast day of the Assumption of the Virgin Mary.

Presumably Diana would be sailing to Halia with the *Pelagos*, but there was no sign of it either at Paleo Limani when they'd left it some hours ago or in the harbour when they'd moored their boat on their return.

Over the last eight days they'd spent as much time as they could in the waters surrounding the Old Athenian Harbour, to the point of exhaustion. They'd had little luck with their search. They'd covered the whole of the off-shore coastline, including the most likely parts of the main island, to no avail.

Joanna had to remind Jake that Diana was bringing the hydrological chart he'd asked for. Maybe it would expose new places to search. Maybe she'd have something more to tell them about this underwater feature, especially as she'd promised to finally reveal the purpose of their quest.

Jake had forgotten about all this. The sole focus of his attention was Joanna and their relationship. Even the search was secondary, being for the most part something they did together, something he didn't question. Everything else that was of importance previously now had a peripheral existence, only fleetingly coming into his awareness, like whiffs of smoke that were easily dispersed.

When Diana did appear, she looked relieved to be back as she greeted them.

"When did you arrive?" Jake asked.

"Only half an hour ago. I'm moored in front of the ferry."

"Are you thirsty? Would you like something to drink?" Jake asked.

"I'd rather we went to Paleo Limani," Diana said. "I've plenty of food and drink on board."

They drained their glasses and left for the ferry pier, walking along the harbour front while Diana told them about her journey from Piraeus. She'd chosen to make several stops along the way, visiting different islands, and she told them what she'd seen.

Joanna sailed with her grandmother and Jake followed in the launch. On arrival, the *Pelagos* anchored in the middle of the bay. The wind had dropped and the sea was calm. They decided to eat out in the cockpit, and Diana had a small fold-up table for this purpose.

It took a while to set everything up. Supper would be a simple array of dips, cheeses and salad, accompanied by sliced bread and washed down with ouzo, water and ice. By now it was dark and Diana had strapped two oil lamps to the deck, above the companionway.

"How was Athens?" Jake asked, after they had poured out drinks, had a toast and begun eating.

"Pretty boring," Diana said. "There were things I had to do concerning my work. But, I'm sure you didn't miss me," she added with a smile. Jake looked embarrassed and Joanna pleased with herself. "You must've been agonising about how you were going to tell me. So let me put you out of your misery. I knew what had happened from the moment I saw you. You both look very happy and I'm pleased."

"Well, now that's over with," Jake said, after an awkward silence, before remembering, "Did you manage to get the chart?"

"Yes, and it's interesting. Being so familiar with the area I never thought of bothering with maps. Now that I've had a look, I've found a few off-shore reefs and shallows which are worth having a look at. I take it you've found nothing so far."

"Nothing remotely possible," Joanna said.

"What we're looking for will be well hidden, but accessible," Diana said.

"Can you describe it again?" Jake asked.

"I've never seen it, but I can guess that it will be a circular entrance, at least two metres in diameter. Rocks or boulders would have hidden it but the recent earthquake would've dislodged these and revealed it. This main entrance will be sealed with some sort of stone door, but there will be a secondary entrance, accessible on land. It might look like a well."

"Wouldn't it have been easier to look for that?"

"No, the islands are riddled with them; besides, this one would be sealed, overgrown or possibly disguised in some other way and, don't forget, we're right under the noses of the army. If we can find the main entrance, we'll find the secondary one. It'll be nearby."

"I'd like to look at that chart," Jake said.

"I have it below," Diana said. "In the morning, after you've had a look, you can tell me what you think."

Jake and Joanna started eating, but Diana just stared out across the water.

"You must be hungry, Gran, you've been at sea most of the day."

"I am, I'm gathering my thoughts. Preparing for what I'm about to say."

"Just take your time," Jake said, remembering what she had promised. His rekindled curiosity, combined with Diana's distracting presence, had cleared his mind considerably.

"You see, it will involve a suspension of disbelief on your part. Can you do that, Jake?"

"I think I can," Jake said, looking over at Joanna. "You know, don't you?"

"I'm sorry," Joanna said. "I was made to promise to pretend that I didn't."

"I don't mind you asking questions, that's fine," Diana cut in, interrupting an awkward moment. "Just don't shoot me down. It will all be clear by the time I've finished."

"As long as we have plenty to eat," Joanna said.

"And drink," Jake added.

"I can't tell you everything I know. That would take days. For now it will be what you need to know." Diana had a sip of ouzo before taking a deep breath. "My story begins twenty thousand years ago. A snippet of time for the geologist and the palaeontologist, as you will appreciate Jake, but an eternity for the archaeologist. The earth, at that time, was in the throes of the last glacial period, or ice age. Most of the world was a hostile environment. Everywhere humans lived involved a fight for survival; well, almost everywhere.

"There was one area of the globe where conditions, for that time of the earth's history, were favourable. As we know, whenever humans have the opportunity to divert their attention away from their everyday needs, they become civilised and make progress.

"Such a place and such conditions existed on several archipelagos of islands in the Atlantic. At that time the sea level was much lower, as much as four hundred feet, and the number and size of these islands was subsequently greater.

"Due to the moderating influence of the sea, their climates were equable, the rainfall regular, and the soils, being volcanic, fertile. Because the inhabitants felt safe from predators and invaders, it was on these islands that horticulture first emerged. Also, and more importantly, there was the sea; the greatest of all providers.

"It was the inhabitants of these islands who became the legendary sea people. Many others adopted or were given that name at later times, but these were the first. They learnt to navigate great distances and, over thousands of uninterrupted years, evolved a great civilisation. I am, of course, talking about what has now become labelled as the Kingdom of Atlantis."

"But there's no evidence to suggest such a civilisation," Jake said, wondering what it had to do with their particular quest.

"That's because Atlantis hunters have been looking in the wrong locations. Atlantis was not one particular island or place. It covered a huge area of island groups. That's why the accounts said it was bigger than Libya and Asia put together. That referred to the area covered, even though most of it was sea. To the sea people, the sea was as much their home as the land. Their mastery of this environment was one of the major aspects of their civilisation.

"The geography of Atlantis meant that it was a group of kingdoms split into two main components. The Eastern section, which was closest to Europe, comprised what are now the Azores, Madeira, the Canaries etc... and the Western, much larger one, included the islands of the Caribbean, the Bermudas, Bahamas etc...Although I said Atlantis was a group of kingdoms, it had one seat of power, a divine ruling council, which was located on an island off the north western coast of North Africa."

"Wait a minute," Jake said. "Sorry to interrupt again, but the area you're referring to had no islands, past or present, that could have supported the landmass that Plato described."

"That's because the Atlantis Plato described was a fiction. Not Plato's fiction; he was just describing what he'd heard, but a fiction nonetheless."

"Why shouldn't all of it be a fiction?" Jake asked.

"As I will explain later, Atlantis waged war on the civilizations of the Mediterranean. Their over-inflated self-description was propaganda intended to daunt. It's a ploy that's been used often throughout history by aggressors trying to intimidate their enemies."

"I see," Jake said, unconvinced.

"Many theories have been put forward about Atlantis, involving strange mysteries, and even extra-terrestrials. Most of these are nonsense. Given the amount of time it had to evolve, it's not surprising that it developed an advanced civilization. Nevertheless, there was one remarkable feature about Atlantis, something that I will come back to.

"As explained, the civilization of Atlantis emerged over twenty thousand years ago and evolved over thousands of years. Its history spans a period of time much greater than the present recorded one. These people noticed that the climate was changing and the sea level was rising at the same time as their populations and prosperity were increasing. They realised that they would have to find new lands to inhabit.

"By tradition, the sea people mistrusted the landmasses that surrounded them. They considered them dangerous and uninhabitable, much in the same way as we look upon Mars. Even where the sea people occupied larger islands, as in the Caribbean, they stuck to the coast. The surrounding continents were settled by other races, but they considered them to be no more than savages.

"At the same time as this was happening, differences between the eastern and western ends of this empire were coming to a head. The divine king who ruled in the east was powerful, as I will explain later, but not powerful enough to hold on to the west, especially over such vast distances. In time, the western end went its own separate way and all contact and knowledge with it was eventually lost. The eastern, and now isolated Kingdom of Atlantis, decided to look further eastwards and expand into the Mediterranean.

"As I said, the Atlanteans greatly feared the landmasses, but two factors made their quest easier. The first was geographical. The idea of conquering the Mediterranean, its coastlines and islands appealed to them. They already had detailed knowledge of these parts and they weren't too dissimilar to what they were used to. The second was the establishment of other civilizations, especially the Egyptians and the Hellenes. Their goal was to conquer, subjugate and enslave these people and, in due course, their armies were prepared and the invasion began.

"At first, all went well, with the Atlanteans progressing along the north shore of the Mediterranean as far as the west coast of Italy and to the borders of

Egypt in the south. Despite the propaganda and the Atlanteans' arrogance at believing themselves to be superior, in the Hellenes, particularly with the Athenians, they met their match and were soundly defeated, before being driven back.

"These events took place around 9000 BC, that's eleven thousand years ago and, despite being entirely forgotten, were one of the major turning points in history. For the Atlanteans it was their second major disaster, the first being the splitting of their empire. The third, final and greatest catastrophe was yet to come."

Diana paused. She had a drink of water and, finishing off what was left of her ouzo, retrieved the bottle from the net slung over the side behind her and replenished their glasses.

"This is all very interesting," Jake said, "and I could sit here listening all night. As a geography teacher, I can't tell you how many different theories I've heard about Atlantis. This one's good, but what does it have to do with our situation?" Then he recalled all the books his father had on the subject in his study in Athens.

"It has everything to do with it, as you shall see. As I said, the third and final catastrophe was yet to come. In what I now speculate was a cataclysmic eruption of the Mid-Atlantic Ridge, the seat of power of the Eastern Kingdom, off-shore from the coast of what is now Morocco, was first razed to the ground by an earthquake and then swept away by a tsunami. This catastrophe was so great that it set off a chain reaction of quakes and eruptions straight across the Mediterranean, destroying the Greek civilizations as well."

"That's a great story, similar to the one Plato relates in his Dialogues, but for which there is no evidence," Jake said.

"Given the manner of its destruction and the length of time since then, it's no wonder," Diana said. "Like many other civilizations, the circumstances were right for it to thrive and it did. Over time it grew in sophistication. At the end it suffered a period of decline and then was destroyed by natural forces. There have been many similar scenarios throughout history and new ones are being discovered."

"I agree that's possible, but I'm not convinced about Atlantis," Jake said.

"There was one aspect of Atlantis that was unique," Diana continued, "something that will never be known. This involved the divine ruling family. There was one legend that held some truth. It has been postulated, in some quarters, that the Atlanteans harnessed the powers of crystals and used them to make lasers. The truth was, they used a certain crystal that was found in only one location; in a subterranean mine. It allowed them to harness the powers of the mind, to focus thought. But this was not in isolation. Another ingredient was involved; the hallucinogenic root of a certain flowering plant, which at that time grew on their islands, that, when used in conjunction with these crystals, enhanced mental powers dramatically.

"I should point out that crystals and flowers have spiritual significance in certain beliefs to this day. Together with birds, they represent the highest evolution reached by rock, vegetation and animate creatures respectively. You will see later on that a flying creature was also critically important to the Atlanteans.

"This use of the crystals and plants was reserved for the ruling family and, over many generations, techniques were refined and powers optimised. This is how it worked. When a royal baby was born, it was given its birth crystal, which it wore around its neck, or on a bracelet or something similar. It was thought that, as the baby's mind grew and developed, the crystal's properties changed to mirror and enhance that development. It was certainly true that one influenced the other because if a crystal was taken beyond a certain distance from its owner, the host retained some powers but lost a considerable amount as well.

"Part of the child's training involved taking the hallucinogenic root, learning to control the hallucinations through meditation and thus, together with the crystal, develop mental abilities. At first, the sorts of powers we're talking about were telepathy, precognition, management of bodily functions and limited control of other minds, but nothing spectacular.

"Every now and then an individual would be born with special physical and mental aptitudes, as happens now. When further enhanced by the drugs and crystal, it made them appear superhuman or what the Atlanteans came to label the Immortals. Certain individuals were able to control their minds and bodies so completely that they could prevent aging. It was also observed that these abilities were inherited and could be passed on and further enhanced by selective breeding.

"So, at the time that Atlantis was nearing its destruction, it was being ruled by an elite of Immortals…"

"If they were so superior, how did the Athenians defeat them?" Jake asked.

"Quite simply, at that time, not only had the Immortals never left their island home, but they thought it beneath them to be involved in anything as crude as fighting. This was about to change.

"Shortly before the destruction, the Immortals had dreams and premonitions of the impending disaster. When the invasion had failed and the cataclysm was imminent, the ruling family had no choice but to flee, crossing over to the mainland.

"For years they wandered incognito along the north shore of the devastated Mediterranean, visiting the islands along the way, until they entered what is now Greece and the home of their former conquerors. Not only did the Immortals admire the Greeks, those who were left, but they felt that here they could find a home that was secure and familiar.

"After months of searching and island-hopping, and after coming close to desperation, they finally found somewhere that met their requirements. Somewhere their hallucinatory roots could grow naturally, somewhere that was remote and secure, where they could cultivate the food and wine they needed. After they'd settled in, they used their powers to rule over their new country of residence, not in any direct way, with force, like kings or queens, but more subtly, as deities. In time they became recognised as the Greek Gods that we know from the Greek myths and legends.

"And where was this new home that the survivors of Atlantis came to and became the Greek Gods? I'm sure you've already guessed. It was here," Diana said, with a sweep of her hand. "They lived here for thousands of years, surviving the later destruction caused by the eruption of Thera around 1,600 BC, right up until just after the Trojan War."

Chapter 28: The Betrayal

"So, what did they do here, you might ask," Diana continued. "Well, very much what we do: fall in love, have families, go on adventures. A few decided they no longer wanted to be immortal, so they surrendered their crystals and left. A community of workers who attended them also lived here. They cultivated the land, cared for livestock, prepared their food, built and maintained their dwellings, produced their wine and clothes, built the harbour near to your father's house, operated an indigenous fleet, manufactured and maintained their spears, shields, helmets, bows and arrows; just what you'd expect from a royal household. The Gods travelled far and wide to extend their influence, have affairs with mortals and generally cause mischief, but always returned here to eat their divine ambrosia."

"I thought that in mythology they were able to turn up wherever they wanted and in all sorts of guises," Jake said, remembering his mother's bedtime stories.

"They did this in a number of ways. They could communicate and influence people through dreams and telepathy. They could manipulate them by invoking visions and emotions. Some could strike a weak-willed person dead just through thought. Some hardly ever left the island, notably Hestia and Hera of the women and Hephaestos and Hades of the men. The more active ones had powers of remote viewing and sensing and could travel through their ability to transmutate. They were able to transform into any animal for the purpose of using its abilities to fly, swim, run or fight."

"Transmutate? What bullshit is this?" Jake said, looking over at Joanna, seeking moral support, but instead she glared back at him disapprovingly. Then he remembered the dreams, the incident at sea and his encounter with the fog.

"So, it was from here that the Gods ruled over the Greek world and the deeds of the Immortals became the basis of Greek mythology," Diana continued unperturbed.

"But I thought the Gods ruled from Mount Olympus," Jake said.

"That's what they led people to believe in order to divert attention away from here. Gods always rule from a high place, not some insignificant island. The servants who lived here were sworn to secrecy. Have you never wondered why throughout history so little is known about this place? This was an exclusion zone."

"Pity Stephanos isn't here," Jake said.

Diana ignored him. "Now, I must tell you something about the characters of some of these Immortals, so that you can understand what happened next. By the end of their era, there were fifteen main Gods and Goddesses. There were six from the older generation, who were the direct descendants of the survivors of Atlantis, and nine adult children. The former comprised Zeus, Poseidon, Hades, Hestia, Hera and Demeter, who were siblings.

"Zeus was the appointed leader; you could best describe him as an authoritarian father figure. He was ambitious and there was no way he was going to be anything but number one. He was also a serial adulterer. He felt entitled to seduce whomever he wanted, whenever he wanted. He didn't just restrict himself to women either, with terrible consequences, as you will see.

"Poseidon, his brother, was similar in appearance and a lot more dangerous. He was bad-tempered, vindictive and violent; a real grudge-holder and relentless enemy if crossed. He believed he should've been the ruler and thought Zeus too affable. He loved the sea and spent most of his time in the water, so much so that he constructed underwater grottos in several places. He was also a philanderer and indiscriminately promiscuous. Although he often used brute force on his enemies, he could cause them emotional pain to the point of suicide. In other words, he could influence and direct their emotions.

"Hades, on the other hand, was the opposite of the other two. He kept himself to himself to the point of invisibility. In fact he had a Cap of Invisibility. He spent most of his time as a recluse. He chose for himself the title of God of the Underworld, so that he could have nothing to do with the world of men.

"Of the three women of the older generation, Hestia was the maiden aunt; she never married or had a partner but was the homemaker for the others. She spent most of her time in solitude and meditation and didn't meddle in the affairs of mortals, considering it immoral to do so. We visited one of her temples in Lichas."

"If I'd known she *really* existed, I would've left an offering," Jake said, tongue in cheek.

"Demeter was similar in her attitude to interference. Hera was Zeus's mate, his Queen, by name at least. Despite her husband's elicit behaviour, which made her insanely jealous, she remained faithful to him. She was active, despoiling his relationships and taking revenge on her rivals.

"The Gods of the younger generation were Apollo, Hermes, Ares, Hephaestos and Dionysus. It isn't relevant to know anything about them except to say that Apollo was the God of divination, establishing the oracle of Delphi, amongst others, although only prophesying once.

"The Goddesses were Artemis, Athena, Persephone and Aphrodite. Again, I will not dwell on any of them, apart from mentioning that Artemis was the goddess of hunting and archery.

"There's one other individual to take account of and that's Ganymedes. He was the son of Troas, the founder of Troy. He was considered the most beautiful youth ever born and was the subject of affection from Zeus, who abducted him and forced him into being his lover. Afterwards he was appointed the cupbearer of the Gods, and Zeus made him immortal by allowing him to have ambrosia, nectar and his own crystal.

"Halia was also the home to the divine mares. They belonged to the original royal household of Atlantis, accompanying the survivors to the island, and were immortal. Throughout the generations they had a psychic link with the Gods. It had been said from long ago that they were a spontaneous and divine creation of the Gods' imagination and, as long as they remained untamed, inviolate, unharnessed and free, the Gods would retain their powers and authority. They could also fly, which gave them the spiritual significance I referred to earlier.

"I should also mention the centaurs. They were half-human and half-horse. They were violent and wreaked havoc wherever they went, until Hercules all but wiped them out. The survivors were allowed to live on the island in peace, provided they protected the trees, vines, blossoms, ambrosia and nectar, but they were not allowed to enjoy this drink, as any form of intoxication would set them on the rampage.

"Now is a good time to mention the nature of the immortality of the Gods. By strict definition it means to live forever, but that's just not possible. What it meant biologically was that the combination of ambrosia and the influence of the crystals prolonged life indefinitely, in theory. When I say in theory, I mean for as long as the Gods had the will to live. Most had had enough after a few hundred years and that's why there weren't that many Immortals left in the end. They were protected from serious illnesses, but the longer they lived the greater was the chance of having an accident. No matter how amazing their recuperative powers, a serious injury could kill even a God.

"So, I've now told you about Atlantis and the Greek Gods and you're wondering what this has to do with anything. Well, I'll now bring everything together.

"The date is 1200 BC, just over three thousand two hundred years ago. Imagine what this island must've been like, inhabited by the Immortals and their servants, grazed by the beautiful divine mares, protected by the centaurs. The Gods, ruled by Zeus, each had their own areas of interest and influence and, to a greater or lesser extent, would come or go as they pleased, returning here to eat their divine ambrosia, which, as mentioned, only grew here. This was washed down with nectar, a fortified wine made from locally cultivated grapes to which was added the honey from bees, which fed on fruit tree blossoms. It should've been a paradise.

"But there were occasions when one God clashed with another. Whenever there were conflicts amongst mortals, the Gods would take sides and support their favourites. For them it was like a chess match, with humans as the pawns. Most of these events were minor and local. The Trojan War was on a different scale and involved the whole of the Greek world. Here the Gods themselves were as much at war as were the mortals, and were seen to have not only initiated the conflict but also to have deliberately prolonged it, with devastating effects.

"Add to this the fact that the Greeks had become more sophisticated and began to see the Gods as interfering rather than protecting. The Immortals recognised that it would not be long before their home and true nature were discovered. The majority thought that it was time to move on and leave the Greeks to their own devices, whereas Poseidon and Ares believed, unrealistically, that the mortals should be put in their place and that the Gods should rule forever.

"Ganymedes, the cup bearer, had not only been kidnapped and raped by Zeus but had now seen his abductors preside over the destruction of his homeland Troy. He was taken for granted and no one imagined him capable of treachery, apart from Poseidon.

"Poseidon saw this unrest as an opportunity. As I mentioned earlier, he had harboured resentment over the decision to appoint Zeus as ruler. He knew that Zeus's weakness was his vanity. He was also aware that the centaurs, Halia's security guards, secretly lusted after the divine mares and were therefore amenable to suggestion.

"It was during a regular gathering on the island that Poseidon hatched his plan. At that time, their meeting place was on the beach at Paleo Limani, the one from which I picked you up with the launch, where they had a lavish pavilion. As the Gods were enjoying eating and drinking, Poseidon mocked Zeus that he didn't hold dominion over all things. Zeus, becoming ever more intoxicated, insisted that he did.

"Poseidon replied that if that were the case, how was it that the divine mares were said to be untameable? Zeus replied that he had ordered them to remain on the island and they did. Poseidon retorted that that wasn't the same thing as the mares were happy to be in a place where they would be protected and unmolested by mortal man. If he was all powerful, could he contain them on one of the smaller off-shore islands, the flat topped one in the bay?" Diana pointed to the third island clockwise from the northern entrance. "At that time it was divided into pens and used to hold goats and sheep in preparation for ritual slaughter.

"Because of the combination of ambrosia, nectar and innate vanity, Zeus forgot what the mares symbolised. He commanded that they be rounded up, boated across to the island and confined in separate pens until such time as he ordered their release. As soon as this was done and all the mares were contained, they became distressed. This in turn affected the Immortals and they also became confused and frightened. Unwittingly, Zeus had neutralised most of their powers.

"At the same time, a powerful poison that Poseidon had introduced into the nectar, with the help of Ganymedes, took effect, and the Gods fell to the ground paralyzed. He sent for the centaurs and ordered them to bind their limbs with hide, just in case some should be resistant to the drug. In fact, before Apollo had succumbed, he uttered the following prophecy, the only one he ever made, 'As you have betrayed your kind, so your kind will betray you'.

"Poseidon intended to dispose of all the Gods, but Ganymedes, in return for his cooperation, demanded that Hestia should not be harmed. She never interfered in human affairs and therefore had no part in the conflict over Troy. Poseidon was happy to comply as he knew that Hestia would not harm him, having taken a vow of non-violence. She rarely came to the gatherings anyway, having her own retreat at the other end of the island. As soon as she had sensed what was happening, she had made haste to Paleo Limani, but was too late. Without being given the opportunity to mourn or to collect her possessions, she was escorted straightaway onto a boat with Ganymedes and they were taken to a place of their choosing. I believe it was the east coast of Evia.

"Poseidon then gathered the centaurs, ordered them to round up the servants, and forced them to construct thirteen wooden coffins before moving the bodies, together with their possessions and treasures, into one of his grottos. With the interment completed, they worked for days transporting boulders from all over the island and, with the use of boats, dropped them over the underwater entrance to the cave until it was concealed. Once this was done, all the servants and their children were slaughtered and their bodies disposed of in a mass grave.

"Poseidon intended to leave even fewer witnesses though. Remember, the centaurs lusted after the divine mares. Only the head centaur was completely loyal to Poseidon. The rest, their gruesome tasks of slaughter and mass burial being accomplished, were allowed to fall upon the mares. They tried to rape them, but as he had foreseen, the mares trampled them to death.

"I believe the surviving centaur was commanded to guard the landward entrance to the tomb. As a further precaution, Poseidon positioned Athena's aegis, containing the head of the Gorgon Medusa, within the tomb itself.

"The crystals of the deceased Gods and Goddesses were placed in Hades' Cap of Invisibility. Poseidon believed that this would prevent them from exerting an influence on the outside world. I'll explain what I mean by this shortly."

"So, by looking for this cave, we're tomb raiding," Jake said.

"No, there's more to it," Diana continued. "You see, Poseidon, having disposed of the others, went on to create his own ruling class. He's established an international web of influence. You could say he's a sort of godfather of the business world, having amassed a fortune. His international yachting business is only a cover. Although much diminished in power, he can still coerce and influence events for himself and those who work for and with him."

"Wait a minute," Jake said, sitting up to attention. "You talk as if he's still alive." Diana remained silent. "If these events you're speaking about happened over three thousand two hundred years ago, then Poseidon must be older still."

"That's right; nearly double that age."

"You're not expecting me to believe this, are you?"

"Poseidon, with the help of ambrosia, his crystal and his willpower, has been able to keep going all this time."

"Are you saying this plant or root still grows here?"

"No, not any more, but there are alternatives. A certain type of mushroom, I believe."

"Assuming that this was possible," Jake said, shaking his head, "how can someone do this and not be noticed?"

"Look at the example of the Mafia godfathers. Why are they so powerful and untouchable?"

"I can't say I've looked into it."

"Because they're surrounded with trusted colleagues who do all their dirty work. They're unseen and in most cases unknown."

"It's not the same thing. Wouldn't these people notice that he doesn't age or change?"

"Of course they do. They all do, but that just adds to the mystique. Participation guarantees wealth and power. All you have to do is follow the rules. The rules are that you're always striving for the cause, always working towards furthering its objectives. In return you get whatever you want; power, wealth, sex or all of these. From the perspective of the individual, you see nothing wrong with what you're doing. You're one of many working for the organisation and you have its power behind you. You feel privileged."

"Okay, I can see how it could work, but I'm not even starting to be convinced that such an organisation with Poseidon behind it exists."

"Well, he's not going to be called Poseidon, is he?"

"It's not this Kephalas?"

"Oh no, not him. He's his deputy. Poseidon is someone else. He's currently known as Basil Protopapas."

Of course, how could he have forgotten? Maria had already mentioned him. "Seriously though, it isn't possible for someone to hang around for hundreds, let alone thousands of years, and not get noticed," he insisted.

"The fact is that he's not hung around the same places for long, neither has he been known by the same name."

"You're asking too much to believe in a secret society run by somebody who's six thousand years old."

"I'm afraid there's more to tell and it's going to get worse."

"I believe you."

"You see, the crystals are still an influence," Diana said, leaning towards Jake and resting her elbows on the table, "despite Poseidon placing them in the Cap of Invisibility."

"In what way?"

"Because each has retained the personality and memories of the God to whom it belonged. You see, in the early days of Atlantis, when one of the Immortals died, their crystal was buried with them. People started becoming possessed by the deceased and acquiring some of their powers, to the extent that they went and sought out the buried crystal in order to be reunited with it. This had the effect of the Immortal living again, but in the mind and body of someone else. When this was realised, the practice was that the crystal had to be destroyed when an Immortal died. Poseidon thought that by placing them in the Cap of Invisibility that wouldn't happen here. But it has nonetheless. The spirits of the Gods have possessed some of the locals, those of us who have complimentary psychological and personality traits. The crystals want to be found and they want to be released."

"So you're saying that some of the people walking around here think they're one of the Gods?" Jake asked, remembering what Maria had told him on his first visit to her taverna.

"Not think, know; for example, I'm Artemis."

"I'm sorry Diana, but you've gone well past my credibility threshold. This is too far-fetched," Jake said, his mental clarity having fully returned. "The idea of immortality, solely because of the effect of a drug and crystal is bad enough but to claim that I'm sitting opposite someone possessed by the Goddess Artemis is totally preposterous."

"I realize this isn't easy," Diana said, "but in order to go further with this, I need you to take me seriously. I must have your trust and belief." She scanned the water, as if looking for something. "The water here is shallow."

"So?" Jake said, glancing at Joanna, who was smiling at Diana knowingly.

"Dolphins would rarely come in here," Diana said.

"Oh, really?" Jake said, his mind in turmoil. His natural scepticism was under assault from a combination of what he was hearing from Diana and what he'd experienced since coming to Halia.

"As Gods our powers were great. Now, inhabiting the bodies of mortals and physically separated from our crystals, we're much diminished. The Cap of Invisibility has a further muting effect. But some abilities remain, more subtle ones, mainly intuition and telepathy. The ability to communicate with animals is one of mine. I'm particularly fond of birds of prey as well as dolphins; they're hunters too, just like me."

"A pair was sighted off Perivoli," Jake said.

"There used to be a lot more, when the Med had more fish, now they're only a few pairs in the area. All on the north side. One's not far."

They fell silent. The breeze had started up again. He thought of his father. Did she really know him? Did they also have this conversation? Was it this knowledge that had led to his demise?

"They tend to sleep at night," Diana continued. "Do you know how they sleep?"

"I don't," Jake said, deep in thought, only vaguely listening to her.

"They rest one brain hemisphere at a time and close the opposite eye," Diana said. "It allows them to breathe, be alert for predators and keep on the move. But they also have an active period when they hunt for nocturnal creatures, like squid. Both the nearby pairs are active just now."

A violent swish in the water made Jake jump. He was facing the port side and the sound came from behind him. He turned. At first there was just turbulent water and then he saw the two dark fins surface side by side, followed by the whoosh of out-breath. Diana was sitting staring at her lap. "The others have arrived," she said. Within seconds the other two also surfaced. For several minutes they circled the boat, rocking it gently with their wakes.

"How did you do that?" Jake asked, astounded. Both Joanna and Diana were laughing, as much from his amazement as from the playfulness of the dolphins.

"Dolphins are intelligent and curious. They come when you reach out to them."

"Yes, but how?"

"It was something I always knew how to do; or rather Artemis knows how to do. I am aware of nature around me. I can feel life. I can sense where these animals are. I can send feelings and mental pictures to them. Then they know where I am and come. They're getting bored; they'll leave soon."

"Hey, can't they find this cave?"

"Don't you think I've thought of that?"

"I thought you could control them."

"Communicate, yes. Control no; unfortunately, that's one of the powers I've lost. Besides, I've tried. They do not acknowledge the existence of a cave. In fact, they generally avoid these waters. I think they have a bad feeling about them. They sense atmosphere, much like us. Otherwise they're helpful. I'm wishing them well."

Then it was quiet again and the waters were still.

"I owe you an apology," Jake said.

"Let's continue," Diana said, nodding in acknowledgement and acceptance. "As I've said, Poseidon over the centuries has built a dynasty, which has spread to many parts of the world. He doesn't stay in one place for long and has frequently changed his name, his nationality; whatever is necessary.

"Soon after the demise of the Gods, the ancient Athenian harbour was established. Little did the builders of it know, but the houses they demolished for their marble and other materials were once the homes of their deities. Apart from this brief interval, Halia remained uninhabited, apart from the occasional pirate that is. It was only during the late nineteenth century that a permanent population established itself. Poseidon started keeping an eye on Halia, from a distance, as it wasn't until then that the phenomenon with the crystals started manifesting itself."

"Why not when the base was here?"

"Because a receptive host needs to be a child, preferably before puberty," Diana replied. "Naturally, once the possessions began, the disembodied Gods started seeking Poseidon out. It was Ares, or Kephalas as he has become, who first found him. He was meant to be our representative, until he became his lackey." Diana sounded bitter. "Anyway, as much as he'd like to, Poseidon can't avoid the place now. Having in mind Apollo's prophecy, the one thing he took care not to do was have offspring. And, with one exception, he succeeded. As you know, Jake, your father was adopted."

"I know."

"Now, I want you to keep Apollo's prophecy in mind when I tell you this. Your father was Poseidon's son."

"My father?" Jake said, shocked. "Poseidon, this man called Basil, is my grandfather? How's that possible?"

"I'm afraid I don't know the details. Just that Basil fathered a son and convinced your grandparents to adopt him."

"That would explain many things," Jake said, almost to himself, trying to digest the significance of the revelation.

"To make matters worse, your father didn't want to conform and be part of his clan. He wanted to go his own way, which was fine, as far as Basil was concerned, as long as he didn't pose a threat.

"Now, you may ask; why didn't Basil just have you both killed? Well, what did the prophecy mean? It didn't say 'your blood'; it said 'your kind'. That could include your father, you, Kephalas, any of us, or all of us working together. He couldn't have us all eliminated. But for reasons I will come to in a minute, he had to be particularly careful about his offspring. So he set out to destroy you as a family. I'm sure he arranged the accident in which your grandparents were killed. I think it was meant as a warning and your father was forced to distance himself from you and your mother."

"So when did my father learn that he was adopted?"

"Probably when he came of age. But your father still defied Basil's expectations, he continued to be successful in business, he continued to support your mother and enjoyed the good life; all without the help of his father, the master. I can't be sure, but in the end, I think your father must've done something to push him over the edge, incite one of his rages."

"How did he do it?"

"It's difficult to tell. It wouldn't have needed his physical presence or that of anyone else. He could've made him imagine he was being attacked. He could've caused him to walk off the cliff. Maybe he caused him to have a heart attack. Maybe the centaur was involved. I don't know. His powers are considerable, but I don't know to what extent he can still control natural conditions."

"Can he still, you know, transmutate?"

"With the confinement of the divine mares, this ability was lost."

"The powers he does have, would their range be limited?"

"He needs the proximity of water."

"What about the woman who was with my father?"

"Who knows? Was she still with him at the time? If she was, maybe he left it to the centaur to dispose of her."

"I don't suppose there would be any point in trying to prove anything."

"If there was any physical evidence, it would've been found already."

"So, how can he be stopped?"

"With great difficulty and I will come to that in a minute. But let me continue. This connection to the island was unforeseen by Poseidon. His intention was to get rid of the others and go somewhere else, some other island, taking the divine mares and establishing a new power base, but he forgot one very important thing. The divine mares originally only answered to Hestia, the first born of the Olympians. Because she had no interest in ruling, she ceded this authority to Zeus. With Zeus dead, this would have reverted to Hestia. I'm sure he tried to find her, but by then, she'd vanished."

"Does that mean she could still be alive?"

"It's generally accepted that she's dead and that the mares have dispersed. We've all tried to find her at some time or other, travelling all over the world, but no one has even sensed her presence.

"So, here's Basil's dilemma. He can't enter the tomb and get the crystals in case we somehow get hold of them and overthrow him. On the other hand he can't have them destroyed, because that could nullify his powers even further, like the destruction of the divine mares did. You see, we all knew we depended on each other. That's why we never anticipated what Poseidon did."

"But if you were all connected, as you say, why didn't you sense his intentions?" Jake asked.

"Because Poseidon was always angry and resentful, but he always took it out on mortals. We never imagined he would turn on us and he wouldn't have succeeded without Ganymedes."

"Who was abducted and raped, then you killed his family and destroyed his homeland," Jake said. "It was pretty stupid not to consider him a threat."

"I agree. We were overconfident."

"But going back to the crystals, why didn't Poseidon just take them with him, instead of burying them?" Jake asked.

"I think at the time he saw no use for them and he feared they might torment him."

"Could he not have destroyed them at the outset?"

"Their destruction required the performance of a ritual involving the divine mares, which was no longer possible."

"So where does that leave us?" Jake asked.

"The crystals must be found and retrieved; that's the key."

"What then?"

"When I, Artemis, and the other Gods have our crystals, we can overthrow Poseidon; we can restore the balance that existed previously. Remember that I said that he had to be particularly careful of his offspring?"

"I do."

"You Jake, as an inheritor of divine blood, could enter the sacred tomb, immune to the effects of the head of Medusa, unaffected by the concentrated proximity of so many crystals, and retrieve them. None of us, as mortals, can do this."

"If my father knew all this, and in view of the fact that his family was in danger, why didn't he pursue this quest?"

"Because he saw it from a different point of view. He would have too much to lose if he took action against Basil and failed."

"So what this boils down to is that, apart from Basil, I'm the only one who can enter this chamber or tomb. But what if I were to decide not to undertake the task? Like my father did."

"Then you will always have Basil breathing down your neck, especially if you have children."

"That reminds me, there's something I must mention. Do you remember the incident when someone tried to break into the house?"

"Of course."

"Well, the Saturday night before Joanna came, I went with Nicos on his yacht to a club on the north coast of Lichas. The one that's in the underground cave. Do you know it?"

"I've not been, but I've heard of it."

Jake recounted the incident on the beach and what led up to it.

"This is puzzling," Diana said. "I can see how Kephalas would arrange with Nicos and that girl to get information out of you about our interactions, but the attack just doesn't fit in."

"Why not?" Jake questioned. "Why not coerce as well as interrogate?"

"To start with, why not just frighten you off? Why bother with the other charade? Also, Basil has more convincing ways of doing this that wouldn't involve witnesses. I have to admit, I have no answer to that one."

"There's more," Jake said, as he recounted first the dream, then the incident at sea and, finally, the episode along the road.

"I thought I told you not to leave the town alone," Diana said angrily.

"I'm sorry. But it didn't prevent the vision."

"They're not the same. In the first he's communicating with you telepathically. In the second he's directly manipulating the environment."

"Does that mean he's on the island?"

"No, he doesn't have to be that close. What matters is the proximity of water; the sea especially. You did right to climb the mountain, although I'm certain he was just trying to scare you. You're also safe here with us or in the town amongst the others."

"Does it mean he's on to us?" Joanna said, breaking her silence.

"No," Diana said definitively. "He still has all the cards, or believes so. He knows nothing of the earthquake and its effect. He believes his grotto cannot be found. He'd rather Jake wasn't here consorting with us, but that doesn't mean we pose anything more than an annoyance."

"So, the bottom line is finding this cave," Jake said, looking at his watch. It was two in the morning. "We'd better get back. What time do we start tomorrow?"

"I'm sure we can manage the usual time," Joanna said.

"But with added care," Diana said. "Basil's on his way to Lichas, so he will be keeping an even closer eye."

"How does he keep track of us?" Jake asked.

"We used to spy on mortals through animals," Diana said. "So our ears and eyes could be the bird on the nearby tree, or your pet dog. Basil can still do the same; however, he can't do it in our presence, we would sense it."

"So, when I've been on my own, he could've been spying on me?"

"He might've been watching you, sure. Whether close enough to hear conversations is a different matter."

"Can he read my mind?"

"Not without an empathic link, which is highly unlikely; maybe a one in a hundred chance. But he can give you thoughts, provoke emotions and cause you to dream."

"So who are the others?"

"I can't tell you," Diana said. "None of them want their identities revealed to you at present."

"I see," Jake said. He could probably deduce some of them from what Maria had said. That would include the mayor and that doctor he hadn't met yet. He looked over at Joanna. "Are you one of them?"

"Not everyone who's an ally has been possessed," Diana said.

"One thing puzzles me. Just because I'm Basil's grandson, why should I be able to enter the tomb? I've never handled a crystal nor taken the drug, whereas you, at least, are under the influence of one of the so called Immortals?"

"There are two aspects to the answer. The first is genetic. Through many generations of breeding amongst themselves, the Immortals have developed certain mental and physical strengths, which would be latent in you. The second aspect is more difficult to explain. You see, the supernatural, the magical part, still exists in some measure. Why you should be able to look upon the face of the Medusa, who after all is only a shrivelled head belonging to someone who's been dead for thousands of years, and remain unaffected, while Joanna and I would turn into a pile of minerals, is inexplicable, a paradox." Diana looked reflective. "You realise that amongst the buried crystals are some that haven't been assigned?"

"I didn't realise," Jake said. "It makes sense there would be."

"Not many. I think only six or seven remained."

"I thought you said that you had to be a child."

"Only if you were being possessed. But with a fresh crystal and the correct training, who knows how far you could go. Think about it." She paused a few seconds to let the idea sink in. "Why don't I meet you at yours at ten? Then we can have a look at the map before we set off."

"Sounds okay to me," Jake said.

They helped Diana clear up before returning to the town harbour in the launch.

Chapter 29: The Map

Friday, 17ᵗʰ August

Jake was barely aware of the knocking. At first he thought he was back in England. Who could want to see him? Nobody visited since Charly left. But he was awake now and shot out of bed. He glanced at Joanna sleeping face down beside him, her golden hair covering the pillow. He pulled on his shorts and a tee-shirt and went to open the front door. It was Diana, carrying the rolled up map.

"God, is it ten already?" he said, letting her in. The morning light was blinding.

"Eleven actually," Diana replied, checking her watch.

"We're still in bed," he said. He heard footsteps behind him; Joanna came out of the bedroom bleary-eyed.

"You don't look much like a descendant of the Gods," Diana said.

"That's ouzo for you," he said.

"Which is why I'm late. At least we can have breakfast together. I'm starving."

"We've got figs for you to start with while we're dressing," Joanna said.

"Yes, they were brought by the lady who looks after my father's orchard."

"I know," Diana said. "Have you spoken with her much?"

"She was at the memorial service," Jake said. There was something else about her that he should've remembered, but wasn't able to. He folded back the patio doors so that Diana could sit outside while she waited. They joined her fifteen minutes later.

"They say fig trees can grow for hundreds of years," Jake said. "Could these have had the benefit of manure from the divine mares?"

"I don't think so," Diana replied. "Are you teasing?"

"Sort of. That doesn't mean I don't believe you. It's just that in the light of morning and with a mild hangover it does seem improbable."

"Let's have a look at that map," Diana said after they'd had cornflakes, toast and tea. They cleared the table and rolled it out.

"Why do you believe the cave's in this area?" Jake asked, pointing to Paleo Limani.

"As Artemis, from where I was lying on the beach, and before I lost consciousness, I heard the conversations of the servants as they loaded the first coffins on boats and rowed them out."

"What happened afterwards? You know, after you lost awareness?"

"There was a period of nothingness. Then consciousness began to return. I was aware, or rather we were aware, of being able to sense each other. It was as though we were in a dark room, but unable to touch or speak. In time we were able to reach out to other consciousnesses on the island."

"Fascinating, I'm sorry I interrupted you," Jake said. "What were we saying?"

"We were talking about the interment. I was about to say that, in view of the fact that there were thirteen coffins to bury, one by one, they couldn't have rowed far. Only this area has the right attributes: low cliffs and steep underwater shelving."

"From what we've seen, I would agree," Jake said.

"It would also rule out an off-shore reef," Joanna added.

"How did they get the coffins in?" Jake asked.

"From the conversations I picked up, the boxes were lowered from boats into the water down to Poseidon, who was in front of the cave and, with the help of ropes that were manned and pulled from the landward end, they were manoeuvred into the tomb."

"You still don't think it would be easier to look for this landward entrance?" Jake asked.

"It's rocky on those islands, with thick bush. It would be too difficult and besides, we'd be in full view," Diana replied.

"Well, there's nothing for it but to go over the same ground again," Joanna said.

"Wait a minute," Jake said. He was pointing to the narrow gap between two of the islands. "This gap isn't like the others. The others are shallow. This is indented inwards, forming a cleft. When the sea level was lower, wave action would have eroded this part more than the others because of weaker rock. Ideal for forming caves. Look here, the water is shallow near the islands, but drops to thirty-three metres in the gap, nearly one hundred feet."

"How could we have missed that?" Joanna asked.

"Easily," Jake said. "We would've just swum by, assuming it shallowed gradually like the rest of the coast. I wouldn't have expected an underwater gorge. It looks an ideal place to deposit scree to hide an entrance as the topography would hold it in place."

"Would a collapse of scree here cause sufficient disturbance in the silt to effect the seabed all the way down here?" Joanna asked, pointing to the site of the ancient wreck.

"If the landslide was large enough and the currents in the right direction, sure," Jake replied.

"We didn't see evidence of scree anywhere. Also, this gap faces southeast. Apart from the morning, it's in shadow," Joanna commented.

"So, we should really explore it in the morning, preferably around ten," Jake said, looking at his watch. "It's twelve now."

"If the entrance is deep we wouldn't see it anyway," Joanna pointed out.

"Not with masks and snorkels," Diana added.

"If you look at the map," Jake said, "it's the only feature close to shore that has sufficient depth and therefore the only place we could've missed without scuba gear."

"So where do we get such equipment?" Joanna asked.

"Lichas," Diana replied.

"You dive?" Jake asked.

"We both do," Diana confirmed.

"So why, in all these years, haven't you looked for it yourself?" Jake asked.

"I never imagined the cave was so deep," Diana replied. "Not knowing its precise location, I would've needed weeks of diving. That would never have passed unnoticed either by the army, the coast guard or Poseidon. Besides it was under a mound of debris."

"If you were unsure where the entrance was and had little hope of finding it before the earthquake, what did you hope to achieve with my father?"

"After the discovery of the wreck south of Paleo Limani, there was the realistic expectation that there would be an underwater survey in and around the Old Athenian Harbour, until the money ran out that is. I would've been able to pull a few strings with my friend."

"But that's irrelevant now," Joanna said. "You're sure the underwater entrance will be sealed?"

"Yes, and you can be sure there's a sentinel guarding it. Just like with the landward entrance."

"Aren't we therefore taking a risk looking for it?" Jake asked.

"No, because if that were the case, every fisherman, yachtsman or swimmer who passed by would be killed," Diana replied. "You would have to try to break in and we don't want to do that. At least with the centaur we know what we're dealing with."

"Basil must suspect we're looking for this cave, surely?" Joanna asked, frowning.

"He'll be keeping a close eye on us now that Jake's here," Diana said. "But he must feel confident that the tomb is impossible to find or break into."

"You're not going to be able to do this dive in daylight, are you?" Jake asked.

"I know," Diana agreed. "So we mustn't forget to hire a couple of torches. We're only going to get one shot at this so we need to get it right first time."

"So, assuming we eventually find this landward entrance, how do we get in and past the centaur?" Jake asked.

"Don't worry about that now; I know how to deal with it," Diana said.

"You know, there are a few things about this that are troubling me," Jake said. It had been on his mind for most of the night. Now that he was thinking clearly again, he'd realised that he had achieved what he had set out to do: discover the truth about his father. "I know this sounds pretty obvious, but as far as I'm concerned, overthrowing Poseidon, Basil, will not bring my father back. Will you answer some questions honestly for me?"

"As best I can," Diana said.

"You keep saying that by retrieving the crystals the status quo will be restored. What does that mean?"

"To say the status quo will be restored isn't quite accurate. Physically, genetically, we're not immortals. It would take many generations to restore that. The Gods will never be the same force they used to be, but at least our combined powers will overcome Kephalas and Poseidon."

"So, each one of the Gods has possessed someone. You mentioned that in the past those who were driven to retrieve the crystals believed they were that person."

"Yes, I did."

"So you, Diana, or whoever you were previously, would be destroyed."

"I don't think it's quite that drastic. Artemis and I have been integrated for so long, I can't remember a time before."

"But if you become more of Artemis, could retrieving the crystals therefore be a form of murder? Won't I be murdering Diana and the others, whoever they may be?"

"That's absurd."

"Is this quest not more to do with your desire for revenge?"

"Well, yes, we want justice first and then peace," Diana replied, seeming uncomfortable. Joanna, sitting on her right, mirrored her. "The only way we're going to get that is by a return to a balance of power. But there's something else you're forgetting. Buried together with the bodies is the greatest treasure of gold and other artefacts that could ever be found, not to mention the unassigned crystals."

"I don't need any more wealth, nor do I lust after being immortal. My father's properties on Halia are going to his siblings. If I let it be known that I was leaving this island, only coming back maybe once a year to visit my father's grave, and went to live in Athens, going about my business there, would Poseidon not just leave me alone? After all, he's had plenty of opportunities to kill me in the last few weeks."

"He would probably leave you alone. No guarantee of course," Diana said. "Especially if you had children."

"I'm still not quite sure why Poseidon would've killed my father. Just because he made it on his own doesn't seem like grounds enough; he was his son after all. For every one like my father there are a hundred who would prefer to take the easier way and cosy up to someone like Basil." Jake noticed that the two still looked strange. "Now that I have the facts, I can see that this quest is highly dangerous and not just to me. Like my father, I now also have something to lose. Basil used me and my mother to blackmail my father. He could use Joanna against me." He looked lovingly at her.

"He's right Gran," Joanna said. "We're in love and we have a life together. I've found what I've been looking for and don't want to lose it. I also don't want to lose you." She looked back at Jake. "Now that we know everything, it's unfair to ask us to risk our lives without even thinking about it. It's too late to go searching today anyway. Why don't you give us the rest of the day together? We'll talk it through and meet you tonight for supper. If we decide to do it, we'll go to

Lichas tomorrow morning for the diving equipment. How's that?"

"You're both right," Diana said, looking relieved. "I've steamed on ahead, driven by my motives and those of the others. Maybe it's time for me to have some time to think things through too. I'll leave you. Say we meet again at ten tonight at Paralia?"

"Sounds great, Gran," Joanna said. They saw her to the door.

"I'm glad you agreed with me," Jake told Joanna when they were alone, although he was surprised at how quickly Diana had accepted it. Maybe she realised what he said made sense. "I was afraid you'd be disappointed."

"Why wouldn't I agree with the love of my life?" she said, looking at him lovingly.

"You mean that?" Jake said, moved. "That's how I feel about you."

"We have to consider our future together, darling. I don't want to risk it without good and just cause."

"I agree," Jake said. He felt like crying for joy.

"This love that's growing between us, it's getting stronger every day. Don't you feel it?" she said. She was looking at him with those piercing eyes; they were devouring him.

"I do, I do," Jake said, feeling elated. He wanted her so much; it felt as if his heart would burst. Ever since Diana had started telling the story, he had concentrated on that and had forgotten how strong his feelings were.

"I love being close to you, darling," Joanna said, embracing him and gently kissing his lips. "I want to get closer still, I want you inside me, part of me; come, let's make love. Nothing else matters."

Nothing else did, just his overwhelming desire for her. He followed her, having forgotten about everything else.

Chapter 30: Basil

He walked onto the aft deck and into the newborn night. The last rays of the sun had disappeared behind the mountains and the warm dry breeze ruffled his hair and beard whilst also carrying the sounds of the harbour: cars, motorbikes, voices, music and the play of waves on rocks, jetties and boats. Then there were the different lights: street lamps, the headlights of cars, those of houses and the illuminations of bars and restaurants. He could see the crowds beginning to build nicely.

He breathed in the air, closed his eyes and interpreted the aromas. They were those of a night of promise; the guarantee of food, drink and casual company. He glanced to his left at the smaller yacht berthed next to his. Kephalas and his family had gone out for the evening. He'd declined a meal on board and had let the crew stand down and take the night off. They would be busy tomorrow evening and needed a break. Only the security team were, as always, on duty. He would go out shortly and wander around the harbour front.

He returned to his state rooms. Of all the yachts he'd owned over the decades, this was his favourite. It was spacious and luxurious but not too big so as to attract media attention. The last thing he wanted was someone photographing him and wondering who he was. With a smaller hull he could visit the more out-of-the-way places and maintain his anonymity.

A more compact yacht also meant less crew; less chance of a loose cannon. Security was always a nightmare, especially now. At least there were only a couple of weeks to go before the present emergency was over.

He felt nostalgia for the days of old. At that time, if someone gave him a problem, he eliminated them; end of story. If somewhere was troublesome, he just razed it to the ground. A good earthquake followed by a tidal wave usually did the trick, preferably in the middle of the night. Was it worth giving up all those powers for what he was now left with? Well, as things turned out, no. But who could have predicted this outcome? Who could have known that a tiny island in the middle of the Aegean would be inhabited to such an extent? Who could have foretold the return of his formally deceased brothers, sisters, nieces and nephews?

But there was no going back. No return to the former glories, even if he wanted to. History had proven that the reincarnated souls were not replicas of the originals. They were still powerful, but once they got hold of the crystals they went a bit crazy and delusional. There was no way he was going to cede power to a bunch of zombies. Try explaining that to them.

In his cabin he opened the wardrobe, parted the hanging clothes, removed an invisible panel and unlocked the safe behind it. He found the wallet that contained his valuables. In one pocket were his current Greek passport and driver's licence. In another was cash; euros and dollars. He took out five hundred euros, which would be more than enough for a place like this. Had it been Monte Carlo, it would have needed to be ten times as much.

This was his official safe; the one customs and other nosey officials could look into. In a separate location he had his other passports: American, British, Canadian,

Australian and Swiss. Some were in different names. There were also several drivers' licenses and birth certificates. In addition he had details of his many accounts, all in different names and in different banks throughout the world, all fed from Geneva.

He put everything back, closing the safe and wardrobe. Leaving the cabin and yacht, he passed a few of the security guards on his way out into the night and the crowds.

This harbour, one of the hundreds he knew, was not particularly exciting, but still boasted over thirty bars, so there was bound to be something for him. Starting from the southern end, he started to go through each one. The first few were empty. From the fourth onwards they started to fill. He went through several of these but found no target. Then there was one with just the right woman but she was Italian and had her husband with her. In Mediterranean countries you could not get away with trying to seduce a married woman or one with a fiancé. Conversely, it was different in Northern Europe and North America. There extramarital affairs spiced up relationships for some, and the seasoning of betrayal made for the best sex.

A few bars later, he found what he was looking for: a German or Scandinavian-looking tourist; fair, blue eyes, buxom and athletic. She was with a female friend and two British men, who were trying to seduce them. They'd met on the island and had already spent the last few days together. Something was blossoming between his choice and one of the men. He sensed that she was highly excited and would be receptive. This was perfect. It was a familiar scenario that he'd encountered thousands of times.

He bought a bottle of beer from the bar and sat where he could watch her, waiting for the right moment. He reflected that sex and business were the only realms left where a man could express his need for conquest and the vanquishing of an opponent. Sex was the most immediate. The taking and seduction of someone else's woman. He had to admit that this aspect was better than before, for there was now an element of danger and he had to work for it.

When she went to the cloakroom he prepared himself and, as she was on her way back, he approached her. "Hey! Fancy meeting you," he said to her in English, mocking surprise.

"Why yes, Basil?" she replied.

Of course, they had never met, but he had implanted the feeling of recognition and his name in her mind. He took her hand and kissed her on either cheek. He could feel her already responding. He looked into her eyes; hers were fixed on his.

"You'll have to remind me of your name, it's slipped my mind," he said in German. He had recognised her accent and he could manage most of the European languages.

"It's Anna," she replied.

"Of course," he said. "Are you here with friends?"

"Yes, just over there."

"Could I steal you from them briefly?" he said. "It would be great to catch up."

"Why, of course, just wait here." She went to speak with her companions. She told them she had met an old family friend and would go and speak with him for a few minutes before coming back. The two men looked suspiciously over at him. He stared them down. Despite his greying hair and beard, he was a big man. Well over six feet and with a muscular physique. Both of them together would have no chance against him.

When she came back to him, he took her outside to a table on the pavement, away from the loud music, and ordered some drinks. They started talking. Already he felt that she was interested in him, drawn to him. All the sexual energy that had built up between her and the other man was now focused on him. He could take her now if he wanted, but he would tease her a bit and build the bond between them.

He understood women better than most men. He'd had many years' experience, of course, but, most of all, he could get into their heads, quite literally. There had to be a mind game involved, with the risk of failure, and occasionally he did fail. Unfortunately, rape was no longer an option.

Women were not drawn to him because they fell in love. There was a certain degree of infatuation involved, but it was more to do with being attracted to power, particularly when exuded with confidence.

And what about love? Well, it never came in to it for him. In the numerous encounters he'd had, it had only reared its head once, and look where that had got him. Sure, there were thousands of women who wanted to stay with him, but he never had a problem shifting them. There was just the one little mistake that he had made. He had paid for it, but pretty soon that would be behind him and things could return to normal.

After a while he felt hungry and asked Anna if he could take her for a meal. She immediately accepted. She went back to her friends to inform them. The men looked put out and the friend seemed upset. Maybe if this Anna checked out he could bring her into it as well.

It was a while since he had enjoyed two women in that way.

When she came back to him, they took a cab to a restaurant in the suburbs to the south of the town, near the beach and the sea, where they could hear the waves and where he felt at home. He went through the usual routine. By the end of the meal, after some expensive food and wine, she was ready. There was no need for an invitation to the yacht. In the back of the cab, as it headed for the harbour, she was responding to him with excitement.

The next morning he was up at eight thirty. The girl was in a deep sleep and probably would not stir for a few more hours. She'd been good and appreciative. There was more to explore with her so he decided he might keep her for a while. He pulled on some clothes and went out into the lounge, where he found Kephalas waiting, having a coffee out on the aft deck.

"You decided to come over this morning," Basil said. "Have you been waiting long?"

"I didn't want to disturb you."

"You must have something to tell me."

"It appears our little friend and her entourage have decided to pay Lichas a visit. Jake and Joanna were on the ferry this morning and Diana has sailed with the yacht."

"Coming here too?"

"Probably."

"So what do you think? Are they up to anything?"

"Not that I can see, maybe they're just bored and have come for a few days. What do you want me to do?"

"Just keep an eye out as usual, make sure they're not playing any games. But wait, I'd like to meet them. Arrange for them to come for drinks, before the other guests."

"I'll see to it," Kephalas said. He finished his coffee and got up to leave.

Basil went up to the bridge and sat for a while. Of course, he knew exactly what they were up to, including Kephalas's part in it. Unfortunately for them, he had foreseen everything and had a surprise planned.

The chance of them carrying out their strategy was pretty remote and, even if they did try, the only threat was to Jake. He was not as stubborn as his father, neither did he have his strength of will, and was being manipulated. Admittedly, he'd shown initiative escaping the encounter on the road, but that was just meant to scare him, and after the twenty-sixth he would either be leaving Halia of his own free will or in a coffin. Poor boy was oblivious to the danger. He would fail and that would be the end of their opportunities for the foreseeable future.

He wasn't particularly interested in seeing Jake. He couldn't afford any sentimentality, as with George. It was Joanna he wanted. He'd heard she'd grown into a beauty, doing justice to the original. He'd have her and he knew she wanted him.

He decided to go back to the girl. She woke as he entered the cabin and smiled with anticipation.

Chapter 31: The *Trident*

Saturday, 18th August

They caught the eight o'clock ferry and sat outside on the aft deck under the tarpaulin. It was one of those mornings with no breeze and the sea was flat calm, which reflected Jake's mood. The ferry was crowded and noisy, full of Saturday shoppers, but he hardly noticed. He sat beside Joanna, holding her hand, facing starboard, watching the water sliding by in contented silence.

They would stay in Lichas two nights. Today, Saturday, they would acquire the diving equipment Diana and Joanna needed. The dive shop was on the outskirts of town, near to which was a small and discreet marina where the *Pelagos* would be waiting to take the equipment on board. After that, Diana would sail back to the main harbour to pick up more general supplies and provisions. They would spend the morning with her, she would then sail back to Halia and they would have two more nights and a whole day to themselves.

Joanna wanted to return and get started right away, but the Greek Navy and Coast Guard were conducting exercises in the waters surrounding Halia, part of their efforts to deter illegal immigrants, and Diana felt that, as a consequence, their chances of being detected were too high.

Jake was looking forward to this time with Joanna. They were getting so close. Whenever he thought their relationship could not get better, well it did. He was so certain about everything when he was with her. Yesterday afternoon and last night he saw the bigger picture. It was a time of such intense feelings and passion that little needed to be said. He felt sure that his union with Joanna was for life. She said things to him, expressed feelings for him that he never thought he would hear.

The matter of the retrieval of the crystals, although not directly spoken, became symbolic. They became a token of his commitment to her, to Diana and the others. He could see himself in the future, married to Joanna, with a family, living in Greece and being part of this community.

"It shouldn't take long to get everything done," Joanna had said. "Then we can just concentrate on being together."

After the ferry arrived, they managed to bypass the throng and disembarked easily. They walked up the quay with their rucksacks on their backs, before finding a taxi to take them the short drive out to the north of town and the dive shop. From there they rented two sets of equipment: tanks, weights, lifejackets, demand valves and a small compressor, as well as the underwater torches.

They loaded up the taxi and took everything to the small marina where Diana was waiting. After transferring the equipment on board the *Pelagos*, they took the taxi back to the Meltemi. Doros had booked them a room at the front and they were able to watch out for Diana from the balcony. They'd only just unpacked when they saw her entering the breakwater.

They walked over to the southern part of the harbour, reserved for smaller yachts, and helped her tie up, after which Diana said, "I'm dying for a coffee; a nice cappuccino."

"Let's go and have one," Jake said.

"I can't leave;" Diana said. "I've had a call from the chandler. He'll make the delivery within the next hour or two, so it's best if we have it afterwards; and what better place to enjoy it than here on deck."

"I'll stay and help Gran with the stowing," Joanna said. "You mentioned wanting to buy swimming shorts, so why don't you go and look for them and I'll text you when the delivery's arrived; then you can pick up the coffees on your way back."

He headed off towards the town. As he left the marina, he started along the quayside, where he passed the large boats. Here, amongst them, he recognised the *Warrior*, moored at Kephalas's pier the day he'd swum to Seal Beach. As he approached, he saw the man himself sitting on his after deck by the gangway looking in his direction. "Hey, Jake," he said, "good morning, what are you doing in Lichas? Business or pleasure?"

"One hundred per cent pleasure," Jake replied, stopping at the foot of the gangway.

"Then come on board and let me treat you to a coffee or a drink."

"Actually, I was just going shopping and to get coffees for my friends," Jake replied, taken back by his friendliness.

"Tell them to come as well."

"Unfortunately they're expecting a delivery."

"The inevitable consequence and inconvenience of having a yacht," Kephalas lamented. "Still, here's a better idea. My friend Basil, who resides on this yacht next door," he pointed towards the sleek monster moored to his left, "wants to meet you. What about the three of you coming for drinks at eight thirty? Then you'll have time to go somewhere else afterwards."

"Sounds perfect, except there'll just be two. Diana will be sailing at midday."

"That's fine, come straight on to the *Trident*; that's where we'll be."

"Okay, see you tonight," Jake said before continuing on his way. He certainly could not turn down the chance of meeting his grandfather, the bastard who had murdered his father, soon to be toppled himself.

He wandered aimlessly into town and was soon engrossed in his thoughts of Joanna again. He imagined their life together in Athens, having a beautiful family, growing old together, always in love. He saw himself retrieving the crystals and being a hero, then running his father's business and all that that entailed.

He was so focused on these thoughts and feelings that he didn't notice that he'd wandered away from the shopping streets and into the old town. His walking appeared purposeful and brisk; straight ahead here, bear right there, turn left somewhere else. The crowds dissipated and the streets turned residential and narrowed, just as on his previous visit. To all this he was oblivious.

Eventually he came to a lane without pavements and with tall stone walls on both sides. Two thirds of the way up, he turned down an alleyway to the left. At the end, he opened and walked through an unmarked wooden door and into enclosed grounds. In the middle was a two-storey house rendered in a creamy warm-coloured stone with a red terracotta-tiled roof and metal railinged balconies on the upper floor. It was surrounded by a luxuriously abundant garden. A mixture of rich sensuous scents surrounded him as did a dense cacophony of bird and insect sounds. As he stopped in front of a dark varnished wooden door, his awareness returned, as if he were coming out of a trance.

He stood there, looking around him, disorientated. He was about to flee when the door opened. The first thing he noticed about the woman who stood on the threshold was the warmth in her smile and eyes. She wore a yellow blouse and black skirt covered with a bright, flower-patterned apron, like on one of those cheesy American television commercials for cookies. It was impossible to distinguish her age. She had shoulder-length, auburn hair with no hint of grey. From her complexion she appeared to be in her forties and her skin had an almost amber glow. She was tall, close to Jake's height, slim and shapely, and attractive in a sweet, motherly way. As if to reinforce this impression, a strong smell of home baking enveloped him.

"Please come in," she said, standing aside to let him pass.

"No, I'm sorry this is a mistake, I'm lost. You couldn't tell me how to get back to the harbour?"

"All in good time, Jake. I've been expecting you."

"Expecting me?" Jake was startled. His first thought was that this was some sort of trap. He wanted to leave but found it impossible to move his legs. His gaze was riveted to the woman's amber eyes. She raised her right hand, the palm facing him, and her pupils narrowed. "I mean you no harm," she said with authority. He felt a wave of benevolent compassion that made him relax. "Come in and be welcomed."

His legs obeyed, quite independently of the rest of him. Once inside, the smell of baking became more intense. It had a rich, sweet aroma and was accompanied by the scent of coffee. It made him hungry.

After a plain entrance lobby, they entered a spacious sitting area with three settees arranged in front of a stone fireplace, blackened with use, but now containing a display of bright orange and red flowers in a ceramic vase. There were embroidered cushions on the settees and at their ends were wooden side tables with colourful shaded lamps. In the middle was a glass-topped coffee table, below which was a shelf of magazines and books on cookery, gardening and home furnishing.

On both sides of the fireplace were free-standing bookshelves with volumes covering religious and spiritual topics.

Beyond the sitting area was a dining room table, to the left of which was a door to what Jake assumed was the kitchen. There were noises coming from that direction, which indicated that there was someone else in the house.

Glass doors from the dining area opened out onto the rear part of a perfect and beautiful garden with an improbable concentration of flowers and flowering plants. From a marble fountain came the sound of running water. There were benches and tables, and he could hear the chatter of birds. Colourful butterflies coasted from one blossom to another, sharing them with countless other insects. Then he remembered. The flowers that were sent for his father's grave. This was where they came from. How could he have forgotten? This was the house at the end of the alley to which he had followed Photis the other day.

"Please sit," the woman said, indicating the settee facing the hearth. She positioned herself on the adjacent one. "Would you like coffee or tea? I can also offer herbal tea that I make myself."

"I don't know why you say you're expecting me; I wandered here by accident."

She looked at him and her smile broadened. "You're here because I summoned you. You know this is so. I know you've been looking for me; for us." She looked towards the kitchen. "You've just forgotten. That's why I thought I'd intervene."

"But why? Besides, I've got to get back." His legs wouldn't obey.

"I know. Your friends won't miss you, just yet. This first meeting won't take long. Please sit."

First meeting, he thought, still standing. Then footsteps approached from the door to the kitchen. A tall slim man in black trousers and a black short-sleeved shirt entered. He had short dark hair that was starting to go grey around his ears and temples. He was darkly tanned with weathered skin. His face was clean-shaven and handsome, although unsmiling and subdued. He was carrying a tray, which he placed on the table. On it was a cafetière, a pot of tea, three mugs and a plate of biscuits, which looked freshly baked.

The man looked at Jake expectantly. It was the man he had followed from the ferry, the man he'd met for the first time at his father's funeral. It was Photis, his father's companion of many years.

Jake extended his hand, which Photis took in both of his. Once again, he expressed his condolences, in Greek, looking emotional, looking as if he wanted to embrace Jake, before sitting down. Jake also sat.

"I'm afraid Photis doesn't speak English at all well. He was expressing his regret at your father's death. But I think you can speak some Greek."

"Indeed," Jake said, "and I thank him for it, but I still don't know who you are."

"Ah yes, me," she said. "In the last few days you've surmounted many hurdles of plausibility. Hopefully, this one will be relatively easy."

"I can't imagine who you could be. But I'm bracing myself."

"That's because the accepted wisdom of those you've spoken to is that I'm either dead or beyond reach," the woman said looking down at her lap. "I'm Hestia."

"Hestia!" Jake was about to break out laughing but stopped himself as he felt he could not do so in front of Photis. "I suppose if I've accepted some of the other things that've been said, then I should entertain the possibility that what you say is true. So, if you're Hestia, you must also be six thousand years old and a goddess."

"The only one left. I'd prefer you to call me Virginia. I go by that name these days."

"And does Photis also know this?"

"Of course."

"So why have you brought me here?"

"Two reasons really. Firstly to have some of the gaps in your recent education filled and secondly to give you a reality check."

"A reality check? I don't think I need one of those."

"I'm aware that you're short of time," she said, ignoring his last comment. "There will be an opportunity for us to meet again, but for now I'm going to get right to the point. I'm afraid you're not going to like some of the things I'm going to say. They'll just have to sink in. I imagine you've been told about your father's parentage?"

"Yes. Do you want to add something to it?"

"A bit. And about the prophecy?"

"That too."

"Basil, Poseidon, my brother, despite his philandering, was careful not to have any offspring," she said, pouring out the coffee. "He succeeded remarkably well, with only the one exception, your father, as you already know. During the last war he left Europe, moving to the United States. There he met a married woman, of Irish descent, with whom he had the nearest thing to a relationship in recent years. By the end of the war, he'd tired of her and returned to Europe and Greece. Sometime later, the woman came looking for him and presented him with a son.

"I believe, although I can't confirm, that he had one of his rages and killed her, probably unintentionally, because she was not seen or heard from again. As for the child, his anger vented, he found it impossible to harm it. At the same time he wanted to keep it close, where he could keep an eye on it. He looked around for an island family. At that time, your grandmother had just given birth to her second stillborn baby, and it was thought that she wouldn't be able to have children of her own. Basil turned up at the hospital and, with the help of a financial inducement, convinced your grandparents to adopt. Basil tried his best to keep this secret, you understand."

"How did Diana and the others find out then?"

"It was Kephalas who figured it out and subsequently let it slip. He has a tendency to drink and talk too much. You must also now be aware of how the crystals work? How they are expressing themselves?"

"I know about Diana, she's Artemis, but she's not told me about anyone else."

"Kephalas is Ares, and Phivos is Apollo, Diana's brother. Do you think Kephalas is happy working for Poseidon? Do you not think they want to regain the glories of the past?"

"Yes, but why would Poseidon employ him?"

"You've heard the expression 'keep your friends close and your enemies closer'? Poseidon's no fool. He knows exactly what's happening and what they're all playing at. It's a power game that's been going on amongst them for thousands of years. A game that's cost many lives."

"Including my father's?"

"Yes, but not for the reason you think."

"I don't understand. Diana suggested that my father was killed because he was planning to help them."

"That's what Diana would like you to believe, but it certainly wasn't the case. His agreement with Poseidon, which guaranteed your safety, was that he should not take sides."

"Did my mother know this?"

"Yes."

"So, why did my father leave us?"

"It was the constant hounding by Diana, Phivos and the others that made it necessary. Your parents were worried that Basil would interpret it the wrong way and retaliate."

"So why did Poseidon kill him?" Jake asked. This last remark of Virginia's caused him to remember Maria, the fisherman's wife, and what she'd said about Diana and the others.

"There's only one reason I can think of that seems to fit the facts. If the woman that your father was seeing at the time, the one he brought to the island, if she was pregnant, that would've been enough provocation."

"That would've been three members of his blood line to contend with," Jake reflected.

"That's why I think no trace will ever be found of her. Although I'm still surprised he killed your father. I think his anger got the better of him once again."

"So where does that leave me?"

"That leaves you as the only person alive who can retrieve the crystals."

"So why not kill me too?"

"The prophecy was vague, and because he doesn't believe you'll ever find his grotto, he's holding back, for now. Also, as far as I know, your father kept his side of the bargain where it came to you. He left you fatherless for most of your life and disenfranchised you from the island properties. So, provided you leave the island after your holiday and never come back, he'll leave you alone."

"But the souls of the Gods want me to retrieve the crystals and give them to their adopted hosts, or whatever they are, so they can regain their powers and hold Basil to account."

"There's more to it than that. When they get the crystals, they will also become like gods, they will live again, after a fashion. Past experience has shown that the fusion of personalities within one mind causes madness. They will not destroy Poseidon, they can't. Instead they will reprimand him and the status quo will be re-established. So, instead of having one megalomaniac loose in the world, you'll have fourteen, all working together, most of who will be crazy. This cannot be permitted."

"Why are you saying this? You're one of them. They're your blood."

"I never took part in any of their manipulations and excesses. I loved them dearly and still do, but know that instead of resurrection they should be put to rest."

"Hold on, this is none of my business. I'll do like my father and refuse to take part. I'll leave the island and not come back. From what I can see, you're just as bad as the others. What I say is, deal with it amongst yourselves. If you're the only Goddess left, you go to the island and sort it out."

"I can't do that. I can't raise my hand against them. It's not my way."

"So, instead you get other people to do it."

"No, that's not so. I just want to do what's right. I don't want you to be added to all the countless innocents that have died. I will not tolerate anyone else getting hurt."

"Who says I'm going to die? I'll simply choose not to take part."

"Unfortunately, you have no choice."

"Are you going to force me, like you made me come here?"

"No, I shall not be forcing you to do anything further, I promise," Virginia said. "Why do I say you have no choice? Because of all those around you on the island, influencing you in some way, including Diana. Their effect is modest. But there's one who's overpowering and deadly, one who you can't overcome, not without help, not without insight. I'm talking about Aphrodite."

"Aphrodite? I've not met her yet."

"The fact that you're not aware of her presence demonstrates the control she has over you. Joanna is Aphrodite."

"Joanna? That's ridiculous, she's only a girl," Jake said standing up. "But so what? We're in love. She's the love of my life and I'm hers."

"That's Aphrodite's influence. She was the Goddess of love. Her powers were that she was able to inspire love and devotion in any man or woman, or should I say blind love and devotion. She's distorted your reality."

"I don't believe that; I know what I feel; I know what she feels. It's real."

"It may be real to you but, as far as she's concerned, you're just a means to an end. Even when she does fall in love, it's temporary, she soon moves on to someone else."

"Whatever. I'm leaving now," Jake said. He had not touched the coffee nor did he want to hear any more.

"I haven't finished yet."

"I have."

"I haven't told you about Teresa."

"Teresa? What does that fraud have to do with it? She's the one who sold herself out."

"Teresa was no set-up. That relationship was real."

"That's rubbish. So why didn't she turn up?"

"She did Jake; in fact, she's still here."

"What?" Jake felt as if his head was going to explode. "I don't understand."

"The day you arrived, Diana knew about her coming. She'd found out her name from Doros, when you made the reservation for the room. She sent someone on board to look for her. There was no way she could be on the scene. She had to be got rid of to make way for Joanna, Aphrodite."

"So, what do you claim happened?"

"Between Piraeus and here she was abducted, put in a car and taken off. You see, Diana knows that Joanna can impose total control over you. What she's not certain of is whether Joanna will stay on the beam and not wander, so she's taken Teresa as insurance. She's a prisoner on Halia."

"That's absurd. It's been three weeks."

"I know, she must be in a terrible state. Diana's going to keep her until she has the crystals and, when she doesn't need her any more, she'll dispose of her."

"I don't believe you. You set me up with some truths I can agree with, just to get me to swallow the rest. You can't fool me. I feel sorry for Photis." Looking over at him, he could see that he'd lowered his head. "My father was fond of him. If I had the time and spoke Greek well enough, I'd soon put him straight. So, go sort out your own problems. After tonight Joanna and I are taking the first flight out."

With that, Jake left, without looking back or shutting the front door. He followed the contours downhill as well as he could remember, back to the harbour. He was angry and his head was spinning. He was relieved when his mobile rang. It was Joanna to tell him that the delivery had taken place and that he should return. He looked at his watch. It was 12:30. He'd been gone for an hour and a half. All he could think of was getting back to her, getting her alone and holding her. He'd tell her that he'd made up his mind to go and that was it. It was only out of kindness that he was prepared to help the others but not at the risk to their lives.

He stopped off at the café nearest to the marina to buy the coffees. When he arrived back, Joanna and Diana were busily chatting away and never asked how he'd passed his time or said anything about the fact that he'd not bought any swimming shorts. The first thing he mentioned was their invitation that evening.

"You're honoured," Diana said. "Either that or he's suspecting something."

"I hope you don't mind my accepting the invitation?"

"It was the right thing to do," Diana said. "Just try and act normal."

"As long as we can go to that restaurant afterwards," Joanna said.

"You've not been?" Jake asked.

"No."

"Gosh, look at the time," Diana said. "It's nearly one thirty. You'd better go if you're planning to swim."

They went back to the hotel, changed into their swimming gear, packed what they needed in a rucksack and took a taxi to the nearest beach. There they had a swim and sunbathe, followed by a light salad lunch, before going back to the hotel.

When Jake sat on the balcony, he felt a lot better. The swim had cleared his head. It was obvious what was going on. Everyone around them had their own interests in mind. Basil wanted to maintain the status quo, Diana and her team had their revenge agenda and Hestia had hers, whatever it was. The only way she could get any leverage against him was to have Photis there. Then it was one ridiculous claim after another.

In the middle were Jake and Joanna. How could Hestia say those things about her? You only had to look at Joanna to know that she was wrong; her beauty, her sweetness. All that love and passion they had for each other.

"What is it Jake?" Joanna said, coming out onto balcony. "You seem distracted."

"I was thinking," he said. She knelt down on the floor between his legs. "It's what I was saying yesterday. This isn't our argument. This concerns something that happened thousands of years ago. We should let them sort it out."

"Gosh, that's not what you were saying this morning. We've gone and hired all this equipment. What's happened?"

"Well, I paid for it didn't I? Let Diana and her friends look for the cave. All these people wanting us to do things for them, for their reasons. Honestly, we should leave them to it. We've got our own lives to lead."

"Of course, my darling. I've told you before, we'll do whatever you want." She embraced him. "I love you."

"I love you too," he said. How could that stupid woman say that Joanna was manipulating him? If anything he was manipulating her by changing his mind all the time. She pulled away from him slightly, looking at her watch.

"We've got three hours until we need to get ready," she said, her blue eyes widening. There was a fire in them and he knew what that meant. This just went to show how wrong Hestia was. The more assertive he became, the more she wanted him. His excitement and anticipation grew. "I just want to be with you, for ever and ever, you and me, closer and closer." She kissed him. "It just seems to get better, doesn't it?"

"It does; I just can't believe it," Jake said. He had forgotten everything they'd just been talking about. The only thing in his mind was how much he wanted her.

She stood up and took his hand. "Let's go inside."

Shortly after eight, he was on the balcony again, dressed and ready for their visit with Basil. He was so happy; what a wonderful day it had been. As he relived it he was aware that there was something unpleasant about it earlier on, but he could not put his finger on it. He shrugged it off. It couldn't have been important.

When Joanna came out, she looked stunning. She wore a light patterned dress with blue in it that brought out the colour of her eyes. He couldn't understand how anyone could be so beautiful. "You look amazing," he said.

"You like it?" she said, twirling round in front of him. "Come on, let's go."

At eight thirty precisely they boarded the *Trident III*. As they walked up the gangway, a deck hand, who was sitting by the ladder, stood up and asked if he could help.

"I'm Jake Philo; I think we're expected."

"Certainly, sir," he replied. "Please remove your shoes. There's a selection of cloth footwear for you to choose from." The man pressed a button beside the gangway.

"Thank you," Jake said. As they found suitable slippers, he noticed a man, dressed in white, walking towards them from within.

"My colleague will show you up," the guard said.

They walked through the open smoked-glass doors into a lounge. This was large by land standards and encompassed most of the deck. The space was being prepared for a reception or a buffet. On the left there was a banqueting table covered in a white tablecloth, with hotplates on it. There was an assortment of armchairs and settees, and several side tables. The finish was in dark veneer, which matched the trim of the windows. The carpet was a deep pile that they sank into with every step.

Two thirds of the way in was a double staircase. They followed the steward up and found themselves on the next deck, which had a row of windows that ran the width of the yacht. They went round the staircase aft and immediately behind the casing was the bar. The rest of the deck consisted of another lounge, this time finished in a dark mahogany. Beyond this and aft were sliding glass doors that led out onto an area of deck containing a round table with chairs. There were three men outside; two were seated and the other, also dressed in white, approached them.

The deck hand greeted them and led them outside. One of the seated men was Kephalas, the other Jake had never seen before.

"Jake, good of you to come," Alexander said, standing up.

"It was kind of you to invite us," Jake said. "Let me introduce you to Joanna Charles."

"Of course we know of Diana's granddaughter, although we've not seen you since you were a young girl. Please come and meet Basil."

The other man stood up. He was well over six feet tall and big in every respect. His large head had long dishevelled locks of greying hair and a noticeably whiter beard. He was wearing navy shorts and a white open-necked tee-shirt. His exposed arms and legs were muscular and the skin tanned and weathered.

He greeted Joanna first. "I'm glad to see you again," he said in a deep, smooth voice, "although I only remember you when you were young, and look how beautiful you've become. Much like your mother."

"And her grandmother," Kephalas added.

"Of course," Basil said "and how is she? I believe she was here earlier."

"She was, but she's left now."

"Pity, I rarely see her," Basil said. "She hasn't slowed down with age." He turned to greet Jake. "I'm glad to meet you, Jake. I'm sorry for the loss of you father. Please sit down both of you. What can John get you?"

"I'd like a dry white wine," Joanna said.

"I'll have a beer," Jake added.

"So what do you do for a living?" Basil asked Joanna.

"I work for the European Commission; I'm an interpreter."

"You have a talent for languages then, like your grandmother. So do you translate documents too?"

"No, I'm a simultaneous interpreter. I interpret for delegates during sittings of the parliament."

"I believe this is most demanding and requires special abilities," Basil said. Joanna feigned embarrassment. "There's no need to be shy about your talents. We know a lot about you already, but little about Jake."

Jake answered questions about himself; where he lived and what he did. Meanwhile the barman had brought them drinks and some canapés. Throughout the time Jake spoke, Basil kept his eyes on Joanna. It was making Jake feel uncomfortable. "How well did you know my father?" Jake asked.

"Well enough to tell he was quite a character," Basil said.

"Unfortunately, you probably knew him better than I did," Jake said. He saw that his statement caused an uncomfortable shift in Kephalas, but Basil was unmoved.

"The departure of a parent, for whatever reason, is difficult and perplexing," Basil said. "I didn't know either of mine when I was young. Both of them were too busy with their social lives. I was brought up by governesses. I think it's made me more cynical. In the end we each have to find our own way."

"Quite so," Kephalas added.

"I think by now everyone knows that your father has left you his business," Basil said. "Have you formed any impressions about our way of life?"

"It's not what I've been used to," Jake replied. "Although I haven't entirely decided what I'm going to do, I think I'll be moving to Athens in the near future."

"Good, excellent. We'll look forward to seeing more of both of you," Basil said, looking over at Joanna as if he meant the words only for her. "You know," he continued, turning to Jake, "this is a community of cooperation. It's what makes us strong. We try to help each other without hesitation. It's a difficult concept to grasp, but in time you'll understand."

"I'm sure it won't take me long," Jake said.

Basil took no further interest in him and instead talked to Joanna about the many islands he'd been to. "You have an attractive boat," Joanna said.

"Thank you," Basil said. "Why don't I show you around?"

"I'd like that," Joanna said.

"I'm sorry," Kephalas interrupted, "but it's coming close to nine thirty."

Jake had a look at his watch. The time had flown and it was now dark.

"I'm afraid I must go and get dressed," Basil said.

"And so should I," Kephalas added.

"We're expecting a number of guests tonight," Basil informed them. "I apologise for not inviting you too, but all are accounted for, and space, even on a big yacht, is limited."

"Next time," Jake said.

They stood up and said their goodbyes. They were escorted to the gangway by the barman. From the yacht they walked to the hotel, where they ordered a taxi to take them to the restaurant.

"When will you be going back to Brussels?" Jake asked once they had settled at their table and ordered their food. They had already been brought water, ouzo and ice.

"The European Parliament is adjourned. Consequently we get long holidays. Four weeks to be exact. But I think we should discuss our future."

"You're right. Things have been moving so fast and with all that we've been dealing with, we've not had time to reflect."

"There's not that much to reflect on," she said, taking his hand in hers. "I love you."

"I love you too," he said, but couldn't help feeling uneasy.

"You say that, but you're not happy about something," she observed.

"I don't know, it was something that happened earlier today."

"I know what it is," she said, smiling mischievously. "You're jealous; you're jealous of the way Basil was looking at me. I must admit it was very lustful."

"You seemed to be encouraging him," Jake said. Maybe that was what was bothering him and he didn't want to admit it. He certainly felt foolish now.

"I was teasing him, which is what he deserves; trying to come on to a young girl, and in front of you and Alexander." She paused, waiting for him to look at her. "The fact is I can't live without you. I need to be with you all the time."

"I feel the same," Jake said. Foolish jealousy aside, this was the happiest moment in his life. "I have to go back and make some major changes; wind up my life in England, sell the house. I don't know what I'll do with the Kensington flats though."

"You'll want to keep one of them. So we can visit."

"You're right. I could sell the larger one, the one where I lived with my mother, and keep the smaller one for us. On the other hand, I don't need the money, so I might as well keep both. One can pay for the upkeep of the other. While I'm doing that I can be visiting you in Brussels for weekends."

"That's mandatory, although I'd like to visit London too."

"I guess by Christmas I could be living in Greece. That's a bit farther from Brussels. I don't know what'll happen then. What do you feel about Athens?"

"I love Greece. My feelings about Athens are more mixed, but I'll be with you and that's what matters."

Chapter 32: Virginia

Sunday, 19th August

Jake woke early; he couldn't sleep. He could see from the shafts of red light coming horizontally through the gaps in the shutters that it was dawn. Careful not to wake Joanna, he got out of bed, put on his dressing gown, carefully unhooked the catch holding the wooden doors and went out onto the balcony, where he sat on one of the chairs to watch the sunrise.

As he stared into the glowing orb he tried to pin down what was making him feel uneasy. Was it this jealousy thing with Basil? Surely he must have got over that. Joanna had made it so clear how much she loved him. During the meal, they'd planned their future. Back at the hotel afterwards they'd agreed that as soon as the crystals were retrieved, they would leave and start their life together.

Joanna was so good for him. It seemed that nothing negative could break down the love they had for each other. She'd sensed he was unhappy about something and she had made him feel so much better. Last night was so intense; so ecstatic. It was as though he was in a dream. And yet?

Maybe he was just afraid of losing her after that episode with Basil. Their love was so perfect, so pure, and powerful. It was nothing like that with Charly. And that loser Teresa, how could he have fallen for her?

He'd rarely thought about Teresa since meeting Joanna. When he did, the thought just passed, but today it dropped into his subconscious and exploded. The detonation cleared the fog that surrounded him. He remembered what was making him feel uneasy. It was the encounter he'd had with Virginia. It was their conversation, which he seemed to have forgotten.

The consequences of this revelation took some minutes to sink in. A period of time when denial tried to fight what could no longer be ignored. From the moment Joanna had stepped on the island, he'd been sinking deeper under her spell. He realised that now. Whenever he showed any signs of resistance, she would subdue him. It was so easy to respond to her. She was so beautiful, so seductive, so convincing, and so intense.

But none of it was real, Teresa's ordeal was. Teresa had trusted him and he'd betrayed her; not the other way round. Irrespective of their feelings for each other, she was his responsibility. If she was being held against her will, he had to do something about it.

The wind was still and the sea calm as it usually was first thing, but his mind was in turmoil. He had to get back to Virginia. He remembered that last night, when he was paying for the taxi, he'd mentioned to Joanna that he was running short of cash and a trip to the ATM would be necessary. He went back inside. Joanna was stirring.

"Darling, why aren't you in bed?"

"I don't know, I'm not tired."

"What's the time?"

"Gone seven thirty," he said, hoping she didn't sense a problem.

"Seven thirty? We can't have gone to sleep much before two. Why are you getting dressed?"

"I'm feeling restless. I thought I'd get some money from the cash till in the centre of town. Easier than going to the bank on Halia. There's also a newsagent on the harbour front that sells English papers. I'll only be twenty minutes."

"You'll come back to bed when you return? I know just how to deal with that restlessness. I'll have you sleeping till lunchtime."

"I'd better hurry then," Jake said, feigning enthusiasm. When he'd finished dressing and taken what he needed, he bent over to give her a kiss, but she was already asleep.

He left the room, ran down the stairs, passed the bemused night receptionist, and went out on to the street. As best he could, he tried to retrace his movements of yesterday.

Being Sunday, the streets were relatively deserted. He walked along the harbour front and then through the entrance to the old town. He was about to retrieve the directions he'd written for himself as he proceeded into the first square when he saw, at the other end of it, a figure in black approaching. As they neared each other, he recognised Photis.

Before he could get to him, Photis turned down a side street and kept a distance in front. Jake understood and kept far enough away so as not to give the impression that they were together. Soon Photis had walked through the entrance to the garden and Jake followed. The front door of the house was open and he walked in, closing it behind him. There was that smell of baking again as he entered the lounge. He saw Virginia and Photis coming in from the garden.

Virginia was beaming as if she was about to greet one of her children. "Welcome back, Jake. Photis has been beside himself ever since I told him you were on your way. He knew you would return. Like father like son, he said."

"And you?" Jake said, trying to control the emotion of being compared with his father.

"I admit I had my doubts," Virginia said, seriously. "Had you been dealing with the fully-fledged Aphrodite, you could not have been convinced. Nobody could."

"You could say I saw the light this morning."

"Then the Fates are indeed with us. Please sit," she said, while Photis went into the kitchen.

"I've been foolish and weak."

"On the contrary, you've been strong and brave. It takes courage to acknowledge the truth and face the pain."

"Was she used against my father?"

"Joanna was too young to be used with him. But your father was more prepared."

"So, if I'm going to rescue Teresa, I assume I'll have to pretend I'm still under her spell. I hope she doesn't notice I've changed."

"If you're clever, she won't, and I'll give you some guidance; but first I would like you to imagine what it would be like if the Aphrodite you experienced was magnified a hundred times."

"I'd be a vegetable."

"Anybody would. Can you imagine such a woman loose in the world? What about Apollo, with the power of prophecy? How rich could he become? Or Ares, the God of war, with the desire and need for conflict. What would life be like?"

"I think I understand what you're getting at."

"I'll say one more thing. Imagine all these Gods, with all their powers, working together."

"World domination."

"Yes, eventually. And as time passed, the crystals would drive them insane, as I've already explained. But there's something you should understand. At the moment they're not all bad, but few would resist the temptations of power."

"You did."

"I have taken a vow of chastity and non-violence. The only other two who would not be interested in power are Demeter and her daughter Persephone."

"And who would they be?"

"The pretty Russian girl, Natalya, and Stavroulla, the nurse and your neighbour."

"Natalya?" Jake said. So she was one of them, like she said. He felt deep disappointment. Despite what Virginia said, she was still one of them. "What about the others?"

"I don't think I should tell you who they all are, otherwise you might treat them differently. You must be wary of everyone. We can't afford any mistakes. There's too much at stake."

"So how do we stop them and rescue Teresa?"

"With great difficulty, but there is a way. For it to work the crystals must be destroyed."

"How many are there?"

"Thirteen are buried together with a few that were unassigned, and I have mine. The problem is getting Poseidon's."

"That's impossible. We went to see him yesterday. Not only does he have security but, even if he didn't, it would take two or three strong men to subdue him."

"More than that Jake. He's a God remember? Even though greatly diminished, it would be impossible to overcome him physically."

"Can't he be killed?"

"With difficulty whilst he's near to or wearing his crystal."

"What to do then?"

"Remember, Poseidon isn't a God in the divine sense, just superhuman. He has weaknesses. His biggest is women."

"Sounds familiar."

"There's no comparison between you. You, like everyone else, are looking for love and intimacy. For Poseidon it's a question of dominance. He gets pleasure out of conquest. It's an addiction, a sickness. He's always been like that."

"How does this help us?"

"It does so in two ways. To start with, he doesn't wear the crystal or keep it with him constantly, especially when he's with the others or with his women. He wouldn't need to anyway."

"Are you sure about this?"

"Absolutely," Virginia said. Photis had come back and brought them coffee and freshly baked biscuits. He served them and sat. "He doesn't need to commune with it all the time."

"Where does he keep it?" Jake said, taking a sip of coffee and a bite of biscuit.

"He has a special place. In his stateroom there's a safe, which he uses for other valuables. Photis and I have managed to get plans of the yacht from the builders. There are most likely other hiding places that we don't know about."

"That means I have to get into his stateroom and have time to break into them, assuming I can find them."

"Correct."

"Well, that sounds pretty risky since I've no idea how to open a safe, not to mention the fact that he could turn up at any time."

"This is true. But there are things we can do to put the odds in our favour and we have an ally."

"How?"

"Think about it, Jake; think about Poseidon's weakness and think about what you've got; probably the most irresistible bait in the world."

"Aphrodite."

"Yes, Aphrodite. All the Gods lusted after her. Most had a relationship with her, apart from Zeus, her father and Poseidon, her uncle. As far as Poseidon was concerned it wasn't through lack of wanting or trying. Did you not notice anything yesterday evening?"

"Yes, and it made me uncomfortable."

"And he knew it. It gave him pleasure to make you jealous. He sees it as another way to neutralise you, humiliate and demean you. Aphrodite for her part wants him too. She knows that the quest for the crystals is risky. However, her seduction of Poseidon will give her dominance over the others and guarantee her future, so she believes. Part of what you have to do is create a situation where she will distract him, temporarily at least. This is crucial."

"How and when do I do that?"

"You'll have just one chance. This Saturday is the annual football match between Halia and Lichas. Afterwards there's going to be a street banquet with live music. Everybody will be there. But later in the evening, Basil will have his own party on board the *Trident*, for specially invited guests."

"But that's too late. By then, I would've been expected to have retrieved the crystals."

"No. Why do you think Basil's so relaxed? He knows that you've just loaded diving equipment on board Diana's yacht. This morning he'll be leaving for Halia and is planning to be anchored in Paleo Limani until Saturday. Nobody's going to be doing any diving."

"I just feel sorry for Teresa having to wait that long."

"I know; that's regrettable, but you will be making good use of your time."

"Where are they keeping her by the way?"

"The last place you would ever think to look."

"The house, my father's house."

"Very good, Jake."

"How did they get her there?"

"It was Phivos, the doctor, who was on the ferry when Teresa boarded it in Piraeus. He's Apollo, by the way, and Artemis's brother. He sedated her and got her off in his car at Lichas. They moved her to Diana's yacht and kept her there until nightfall when they could transfer her to the house."

"I thought so," Jake said. "I remember the marks on the stern of Diana's yacht, as I climbed on board that evening at Paleo Limani; the damaged jetty made them. Do you know where she's being kept?"

"In the basement I'd imagine. The walls are thick, there are no windows and your father had two or three lockable store rooms."

"Is there someone on guard all the time?"

"I can't imagine so, and certainly not at night."

"Virginia, something's bothering me; surely Aphrodite must realise she risks the recovery of the crystals if she betrays me with Basil."

"She realises nothing of the sort. She's never lost a lover through her infidelity. They always wanted her back. That's her weakness, she thinks she's invincible."

"How do I keep myself from falling back under her spell?"

"You have become stronger already, more resistant, but it's important you give her the impression of being completely subdued and enfeebled. This will cause Joanna to feel overconfident as well as bored. At the same time you must be careful not to make Diana suspicious."

"I hope I can pull that off. So what about you? How is it that you're here, within twenty miles of Halia and none of the others know?"

"I will explain. As you know, when the murders took place, I was spared and, together with Ganymedes, escorted to the coast of Evia. At that point we parted company. He went back to Troy to try and rebuild it after its destruction, but he was hounded and chased away. Eventually, together with a group of other survivors, led by a man called Brutus, he ended up in the west of England."

"The west of England?" Jake exclaimed.

"They landed in a place called Totnes."

"I know it. Why there of all places?"

"He had heard that Hecate lived there. She was the Goddess of witchcraft and did not reside on Halia or in Greece, instead travelling the world in order to teach her craft. She took up residence in the southwest of England because her father and the other surviving Titans were exiled there."

"Did these Titans have crystals too?"

"Indeed, but the Titans were not as sophisticated and powerful as the Olympian Gods."

"Didn't you bare a grudge towards Ganymedes?"

"That emotion has no place in me. Besides, my family was responsible for the slaughter of his family, acquaintances and compatriots. It's rather difficult to be judgemental. Anyway, as you know, it was Kephalas who first sought out Poseidon, wanting to convince him to retrieve the crystals. He wasn't difficult to find, as he was always going to be rich and powerful. Of course, this was before they realised he'd had a son. Poseidon wouldn't cooperate, so when they learned about your father, they decided to try and find where the tomb was. The only people who would know this, other than Poseidon, were Ganymedes and me. We were the only witnesses. So Kephalas and the others tried to track us down as well. I was wise to this as I was already observing them, so they had no luck finding me. I have lived here in the citadel for many years, waiting."

"What happened to this Hecate and Ganymedes?"

"Hecate died a long time ago in the region of Devon and was buried in the uplands. Her crystal was found and briefly caused some problems, but it was neutralised in the early '80s. Ganymedes passed away soon after Hecate and was buried at sea with his stone. It's in a deep place and out of reach. The Titans also died out and their crystals were scattered and are still unaccounted for."

"Can't Basil or the others detect you or sense your presence, or that of your crystal?"

"As I explained, I took a vow of chastity and non-violence. My life has been devoted to passivity and meditation. I am infinitely receptive, therefore aware of everything, but entirely unobtrusive and disturb nothing. I leave no footprint, physical or otherwise. My crystal reflects this."

"I suppose you know where the wellhead is then?" Jake asked, aware of the passing time.

"I do, but if you don't mind, I'll keep it to myself for now."

"Was it Kephalas who arranged the attacks on me? You know which ones I mean?"

"Yes, I do and no, he wasn't. There would be no reason for him to do so."

"Who then?"

"It was your aunt and uncle who arranged them, I'm afraid."

"I guess they have a lot to gain if I sell the business," Jake reflected. "It was you who was there, wasn't it?"

"It was."

"What if Emma hadn't been available?"

"Photis would've had to deal with it. He was standing by and is quite competent, from what I understand."

"But who alerted them? The outing was only arranged the night before."

"It was Panagos."

"But I thought he called Alexander."

"Him too. Panagos is hedging his bets."

"Poseidon did give me three warnings of his own. A sort of dream, an incident at sea and the luminous cloud or fog."

"This is more serious, but a mistake on his part."

"Why?"

"Because he showed his hand too soon. Without it you would've been more sceptical about what Diana told you."

"And I might still be under Aphrodite's spell."

"There would be more chance of that. Have you been on board your father's yacht?"

"Not yet."

"You have the key, I presume?"

"Yes, at home."

"Good, we may have a use for it."

"You mentioned an ally?"

"That and the plan is what we'll talk about next."

Chapter 33: The Wait: Monday

Monday, 20ᵗʰ August

Jake was trying to show sympathy as they sailed back to Halia.

Up until that time he was struggling with his role. How was he to be? Submissive and hasten her boredom? Or would that seem too easy and raise suspicions, especially Diana's? Perhaps he should continue showing resistance, but then that risked attracting Joanna's focused attention.

He was considering this when the call came. It was Diana and, judging from the swiftness with which Joanna's cheerfulness vanished, it was obvious why.

"It's a disaster," she said, after she had hung up.

"Why? What's happened?"

"The *Trident* has anchored at Paleo Limani."

"Why would Basil do that?" Jake asked, trying to appear surprised.

"To piss us off, I don't know." She was incensed.

"Does she know how long he's staying?"

"Gran will try and find out. She'll meet us at the quay."

"Maybe the news won't be that bad," Jake added, trying to take her hand in consolation. She didn't respond, so he left her alone. He imagined all of them would be panicking right now, apart from Basil, who would be smugly pleased with himself.

He felt like laughing, but remembered Virginia's warning, not to take Joanna for granted. She would hold sway over him were it not for the fact that she was getting restless.

What he wanted the most, he knew, was to pretend to resist, to pretend to rebel, so she could seduce him and once more take him to that place of abandon and pleasure. That would be a disaster if she persisted. He would forget everything; Teresa, his father, everything. He wouldn't come back to his senses until he was either coerced into retrieving the crystals or died trying.

As they were entering the harbour, he remembered what Natalya, sweet Natalya, had told him when they'd last spoken, that she'd be back in Halia on the nineteenth. He looked out for the yacht but couldn't see it at the pier. It was twelve o'clock and they had probably sailed to one of the beaches for the day.

As they docked, Joanna was up and looking for Diana. They spotted her sitting on the wall of the flower bed. As soon as the ramp went down, she was pushing her way through the queue, with Jake close behind her.

"Well?" Joanna said as she stood over Diana.

"I couldn't find out anything," she said. "At worst, he'll come back into the harbour on Saturday, in time for the celebrations."

"Great," Joanna said. "So I'm stuck in this shit hole for another week."

Diana visibly tensed. She looked at Jake, searching for a reaction. It was time for a bit of mischief. "We could always go back to Lichas or one of the other islands for a few days," he said, looking down at his feet.

"It's only a week, darling," Diana said to her granddaughter. "I know you both can't wait to get away and be together, but you'll have to be patient a few days longer." Joanna looked ready to explode. "Jake, I ordered some last minute things from Lichas, would you be so kind as to get them for me. They'll have my name on them."

"Sure." Jake did as he was told, but knew that he wouldn't find anything. Once on the ferry, he went up to the boat deck and looked towards them from inside the cabin. Diana was now standing and appeared to be giving Joanna a lecture. The severity of the scolding was clear from her body language. Joanna appeared cowered with her head down. He went back downstairs, had a quick look round and came back out. As he approached, he saw that their postures had changed. Diana looked more encouraging and Joanna calmer.

"I couldn't find anything," Jake said. "Why don't you call and see if they put the right name on the package."

"It doesn't matter," Diana said. "They did say it might not be delivered today. Anyway, it's too hot to be standing here."

"I wouldn't mind a swim," Jake said. "Anybody interested?"

"Why don't we go back to the *Pelagos*?" Diana said. "I was planning for you to eat with me tonight, before the arrival of our unwanted guest. We can swim, sleep, eat lots and I'll bring you back in the evening."

"Ideal, I'll take our shopping back," Jake said. "Do we need anything from the house?"

"No, just leave the swim bag," Joanna said, pointing to it.

"Meet us at the launch," Diana added.

It was calm and cool where the yacht was anchored within the bay. He had several swims from there, afterwards lying on his towel on the bit of deck forward of the companionway. He felt that Diana and Joanna preferred to be left alone and they stayed below most of the time. He could only imagine what they spoke about. He picked up his tee-shirt, laid it on his face to shade his eyes, and dozed. In the distance he could hear the sounds coming from the *Trident*, anchored about four hundred metres towards Panagia Island. There was a procession of launches going to and from the harbour, passing close enough to the *Pelagos* for their wakes to gently rock her. Then there were the screams and yelps of those taking swims. What would Basil be like in the water? He was nowhere to be seen.

He fell asleep and did not wake until the sun had disappeared behind the hills of the main island and the loss of heat made him shiver. He had been out for nearly two hours. He gathered his things and went below.

He crept quietly on board and found Joanna asleep, fully clothed, on a bunk bed. She looked so beautiful and innocent. He wondered what the real Joanna would have been like, without the influence of Aphrodite. Diana and Virginia had said that the spirits of the Gods possessed those who had similarities in their characters, so she probably would not be any more likeable.

He assumed Diana was also resting; he took his jumper and book from his rucksack and went and sat back out on the port side of the cockpit, facing the *Trident*, keeping an eye on any activity. Were they being watched? He pretended to be reading, but instead was rehearsing in his mind what he would be doing on board Basil's yacht in five days' time.

Before long he heard the girls stir and, by the time it was fully dark, they came and joined him, carrying a tray with ouzo, water, a bowl of ice, three glasses, a bowl of olives, and cubes of feta and bread.

They spoke little at first. Diana seemed much more at peace, as did Joanna, who smiled at him warmly whenever he looked her way. The girls had their backs to the *Trident*, which was now brightly illuminated, and paid it no attention. Whatever Diana had been saying to Joanna had worked, for now.

As the evening progressed, so did the conversation return. It was like old times, when he believed himself to be loved and in love. It was so easy to push the truth further and further into a corner of his mind until it vanished, until he was back to living the delusion, and finally to believing it.

Supper was a fish feast that only Diana knew how to catch and prepare. They had shellfish with salad to start and individual red mullets with jacket potatoes to follow, accompanied by wine. Afterwards, Joanna snuggled up to him, no doubt demonstrating to her grandmother that she was cooperating.

Towards the end of the evening, Jake asked an inevitable question, "If Basil thinks we're on to something, how are we going to retrieve the crystals?"

"We have a plan," Diana said. "I can't give you the details, but the only way Basil will prevent the retrieval of the crystals is by eliminating all of us."

"But he only needs to kill me," Jake said.

"But he'll have to kill us first," Diana said. "When the time comes, we will protect you, we have to."

Diana had them back at the quay by midnight. Jake was surprised that Joanna wanted to go home and not look for people to socialise with. Instead, they walked hand in hand through the dark streets.

The air in the flat was stale after having been left unoccupied for three days. They opened the windows and shutters and then had a shower together, something they'd not done since the beginning of their relationship.

Afterwards they went into the bedroom and she started saying those things to him, doing those things. While he was still present, he wondered whether he should pretend to be ill or anything to prevent what was happening. But he knew he wouldn't. He was falling into her and knew he couldn't stop it.

Chapter 34: The Wait: Tuesday

Tuesday, 21st August

By midday Joanna and Jake had walked to the beach, the one with the café. In the bay yachts and power boats of different sizes were anchored, each surrounded by its own flotilla of swimmers, floats and smaller craft. One of them Jake recognized as belonging to Natalya's family. He felt excited at the thought of her proximity, that he might see her, even from a distance.

The beach itself was, as always, crowded, both in and out of the water, and Jake soon left Joanna lying on the sand, reading a magazine she had brought from Lichas, in order to go into the water. He swam towards the vicinity of Natalya's yacht, but kept sufficient distance from it as to not make his interest obvious. He circumnavigated it without any luck and came back to the beach disappointed.

Since returning from Lichas he was concerned about succumbing to Joanna again. But something had changed. Yes, there were those moments like last night when she focused on him, when it was like a dream again, but the rest of the time she was distracted, her mind elsewhere. Who or what was she thinking about?

For his part, Jake had only one overriding concern: Saturday; and within him an imaginary chronometer was counting down the days, hours, minutes and seconds. Beneath that, his thoughts were with Teresa and Natalya; Teresa because of the responsibility he felt for her and Natalya because of the growing feelings he was experiencing.

"I'd like to go back," Joanna said late in the afternoon. "Do you mind? We can have a nap and go out again later."

"Sure," Jake said. "When's your Gran coming?"

"Around nine."

After supper at home on the patio, the three of them walked down to the harbour. It was coming up to eleven thirty, the wind had dropped and the town was throbbing with activity, music and conversation. They went to the yacht club. At a table on the right-hand side they found Savvas, his wife Mina, the mayor's spouse Maria and Phivos. They acquired three more seats and joined them. Jake sat between Phivos and Joanna. It was the first time he'd met the former, the scum who, together with Diana, had abducted Teresa. He was tall and well-built, with short dark curly hair. He had a broad open face with well-proportioned features and brown eyes. Jake knew that Diana and Mina thought highly of him.

He was well aware that this gathering was for his benefit, to bring him into the fold, to make him feel welcomed, to confirm Diana's assurance that he was under their protection.

After arriving back from Lichas yesterday to the news that the *Trident* had anchored at Paleo Limani, Jake had anticipated a dampening in the spirits of these Gods in waiting, as he thought of them. But, if what Diana had said at the end of their evening on the *Pelagos* was anything to go by, they had somehow managed to convince themselves that the recovery of the crystals was inevitable, such appeared to be the level of their anticipation and expectation.

There was an awkward silence at first. The waitress came and everyone, apart for Savvas, ordered drinks.

"So how are you settling in?" Phivos asked Jake.

"Just fine," Jake replied.

"I'm sure it must be different from the life you had before," he continued.

"Somewhat," Jake said.

"It's a shame you'll not have a house on Halia. I'm sure you'll want to come back now that you've made friends."

"I suppose so," Jake agreed.

"We'll have to look for one. They do come up occasionally. It may not be near the harbour, but there are some beautiful cottages up in the town."

"Yes, but then he has the hill to contend with and there's never anywhere to park," Maria said. It was the first time Jake had met the mayor's wife. She was of medium height and slight, with large brown eyes and a dyed blonde bob of hair that did not suit her dark complexion. She inhaled deeply from her cigarette, the only one at the table who smoked.

"He's managed without one so far. I haven't got one either," Phivos argued. "I've left mine on Lichas. Don't listen to them, they're lazy."

"Lazy?" Maria protested. "You try organising a social life and then see whether you want to run up and down hills all day."

"Clearly you need to have a car, as well as somewhere to park it. You're the mayor's wife," Savvas said. "Try running a supermarket."

"That's hard," Mina agreed.

"Then why do you want us to start a chain of them?" Savvas asked his wife.

"That's different," Mina explained. "When you open a chain, other people do the work."

"You have no ambition, Savvas," Phivos remarked.

"Everyone has different priorities," Savvas retorted.

"Yes, but when circumstances change, you must change too," Phivos said. "Take our friend Jake. Unfortunately his father died, but he's been left with an opportunity to live a different life. So what does he do? Go back to England and carry on being a teacher, as if nothing happened?"

"If that's his passion, yes," Savvas said.

"Well? Is it your passion?" Phivos turned to Jake.

"As it happens, it isn't; I made a bad choice, but I still agree with Savvas," Jake said. "If I loved it, why change?"

"Jake, Savvas doesn't like being a grocer," Mina said. "He likes being here. He's a loner. So don't use him as an example."

"Besides, your upbringing and background were for something better," Phivos said. "Now you also have the opportunity. Why would you deny yourself?"

"But why does it matter?" Savvas said.

"Because it's human nature to be the best you can and rise above others," Phivos replied. "It's all over the animal kingdom. They have dominant males and females too. Just look at the Olympics. Did you not notice the emotions of the medal winners? If you think any differently it means you have issues."

"Not everyone thinks like you," Savvas remarked.

"And what's wrong with the way he thinks?" Mina said. "If people like Phivos weren't ambitious, we wouldn't have doctors, lawyers and businessmen, let alone Olympic champions."

"I didn't say there was anything wrong with him," Savvas said. "I just said that not everybody wants to be like him."

"Being a businessman, doctor, or whatever, is commendable; I just don't like the social commitments involved," Jake said.

"That's probably because you don't understand them," Phivos countered. "But it's the most important part."

"What?" Savvas exclaimed. "That's nonsense."

"He's right; you listen to him," Mina said.

"You're a doctor because you've qualified; you're a businessman because you've worked damn hard," Savvas said. "None of it comes from socialising."

"No, but socialising and networking reveals your status and, if done skilfully, will move you forward faster than you would otherwise," Phivos patiently explained.

"I accept that what you say is true," Savvas said. "but not everybody wants to move forward that fast, if at all."

"But why would you not want to achieve a better result?" Phivos asked. "Take marriage for example. Women look for men with status. It's a well-known fact."

"What ever happened to love?" Jake questioned.

"Everlasting love doesn't exist," Phivos said. "So why make decisions based on it?"

"It all sounds very depressing," Savvas said.

"Why? Because I don't believe in love?" Phivos responded. "I believe in friendship, though. That's different and it lasts. Perhaps you're mistaking one for the other."

"I agree with you about friendship, but not about love," Jake said. "Yes, that initial intensity and obsession may be brief, but passion can last, and it may not necessarily include friendship."

"How did we get on to the subject of love?" Diana asked. "It's boring."

"You would say that," Joanna said. "You're like Phivos; you can't fathom it."

"And has it done me any harm?" Diana questioned. "I'm perfectly happy without a partner and get a lot more done as a result."

"You were married once," Joanna remarked.

"That was because I wanted children," Diana replied.

"We started off by talking about why social status is important," Phivos said, "not only for finding a spouse, but also for business. That old adage that 'it's who you know not what you know' is perfectly true in every field of endeavour." Everyone round the table nodded in agreement. "I don't see you commenting on that point," he said, looking at Savvas.

"I'm a fair man," Savvas said. "I know when I'm beaten."

"If you agree with him, why don't you put in some effort towards your social skills so we can get a bit further in life than being village grocers?" Mina asked.

"Because I don't see why I have to socialise and put on an act with people I don't like," Savvas responded.

"You serve all the customers that come into your store," Phivos said. "Do you like all of them? I actually don't like all my patients, but I treat them the same."

"It's when you base your actions on emotions that you get into trouble," Diana claimed. "Look at Nicos, what a nice boy, yet barely capable of getting up in the morning."

How true, Jake thought. Without Virginia's guidance, he'd be like that too.

"If it wasn't for his father's millions, he'd be destitute," Maria acknowledged.

"Or most likely dead," Diana added.

"There's a different way of looking at things, Savvas," Phivos said.

"I can't wait for you to tell me," Savvas quipped.

"The sooner you and Mina expand your business to the mainland, the sooner you can get others to do the distasteful work. The sooner you do that, the sooner you can go back to doing whatever you prefer. Just a little sacrifice and compromise on your part."

"It's the time it will take that's the problem," Savvas said.

"It won't take long, just a few years," Mina responded. "Besides, it's not as if we'll be running short of it."

"Quite," Savvas added uncomfortably.

"Diana, what are your plans after the summer?" Phivos asked.

"I'm just going to carry on as before," Diana replied. "What about you?"

"I think the way forward is to expand my practice and offer more services," Phivos said. "And what about you, young lady?"

"I just want to be footloose and fancy free. I want to travel the world and go on adventures," Joanna said. "Depending on what Jake also wants to do," she added as an afterthought, taking his hand in hers. "To start with, I'll be moving to Athens."

"To which I would add that when you do move, you allow me to be your mentor," Phivos said to Jake. "I'll show you the skills you need to hold your own socially."

"He need only emulate his father," Diana said.

"I'm forgetting, your father could've taught us all," Phivos declared.

"There wasn't anyone he didn't get on with," Mina added.

And so the conversation continued, with each betraying their aspirations for the future, once in possession of their crystals no doubt, until, to Jake's relief, Phivos looked at his watch. "It's getting late," he said. "The phone will start ringing in the morning."

"A doctor's never on holiday," Mina commented.

"Even with my relief, patients expect him to check with me before prescribing any treatment," Phivos said.

"Do you still play your mandolin?" Joanna asked.

"Every evening for at least an hour, sometimes two," Phivos said. "Life wouldn't be worth living without it."

"I've heard it on a few occasions, while passing," Jake said. "You play beautifully."

"Thank you," Phivos said. "Anyway, I must go. I'll settle up for the drinks so far and I'll see you all tomorrow. Give my regards to Yiannis."

"I will," Maria said. "He's sorry he couldn't be here."

"Do you mind if I walk with you?" Diana asked. "I must be getting back myself."

"Not at all," Phivos replied.

"I'll go with them and see Gran to the launch and be right back," Joanna said to Jake.

"I'd better be going as well," Maria said. "The mayor's wife never rests. Goodnight all."

"Where is the mayor anyway?" Jake asked, after Maria had left.

"Most likely getting acquainted with the electorate," Savvas replied, turning to his wife Mina, who looked back knowingly.

"What, at this hour?" Jake questioned.

"He likes to have one-to-ones, and they can take some time," Savvas said.

This time Jake understood.

"As soon as Joanna comes back we must be going too," Mina remarked.

"You don't have to wait," Jake said.

"Then I'll just go to the ladies and we'll be on our way," she said to Savvas as she got up.

"Don't pay any attention to what they say," Savvas commented when they were alone. "Do things your way."

"I intend to," Jake said.

"And don't let them manipulate you," he added.

"What do you mean?" Jake asked.

"You're a nice boy, Jake. Just like your father. He just wanted to mind his own business and get on with his life."

"I still don't understand," Jake said. It pained him to lie to Savvas, but he couldn't risk a trap or betrayal. Jake had surmised that Savvas was Hades, the God of the Underworld. When push came to shove, whose side would he take?

"I can't say any more," he said. "Just be careful."

They sat in silence until Mina returned and then left him with his thoughts as he waited for Joanna. He looked over at the yacht pier. The whole row was occupied, apart from a gap in the middle for the still absent *Bacchus*, and the last space, which was probably intended for the *Trident*. He had business to attend to on his father's boat; something he had to retrieve. This was an ideal opportunity, with nobody monitoring him. Even if he was seen, he could always say he boarded her out of curiosity. Nobody would guess the real reason.

He got up, went down the steps and across to the pier. The *Sevastia III* was the first one in the row and not like the others. It was a medium-sized powerboat; just the right size for one person to handle, if needed. Consequently it was the smallest.

After checking that there was no one watching, he pulled on the hawser in order to bring the stern close enough to board. It required a prolonged effort before he was close enough to step down into the stern well, which was sheltered by the navigation deck above. He unlocked the glass-sliding door and stepped inside. It was dark but he dared not turn on the lights. He would have to make do with the street lighting that was filtering in through the windows.

The inside was pretty basic from what he could see. A simple integral lounge, kitchen and diner, but there was no time to explore. Photis would have removed all personal effects. Fortunately, the only thing he forgot, in his distress, was his own set of keys to the basement of the house on the headland. In one of the storerooms of the cellar he kept tools and supplies for the boat.

There were two cabins; the master bedroom was straight through into the prow, and the guest bedroom, which Photis used, was down in the stern, past the toilet and shower. He retrieved the keys from the top shelf of one of the cupboards and made his way back to the lounge. He stopped at the glass door to check if it was safe to disembark.

He quickly retreated into the shadows. Coming from the direction of the yacht club was Natalya with her two younger sisters, arms linked on either side, chatting happily, their golden hair waving in the breeze. God she was beautiful, he thought. Why did she have to be one of them?

His eyes never left her until they had gone up the pier and onto their yacht, after which he left to go back to the yacht club and wait for Joanna.

Chapter 35: The Wait: Wednesday

Wednesday, 22nd August

The next day continued in the same manner. Jake and Joanna went to the beach at noon, and in the evening, after supper on the patio with Diana, the three of them made their way to the yacht club again.

On this occasion they met Stephanos, Niki and, for the first time since their encounter at the bank, Yiannis, the mayor. Now it was Stephanos and Yiannis who were offering their support to Jake, this time in the field of commerce and politics.

"But I thought you'd retired," Jake said to Stephanos.

"I know," Stephanos said, "but I've been thinking about it and I'm getting bored here, while Niki, after having had a taste of local governance, would like to try something more ambitious."

"It's the same for me," Yiannis said. "Local politics is fine but not challenging enough."

"What about your electrical business?" Stephanos asked.

"My sons are now old enough to take over," Yiannis replied. "I'll stay on as chairman."

"Will you and Niki continue to work together?" Jake asked the mayor.

"It's an intriguing idea," Yiannis said. "But Niki's more interested at the municipal level, while I want to go in nationally."

"It's been my ambition to get involved in Athenian politics," Niki added.

"Greece has become an international embarrassment," Yiannis said. "It's time to tackle corruption and bring back national pride."

"I'm afraid I'm not interested in politics," Joanna said. "I can't think of anything more boring."

"I can't see why anyone would be indifferent to the way they're governed," Niki said. "It's a strange view considering your profession."

"I enjoy translating and languages," Joanna said. "Just not the content."

"I'm not particularly interested either," Diana said. "Just environmental and conservation issues."

"A bit narrow-minded, but probably most people's stance," Niki said.

"What do you mean narrow-minded?" Diana said. "What makes you so superior?"

"You're just being self-centred, like Phivos," Niki said. "You'd think you were twins."

"Let's stop it right there," Yiannis interjected. "Everyone's entitled to their view."

"That's interesting," Niki said. "I'll hold you to that one day."

"And what are you going to do?" Jake asked Stephanos.

"I'll stick to business and what I know. I've had experience in finance and marketing. There's a need for independent consultants in the field, especially these days. Businesses will need help to survive, especially if we drop out of the euro. You could be one of my first customers. I don't suppose you know what your father's debt arrangements were?"

"I'm afraid I don't." Jake said. "But when I do, you'll be the first to know."

"And don't forget that Niki and I can also be of help," Yiannis added. "We would love your endorsement and your support and can introduce you to influential people."

"Sounds good," Jake said.

"From what I know of your father's business, he had properties all over Greece," Yiannis commented.

"Thessalonica and some of the larger islands," Jake stated.

"You'll need to be able to get around then," Yiannis said. "You should consider learning to fly. I have my own plane and own a flying school. You should fly with me one day, I'm sure you'll love it."

"I'll try anything," Jake said.

And so the conversation continued for the rest of the evening. Yiannis, Stephanos and Niki dominated it, discussing what policies were needed to rescue Greece from the perils it now faced. Diana and Joanna, meanwhile, who were sitting either side of Niki, said little and did not look as though they were enjoying themselves.

Jake sympathised; all this pretending was tiring. He preferred to concentrate on his two preoccupations, Saturday and Natalya. He was looking out for her, hoping for a chance encounter, even though he knew it would be futile.

Chapter 36: The Wait: Thursday

Thursday, 23rd August

They arrived at the beach at midday. In the bay was the usual assortment of yachts, on the outer fringe of which was Natalya's, but today Jake was surprised to see the *Warrior* amongst them, anchored close to shore.

The strand itself was more crowded than usual and they were forced to settle for an unshaded spot. After they'd laid out their mats and towels, Jake observed a launch, belonging to the *Warrior*, come across and tie up by the floats that sectioned off the bay. The young man in charge of it gracefully dived into the water and swam to the beach. He walked across the sand towards them and spoke to Jake.

"Mr Kephalas saw you arrive and would like to invite you on board for lunch."

Joanna's features lightened considerably at this. She looked over at Jake.

"That'll be great," Jake responded.

"Yes, we'd like to," she confirmed eagerly.

"You can swim out whenever you like. Drinks will be at two followed by lunch," the young man said.

"That'll be fine," Jake replied. This was unforeseen, but unavoidable. Virginia had mentioned to Jake that Kephalas, Ares, was Joanna's, Aphrodite's, long term lover in the old days. It would be disastrous to their plans if they were to get back together. On the other hand, turning down the invitation would raise suspicions.

Nearly two hours later, when they mounted the accommodation ladder onto the afterdeck of the *Warrior*, a much more modest yacht than the *Trident*, the same boy was waiting for them, this time dressed in all whites, and offered them a towel each.

The sun-drenched open deck had sets of tables and chairs with towels and over-garments draped over them, but nobody was sitting outside.

As they walked into the air-conditioned lounge, Jake was relieved to see that there were other guests. There was Alexander, his wife, children and a couple he'd never met before. There was a lady who appeared to be a governess and, to Jake's surprise, Phivos. The latter was also in his swimming shorts, so he must've come from one of the other boats.

An impressive buffet was laid out on a long counter, but the food was still covered under cling film and white towels. Jake and Joanna sat on the only two seats still available, Joanna next to Phivos on a small settee, and Jake next to Mrs Kephalas, on the other side of the lounge. They had separate chairs either side of a small side table. Mrs Kephalas wore a flimsy red beach gown over her bikini. Her dark hair was tied tightly back, showing off her flawless complexion. The nails of her hands and feet were a perfectly manicured ruby red, matching her lip gloss.

Meanwhile, Alexander was sitting on a stool at the bar talking to the unknown couple. He briefly acknowledged Jake's and Joanna's arrival with a nod and carried on with his conversation.

"These are our friends from London," Mrs Kephalas said, introducing them by name. "They're visiting for a few days. We've just brought them over from Lichas."

"They're staying with you at your house?" Jake asked.

"Naturally, we will be going there later, but we thought we'd stop here on our way for a swim and lunch. Unfortunately our bay isn't as nice. It has little sand and few visitors. We plan to come swimming here for the next couple of days. You're both welcome to join us again."

"That's very generous," Jake said. The young man came and asked him what he wanted to drink. Jake asked for a cold beer. "I never had the chance to thank you for the invitation to your reception."

"Don't mention it. Alexander tells me you'll be moving to Greece soon. Will you be staying in your father's apartment?"

"Yes, it's in a nice area."

"It's just right for a couple, I hear, but I imagine you'd be looking for something bigger if you had a family."

"Quite so." Jake wondered whether she was talking in general or referring to him and Joanna.

"How long are you staying on the island? I hear you won't be keeping a house here."

"That's right. By the beginning of September both houses will be owned by my aunt and uncle." The waiter brought him his drink and he took a long sip. "I plan to leave by Tuesday."

"It's too quiet here. A young man like you would be looking for somewhere more exciting," she said with a knowing look.

"True, although my father's buried in the cemetery so I will be making occasional visits."

"Understandably. Your aunt and uncle didn't stay long."

"They only came for the memorial service and left the next day."

"Will they be keeping the houses?"

"I believe they'll be selling them. I don't think they feel at home here."

"We're set in our ways, I'm afraid. We like to see the same old faces."

"Like an exclusive club. Still, coming was a worthwhile experience."

"And you wouldn't have met Joanna."

"That's true."

"A lively girl."

"A handful," Jake agreed, wondering what it was that Mrs Kephalas meant.

"She caused a few scandals at university in London and in Paris," she added, lowering her voice. "But I suppose you know all about that."

"Yes, she does seem to cause mayhem wherever she goes," Jake said. Of course, he knew nothing of Joanna's past. "So, you saw her in London?"

"Not often, only when Diana was visiting and they came together."

"And will you continue having a house there?" he asked, trying to change the subject. "Or will you move to Greece?"

"We spend a lot of time in Greece already. I think once the children finish their education we will be coming for longer. I don't think we'll give up London completely though. It will remain our refuge."

"Your refuge?"

"Athens is too, well, parochial. You constantly feel under observation and under siege."

"Under siege?" he said, glancing over at Joanna who was still conversing with Phivos.

Mrs Kephalas had followed his gaze. "Well, people are always turning up uninvited. Friends and relatives; it's the way in Greece; you have little privacy."

"I hear you have a place in Florida too?"

"That's right; we use it during the European winter," she said, looking at her watch. "Will you excuse me?" She stood up and signalled one of her staff, who went over and helped her uncover the food. Meanwhile, Jake glanced out the glass doors of the after deck, out to where Natalya's yacht was anchored. He could see people on deck and in the surrounding water, but today it was too far away to pick anyone out.

"Please come and help yourselves," Mrs Kephalas announced before sitting back down. "Are you hungry?"

"I am, but I'll wait for everyone else," Jake said.

"You're like me then. You like to delay your pleasures."

Nobody responded at first, but soon they started going up, two at a time. Joanna and Phivos were among the last and still engrossed in conversation. From the little he overheard, they were talking in French. Finally Jake went up with Mrs Kephalas.

The food consisted of meats, pastas and salads.

"I don't know your name," Jake said, as they were serving themselves.

"Louisa," Mrs Kephalas said.

"That's a lovely name".

They continued to talk as they ate. It was obvious that Mrs Kephalas had an agenda, but he just couldn't work out what it was. "Would you like some more?" she asked after he'd finished.

"No, I've had enough," he said. The plates were large and he had pretty much filled his to overflowing. "It was delicious. How do you produce such meals on board? You must have good staff."

"I'm insulted," she said pouting her lips, looking hurt. "I do have good staff, but I do the cooking for guests."

"I'm sorry. Then I must compliment you on your abilities."

"I'm of Italian descent and you can't keep an Italian woman out of the kitchen."

"Still, you must be good. It can't be easy to cook on board a yacht."

"You'd be surprised. My kitchen here is more sophisticated than in any one of my homes."

"Really?"

"Are you interested in cooking?"

"Well yes, I rather enjoy it, although I'm not up to your standard."

"Then let me show you my kitchen, or galley as we should call it. I think you'll enjoy it. Let's go now while they prepare the table for dessert." She took his plate and gave it to the waiter, who she also instructed to clear the food and bring in the next course. "Come with me," she said.

He followed her down a short side passage with portholes on one side and cabins on the other. This eventually opened up into a pantry with cupboards, sinks and work surfaces. On one of the latter were the desserts on serving platters, ready to go out. Through the pantry they entered the galley. It was spacious and all in stainless steel, like the kitchens of famous restaurants he had seen on television. It was spotlessly clean and two of the crew were washing up, while another was wiping down surfaces.

The galley had no portholes, but there was air-conditioning, which kept the space cool. As she showed him round, he only paid vague attention to what she was saying, instead wondering what she was up to. Was she trying to lure him away from Joanna so that Kephalas could approach her? This seemed unlikely as Phivos was there.

"As you can imagine, I just love this kitchen," Mrs Kephalas said at the end.

"Do you wish you could live on board?"

"We do when we're touring the Mediterranean. But it can get claustrophobic. What you gain in the large state rooms and galley you lose in the other cabins. Let me show you a guest room." She led him out the other exit from the galley, down the side passage and then down some stairs to the lower deck. "The master and guest cabins are on the outside and the crew's on the inside." She opened the first door they came to and let him in. She closed the door behind her. "Do you see what I mean?"

He could. The cabin was tiny, just a double bed, surrounded by built-in cupboards, and a separate shower and toilet. The two small portholes let in scant light.

He turned back towards the door and faced her. She was standing close to him, blocking the way. Before he could say a word, she had her arms around his neck, her soft, moisturised lips on his, her tongue forcefully exploring him. For a few seconds he found himself responding; wanting her. So this was what it was about. She would seduce him and that would leave the door open for Kephalas. Or were they acting on Basil's instructions? Whose side was Kephalas on anyway? He pulled away gently but firmly.

"Do you not want me?" she said, breathing heavily with excitement. "I want you very much. I can feel you want me too. We can give each other a lot of pleasure." She tried to kiss him again.

"I'm with someone," he said pushing her away again. "And so are you."

"You mean Alexander? He doesn't mind. Don't you know anything? We have an understanding. He has his affairs; I have mine. You should've worked that out by now. We could have a wonderful time together, especially when you move to Greece. We could be close."

"As I said, I'm with someone."

"Joanna's really got you, hasn't she? I can free you from that. I can show you genuine passion."

"I can't," he said, pushing her away again.

"If you claim to know Joanna, you must realise you're being used. She won't be with you long."

"Nothing's certain in life."

"You poor fool," she said, readjusting her clothes and straightening her hair. "I'm afraid you'll discover the truth soon enough. I'd better get back to my guests."

He followed her out and they were back in time for the desserts. Afterwards Jake spoke to the British guest and Joanna conversed with his wife. Louisa completely ignored him.

At five Mrs Kephalas announced that the yacht would be leaving to go back to Seal Beach, so Jake and Joanna, having thanked their hosts, left and swam ashore. Phivos followed behind them, swimming to a speedboat tied to the floats.

"What is it about eating that makes you more susceptible to the cold?" Joanna said as they came out onto the beach.

"It's because your body's directing blood to your digestion and away from keeping you warm. Alcohol doesn't help either."

"Do you mind if we go home?"

"Not at all."

Later they met Diana at the Paralia taverna for a meal. They spoke about their afternoon on board the *Warrior*, though Jake left out Mrs Kephalas's attempt to seduce him.

They didn't encounter anyone else that evening.

Chapter 37: The Wait: Friday

Friday, 24th August

The routine monotonously repeated itself the next day. At the beach the usual collection of yachts and speedboats had assembled, including the *Warrior*, but Natalya's was absent. Joanna did not express any desire to board, although secretly she would have wanted to. Jake suspected that Diana had had a word with her.

In the evening, after eating at home with Diana, they went to the yacht club to find Mina and Yiannis sitting either side of a newly arrived Nicos. They spent most of the evening talking to him, rather like parents would to a wayward son from what Jake was able to overhear.

Savvas was also there, talking with his sons, not very enthusiastically, about the implications of their moving back to Athens. Meanwhile Phivos, Joanna and Diana walked up and down the waterfront immersed in some discussion Jake knew nothing about.

Jake was glad not be the centre of attention tonight, not to have to be on his guard, not to have to be careful what he said or did. Instead he thought about what he would have to do tomorrow. This did not prove useful as the more he tried to anticipate the difficulties he might face, the more pitfalls he imagined.

The time passed, and when most of them had gone, he was left with Nicos. The latter looked depressed.

"I wouldn't mind a drink," he said to Jake, who had only drunk two beers all evening. Nicos had been abstaining until then. Jake got the impression that Yiannis and Mina had been speaking to him at his father's instigation. "Will you join me?"

"Sure," Jake replied.

"Personally, I prefer the bar. Where's Joanna?"

"She's been walking with her grandmother and Phivos for hours. I see them passing every now and again," Jake said, looking down on the promenade. "They won't miss me." They got up and made their way to the other side of the club.

"What'll you have?"

"Ouzo with water and ice," Jake said, anticipating he needed something to relax.

As Nicos ordered the drinks, Jake looked around. It was the first time he'd been in the bar area. He saw Natalya immediately and she was looking at him. For a fraction of a second, he betrayed himself. He felt a cocktail of feelings that he could not control; love, compassion, tenderness and longing. After all these days of pretending and acting, he had dropped his guard. Irrespective of Natalya's loyalties, he could not afford to betray any feelings for her. He turned back to the bar and Nicos. This was so foolish. He could ruin everything with this carelessness. "How did your trip to Athens go?" he said to Nicos.

"Oh, fine. The girls made it to the airport all right. I visited a few islands and friends and here I am again."

"How long are you staying this time?"

"I'm hoping to leave on Monday," Nicos said. The barman gave them their drinks. They took a welcome sip. "How well did Britain do then?"

"Amazingly," Jake said. He regretted not being able to watch the Olympics more closely. "Are you interested in sport?"

"Not really, but my friends talk about it. I hear you're definitely moving to Greece?"

"That's right. There's not much that's secret around here."

"Tell me about it. It really sucks. I hate it. I can never get away."

"It's only for a few weeks in summer."

"Yes, but for me it's wherever I go. But hey, let's change the subject. When will you be coming down?"

"Probably Christmas."

"That's great, we'll get together. I'll take you to some clubs your father used to go to."

"How come you used to go out with him? There's such an age difference."

"It doesn't matter so much in Greece, but your father was a great guy with a sense of humour. He didn't judge me and I really liked him."

"Was he friendly with any of the others?"

Nicos didn't answer immediately. "I was his only friend here."

"Have you got plans for the future?" Jake asked. He'd heard these from everyone else except Nicos.

"No, I don't have plans. I just make them up as I go along." Nicos looked down rather seriously. "From the discussion I've just had, my father's arranging some sort of rehab, although there may be a way of avoiding it."

"Oh? How?"

"Nothing," Nicos said quickly. "Forget I said anything."

"Does he ever come to the island?" Jake asked, speculating on what he meant. "You know, your father."

"Oh yes, but never in summer. He runs a cruise ship company. Now's the busiest time," Nicos said. He looked behind Jake at someone approaching. Jake turned to look. It was Natalya.

"Hello, Jake," she said.

"Hi," Jake said. "I see you're back. Are you staying long this time?"

"Until Monday probably."

"I've been going to the same beach as you, but I didn't see you swimming."

"I had a bad cold. This is the first time I've been out since Tuesday."

"I'm sorry to hear that."

"I'll be back in a minute," Nicos said. "I'm just going to the restroom."

"Why didn't you come over to greet me just now? It was rude and hurtful," Natalya said, once Nicos was out of earshot.

"You looked preoccupied; I didn't think I should disturb you."

"Didn't you see that I only had eyes for you? I may have been away, but I have thought of no one else."

"Am I supposed to think that means something? Natalya, we hardly know each other. We're barely friends."

"This isn't what your eyes were telling me. When you first saw me you showed your true feelings. This gives me great joy and hope."

"You're imagining things. Besides, I'm with someone else, as you probably know."

"This hope I have is not just for me, but for you as well."

"There's a queue for the john," Nicos said, returning. "Hey! I think I see Joanna and Diana coming up the stairs."

"I'd better go in case they think I've left," Jake said, draining his ouzo. "Thanks for the drink," he said to Nicos. "I'll see you both around."

Chapter 38: The Street Party

Saturday, 25th August

Jake woke early, disturbed by a commotion in the harbour. There was loud hooting, followed by the clattering of the anchor chains of a large yacht mooring. It could only be the *Trident*. He looked at his watch; it was seven thirty. He was surprised to have slept at all, but it was important he tried to rest for longer.

He turned towards Joanna, lying on her side facing away from him. She had the sheet up to her neck and her golden locks were splayed over the pillow. Their relationship had developed much as Virginia had predicted over the past week.

He could sense the contempt and boredom growing in her. He could feel how much she resented being with him. Despite what he imagined was some serious pressure from Diana, Joanna was not disguising her feelings. He was, after all, just one of hundreds of men Aphrodite had seduced. Sex had become mechanical and she was no longer enjoying it. Strangely enough he still was. He put this down to the fact that he was now manipulating her and not the other way round.

He thought about Teresa. How were her spirits? What would she feel about him now? Did she understand why she was being held? In the few minutes they would have together, would he be able to get through to her to a sufficient degree to convince her to cooperate? Would he even get that far? Indeed, would he survive to see tomorrow's dawn?

And what of Natalya? He wanted to believe in her but could not permit himself to do so. Their feelings would have to remain unknown and unexplored. Once the crystals were destroyed, if they were destroyed, she might not be the same woman anyway.

Virginia, with Photis's help, had thought this through, and one of Jake's wishes after it was over was to get to know them both much better, especially the latter. He would have to brush up on his Greek to converse with Photis, but there would be so much about his father he could learn from them.

He closed his eyes and tried to subdue his thoughts and managed to doze for a while.

The hours passed slowly during the day. They went to the beach in the late morning. It was hot, very hot, and the sea was glassy, which was not good, as it would make things more difficult for him in the evening, if it persisted. The air was hazy and lacked its usual clarity. It somehow made things seem unreal, implausible even. Were it not for the suffering of Teresa to keep him focused, he could easily have drifted into despondency.

Now, as the evening approached and he walked along the harbour, with Joanna at his side, he felt more determined. He could feel the knotting of his stomach as his nerves and senses moved to a higher level of alertness. As soon as he entered the arena, the curtain would go up.

The stadium was behind the school, a pretentious affair for such a small island. The pitch had a running track around it and open concrete seating on all four sides. At the entrance there was a flight of stairs leading to a walkway that ran along the top of the stands. Once there, Jake surveyed the audience. At the far end was a group that included Alexander and Basil. He searched for someone nearby with whom he was acquainted. Meanwhile, Joanna had spotted Diana at the other end of the stadium and was pulling at his arm to follow.

Fortunately, in the distance, Jake spotted Panagos with Savvas and Mina, the grocers. He made the excuse that he had to have a word with him.

He walked towards the end of the long row and sat next to Panagos. He spoke to him about the house, mentioning some imagined problems: the plumbing and the patio doors, while his attention was focused on his next target. There in the next block of seats was Stephanos. He was sitting with the banker and the local doctor, who in turn were just below Alexander and Basil. It was essential that he get himself invited to the yacht that evening. For that to happen, he had to give Basil a good reason to want to do so.

He concluded his conversation with Panagos when Stephanos caught his eye and waved. Jake waved back and approached.

"How are you?" Stephanos enquired.

"I'm fine," Jake replied. "And you?"

"Busy, very busy."

"And Niki?"

"The same. I've seen less of her than I have of you, if you don't count the time we're asleep." His friends laughed. Jake saw her sitting with a group that included Yiannis, the mayor, and Phivos. He looked back in the direction of Basil, next to whom was an attractive woman with long fair hair tied behind her head. Jake sat in a position where he hoped to attract his attention.

"So where's your charming companion?" Stephanos asked.

"She's sitting at the far end with her grandmother," Jake replied, pointing back in the direction from which he'd come.

"Diana never did like mingling. Tell Joanna to abandon her grandmother and come and sit with us."

"Better still," one of Stephanos's companions said, "send her over and you stay with the old crone."

"I don't think so," Jake said, taking a quick glance at Basil. He successfully caught his eye and nodded in acknowledgement. Basil nodded in return. This would be his chance. He smiled and walked over to him.

Basil stood up and they shook hands. He did not introduce his companion.

"I'd like to thank you for your hospitality last Saturday," Jake said.

"Don't mention it," Basil replied. "I'm sorry we didn't have the space to invite you for the evening. You must give my regards to Joanna."

"She was also grateful. She was so impressed with your yacht and hasn't stopped talking about it."

"Is that so? It's my own design. I had it custom made."

"Isn't that amazing? You won't believe this, but Joanna could tell right away. She said to me, 'I bet it's his design'. She could see clues."

"Really? Like what?"

"I couldn't tell you because I'm afraid I was sceptical. You know, although Joanna's a linguist, she's very artistic, she appreciates beauty and good design. Anyway, she did say that if she was ever invited again, she would demand that tour you promised her."

"Demand a tour? Well, tell her that she can have that opportunity tonight. Why don't you both come on board the *Trident* after the street party? The festivities will continue on board and we're fine for numbers."

"I'm sure she'll be thrilled when I tell her. What time do you want us?"

"Any time after midnight."

"Thank you so much. I'd better go back or else Joanna will think I've abandoned her," Jake said as he withdrew. He had a final word with Stephanos and then went back to Joanna and Diana just before kick-off.

"You were gone a long time," Joanna said.

"Well, I wanted to speak to Panagos about a few things and it's always difficult to get hold of him. Anyway, then I saw Stephanos and had a brief chat with him and, as he was nearby, I went to thank Basil for the invitation last Saturday."

"What did he say?" Diana asked.

"After I told him how much we loved the yacht, he said that he was pleased and that he'd designed it himself. I'm afraid I lied at that point and said that we could tell. He seemed to want to show us around it sometime."

"You obviously appealed to his vanity," Diana said.

"Did you know that he's hosting a gathering tonight?" Jake continued.

"He has it every year after the match and street party," Diana said.

"I didn't know that," Joanna remarked.

"He said we could go if we wanted," Jake added.

At precisely seven o'clock the match started and the stadium reverberated to the sounds of jeering or cheering, depending on who had the ball and what they were doing with it.

"What did you tell him?" Joanna asked.

"I said that I would ask you, but that you probably would prefer to stay at the bouzouki and watch the dancing."

"We'd be able to hear the music and the singing from the yacht. All we'd miss is old fat men making fools of themselves."

"It doesn't start until midnight so we can decide at the time."

"It's not that simple. We would dress more formally if we were going onto the yacht."

"We can dress to allow for both options then."

"Why did you assume that I wouldn't be interested in going?"

"I just thought you wouldn't enjoy it. We'd spend the night talking to half-drunk men and women."

"What do you mean half-drunk men and women? They'll mostly be wealthy businessmen and their wives. We can't spend twenty-four hours a day stuck to each other. We have to network. Some of these people will have businesses in Athens. You could learn something from them."

"I don't know, the other problem with these parties is that they last till the early hours, you take days to recover and at the end you wonder if it was worthwhile."

"You can sleep all day if you want to. We can't do anything at Paleo Limani until Monday anyway and then not till nightfall."

"But it's still a waste of a day," Jake added. Annoying Joanna was becoming a real pleasure.

"Well, personally, I'm quite capable of sleeping late and getting up early on the occasional day. You need to lighten up, Jake. You have a tendency to smother people."

"What do you mean?" Jake said, trying to sound upset.

"This is not the time or place to be talking about this," Joanna said. "I need to go to the ladies, I'm suffocating here," she added, getting up.

"I need to go too," Diana said. "Do you know where they are? I always forget."

"I'm sure we'll find them."

They walked off. Jake was certain they would be having another talk. Virginia was right about Aphrodite. She would become more and more difficult to control as time went by. Her arrogance had no bounds. He wondered what Diana would be saying to her. It mattered a great deal this time. If it was as predicted by previous occasions, it would be an opportunity for Jake to push her over the edge.

They were away for at least half an hour. By the time they came back, the first half was nearly over. The sun was setting and Jake could see the last rays touching the tops of the surrounding hills. "I'm sorry to be this long, darling." Joanna said sweetly, "but football matches bore us and we got talking to some ladies."

"You haven't missed much," Jake said. "No one's scored."

"Are you interested in the match?" Joanna asked.

"Not particularly," Jake replied.

"Then let's go for a walk," she said, taking his hand.

"What about your grandmother?" Jake said, looking over at Diana, who stared grimly into the distance.

"I'll stay," Diana said, looking at Jake and forcing a smile. "We can meet later in the square."

They left the stadium just as the floodlights came on and went out through the grounds of the school and onto the darkening streets, which, apart from a few young children in the playground with their minders, were practically deserted as everyone was at the match.

"Where do you want to go?" Jake asked.

"Let's go back home for now." They didn't speak for a while. She looked down at the ground as if concentrating on what she was about to say. "I'm sorry about my behaviour, but there are a few things we need to clear up once and for all," she said, taking his hand in hers.

"All right, I'm listening," Jake said, pretending to sound worried.

"I didn't mean to say that you were suffocating me. It's just that we express our love in different ways. I like to mingle; I need to be social. I love being with you and other people. You're more of a loner, but together we can complement each other."

"I understand, and I'm sorry too and, of course, we'll go to the yacht afterwards. I can only excuse my behaviour by saying that it's because I love you so much," Jake said, trying to make it sound emotional. "I can't live without you. I don't want to share you with anyone else or, worse still, lose you completely."

"Oh, Jake," she said, with a sigh, as they were entering the cool dark flat. "What am I going to do with you?"

He shut the door and took her in his arms. "I'm desperate for you; I must have you," he said. "I suppose you'll have to get dressed now."

"There's plenty of time for that," she said, resigning herself to the implication in what Jake said. They walked into the bedroom, taking their clothes off as they went. Once in bed, when he was on top of her, he could see from her face, as she stared into the distance, away from him, that her thoughts were elsewhere.

It was nine thirty when they arrived at the street party. The town square had been laid out with wooden tables and chairs arranged in a semi-circle facing the sea, the empty space within being for the band and dance floor, both of which were on a raised platform. Around the outside of the seated area were long, dressed trestle tables on which the banquet would be arranged and for which stainless-steel heated trays were already in position. At the ends were stacks of plates, cutlery and paper napkin dispensers. Men and women in white aprons were arranging the food and drinks, all provided free by the Friends of Halia.

As they approached the square from the museum end, a waiter holding a clipboard intercepted them and asked their names. They gave him Diana's and were taken to a table for four along the outer fringe.

Most of the other tables were already occupied. The biggest of these, a long one in the centre, sideways to the band and dance floor and behind the one for the dignitaries, was reserved for the football teams. The din of many voices filled the air and overwhelmed the recorded Greek music playing from loudspeakers attached to the surrounding lamp posts.

Their table had a bottle of both red and white wine, which the waiter opened, as well as a bottle of mineral water. He explained that the food was self-service and an announcement would be made when it was ready. If they wanted any more drinks, they would have to buy them from the taverna bar.

"Are we happy with wine?" Jake asked. He would somehow have to disguise the fact that he was not drinking. It was dark where they were sitting and the mortar between the cobbles at his feet had cracked and come away, providing the opportunity to discreetly pour liquids away.

"I can't speak for Gran but I'll be happy with wine," Joanna said. "Speak of the devil. Were your ears burning?"

"Not that I noticed," Diana said as she approached and sat down. She was wearing a short-sleeved cream blouse tucked into dark brown trousers. She hung her handbag on its strap on the back of the chair. Joanna, on the other hand, was wearing a skimpy black skirt and blouse.

"Was the second half worth seeing?" Jake asked.

"Not really," she replied. "It ended in a one all draw."

"At least you saw two goals," Jake said. "I wonder what happens with the cup."

"I think it stays with last year's winner," Diana said.

As they spoke, he noticed that Joanna was turned away from them, in a world of her own. She was looking towards the head table where the dignitaries were gathering. Jake recognised Kephalas and his wife, the mayor, Maria, Niki and Stephanos. Some of the rest were familiar faces that he had seen around but for which he had no name. After they had taken their places, Yiannis stood up and, facing the audience with a microphone, called for attention by striking a glass with a fork before then launching into a speech in Greek. Jake only vaguely followed it but responded whenever there was cheering, laughter or applause.

The good thing about having to play a part over the last few days was that it kept his nerves at bay, Jake reflected. He was continuously concentrating on what he was going to say and do and gauging the mood of those around him. So far so good, but this was only the beginning. The manipulation of Joanna and getting invited onto the yacht were fairly predictable. As far as this initial stage was concerned it was only Diana he had to worry about. She was sharp-witted and observant and he had to be careful in her presence. But she also seemed preoccupied at times, no doubt with the confinement of Teresa on her mind as well as her responsibilities for retrieving the crystals.

It was on the yacht that the uncertainties would really begin. There were so many random factors; too many variables to control. Virginia had said something to him which had helped him keep faith against what he thought were unlikely odds.

He was expressing his concern about the numerous things that could go wrong when she said: "I've had many years to observe fate. When someone, like you, is thrown into a situation where they have little choice in the course of action they can take, I've found them to be the agents of destiny." When this didn't console him she went further. "You must have faith, Jake, faith in me, in Photis and in yourself. When the time comes, you must trust your intuition that you will know what to do. This insight is your gift; what you've inherited from us."

He looked around him. Here he was surrounded by all these normal people and yet amongst them were his enemies and false friends. So far he'd identified Poseidon, Aphrodite, Ares, Artemis, Zeus, Apollo, Demeter, Persephone, Hades and probably Dionysus; he was certain the latter was Nicos. But of the others he wasn't sure. Who were Mina, Stephanos and Niki?

If he was successful tonight, he wondered how it would affect those concerned. They were certainly possessed, but what effect would the removal of the possessing entity have? How it all worked was beyond

Jake's ability to understand and there was not enough time for Virginia to explain.

Retrieving Basil's crystal and leaving the yacht with it seemed a far-fetched endeavour. Virginia warned him not to focus on it, but to take just one step at a time. The task was his and his alone, as dictated by fate. She did say that she would be closer to him than he would know and at those times when he had managed to calm his mind, he swore he could sense her reassuring presence.

With a flurry of applause the speech finished and, no sooner had the mayor sat down, an announcement was made about the food. Then the band mounted the stage and started warming up. At the same time people started queuing at the various serving tables. Neither Joanna nor Diana appeared particularly interested in joining the lines and Jake, for his part, had to take care how much he ate. Alcohol was an obvious avoid, but too much food could also make him sluggish.

Time dragged on. In another hour and a half they would have to be on the yacht. It was half an hour before the crowds had dispersed sufficiently for them to go up and help themselves. Jake stuck to chicken, pasta and salad. In truth he was not really hungry. They ate in silence. The music was so loud that conversation would have been an effort. There was an air of expectancy. Jake was worried that he was giving something away. He tried not to keep on looking at the time and was relieved when Phivos came to the table and asked Diana if she would not rather go to the yacht club with him as he was bored. Diana agreed, wished them a pleasant evening and left.

Although the band had been playing for nearly an hour, the first dancers did not start going up until eleven thirty, when the vocalist arrived. After a warm-up tune, she started singing a popular song. This raised a cheer and two men went up to the dance area. One was Nicos. The way he moved his body was incredibly intense and graceful and the audience started rhythmic clapping. Then a few minutes later, Alexander went over from the main table and joined in. His dancing was equally as good but in a more passionate, aggressive way as opposed to Nicos's, which was more elegant. Others joined in, forming a circle round the two, either dancing or clapping whilst kneeling on one knee.

To Jake's surprise, Joanna got up, excused herself and, without asking Jake if he wanted to join her, walked to the dance floor, straight through the ring and joined Nicos and Kephalas in the centre. They in turn made room for her and took turns dancing with her. Joanna's movements were sensual and suggestive and the audience found the threesome entertaining.

And so it went on. As soon as one song finished it was followed by another and still the three danced, seemingly oblivious of time and place or the comings and goings of others in the audience.

It was coming up to twelve thirty and Jake was beginning to worry. Presumably both Alexander and Nicos were also invited to the yacht. What if they didn't want to go? What if they decided to stay here dancing and Joanna the same? According to mythology, not only was Ares her long-term lover, with whom Aphrodite had children, but she also had an affair with Dionysius. He had to think of something. There had to be a way to get back on track.

He reflected on what Virginia had said about fate and destiny and wondered what answer it had for this one. It was just as he was having these thoughts that

Natalya appeared out of the gloom. "Jake, may I join you?"

"Of course you can," he said, trying not to sound too eager. "I didn't see you at the football match."

"We were there. You didn't see me, but I saw you," she said, sitting in Joanna's place, moving the chair closer to him, so he could hear her. "I take it you're not much of a dancer."

"I certainly couldn't compete with them," Jake said. He could feel her breath buffet the side of his face as she spoke.

"The steps to Greek dancing are simple; it's all in the expression."

"I suppose you're an expert."

"I can't do it like them, but I'm good. Maybe I can teach you how to feel the music one day. But my father's very good, being Russian." Then, after not receiving a response, "I've been watching you, first at the football match and now here."

"I didn't even know you were here."

"I'm sitting over there, towards the harbour, with my family," she said, looking over her shoulder. "It's dark, so you can't see me, but I can see you."

"Sounds boring."

"It's interesting, actually. I've noticed many things. I've seen you filling your glass with wine and pretending to drink. Then, when the others aren't watching, you slip it under the table and pour some onto the ground, into the earth. So why are you doing this?"

"Maybe I like it when those around me have drunk too much and I remain sober. Maybe I always do it."

"Maybe, but I observed something else. I can see that Joanna treats you like dirt and you act like a slave in front of her, but now that she's dancing provocatively with other men, you don't care. You keep looking at your watch, but you don't appear jealous."

"How do you know I'm not jealous? Maybe I just don't show it or maybe I have faith in her."

"Maybe you know better, after all. From the time I first met you until now I think you've learnt much. I think you're hiding things from me."

"Why would I do that?" Jake said, not daring to look at her.

"Because you believe I'm going to betray you," she said, looking at him carefully. "You can't look at me, can you? I think you understand much, if not everything. I know you will not open yourself to me."

"You're a clever girl and a good one; much better than them," Jake said, looking around him.

"I know what is being planned for you," she said, looking down at her hands. "I want to help you."

"But why would you do that? Why would you go against them? You have so much to lose."

"To betray love and lose honour for power is a tragedy. I will not follow them."

"Few people would see it that way and fewer still would not be tempted."

"I know that the first time we met you thought me pointless and stupid," she said, raising her hand when he tried to object. "But I'm stubborn and strong inside, like my father. Also, some things have too high a price. You keep looking at your watch and seem anxious. I think you're planning something."

"I think you're imagining things."

"I *know* you're planning something," she reiterated. "I can see it from your face that you're lying to me and you hate yourself for it."

"I don't know what to say."

"What is it you're so worried about with the time?"

Jake thought about it for a while. "I need Joanna to stop dancing. I need to go somewhere with her."

"I will do this for you."

"You can do it? How?"

"You'll see."

"Well, if you can, I need it done now."

"Okay." She got up, paused as if she had something further to say and then left.

He saw her walking in the direction of the harbour, round the outside of the tables. She got to one deep in the shadows and spoke to someone there. Then a big man got up and escorted her to the dance floor. It was her father.

As soon as they moved in and started dancing together, it was as if a spell was broken. Kephalas walked off mid-dance and left Joanna looking round confused. A few minutes later, more from the Russian table came to the dance floor and then Nicos left as well. Finally, Joanna came back to the table, sweating profusely and looking disappointed.

"Are you okay, darling?" Jake asked.

"Yes, it's a shame we had to stop. We were so wrapped up with the atmosphere and the music, until that bloody Russian and his family came along."

"I don't understand."

"Alexander can't stand him. What's the time?"

"One o'clock."

"We'd better head for the *Trident*."

Chapter 39: The Yacht

At just after one, when they boarded the *Trident*, the party was well under way. There were two crew members standing sentinel by the gangway and, once they were let inside, they walked through the lower salon, where couples sat for a quiet chat away from the noisier gathering above.

Climbing the stairs up to the bar and sun deck, they picked up flutes of champagne from a waiter with a tray and made their way to the open deck area at the stern, where most people had congregated. Apart from Kephalas and his wife, Jake saw no one else he recognised. Most of the other guests were young, being around his age.

The round central table had been removed and in the middle of the open space stood Basil Protopapas. He had a drink in one hand, and clinging to his arm was an attractive blonde in her late thirties, not the same woman who was at the football match. She looked drunk, stoned, or both, and was holding on to Basil more for support than affection.

Basil saw the new arrivals and beckoned them over, presenting them to the guests at hand. Some were married couples from Athens, all with high-powered jobs in finance or banking. Also amongst them were men and women, of various ages, who worked for Basil in some capacity or other in his yachting business.

Jake began to converse with some, automatically asking the usual questions, giving the usual replies, all the time aware of his surroundings, waiting for his cue. Through these exchanges, it transpired that many had come on the ferry to be here, and there would be a special service at nine in the morning to take them back to Lichas. The priority for now was how to get Joanna and Basil together. At the moment they were ignoring each other.

Jake, having exhausted the small talk, sat on the bench seat that encircled the deck, drink in hand, leaving Joanna unattended as she spoke to a woman who ran a fashion business in London. After a while he saw that Nicos had arrived and was stepping out on the deck, joining Kephalas.

"What time do you call this?" Basil reproached him playfully.

"You're lucky we came at all," Nicos said. "If it wasn't for the Russians, I'd still be dancing, and so would you." He looked towards Joanna.

"When I'm in the mood for something, nothing can distract me," Joanna replied, looking in Basil's direction.

"Alexander doesn't share your focus," Nicos said.

"He's easily distracted," Basil said. "Did you enjoy your short stay on Lichas?" Basil asked Joanna, moving closer to her, the blonde still clinging to his arm whilst speaking to another woman on her right.

Meanwhile, Nicos sat next to Jake. "Do you have an issue with Russians?" Jake asked.

"Not me," Nicos replied. "I don't have issues with anybody; not negative ones at least."

"So what's the story there?" Jake asked, keeping an eye on Basil and Joanna. They had moved a few feet away from him, so he couldn't hear what they were saying. The blonde woman was still holding on to Basil as if he were a life raft. The body language seemed positive.

"I don't suppose you've heard of Kephalas' reputation, have you?" Nicos said, sipping his whisky and ice. He looked in the direction of Alexander and Louisa to confirm they were too far away to overhear.

"He seems to have one in many areas. Which are you referring to?"

"I'm referring to his private reputation."

"I've heard that Alexander and his wife lead colourful lives."

"I'm not gossiping by confirming this; it's common knowledge. And you would've noticed that the Russian and his wife are a good-looking couple."

"I saw the Russian from afar, but not the wife."

"Unfortunately for Alexander and Louisa, the Russian's a bit of a prude when it comes to marriage and family. Mrs Kephalas made a pass at him, with a view no doubt to partner swapping, which he politely declined. That's fine; Mrs Kephalas makes passes at many people. The problem started when Alexander's older daughter befriended the Russian's youngest and invited her to spend a few nights on the *Warrior* when they were due to go on a short cruise. The Russian refused saying 'it was not the right moral environment for his daughter'."

"Under the circumstances he could've said worse."

"It was bad enough for Alexander. He wanted to go and beat the crap out of the Russian."

"There's a bit of a difference in size," Jake said. Even at the distance he was from the dance floor, he could tell he was a big man.

"Kephalas is a bit of a scrapper; anyway, Basil intervened."

"I suppose that's why Kephalas has to put up with him."

"Exactly, but he draws the line on the dance floor."

"Why does Basil like having the Russian around?"

"I don't know everything about it, but I think they exchange favours. They don't have any direct interests in each other's businesses, but the Russian has ex-KGB connections. I'm told he can get background on anybody in the western world."

"What does Basil do in return?"

"I don't know, commerce is not my thing," Nicos said, looking distracted. "Look, this isn't any of my business, and you might not even mind, but Basil seems to be hitting on your girlfriend."

Jake looked over at them. Certainly Basil was standing much closer to Joanna. The blonde woman seemed just as interested. "It might be a bit difficult with his girlfriend on his arm."

"You don't know Basil. He'd make Alexander look like a saint. You don't know what's going on here, do you?"

Jake looked back at him blankly.

"Do you see these solitary women?" Nicos said, looking around the place. "Do you know who they are?"

"Guests, I assumed," Jake said. He was too preoccupied to notice, but there were a good dozen unattached women milling around with very little on.

"Guests yes, but apart from the few that are business contacts, the rest are single, attractive and here for one reason."

"I still don't understand," Jake said, bemused.

"They're hangers-on. They're here for the free board, travel, food, drink and drugs. They're here for Basil and any of his guests to enjoy."

"That explains why the others haven't come, especially the Russians."

"They wouldn't have been invited."

"I bet Alexander feels at home."

"Most of these girls are pretty much out of it. To give Alexander his due, he prefers a bit more of a conquest."

"So I could just go up and take any of them down to a cabin?"

"You wouldn't even need to tell her your name and, by the look of things, Basil would be only too pleased if you did?"

Jake pretended to only just realise the consequences of this. "I'd better get Joanna and get out of here." He tried to stand up, but fell back down. "God, I can't get up, I shouldn't have had so much to drink."

Nicos shook his head, "I can't help someone who can't help himself."

"Why do you want to help me?"

"I don't like seeing people get hurt," Nicos said. "Anyway, I've got my eye on those two, just inside on the settee. I'm not like Kephalas; I like things to come easy. I'll catch up with you later."

Nicos left, drifting towards a couple of scantily dressed girls in the bar lounge. He spoke to them; they giggled and let him sit between them. Jake looked back at Joanna and Basil. It was time to play the drunken, jealous boyfriend. This time he got on his feet and went up to them.

"How are you, darling?" he said, putting his arm around her and steadying himself. Pulling her towards him, he planted a sloppy kiss on her cheek. Joanna looked disgusted.

"Your charming girlfriend's been amusing us," Basil said. The clinging woman nodded.

"She's one of a kind," Jake said. "I'm lucky to have her." He gripped her possessively and watched her cringe. "Don't let me interrupt the conversation."

"Margaret and I were just saying how much we think you'd enjoy a cruise," Basil said. "Might we tempt you to join us?"

"When did you have in mind?" Jake asked. Margaret looked as though she wasn't capable of thinking anything. She kept on blinking as if she was about to pass out.

"Early September's a great time to tour the islands," Basil said.

"Unfortunately we have to get back before then. We have plans to put in place. By Christmas we want to be living in Greece together. Isn't that right, darling?" Jake was raising his voice.

"Yes, Jake, but what's the harm in taking the time to go on a little cruise? I've never seen the islands properly."

"I don't like changing my plans; besides, what about your job?"

"I was going to quit anyway, remember? If you can't be flexible, why can't I go?"

"Because we can go together some other time," Jake said, squeezing her until she squirmed. "Is there something wrong?"

"You're being rough," she sneered. "You're obviously drunk."

"I'm not drunk," Jake raised his voice even more, which made the people nearest them turn their heads. He pretended to stagger a little and gripped Joanna tighter.

"Take it easy, Jake," Basil said, grabbing his arm with a massive hand. "Why don't you sit down, you look unsteady."

"I'm fine," he said. "But my glass is empty, I need another drink."

"Only if you sit down," Basil said. "What would you like?"

"Ouzo with ice."

"Now sit down and I'll have it brought to you."

Jake did as he was told and sat in the same place as before. Meanwhile Basil signalled one of the waiters and gave him instructions before returning his attention to Margaret and Joanna. They continued as if the interruption had never occurred.

Within minutes a waiter came to him. It was the head barman who had served them during their previous visit to the *Trident*. He carried a tray with a half-full glass of ouzo in ice and a small jug of water. "This I believe is the drink you ordered, sir," he said in an American accent.

"Just fill it to the top," Jake said, looking up at him. "On second thoughts, I don't know whether I can drink it, I might have to lie down."

"That can be arranged to suit you," the waiter said and walked away.

He focused on what he had to do next and recalled the relevant part of the conversation with Virginia, particularly when he asked about the ally.

"Poseidon has forgotten all about me," Virginia had begun. "He believes I'm dead or that I'm in retreat in some monastery in the Far East.

"Anyway, in recent years I've tried to keep as close to him as I could without being noticed, using whatever resources have come my way to gain advantage. These have been scant, but there is one. As you remember, Poseidon had met your paternal grandmother in New York during the war years. She was already married with two children. He seduced her, had a long affair and then abandoned her just as she fell pregnant with his child; your father. You know the rest.

"All those years, the husband had to bring up the children on his own, never knowing what became of his wife. The youngest of these, a daughter and your father's half-sister, married and had children of her own. One of these, your half-cousin, became a security expert. I approached him some years ago. The disappearance of his grandmother was still a family trauma, especially since the mystery of her whereabouts had never been established. I told him what had happened and who was responsible. I had spent many years gathering evidence, circumstantial at best, but I convinced him. He was willing to help me bring down the man who was responsible. I got him to start working for Basil's Florida operation. He worked his way up to head barmen on their chartered boats. Three years ago he was promoted to the *Trident*."

"That's quite a sacrifice," Jake had commented. "Probably not the life he would've chosen."

"I have compensated him generously," Virginia had replied, "put his children through college, guaranteed his financial security. He's a good man, mid-forties. He's waited a long time for this. Because of his past experience and intimate knowledge of the yacht, he will be able to help you when the time comes."

And the time had come. Jake got up and approached Basil and Joanna. "I don't think I can drink any more," Jake said to Basil, wavering as he stood. "Is there somewhere I can lie down for a few minutes?"

"How pathetic," Joanna remarked, looking away from him.

"Why don't you take him down to one of the cabins?" Basil said to the nearest waiter available. It wasn't the same one who had brought him the previous drink, but he put his tray down and firmly took hold of Jake's arm.

"Do you do this often?" Jake slurred.

"All part of the job sir," the waiter said.

He led him down three flights of stairs until they were in the crew accommodation corridor. They stopped outside a cabin door and he let him in. "Is there anything you'll be needing sir?"

"No, thank you. I'm just going to lie down for a few minutes."

"As you wish," the waiter said, shutting the door.

Jake had to wait an agonising twenty minutes before the door opened again and the waiter he'd seen earlier, the head barman, came in and closed it behind him. "I'm John," he said.

"I'm Jake. What took you so long?"

"An unexpected turn of events. Come we haven't much time. We'd better hurry." He opened the cabin door and looked outside. "Follow and listen." They cautiously exited the cabin, making sure there was no one in the corridor. "Above us is 'A' accommodation deck. The cabins there are for guests and the owners. This is 'B' deck, where the officers and crew sleep." He locked the cabin behind them. "If I lock this and you don't respond if someone knocks, they'll think you've passed out. It might buy us time."

There was no one on the lower deck and, as they passed one of the cabins, John stopped and opened it.

"Wait," he said, entering briefly and coming back out with a hold-all.

They went up to the next deck and, in less than a minute were outside the stateroom door. John unlocked it and they entered the dimly lit cabin, which consisted of two parts. The first was a sitting room, which was the width of the boat. Being so far forward, it was not as broad as the widest part of the yacht, but still contained a settee, arm chairs and a coffee table on the starboard side, and an office area, with a desk and a filing cabinet, on the port side. Forward were open, folding doors leading to a spacious bedroom. This was set into the prow, with the bed amidships.

Jake was startled to find someone lying on it. It was Margaret. John saw his shock. "Don't worry," he whispered. "She's drunk, drugged and more. I could drill her teeth and she wouldn't notice."

"Is this the unexpected event?" Jake whispered back.

"Yep, and it means Basil's unlikely to be bringing anyone in here," John said, unzipping the holdall. From within he took out a black full-length wetsuit and rubber boots, which he laid out on the bed beside the sleeping woman. Jake undressed and started to change into these. He put his mobile into an inside, waterproof pocket. Next John took out a tool kit, from which he removed an electric drill. He plugged this into a nearby socket, then opened a built-in wardrobe, parted the hanging clothes and, after removing the partition on the back wall, started working on the safe. Fortunately, the high pitch whine was no match for the sound of the music that was coming from the deck above.

"Is there anything I can do?" Jake asked.

"No. I'll be five minutes. I can't use a more powerful drill because I might blow a fuse or the power surge would be noticed by someone in the engine room."

"Will they not miss you upstairs?" Jake said, sitting down to catch his breath.

"I'm on a break. I told them I needed a crap."

Jake set to considering their first major problem, something he had been brooding on over the last few days and which had also concerned Virginia. Here they were in Poseidon's cabin, breaking into his safe, about to steal the most precious thing in his life and he's upstairs seducing Aphrodite on an island surrounded by all his enemies. It didn't add up. Poseidon didn't get through the last three and a half thousand years by being lax. He wouldn't have left the crystal in his stateroom and gone somewhere else if he wasn't certain it could not be stolen. As Virginia had suggested, there had to be another hiding place. He remembered her words to him: 'When the time comes, you must trust your intuition that you will know what to do. This insight is your gift; what you've inherited from us.'

"There's another safe," he said to John.

"What?" he exclaimed. "This is the only one I know of. It's in the original plans. No one told me about another."

"You carry on, but listen to what I'm saying. We know that Basil's always picking up women and bringing them in here. The last thing he wants is to be fiddling with a safe in front of them. There's another one, somewhere out of sight." It had to be easy and quick to get to. He started systematically searching the two rooms of the cabin, behind furniture, pictures, underneath carpets; he even prodded the ceiling, before turning to the en suite.

He could not risk switching on the light of the bathroom as it had a porthole, so he borrowed a torch from John and went in to search. It could only be in here. It was the only place he could go and not been seen. As soon as he entered, he guessed where it had to be. Looking at the mirror above the basin, he realised that it had to be behind it. Either as a result of logic or intuition, sure enough, after fiddling around its edges, he managed to find the latch that released it and which allowed the mirror fitting to swing open, revealing the safe behind.

When he returned to the bedroom, John had opened the first safe. "I was told only you could look inside," he said.

"That's great. But there's another one in the bathroom, behind the mirror."

"Shit," John said, picking up his equipment and rushing into it.

Jake opened the cupboard safe and looked inside. He could already hear the drill starting up again. The inside of the compartment contained mostly money, a passport and a few papers. At the front was a black suede pouch, the kind used for carrying jewellery. It was heavy and contained a gold chain. On it was a pendant in which was embedded a small ruby-coloured stone. This was curious he thought, and not what Virginia had told him to expect. Was this a decoy, to stop thieves from looking any further? He sat on the bed and waited.

"Have you found anything?" John asked from the threshold of the bathroom.

"I don't know," Jake replied. He put the pouch in his zipped pocket, closed the safe, replaced the partition, then the clothes, and shut the cupboard.

"I can't open that safe," John said, returning to the bedroom, carrying the holdall.

"What?"

"I can drill it, but pulling the door open will break a circuit, which in turn will set off an alarm."

"How do you know this?"

"I'm familiar with the make. There's no doubt."

"What sort of alarm?"

"It could be every damn one on the yacht or just Basil's mobile. What difference does it make?"

"We're screwed then."

"Not necessarily. I've examined it thoroughly and can't see any wiring."

"Unless it's hidden."

"Unless it's hidden," John agreed. "If there's no wiring, then there's a remote power source."

"What's that?"

"It's a battery-powered unit that transmits the energy to the circuits of the alarm. It has to be nearby, no more than a metre away, especially if the signal has a bulkhead to go through. If I know anything about Basil, he's not going to risk his safe being left unprotected if there's a power cut."

"I agree," Jake said. "But we must still cover that option."

"Of course," John agreed. "I'm going back up to the bar. They'll wonder where I've been. I'll find some other excuse to slip away and go down to the engine room and pretend I'm looking for the electrician. I'll say there's something wrong with the icemaker. I'll have to sabotage it somehow. Meanwhile, you look for this remote power source."

"How do I disable it?"

"It'll be battery-powered. Just move it a metre or more away from the safe."

"So I can open the safe then?"

"Definitely not," John cautioned. "He might be using both systems at the same time."

"Okay."

"When I get the chance, I'll pull the fuse for this cabin, so when the lights go out, you'll have just thirty seconds, that's all. Open the safe, get what you're looking for, then shut it again. And don't forget to put the mirror back."

"Once I find what I'm looking for, how do I get out?"

"Above the bed," John said, pointing at the skylight. "Once you've finished in the bathroom, dismantle it." John gave Jake a screwdriver. "It's wide enough for you to get through."

"What if there's someone on deck?"

"I'll give you what I think is a reasonable amount of time, then I'll go out for a smoke, I'll signal you with three knocks when the coast is clear. The dangerous part will be getting into the water and away from the yacht without being seen. I'm going now. Find the power unit, disable it, then go into the bathroom and don't take your eyes off the lights." John gathered everything up, including Jake's clothes, and left.

"Good luck," Jake said, starting to look for the remote power source immediately; first in the bathroom itself, then all round the vicinity of the partitioning of the en suite, until he came to the office area. There against the bulkhead was a wood veneered, three-drawer filing cabinet. Predictably, all the drawers were locked. It was the only place within a metre of the safe where the battery unit could be.

There was only one thing for it. Fortunately, the cabinet was not attached to either the deck or the bulkhead and, careful not to tip it over, he eased it along the carpet to the other end of the cabin. As a precaution, he checked the desk as well. It also had locked drawers, so he moved this across the room as well.

Jake had to wait a quarter of an hour in the bathroom, every minute of which was an eternity, with every sound posing the threat of Basil or someone else entering the cabin or of Margaret somehow coming back to life again. When the lights went out, Jake was quick to act.

He opened the safe. This one was smaller; it contained several passports and driving licences of different nationalities and a thick wad of dollars. He felt around until he came upon another pouch. This time he knew he had the right one, the one he was told to expect. This bag, which had the texture of fine chain-mail over velvet, was invisible. Removing it and confirming it contained the authentic chain and pendant by feeling inside, he closed the safe and replaced the mirror. Five seconds later, the lights came back on.

He put the invisible pouch, made from material that Poseidon had cut away from the Cap of Invisibility, into his zipped pocket. This was another of Basil's precautions, preventing its precise location from being detected by Hestia or Diana and her accomplices. But, at the same time, it meant that Jake could take it from the yacht without Basil's awareness. Unfortunately for Basil, keeping it thus cloaked also had the effect of dampening his powers.

Back in the stateroom, he moved the desk and the filing cabinet back, making sure not to leave any skid marks on the carpet. Then he stood on the bed, straddling the still unconscious woman, and removed the screws holding the skylight in place, before waiting for the light tapping on the toughened glass. He tapped a reply and the frame was lifted off from above. Then Jake raised his hands through and, with John's help, was able to wedge himself out.

"What happens to you now?" Jake whispered, after checking that the coast was clear and while John was replacing the skylight.

"I'll go back down and put the screws back, then I'll resume my usual duties. I'm to give you an hour and a half before leaving. I've got a scooter waiting for me around the corner and Photis has left a speed boat in one of the coves. Anyway, good luck."

"Likewise."

Outside, the air was cool and the music louder, echoing around the harbour. Jake went to the bow, strode over the rail and lowered himself over the side, gripping the anchor chain with his legs, his hands still grasping the handrail. The metal was cold and slimy, the drop in temperature causing it to attract condensation. He looked back along the deck. John had gone. Sliding down the anchor chain, he lowered himself into the water.

Chapter 40: The House

Jake slipped into the darkness of the harbour, pulling away from the other yachts, the lights of the pier and nearby embankment. The sea was cold and at first he shivered, until the wetsuit's thermal properties took effect. Mixed in with the music from the *Trident* was that of the party in the square, the live group and singer, who would be performing until the early hours. When he was a sufficient distance from the yacht pier and in the centre of the harbour, he could see the crowded square, the dance floor obscured by the band.

He had rehearsed this many times over the last week, while walking along the promenade. He aligned himself with certain lights so that he could head for the meeting point. This was a stony cove located at the foot of the opposite cliff and below a rocky outcrop. When he was close enough, he picked the latter out against the star-lit sky, remembering to be careful not to stand when he came into the shallows, in case he stepped on a sea urchin. Even rubber boots would be insufficient protection against the sharp spines. Once in the mouth of the cove, he started crawling in, seeing no one at first. When he was in one foot of water and beginning to feel the chill of the breeze, a dark figure emerged from the shadows.

Photis waded out, carrying a towel in which he wrapped Jake like a parent would a child as it came out after a swim. Jake stood up and faced his father's faithful companion. "Have you got it?" he asked in thickly accented English.

Jake nodded with a smile. Both men spontaneously embraced each other. It was the first time they were alone and for that brief moment an exchange of feelings took place, one long in the waiting. Photis rubbed Jake on the head affectionately, before turning to walk up the cove.

Jake followed him off the strand, along a path up the cliff, over the crest of the promontory and down the other side. There, beached in another pebbly cove was an inflatable. They soon dragged it into the sea and, once Photis had lowered and started the engine, were on their way again. Jake looked at his watch. It was twelve minutes since he'd left the *Trident*.

Photis handed him a torch, which he used to illuminate their progress forward. The sea was smooth, only lightly rippled by the soft breeze. They easily traversed the big bay to the first headland, before passing the inlet, where he had met Diana, and heading northeast towards Perivoli.

They arrived just out of sight of his father's cove and Jake turned off the torch. It was too dangerous to come up to the pier, in case they were heard or seen. This aspect of the task was the only part upon which Jake and Virginia had differed. She had wanted him to go straight to Paleo Limani and deal with the crystals. He wanted to rescue Teresa first. Virginia saw this as an unnecessary risk. Jake, on the other hand, was worried that, even if he succeeded in destroying the crystals, Teresa might still be harmed, as a form of reprisal. In the end, Jake stood his ground and they agreed that, provided there was no one guarding her, he could spring her loose. The risk then was that the rescue would be discovered before he got to the crystals.

Jake entered the water, this time with mask, snorkel, fins, an underwater torch and a black hood for extra cloaking. He gingerly made his way around the rocks, across the ancient, submerged harbour, and cautiously entered the cove. He saw no one. Coming out of the water and removing his fins, he walked across the pebbles to the cliff edge, the sound of every grinding step making him grimace. In contrast, walking up the path and slope to the front of the house was noiseless. All seemed peaceful and deserted so far. He went round to the back of the building, the side that overlooked Perivoli and where the entrance to the cellars was. He unzipped his wetsuit and retrieved the keys from an inside pocket.

As he passed some undergrowth on his left, he caught a scent in the air. It wasn't natural, and vaguely familiar. He heard a rustle, but, before he could turn his head, a dark figure was upon him, their hand over his mouth. This attacker was much shorter than him and Jake was about to spin round to square up to him.

"Shh…Make no sound." It was Natalya.

"What the hell are you doing here?" Jake whispered.

"Shh…Please." She pulled him across the back of the house, past the cellar entrance and down the road. Hidden from view, a car was parked. They went a safe distance from this and into the undergrowth. "Jake, I knew you were up to something."

"I guess you're with them after all," he said, dismayed.

"No, my darling, I came to warn you. I thought you might be coming here," she said, holding his wet arm. "Diana, she's with the girl."

"Why would she be with her at this time of night?" Jake said. "Besides, as far as I know, you could be the one guarding her."

"I would never lie to you," she said, trying to embrace him.

"What are you doing?" Jake said, pushing her away. "Leave me alone. How did you get here?"

"I walked."

"Another unlikely story. How do I know this isn't your car?"

"This is Phivos's car. Diana's borrowed it."

"If you're not one of them, how do you know all this?"

"I am one of them, but I'm not with them. I've already told you," she pleaded. "They have asked me to participate, but I gave a good excuse. I said that my father doesn't let me out of his sight. They know about this."

His mind was working furiously. "I have an idea. We'll soon see whether you're lying or not." He unzipped his wetsuit and then the watertight pocket and took out his mobile. He dialled Diana's number. She answered on the first ring.

"Hi, Diana? This is Jake. Did I wake you?" he said, trying to sound drunk and upset.

"Er, no, I'm reading in bed," Diana said. "What's the problem?"

"I've just left the *Trident* and am coming to the *Pelagos*. You're at the ferry pier aren't you?"

"I don't understand. What do you want with me at this time of night?"

"I'm sorry, I just need someone to talk to."

"Where's Joanna?"

"Forget about her," he said, trying to sound bitter and emotional. "She's with Poseidon or Basil. I couldn't stand it anymore, I had to leave."

"Look, er, you can't come here. I'm undressed. Let me sort it out and I'll come to you. I'll come to the house."

"Don't bother," Jake said. "I'll go for a walk instead. I need to clear my head. I've heard there's a ferry planned tomorrow morning to take guests back to Lichas. I might pack up and leave this stupid place." He hung up. "Now we shall see whether you're telling the truth."

They didn't have long to wait. They heard someone emerge from behind the house and walk up the drive with a pool of light shining in front of them from a torch. They were on the phone.

"That whore's at it again." It was Diana's voice...... "If I'd tried to stop her, she would've gone anyway."....... "I'm going to leave the car in the square with the keys in the ignition. You get here as soon as you can.".............. "I've got to try and find Jake, he sounded drunk and could wander off anywhere." She paused by the door of the car, listening. "I don't care, I don't want the girl left alone." Diana pocketed the phone, opened the door, got into the car, started the engine and drove off.

"I'm assuming that was Phivos she was speaking to," Jake said. "So, what will happen when he finds Teresa's gone?"

"He will call Diana and tell her."

"And what will she do? I'll be on my way. Will they be able to stop me.?"

"It depends what you are going to do next."

"I'm going to Paleo Limani."

Natalya bowed her head in understanding. "If she thinks you're going there. If she believes you're going to get the stones, she will go to Basil."

"Basil? But he's the one they're plotting against."

"Better to be embarrassed than lose the crystals, Jake."

"Then I'm stuffed. I either have to leave Teresa and try to get the crystals or rescue her and abandon them."

"This girl's important to you?" Natalya said, frowning.

"Not in the way you think. She's an innocent victim and I'm responsible for her being here."

"Then I will help you."

"How?"

"You will see. Let's go, we must hurry."

They walked to the back of the house, unlocked the cellar doors and went down the concrete steps. They descended onto a lobby where there was a desk on which a camping gaslight was burning. There was a chair beside it and, in the corner, a single made-up bed. There was the smell of damp, urine, disinfectant and unwashed clothes. There were three storerooms in front of them. A dim light shone through the keyhole of one. Fiddling with the keys until he found the right one, he took a deep breath, unlocked the door and entered.

The room was dark with only the light of an oil lamp on a table and what now came in from the lobby illuminating it. In front of him was another single bed with a form under a sheet. To the right there was a table, a chair and a freestanding cupboard. The remains of a meal sat on a tray on top of the table with a glass and a bottle of water. There were personal effects scattered all about the room on what appeared to be threadbare rugs. In the furthest corner was a metal bucket with a large floor tile covering it. Beside it on the floor was a roll of toilet paper, a lidded bin and a bottle of bleach.

As he was considering what to say, the girl stirred and uttered a muffled, "Fuck off".

"Teresa, you've got to get up."

It took her a few seconds to react but, when she did, she sat bolt upright. She was only in a short-sleeved tee-shirt and underwear, "Jake, what the fuck are you doing here?"

"I've come to get you out."

"Get me out? I've been here for fucking weeks; where the fuck have you been?" She seemed ready to either cry in despair or scream with rage.

"I didn't know you were here until a week ago. But there's no time to explain, you've got to get dressed now."

"Wait a minute. Where's everybody? Aren't we going to get caught?"

"There's no one here at the moment."

"How do I know you're not one of them?"

"For God's sake, get on with it. There won't be another chance."

"I've not seen anybody's face. Everyone comes in wearing a hood." She seemed to be having a conversation with herself.

"I've come to get you out, so please…"

"But wait. I could get killed. Do these people have guns?"

"I haven't seen any."

"If they were going to kill me, they wouldn't be wearing masks. They must intend to release me at some point. Maybe they're waiting for something."

"It's not like that."

"How do you know so much?"

"I've made it my business. You've got to believe me; our lives are in danger. I've got to get you out now."

"How can you be so certain?"

"I think these people killed my father. So, please, get dressed."

The last remark had the right affect. "Wait outside," she said. "What should I wear?" she shouted back.

"Something lightweight and dark, preferably trousers."

When she stepped out, she was wearing black trousers and a dark brown blouse. Her hair was tied back and she looked pale and grubby. "I've got nothing; no passport, no money; they took everything." She stopped in her tracks when she saw Natalya. "Who the fuck?"

"That's the least of your worries," Jake said. "This is Natalya and she's just about to tell me how she's going to help."

"I will take her place," Natalya said.

"What? So I'm exchanging one hostage for another?"

"Only if you fail."

"But what if they harm you?"

"They won't. They know that if they touch me, my father will kill them all. Now go," she said. "Give me the key. I will lock the doors behind you."

"I'll be back for you, I swear it," Jake said, before turning away.

"Who's the Russian Princess?" Teresa said once they were outside.

"I'll explain everything once we're on our way." He took his mobile out of his pocket and called Photis and told him to meet them at the pier.

Chapter 41: The Tomb

By the time they'd walked down to the old broken concrete pier and Jake had picked up his fins and mask, which he'd left lying on the beach, Photis had berthed. They boarded the inflatable and were on their way again.

"Where are we going?" Teresa asked.

"The Old Athenian Harbour," Jake said, as he took up the torch again and shone it forward.

"Is that supposed to mean something? I don't even know where I am."

"We're not far from Lichas, your final destination when you left Piraeus," Jake said. Photis had manoeuvred away from the rocky coast and was now powering towards Paleo Limani.

"Why don't we go to the police or the airport?"

"Because wherever we go, we will not be safe. What I do now will ensure that we are. We will be there in five minutes. I can't tell you everything in that time, but enough to improve our chances of survival, because you might see things that otherwise shock you." He had rehearsed this little speech for a week. "First you must suspend all disbelief in respect of what I'm about to tell you. Be sceptical when it's over, but not now."

"Okay, I'm listening."

He told her as much as he could, trying to study her face as he did so, but he couldn't see her expression; it was too dark. When he'd finished, Photis was just powering down as they approached the southern entrance to the bay. There was no time for any feedback.

"We must be quiet," Jake said. "It's like an amphitheatre in here." It was windless in the sheltered bay and the engine sounded like a pneumatic drill on a Sunday morning. "We'd better lie on the bottom of the boat, so that anyone seeing it will think Photis is alone."

Handing the torch back to Photis, they lay down side by side and Jake looked up at the starry sky. He turned to Teresa; she looked tense. He searched for her hand and held it reassuringly in his, but she didn't respond. Photis, meanwhile, crossed the bay and progressed out of the north eastern inlet.

When they pulled up to the rocks on the western side of Panagia Island, Photis cut the engine and raised it. Then he leapt into the water and secured the boat by wedging the anchor under some rocks.

"Can I talk?" Teresa asked.

"Sure, I don't think we can be heard from here," Jake replied.

"I thought you said there was a church."

"There is."

"This seems a strange place to get to it from."

"We can't go to the pier, an army detachment overlooks it," Jake said, getting out into knee-deep water. "You stay here; we'll be back shortly, when I've got the stones."

"Are you nuts?" she said, jumping into the water. "I'm scared; I'm not staying on my own."

"It'll be dangerous."

"You're either crazy or telling the truth. Either way I don't want you two out of my sight."

Photis picked up a rucksack, a pick-axe and bolt-cutters from inside the launch. Jake took a rucksack and a holdall. They ascended the hill and soon came to a rough path, probably made by goats, that led in the right direction. Photis led with the torch. Jake looked at his watch. It was one hour since he'd left the *Trident*.

Diana would be looking for him. At some point Joanna would leave the party and join her. Then Basil would go back to his cabin. When would he look for his crystal? Would he go to bed and get it in the morning or would he look for it right away, if only to reassure himself? What would happen when Joanna and Diana started talking, going back home and finding him missing? Would they think he was out sitting on a bench feeling sorry for himself?

As soon as Basil discovered that his crystal was missing he would be here within ten minutes; that was the only certainty. The success of the mission rested entirely on when that happened.

When they'd gained some height, Jake looked back at the entrance to the bay and beyond that the town. All was quiet, so far. Ahead, in the distance, the torch had picked out the church with its white walls and blue-domed roof. He felt his stomach tighten. If he thought the actions on the yacht were dangerous, at least the situation there was controllable. It had been thought out and everything had gone to plan. From now on, though, they were entering the unknown.

They reached the church and, stepping over the low wall, made for the well-head in the middle of the courtyard. This was where, during his attendance at the service, Jake had seen the circular discolouration in the concrete and the proliferation of ants coming out of its cracked surface. Virginia had confirmed that the landward entrance to the tomb was here.

From his rucksack, Photis took out a small hammer and started tapping the area. It made a hollow sound. With Jake and Teresa stepping back, he took hold of the handle of the pick-axe and, arcing it over his head, attacked the concrete with all his strength. After a dozen strikes, the cap cracked sufficiently for them to remove the broken blocks. Underneath, to their relief, was what they were looking for.

The entrance to the well was secured by a rusted round and hinged metal hatch that was padlocked. Photis used the metal cutters and cut through the lock, but did not open the hatch. He looked up at Jake and nodded, before taking Teresa away to the side of the church, amongst the trees.

Jake knelt by the hatch and undid his rucksack. Although there was another way into the cave, the underwater entrance, of the two, this was the safest. The other contained too many variables. Firstly, there was no way of knowing whether that doorway was still sealed and what was involved in opening it. Also, according to both Virginia and Diana, the underwater access was guarded; guarded by what?

He hoped Virginia's guess that this was the entrance was accurate; it had to be. Basil and Alexander of course knew of its location, but the others would have dismissed the possibility of the church because it was so far from the inlet and on such high ground. He would know soon enough because first he had to get the protector out. That was the advantage with this entrance; there was a way of dealing with the centaur. It had weaknesses.

From his rucksack he removed the first item Virginia had given him: a gold bowl with a metal lid held by four clasps. It contained ambrosia, the food of the Gods; a mixture of cooked pearl barley, vine fruits, herbs, spices and a hallucinatory mushroom, grown in Virginia's garden. Next to come out was a gold chalice; the cup from which Ganymedes used to serve the Gods their nectar. He'd given it as a gift to Hestia when they parted ways in Evia. Nectar was mead, made from white grapes and honey. It was very potent and centaurs were denied it because it provoked violent and uncontrolled behaviour. For this reason, they desired it all the more.

Lastly, he pulled out a goatskin wine carrier and poured the nectar into the chalice. Then he opened the bowl with the ambrosia and finally the hatch of the well. He stepped back and joined the others over the low wall at the side of the church and behind some trees. They crouched down on the ground.

"What's meant to happen?" Teresa said. "You didn't say anything about this."

"When you see what I'm expecting to happen, you'll understand why," Jake whispered. He could see fear in her eyes. "Just stay still, calm and quiet." He looked at his watch. They had passed the one hour and fifteen minute mark. What the hell was going on aboard the *Trident*? All he could hear was the sound of goats' bells coming from the main island.

At first nothing happened. The minutes ticked by and they were conscious of each other's breathing. Here in the shelter from the breeze, Jake felt hot and clammy.

Then he noticed something. A fine black filament came out over the lip of the well-head and ran along the ground. It was followed by another, then another. Jake understood what Virginia had meant when she said that the centaur needed no entrance to come and go, just the smallest hole or gap or crack. The filaments ran a few yards and began tangling together, forming clumps. It reminded Jake of ink in water. As the clumps gained mass, they coalesced and started rising, forming an amorphous opaque mist about two metres across. It began to glow, just like he'd seen in his dreams and on the coast road. Then it began to condense, moving from diffuse cloud to solid object. Teresa had grabbed hold of his arm and was digging her nails into it. She was hyperventilating.

Jake's idea of a centaur was a human torso on the front end of a horse. Paintings and drawings he'd seen depicted a good-looking, fair-haired and fair-skinned man with horns. He wasn't prepared for what took shape before him.

The horse part was big and muscular and, in the subdued light, completely black with a luxurious tail that nearly touched the ground. They were looking at its profile as it was facing towards their right. Although the human-like torso started from where the head of the horse should have been, it too was black and had a shaggy main. Above, where the front legs joined the body, were its arms. These were short, thick and covered in black curly hair.

The beast turned, looking around it, seemingly oblivious of the offerings on the ground, first looking away and then towards them. As it faced their direction it was apparent how broad and powerful the creature was. The chest was a dark chocolate colour. The head was huge, with the top also covered in thick, dishevelled locks, out of which protruded two short grey stumps.

The face was pure malice and evil. The lips were drawn and the nostrils flared. The red eyes darted about. At one point they seemed to be on them, and then went to their offering and back to them as if trying to decide what to deal with first.

For what seemed like eternity, it just stood there, while they remained frozen in fear. Teresa had put one hand over her mouth as if trying to stifle her own scream. For the first time that evening, Jake felt in mortal danger. If the centaur went for them, they could never outrun or outfight it.

But it did not. It behaved exactly as Virginia had predicted. First it collapsed its front legs, then its back legs, then it picked up the chalice and drank the contents in one. It raised up the goatskin flagon, removed the cork and refilled the chalice with mead. Again it drank it all in one go. It refilled the chalice a third time. Then, putting down the goatskin flagon, it picked up the gold bowl, opened it and sniffed the contents. Satisfied, it took the golden spoon and started eating. After a few spoonsful, it had more mead.

Following some more eating and drinking, it started to talk in a language they could not understand. It looked about itself as if imagining it was in company and conversing with companions. At times it would raise the chalice as if making a toast. At others it would spill mead on the ground and look heavenwards as if offering libations to a God. It carried on in this way and Jake wondered if Virginia had remembered to administer the drug. She'd said that if she used something too quick-acting, it might not drink or eat enough to keep it out for as long as they needed.

Even though they couldn't understand what the centaur was uttering, it became apparent that its speech was slurring. Eventually it began to sway from side to side and its head kept dipping forward as if on the verge of falling asleep. In an instant, it put down the chalice and bowl and rolled on to its side.

After it didn't move for a few minutes, they approached. Even in sleep it looked ugly and menacing. Jake looked at his watch. It was an hour and a half since he'd left the deck of the *Trident*. When they were satisfied that the centaur was unconscious, Photis unpacked the rest of his rucksack and unfurled a rope ladder, which he tied to a nearby tree and lowered down the shaft. He nodded at Jake, put something in his hand, gave him an affectionate smile and squeezed his arm. It was time to go.

"Shouldn't we tie this thing up?" Teresa said.

"Unfortunately, it can't be bound, or killed for that matter; not by conventional means," Jake said, stowing what Photis had given him in his zipped pocket and putting the empty rucksack on his back. "I'll be back as soon as I can."

The smell started as soon as he lowered himself below the lip of the well and grew worse as he descended. The bore was circular and wide enough, but the walls were rough and hard. He constantly bumped and scraped most parts of his body, especially his knees and back. It was awkward and every step down was painful. Soon he didn't notice the pain; the smell was becoming so strong and putrid as to make it difficult to breathe. It was a smell similar to bad fish and rotten meat and he wondered if he'd be able to hold onto the contents of his stomach.

After a while he feared that the ladder wouldn't be long enough, but eventually he descended out of the well bore and into a chamber. This made things even more difficult because it was pitch black and awkward trying to get his feet onto the next rung of the ladder. Finally, his lower step came onto solid ground and he was able to stand. From his belt he pulled out a heavy, rubber torch. He put the strap round his wrist and switched it on.

He stood in a circular chamber carved out of the rock. It was about seven feet high and eight in diameter. There was a single exit tunnel, which Jake guessed went south. The side walls were weeping water and, were it not for the tunnel, out of which it trickled, it would certainly have filled the bottom of the well. For some reason the smell was not so bad, or had he got used to it? There was a draught coming from the tunnel. This seemed to suggest a second land-based entrance.

The flow of the water meant the tunnel sloped downhill and, after passing through twenty metres, he entered another larger chamber. As soon as he did so, the smell became so intense that he retched violently. It took him a few moments to compose himself and begin to breathe normally again. A quick scan of the space with the torch revealed things he could not identify and it was only when he looked more closely that he understood the horror of what he was seeing. He was looking at body parts strewn all over the floor and in various stages of decay. He assumed that most were goat as there were many hides and skulls. There were also two other exits from the cavern. He had a closer look at the one on his left. This seemed to ascend sharply and he could sense the movement of air. This must be the other entrance, otherwise how did the centaur get these animals down here? The other exit was a tunnel immediately opposite the one he had been in. It carried on gently downward and would be the one that would lead to the tomb. He continued forward, but before he entered, something on his right, in the corner of the chamber, caught his eye.

It appeared to be a bed of straw. When he shone his torch on the part farthest away from him, he couldn't hold himself any longer. He felt a sudden up-rush from his stomach and was sick on the part of the bed nearest to him. When he'd finished he forced himself into the tunnel and walked as fast as caution would allow, while in his mind was etched the image of the shrivelled, decomposed body of a woman in the foetal position, facing away from him, her skin a sickly yellow. But the hair, the hair was long and a chestnut colour, in perfect condition and looked as if it had been recently brushed. Was this Denise? Was this Denise with the remains of his step-brother or sister still inside her?

He stumbled down the passage, which seemed to have no end and, at his feet, the trickle of water streamed. The tunnel went on, but at least the smell had dissipated. In his mind he imagined himself walking under the camp with the soldiers, towards the inlet.

In time, the smell of fetid decay was replaced by a different one entirely. It was still the smell of death, but it was spicy and sweet. Eventually, he came to what was once a wooden door but was now a jumble of rotted wooden planks that were held together by rusted metal braces. When he pushed on it, it fell to the stone floor and disintegrated.

Beyond this, and blocking his way, were two stone pillars, chest height and roughly hewn into irregular shapes. He tried to squeeze himself past them, but inadvertently pushed one over and, as it toppled to the ground, it disintegrated into a powder.

He was in another chamber but, no sooner had he shone his torch forward, than his heart nearly stopped. In front of him, at the end of a metal stake, secured into the ground, was a shrivelled head. It had thick black strands coming out of the top of its cranium; then he understood. This was the head of Medusa, guarding the entrance. So it was true. Any mortal that looked upon her, even now, would be turned to minerals. Curiously, beside Medusa was another one of those pillars, this one more recognisable as the figure of a man, with an arm raised in the air. Was it about to strike the shrivelled head before it too was turned to stone?

So, he wasn't the first to enter the tomb. At least two had tried before him, not getting any further than this entrance. He proceeded forward.

This chamber was much bigger than the ones before. At his feet, the stream that had passed through the tunnel behind flowed through the middle of the hall and out through yet another tunnel opposite. The only difference was that this other passageway was much higher and wider.

Apart from the gap through which the water flowed, everything else was chaotic and, because of the narrow beam of the torch, which only allowed Jake to see small areas at a time, it took a few minutes for him to get his bearings and confirm that he had now entered the tomb.

Jake had been told that when the Gods were drugged and tied, their bodies were placed in wooden boxes, which were brought into this chamber via the seaward entrance, the broader passageway opposite. He had imagined seeing these coffins laid out in an orderly fashion, showing some sign of the respect that deities should command. He'd imagined seeing something dignified and regal, not what now confronted him.

The boxes had been stacked in the left-hand side of the room and, because the wood had disintegrated, the bodies were left piled on top of each other, still wearing their clothes. They'd mummified, much like the Egyptian remains he'd seen on television and in museums. Dark, shrivelled, leathery skin drawn over skeletons, with no sign of the perfection and beauty they were supposed to have once possessed. Strangely Jake didn't feel sickened by them, as he had with the body in the first chamber. As he approached, he could appreciate that they were once very big, like Poseidon, and he could tell the men from the women. He was tempted to examine them further, but was aware that he was short of time.

On the other side of the room their personal effects were laid out: clothes, footwear, armour, furniture and gold; gold cups, gold bowls. There were open chests full of jewellery. Here were countless and unimaginable riches. Why would Poseidon not want to keep them for himself? Perhaps he had nowhere to store them and intended to come back. But it all looked undisturbed and there was a certain melancholy to it all, a sadness that it should end as it did.

There was no time for reflection. He had to find the crystals. Remembering Virginia's instructions, he removed her crystal, the stone that Photis had just given him, from his left-hand pocket. The stone was glowing faintly; it had sensed the proximity of its companions. He moved towards the side of the room with the bodies. The glow grew fainter. Then he moved in the other direction. There was a definite increase in brightness.

Then, through trial and error, by constantly turning the torch on and off and moving in different directions, he narrowed the search down to one corner of the chamber. Now the difficult part: finding something invisible inside something invisible. This section of the room contained clothing laid out in piles on the floor; the perfect place to hide something like this, as normally one would expect it to be amongst the other solid objects. He scanned the crystal over the vicinity but it was too small an area to show any difference. There was nothing else for it; putting Virginia's stone back in his pocket, he got on his hands and knees and started searching systematically through the clothes for solid objects.

As he started doing so, he could not stop thinking that these were the garments worn by the Gods of mythology and yet most of the time they just disintegrated in his hands, leaving nothing but clouds of dust. Soon the air was full to choking. Every time he moved to a new pile, he would put down the torch, so he could use both hands. On one such occasion the torch pointed towards the rocky wall and something caught Jake's eye. It was a shape that was out of place. The shadows cast by the rocky surface were rough and angular. Here was something round and smooth. He picked up the torch and approached. There on a rocky ledge was what looked like half a football, sitting upside down and covered in dust. He blew this layer away and it vanished. This was it; the settling dust had revealed it. Picking it up, he was surprised by how heavy it was. It did indeed feel like a metal helmet with a rim going all the way round, and was covered in the same fine mesh as the pouch he'd retrieved from Basil's safe. He knelt down and placed it on the floor, holding the invisible object with his left hand. He put the torch on another ledge and angled it towards the ground. With his right hand he felt inside.

As soon as his hand passed the lip of the helmet, his body disappeared, including the clothes he was wearing. He pulled away as if his hand had been singed by a flame. He'd prepared for this for days, rehearsing everything in his mind and yet, facing the real centaur, the real Medusa, the real bodies and now the helmet of invisibility still unsettled him.

He put his hand back in. In the helmet was a pouch. Without taking it out, he undid it and felt inside. There they were; the crystals. Not all on chains like Poseidon's, but embedded in something, like brooches or rings, most certainly of gold. So the set was now complete. He, Jake, now had all the crystals in his possession.

It occurred to him, not for the first time, that he too could now be a God. There were extra crystals in the cap; Diana had said so and Virginia had confirmed it. He could bring all the other Gods back to life and he could become one of them. He could learn their secrets and become immortal too. He could be their hero. He wouldn't want to rule, he would let the others sort that out amongst themselves. He could have whatever he wanted; anything and anyone. Women would come to him, he would be the one choosing, and he would do the rejecting. Together they would be invincible; and if anyone dared to stand in their way…?

He remembered his mother, and tears welled up in his eyes. He remembered how she had died, how she'd withered away, how she was in pain. He wouldn't have to face any of that. He wouldn't have to face old age at all if he didn't want to.

This was the crystals talking to him, just as Virginia had predicted. They were talking to him and tempting him. They were telling him what could be and Virginia could not deny that what they promised was not true. She said that he would have a decision to make, a difficult and solitary one.

He took off his backpack and put the helmet inside. There was little time. He put the rucksack back on his back and, with the torch beam to guide him, ran back the way he'd come.

Chapter 42: Confrontation

"You took your time," Teresa said as Jake emerged from the well-head. Photis stepped forward to help him out.

"Anything happening?" Jake asked, looking round.

"I don't know what, but there's been a lot of commotion going on in that direction," Teresa replied, pointing towards the harbour.

"Then it will soon be coming our way," Jake said. "Let's get going."

"Do you have them?" Photis asked, looking worried.

"I do," Jake replied. "Let's go, my friend."

Picking up their equipment and leaving the unconscious centaur, they ran down the path and back to the boat. When they reached it, they threw everything inside, pushed it off the rocks and stepped on board. Photis lowered the engine and had it started on the second pull. They sped away and left the bay from the northern entrance. The plan was to run round the outside in the open sea to the third island along, thus avoiding the army camp. It would only take a few minutes.

The wind created by the speeding boat blew away the memory of the stench of that first chamber, the one he'd had to go through again. It wasn't all horror and decay, though, not as far as the tomb was concerned. There was beauty as well. He thought again of the Gods and their treasures, the possessions they'd accumulated over thousands of years, doubtless some coming from Atlantis itself. He now had a decision to make. Would he send the crystals into oblivion or would he save the Gods and become one himself? There would then be no limit to what he could achieve. He looked at Photis's proud profile. Jake would see to it that this wonderful man was rewarded too, beyond his wildest dreams.

Each God was renowned in a certain field, be it love, commerce, wine and dance, or prophecy. The latter appealed to him. His intuition had served him well so far. How much more could his abilities be improved?

They rounded a headland and began to approach the next inlet, the cleft at the base of which was the underwater entrance. As they approached the mouth of the isthmus they encountered a few small waves. The boat jumped slightly and he could feel the weight of the helmet in the rucksack against his back.

He became aware of a gnawing unease, which quickly escalated into an unexplained panic. He had forgotten something. While he was fantasizing about becoming a God, he had overlooked something. What was it? He had memorised everything that Virginia had told him, but nonetheless something had been overlooked. Something to do with the stones.

It came to him and, as the thought formed in his mind, he turned towards Photis, who was concentrating on what he was doing, quite oblivious to any imminent danger. There was no time to explain anything. There was just enough time to act.

They were just beginning to cross the mouth of the inlet when Jake grabbed the tiller with both hands. With his left he pushed as hard as he could, which veered the inflatable to starboard. With his right he turned the throttle to full.

Photis was startled and braced himself. Teresa, who was sitting on the bench amidships, facing forward and holding their torch, fell backwards as the prow lifted and swerved to the left. She bounced off the side of the boat and fell on her back at Jake's feet.

Photis, thinking that Jake had gone insane and seeing that they were now heading at speed for a cove within the inlet, tried to reassert control with both hands. They made another crazy turn to port and this time it was Jake who lost his grip on the tiller. Owing to the weight of the rucksack on his back, he began falling backwards and had to grip the bench underneath him with both hands to stop himself falling into the sea.

Just as Jake was beginning to sit upright again, the top of the water to his left and behind the boat began to blister as if an enormous bubble of air was breaking the surface. The boat began to lean over on its starboard side and once again Jake struggled to keep himself from falling overboard. He was vaguely aware of Teresa, still lying in the bottom of the boat, screaming.

Photis had the presence of mind to turn the boat once more to port, so as to reduce the chance of tipping over. They both looked behind them to see what was happening. The water kept on rising as if it were a column, before it began falling back again, but, as it did so, something from within was revealed; something dark that blacked out the stars. The form, like an enormous bulbous torpedo, kept on rising. Only when it came clear out of the water and Jake saw the tail, did he understand what it was: a Great White shark. It began tipping downwards from the front, the tail still swishing, as if trying to make headway through the air, before impacting onto the surface of the sea.

The first wave, caused by the monster rising, passed underneath them. When it fell back into the water a few seconds later, the next wave it created was like a wall rushing towards them.

Photis and Jake looked forward simultaneously. The boat had managed to right itself for the second time, but now they had no choice but to head for the inlet and the cove.

When the wave struck the boat, it swamped it and pushed it forward. They were in the foam of the wave, unable to see and holding on for their lives. Jake feared for Teresa. Their only hope was that they would be beached in the cove. As they rushed towards it, they were accelerating. Then abruptly the boat spun round, having probably winged a rocky outcrop, and they were facing the other way, being pushed backwards.

This was the worst possible outcome. As the prop hit the bottom, it slowed them to a stop and the onrushing water raised the prow up over their heads until the boat overturned. Jake and Photis fell on the engine, holding on to it until they somersaulted and fell on their backs on the coarse pebbles with the boat on top of them. At first they were underwater and, as the wave rushed back out to sea, the coarse sand from farther up the cove was drawn down and partly buried them.

When the sea finally receded, Jake and Photis were able to lift themselves out of the sand, crawl from under the boat and scramble to their feet. Jake seemed to be alright, apart from a cut on his forearm that was slowly seeping blood. Photis too was unharmed. They frantically looked around for Teresa, but couldn't see her. Realizing she was still under the boat, they tried to right it and, with one simultaneous heave, they succeeded. Amongst the scattered contents, Teresa was lying prone on top of the fuel tank.

Jake turned her on her back as Photis started throwing things back into the boat.

"My ribs and side really hurt," she said, in a weak voice.

"Just relax," Jake said. "Show me."

"I can't, it really hurts."

"Let me see," he said, removing the rucksack, miraculously still on his back, and taking out the other torch. He lifted her clothing. She seemed to have struck the fuel tank on her lower left-hand side. The area was red and swollen and felt hard. "Just rest," he said, pulling her top back down.

Jake looked over at Photis and undid the rucksack again. He took Hestia's crystal out of the wetsuit pocket as well as the pouch containing Basil's precious stone, and placed them safely in the Cap of Invisibility with the others. This was what he had forgotten to do. Having passed over the isthmus, the protector of the underwater entrance had detected Hestia's crystal and, suspecting a theft, was induced to attack.

Photis had already put everything back in the boat and seemed to understand what had happened. Hopefully it would be safe to continue now; it had to be. They would be dead if they stayed on that beach. Jake looked at his watch. The glass was cracked and the display had gone. The time was irrelevant now. He helped Photis move the boat back in the water. Miraculously the prop seemed to have survived the grounding. He went to get Teresa.

"How do you feel?" he asked.

"I don't know," she said. Her voice was weak and she was trembling. "Along with the pain under my rib cage, my left shoulder's also aching."

"We'll help you back to the boat," he said. He looked at Photis and waved him over.

"I can't; I don't know. What happened anyway?"

Jake realised she hadn't seen the shark. "We were hit by a freak wave," he said. "There are often earthquakes in this area. It's unlikely to happen again anytime soon and we can't stay here."

"Something to tell your geography class, eh?" she said trying to get to her feet. "You'll have to help me; I don't think I can walk."

They lifted her up, carried her to the boat and sat her on the bottom, her back against the bench. It took several pulls to get the engine started again, but they were eventually on their way.

They rounded the final island to cross the last stretch to their destination. As a precaution, Photis proceeded slowly and clung close to land, crossing the straight at its shallowest point. Jake held the torch to guide them. These were all areas that he'd snorkelled with Joanna and he knew they were not more than two metres deep. At least if the shark came again, it could not strike them from below and they'd see it approaching.

Photis made landfall on another cove. He raised the engine as they leaped out into the shallow water, while grounding the boat. Teresa had stopped moaning, but was now panting. She'd gone pale and, in the starlight, looked like a ghost. She was close to passing out and Jake was concerned she had internal bleeding.

"Hang on Teresa; I'll be as quick as I can," Jake said, not knowing whether she'd heard him. With the rucksack on his back, he charged up the rocks of the beach, onto the flat top of the island, and started walking inland, towards its centre. It was overgrown and he was up to his ankles in vegetation. But amongst the growth, under the starlight and the beam of the torch, he could make out the remains of the ancient walls that once crisscrossed the crown of it. It was no more than five hundred metres across and was where the Gods had kept their livestock. Virginia had explained that this was so as not to pollute the main island. This was also where, over three and a half thousand years ago, Zeus had confined the divine mares, the event that had led to the downfall of the Gods.

Jake would now have to perform the final ritual of death, the one carried out from the old days of Atlantis, for the last time. As he continued to proceed inland, he remembered what Virginia had told him about it.

"In the olden days of Atlantis, when an immortal died, their crystal was buried with them, until it was realized that the living were being possessed by the spirits of the dead; just as was happening now. In those days there was no Medusa's head to protect the tombs and the possessed tried to rob the crystals from their graves in order to regain their power. It was found that the new personalities were malevolent and caused many problems. Dead kings would try to reclaim their thrones, dead spouses their husbands or wives and so on.

"It was decided that the crystals of the deceased had to be destroyed. It was long assumed and intuited that they were created from the fire in the bowels of the earth before rising to the surface. To the fire they would have to be returned. This became the job of Anippe, the queen of the divine mares, in a ritual that evolved over many centuries. She never revealed where she took the crystals, but it was thought to be the depths of the Atlantic, from where Atlantis and its crystals first rose.

"This time she will be returning the remaining crystals, including mine. The cycle will be closed. Once they are destroyed, the souls of the Gods will be released from bondage, the centaur will be no more, and the divine mares will pass on from this existence."

So, the moment of truth had arrived. In what Jake judged to be the centre of the island, there was a rocky clearing. He took off the rucksack and put it on the ground. He knelt on one knee, closed his eyes, lowered his head and cleared his thoughts. In his mind he called the name and said the words Virginia had made him memorise. After a while he opened his eyes again and waited.

A great stillness fell upon the island as if the wind had dropped, but when he looked out upon the water, he could see that the wind waves were still streaking across the sea. Slowly a mist started to form on the ground. It rose from the rocks and exuded from the vegetation. It continued to do so until the surroundings were obscured. This mist had no feel to it or smell, nor was it cold or damp. It was radiating silver, as if it had trapped and magnified the light of the stars.

He stood and, as he looked upwards, the dark sky became obscured as well; he was completely enveloped. When he looked down and about him, he saw amorphous, bright shapes on all sides, initially at a distance. Then in front of him, one of these entities approached. The mist parted and there she was. At that moment he thought a creature so perfect could not exist. Anippe, for this was what he assumed he was seeing, had the recognizable shape of a horse and yet was not an animal. She was somehow not completely solid but slightly blurred, as if straddling both realms of spirit and matter. The startling blue eyes, the only part that was not a radiant silver, gazed upon him.

Virginia explained that he could not speak to Anippe, nor she to him. He had to empty his mind and he would hear her voice in his head. She would speak to him when they were both ready. Jake had no problem with this as he felt complete peace in her presence.

"Iacovos, son of Giorgios, grandson of Poseidonos, why have you summoned me?" A voice indescribably sweet and compassionate addressed him.

In similar fashion Jake had to talk back with his own mind. "I have come to request you to perform the final rites for those who have departed and to destroy the remaining crystals."

"It is my sacred duty to do this and you have the authority to command it of me," came the reply.

Jake got on his knee, opened the rucksack and took out the large pouch from the helmet. "Here they are," he thought.

"Within are two that are not dead," he heard Anippe say.

"The one has surrendered hers for the common good. The other has had his taken, again for the good of all concerned."

"Place the bag over my neck," Anippe instructed him.

Jake did as he was told. He extended the strap and put it over Anippe's head. The pouch with the crystals rested on her chest. As he did so his hands and forearms brushed against the hairs at the back of her neck. The right forearm, the one that had been cut during the incident with the shark, felt warm and tingly. When he withdrew, he looked at it. There, before his eyes, the whole process of healing, which would normally have taken a number of days, took place before him in a matter seconds. He touched his skin; there was no trace of the injury.

He stared open-mouthed at Anippe, his mind racing. He struggled to put the thoughts he was thinking into words in his mind. But before he could do so Anippe replied.

"Bring her to me."

He did not hesitate. Leaving the rucksack on the ground, he turned and ran back the way he'd come, guessing the direction through the mist, through the vegetation and down the slope onto the beach. There in the boat Photis was cradling Teresa in his arms. He was talking to her, comforting her, stroking her hair. She was showing signs of shock, and seemed confused and anxious. Photis looked up at him gravely, shaking his head.

"Come, we must take her up the slope," Jake shouted.

Photis responded instantly. Jake carried her under her armpits and Photis under her knees. Once they had battled their way up the rise, they ran towards the clearing inside the mist, where he'd left the rucksack. They put her down on the ground. Photis looked around puzzled. The mares were nowhere to be seen. Jake told Photis to go back to the boat and wait. When he was out of sight, the bright shapes re-emerged and Anippe reappeared. She came over to them and lowered her head. The hair on her main fell over Teresa, who at this point was shaking violently. When Anippe raised her head a few seconds later, Teresa had fallen asleep.

"It has been done," Anippe projected.

"Thank you, Anippe," Jake thought. In the distance he heard the sound of a large engine powering up. He couldn't see out through the mist but could guess what was happening.

"Until the crystals are destroyed, they will not know that I have them," Anippe revealed.

"I understand," Jake thought. "Now you must go, but it grieves me that I will never see you again."

"My thoughts will be with you," she passed on. "Be aware, once I go, I can never be recalled and can be of no help to you. That which I am will no longer be of this earth."

"I know, Anippe. Go now. Go quickly," Jake thought. As soon as he'd finished the thought she vanished, and the surrounding mist lost its luminosity and began to disperse, being blown away by the breeze.

"What am I doing here?" Teresa said still lying on the ground. She started to get up, at the same time feeling her side. "I don't understand."

Jake was about to say something when a floodlight scanned the island. He looked towards the harbour entrance and saw a large yacht approaching with a few smaller speed boats and launches in attendance. "Here they come. You go back to the boat. I'll be with you in a minute."

"Which way?" Teresa said.

"That way," Jake said, pointing behind him. Teresa turned to run and Jake knelt down and started picking up stones, which he put in the still invisible helmet. When he'd finished, he put the rucksack on his back and ran down to the cove. Photis and Teresa were waiting to get back into the boat, but it was too late. The strait was blocked at both ends. The end that led to the bay was closed by a launch, and what looked like the *Warrior*, Kephalas's yacht, was approaching the seaward entrance and was in front of the cove. There were several other smaller boats milling around.

When the *Warrior* was as close as it could get, it swivelled its two front spotlights and aimed them at the cove. At the same time the launch also turned on a spotlight. Behind it was another boat. The passengers had torches. The dark background and the blinding light meant that Jake could not make out any faces. From the *Warrior* he could hear the squeal of a loudspeaker being switched on.

"Hand over the stones and maybe I'll let you live long enough to tell me how you got to them and who helped you," Basil's voice boomed across the bay.

"I don't know what you're talking about," Jake shouted. "In fact, we're really glad you showed up. We've just been attacked by an enormous shark."

"I don't think he can hear you," Teresa said. She stood close to his left while Photis was on his right.

They could hear the whine of the engine of an approaching boat, which appeared in the light of the foreground. It was a launch similar to their inflatable. It had two crew members dressed in white. When they were in the shallows, they stepped out; one was carrying a loudspeaker in one hand and a gun in the other. The second man was carrying a torch and another gun. They walked up the beach to Jake. "You are to hand over the stones to me," the one with the loudspeaker said, pointing the gun at him.

"Tell your boss that I don't know what he's talking about, we've just nearly been killed by…" Jake was saying; but the man did not wait to hear the rest, instead turning towards the yacht and speaking in the loudspeaker.

"He's not cooperating, sir," he said.

"Just hand them over or I'll blow your friends' heads off," was Basil's reply. The man with the gun turned back to him.

"Why should he hand them over to you?" A male voice came from one of the other boats. It sounded like Yiannis, the mayor. "Now's a good time to put right the atrocities you've committed."

"Sorry if I don't quake in my boots, but I don't see your thunderbolt coming my way," Basil responded.

"He's right," another voice said. "You've had three and a half thousand years your own way. All we're asking is that you restore the old order." This could only be Phivos, and Jake could discern the mutterings of approval.

"I hate to point out an inconvenient fact, but you're all fucking dead, so toddle along before I decide to blow your zombie heads off," Basil said.

"You can't kill us all." This time it was Mina. "Not all of us want to restore the old order. Just give us our crystals and we'll go far enough away not to trouble you."

"That's right." It was Diana this time. "You know me. I'm not interested in a new or old order. Just give back what you took and I'll be on my way too."

"You probably think I'm pretty stupid, nature girl; you're probably behind all this," Basil said.

"I'll admit I've been trying to retrieve the crystals, but none of this is my doing," Diana said.

"Well, who then?" Basil raged. "Who will step forward and admit to it?"

"And what will you do to them?" Phivos asked.

"Stop wasting my time," Basil said. "Hand the stones over or I'll shoot you all and take them anyway."

"You do that and even you will end up in jail," Phivos said.

"The next one of you to speak will be shot," Basil shouted.

Jake asked the henchman with the gun for the loudspeaker. He handed it over. "Do you think I'm stupid enough to be carrying them with me? I've hidden them up there." He pointed up at the island. "Your man can search us, if you want. You know you can't find them without me. Let the man and girl leave in the launch and I will take him to them."

"Actually, I can find them quite easily," Basil said. "Search them."

The henchman grabbed back the loudspeaker and, with the help of the other, frisked them and went through all their things. He emptied the contents of the rucksack on the ground. The invisible helmet dropped on to the pebbles and the rocks he'd picked up fell out of it. The man with the loudspeaker reported back to Basil.

"I've got a slightly different proposition, only to save time," came the response from Basil. "Retrieve the stones or I'll have the man strung up and gutted before your eyes, then I'll have the same done to the girl. One of my men will accompany you."

Jake and the lackey had just turned to go up the slope when Jake heard many voices talking at once. It was like people in panicked confusion. He looked down at the ground and could see the helmet, he could see the fine golden chain covering its dark metal. It had lost its invisibility. Then he knew it had been done; the crystals were no more.

"You stupid, stupid man." Poseidon's voice was livid with rage, he was practically screaming. "What have you done? Who gave you the right? Kill him. Kill him now."

Jake turned to see the two men in white approaching. The leading one with the loudspeaker was raising the gun. At the same time, from the corner of Jake's eye, he saw movement from Photis, who was now standing to Jake's left, between him and the crewmen. By the time he'd turned his head towards him, Photis, in one movement, had taken something out of the belt of his trousers with his left hand and, with a sweep of his arm, made an arc that passed across the front of the crewman's throat, leaving a dark gash.

As the dying body collapsed to the ground, Photis stepped past it and, in the time it took for the other crewman to understand what had taken place, Photis had plunged the knife into his stomach.

He heard more confused voices and shouting. Then there was a loud report and something tore into Jake's left shoulder with such force as to cause him to spin round and fall onto the ground on his front. He heard Teresa screaming and then a heavy body fell on top of him, forcing the wind out of his lungs. This was followed by another report and a second sharp pain, this time in Jake's upper back. He passed out.

Chapter 43: Natalya

Monday, 27th August

The first sensation Jake had was the pain in his upper chest on the left-hand side and another separate one located above his right shoulder blade. He was also aware of someone holding his left hand in both of theirs.

He opened his eyes and saw Virginia, smiling warmly. "Welcome back, Jake." she said.

"How long have I been out?" he replied, hoarsely.

"About thirty six hours. It's mid-afternoon on Monday."

"Where am I?" he said, clearing his throat.

"Lichas General Hospital."

"My mouth's dry."

"Wait, I'll fetch something."

Virginia left the room and, while she was gone, he looked around as best he could, and found himself in a plain, light blue painted room, big enough for the bed and a few chairs. A drip was attached to his right arm. There was a vase of flowers on a table at the foot of the bed and two cards on the table beside him. He was not mobile enough to reach for them.

It was not Virginia who came back, but two nurses, quickly followed by a doctor. They gave him a thorough examination, changed his dressings and administered a painkiller with some water, before leaving and allowing Virginia to return.

She sat down again and offered him some more water from a cup with a straw that was now on the bedside table. He tried to raise his hand, but stabbing pains made him groan. He let her put the straw to his mouth for him. "What happened?" he asked, after a few sips.

"You were shot twice, once in each shoulder. The first from the front, then another from behind. Both were flesh wounds, but the second severed an artery and you lost a lot of blood." Virginia had replaced the cup and taken his hand again.

Jake thought for a while. "I remember being shot the first time, then someone falling on top of me and then being shot again."

"That was Photis; he fell on you to protect you," Virginia said. "The second bullet passed through him first."

"How is he?" Jake asked anxiously, trying to raise himself and grimacing in pain.

Virginia lowered her eyes and tightened the grip on his hand.

"Oh, God, no. Tell me it's not true." He felt tears welling up in his eyes. He wanted to say something more, but the words were being choked in his throat and his lips trembled.

"Easy now," Virginia said gently. "You're still weak. Don't be so sad. Photis died in the most honourable manner he could have chosen. He was struggling to get past the death of your father; not being there for him."

"I didn't get to know him, I didn't spend enough time with him."

"But what you'll remember will be the best of him."

"When's the funeral?"

"His body will be flown to Athens today and the funeral will be tomorrow."

"I won't be able to make it, will I?"

"No, you'll still be here. I'll be going for both of us."

"Teresa?"

"She's okay. She's still helping the police. She was in to see you this morning. One of these cards is hers. She's flying back to England this afternoon. We had a long talk. Don't worry, she doesn't blame you for anything."

"I'm pleased. She's been through so much," Jake said looking thoughtful.

"She wanted to stay longer. But I thought if she did, things might have been awkward."

"Awkward? In what way?"

"Well, she'd have been obliged to be grateful to you and you would've felt guilty about her. Better you meet again in England."

"I guess you're right. I think our feelings have changed, as a result of events."

"I sensed that right away. She's a wonderful girl. I've got her address and telephone number. I'm sure you'll make great friends."

"We were lucky to get away with it."

"You can thank our Photis for that as well. When he came into the harbour on Saturday night, before he went to wait for you at the cove, he sneaked on board the *Sevastia* and waited. While you were making your way on board for the party, he dived under the *Trident* and fouled its propellers with chains. Sheared the blades right off when they tried to leave for Paleo Limani. They had to drive to the *Warrior* and take that round instead. This alerted the others to what was going on and that's why everyone turned up at once."

"It bought us those precious few minutes. Dear Photis. So what's happened to Basil and the others?"

"Well, soon after the shots were fired, the coast guard turned up. They were patrolling nearby and were alerted by the troops on the island when they saw all the boats and flashing lights. They thought some drug smuggling operation was taking place. Basil, Alexander and the crew on the *Warrior* are in custody. Basil fired the shots, so he'll be going down for murder. Someone must've grassed on Diana and Phivos because they're under arrest for kidnapping. I don't see their future being too promising. Joanna, Yiannis and Mina are confined to Halia and are being questioned. None of the others have been implicated. The police are trying to make sense of it all."

"Good luck to them," Jake said. "Do you think the tomb will ever be found? Won't they suspect something if they see the cracked concrete and the open well in the churchyard?"

"I doubt it. I don't see anyone going down there, so I'm hoping that part will be passed over and my family will rest in peace."

"I suppose they've changed, now that the crystals have been destroyed."

"Probably feeling lost and confused; or so I've heard. All but one that is."

"Who?" Jake asked, although guessing who Virginia was talking about.

"One young lady who knew exactly what she wanted, and still does," Virginia said. "She was here yesterday afternoon, before going back to Athens."

"How was she?" Jake said, feeling emotional again. "Do you know what she did?"

"She seemed fine. As soon as Phivos got called to go to Paleo Limani, she made her escape. She also bought you precious time. I filled her in on all the other details. Of all of them, she was the least affected, the one who resisted the most, and she's so proud of you."

"Did she tell you what else she did? How she helped us at the street party?"

"I know what she did. You realise she's in love with you?"

Jake reflected on this. "I was afraid her feelings would've changed."

"They haven't, but it's now up to you to make your feelings and intentions clear to her. She's a wonderful woman from what I can see."

"I know."

"I must also tell you that it was her father who brought you here with his yacht. Made the crossing in forty minutes."

"I owe a lot of people. And you. How do you feel about losing your immortality?"

"This morning was the first time I got up with aches and pains. I'm going to experience growing old, but I will do it gracefully."

"What will you do?"

"I will live out my days here. I love my home. I expect to spend much time with you too, I am your great aunt, after all."

"I would love to have you in my life."

"That's just as well because I've asked for you to be moved to my home as soon as they feel they can discharge you. I may not be a Goddess any more, but I know a thing or two about healing."

On the third Sunday in September, Jake stood in front of the gates of the mansion and spoke into the intercom. It was early evening and the sun was close to setting. The oppressive heat of summer still prevailed in Athens, but out here, in the far suburbs, it was pleasant.

He'd stated the name of whom he wanted to see, given his own and was now waiting for a reply.

He was feeling tense; he relaxed his shoulders. They were still sore from his injuries and he would need physiotherapy, followed by many months in the gym to build up his strength.

He'd thought of calling, but just couldn't bring himself to do it; it somehow didn't seem appropriate. Today, he'd gone to Zacharias's for lunch. Beforehand, the man who used to be his father's solicitor and now represented Jake, kindly took him to the cemetery where Photis was buried, somewhere in the centre of Athens. He must have cried on his knees for fifteen minutes, not only for Photis, but his father as well. Then they went back to Zacharias's house to eat, before he drove here in his father's Mercedes.

The reply from the intercom was affirmative and the gate swung open automatically. He saw a short drive that led to a fine two-storey brick house, surrounded by well-tended gardens. As he approached the front door, it opened, and Natalya's father was there to greet him.

"You are welcome to my home," he said. "I hope you have fully recovered."

"I have a way to go still, but thank you for taking me to hospital."

"It was my pleasure. I know my daughter's been waiting every day to hear from you. I would let you in the house, but then you would have to meet our family before you could be alone with her. Now, if you walk round to the back, you will find her right away. Maybe afterwards you can both come in."

"Thank you," Jake said.

He walked round the house and with every step became more nervous. This seemed as bad as when he was boarding the yacht or entering the tomb; when his life was in danger. His fear now was that Natalya had changed, that she wasn't the same woman he'd fallen for; or that she didn't think the same way about him, despite what Virginia thought.

When he reached the back garden, he saw her. She was seated on a swing, hung from a tree branch. She was facing away from him and into the setting sun, wearing a light cream skirt and blouse, with sandals dangling from her feet. The rays were playing with her shoulder-length hair, a brilliant gold.

He approached, but didn't call out until she heard him and turned, her sandals falling to the ground. Her blue eyes widened and her smile broadened. Seeing her stopped him in his tracks. He couldn't imagine anyone more beautiful. They looked at each other, many expressions crossed her face, and doubtless his as well, but they still didn't speak, as if carrying out a dare.

"You have nothing to say to me?" Natalya finally asked.

"I have too much to say to you."

"This could take a long time."

"Maybe even a lifetime," Jake said. At this Natalya closed her eyes as if digesting the words. Her lips quivered with emotion.

"Promise me something right now," she said, regaining her composure.

"What?"

"Promise that you won't come any closer."

"But why?" Jake was distraught.

"Promise."

"I promise. Why, what have I done?"

"You've made me the happiest woman in the world," she said, her features again distorted with emotion. "I could hug and kiss you all night."

"Natalya, what's wrong with that?"

"Do you know how many people in the house are looking at us right now? My parents, grandparents, sisters, my aunts and uncles, cousins. I can see their faces from here. They're looking through the windows, maybe they're taking pictures with their mobiles or cameras; waiting to see what we're going to do. They're waiting for us to do something dramatic, like in the movies, so that they can post it on Facebook."

"This is not what I anticipated, not as romantic. We're supposed to fall into each other's arms and live happily ever after."

"We'll spend a lot of time in each other's arms, don't worry. Maybe we'll live happily ever after too, God willing."

"I'm sorry about what happened back on Halia; that I didn't tell you the truth; that I didn't trust you sooner. I will never doubt you again."

"I know how difficult it was for you."

"So what happens now?"

"First, we'll go into the house and I'll introduce you to everyone. This will take some time, so you must be patient."

"Okay, I can do that."

"Then we can go out for the first time together," Natalya said, shivering with excitement.

"Where shall we go? I'm not fully recovered yet. I may not be up to much."

"I'm sure we'll think of something," she said with a wink. She got off the swing, absentmindedly leaving her sandals behind and walking barefoot. She linked her arm into his as they started walking back towards the house.

From the author

Coming from a seafaring background, I have always loved the sea. My ancestral home is a tiny island in the Aegean. It is mentioned in the Bible, but there are periods of time for which there is no recorded history, no explanation for some of the ancient remains that exist. It is wild and beautiful and its eerie atmosphere was the inspiration for 'The Sea People'.

Although I was born in New York City, I spent the first six years of my life on a working cargo ship with three generations of my family. My parents moved to London when I was twelve and, when I finished my education, I worked in shipping, managing my father's ships up until the time of his death, when the business was wound up. Over one two-year period we were frequently in the local news in the south west of England, where I now live with my wife, but you'll have to wait to hear about that in my next book!

If you would like me to let you know when this and future books are to be published, please visit my website, www.theo-lemos.co.uk and sign the mailing list.

I do hope you have enjoyed reading my first novel and, if you have, please tell your friends..Also, if you would be willing to post a short review on Amazon, I'd be extremely grateful.

Theo Lemos
South Hams, England, 2014